1922

g heavily. Ghastly concoctions like pink ladies, gin
ge blossoms, out of bottles libellously-labeled gin,
, and rye. I spent fewer hours at Molekamp and more
in salon and speakeasy, carousing around town with
d of anesthetized fervor, deliciously seasoned with
I convinced myself that it was a binge well earned after
old and hunger and being executed several times.

ME BANDY, YOU CISSIE

1923

decide whether to kill myself or have a nice cup of tea.

ME TOO

1924

ost all belief in God, church and state, in the inherent goodness
n, in outwardly imposed discipline, in authority, even in virtue
; but these were minor penalties compared with the furies and
rs that beset so many former fighting men.

THIS ONE'S ON ME

1926

Anyway, I'm not thinking of changing too much," I said, lifting my
ead to kiss Sigga's plump, juicy lips, then turning over and uttering a
contented sigh, secure in the knowledge that the anger was over with,
and that I had regained that amazing human phenomenon, belief,
which could triumph over demolition as surely as a flower emerging
from a crack in the concrete.

ME SO FAR

The Ba

"I've had a snea
what they're doin
know, here and the
month, and orderin
way, and sending the
in returns on how man
from leprosy. That kin
finger on. But making $
That's really something."

I looked at those four men, figh
there was nothing else to do, and
the other privates and sergeants an
misery and suffering without comp
because they hated the enemy but so
families down. And I was suddenly ove
and sadness, and something like sham
strutting and smirking through the confl
spearian porter or gravedigger.

THAT'S

1920

I was a nasty reminder of the conflict, for I was
too-familiar cloth the color of horse-dung; worse, it
ously ornamented uniform of the class that had mad
of the war; bloody red tabs and overbearing braid,
crossed sword and baton of my rank rank.

No wonder the civvies glared.

IT'S ME AGAIN

I started drinki
bucks, and ora
scotch, bourbo
and more time
Dash in a ki
Puritan guilt.
two years of

I couldn'

I had
of ma
itself
terr

ME SO FAR

VOLUME VII

The final volume of
THE BANDY PAPERS

Donald Jack

Doubleday
Toronto New York London Sydney Auckland

Canadian Cataloguing in Publication Data
Jack, Donald, 1924–
 Me so far

(The Bandy papers ; v. 7)
ISBN 0-385-25222-6

I. Title II. Series: Jack, Donald, 1924– . The Bandy papers ; v. 7.

PS8519.A34M38 1989   C813'.54   C89-094050-9
PR9199.3.J32M38 1989

Library of Congress Cataloging-in-Publication Data

Jack, Donald Lamont.
 Me so far / Donald Jack.–1st ed.
  p. cm.
  ISBN 0-385-25222-6
  I. Title.
  PR9199.3.J3M38 1989
  813'.54–dc20

Typesetting: Trigraph Inc.
Design: Lesley Styles
Illustration: Kim LaFave

Printed and bound in the USA
by Arcata Graphics

Published in Canada by
 Doubleday Canada Limited
 105 Bond Street
 Toronto, Ontario
 M5B 1Y3

Contents

PART I

A First Class Passenger

I fear that I have antagonized a goodly number of persons in my time despite my most determined efforts to remain as nice as pie—and no one was to be more antagonized than the Viceroy of India, who was also traveling, appropriately enough in his case, on the *Viceroy of India*.

Earning his displeasure was especially regrettable as it was to his bailiwick that I was about to repair, if repair is the right word for any activity in which I was likely to be involved. I was journeying to India to join the Maharajah of Jhamjarh's new air force. The damnable thing was, I would have avoided the encounter had I stuck to my original plan, which was to travel to India at a later date. I had brought forward my travel arrangements partly in order to keep an eye on Prince Khooshie, the Maharajah's eighteen-year-old son and heir. Khooshie had already booked passage on the liner. He had met a girl at some diplomatic shindig, and was so smitten that when he heard she was leaving for Asia on the following Saturday, he had immediately booked passage for himself on the same ship, securing the finest accommodation available, a suite on the port side that included two staterooms (from the Latin, *status*). Which was lucky for me. Applying at the last moment I was unable to obtain any accommodation whatsoever, and Khooshie kindly offered me one of his rooms.

Actually he didn't offer it all that kindly. In fact he grumbled quite a bit. "Dash it all, Bartholomew, I thought I was going to get away from you for a few weeks," he stormed. "All my life I have been fussed and tutted over by nurses and relations, smothered by *ayah*, loomed over by *chowkidar* and drilled by *chaprassi*, not even being allowed into the back garden half the time in case I fell and hurt my little self. Then I come to England and, oh, it is wonderful, I will be free, free at last from all the cosseting. And then I find that you are to be my nursemaid. And now you are wanting even to sleep with me. It is intolerable."

"All I'm asking for is one measly stateroom," I replied. "However, if that's too much to ask," I sniffed, "I'll descend into the bowels of the boat and travel steerage in utter misery and degradation for the entire voyage. Then you'll be sorry. That'll teach you a lesson."

"Here, wait," Khooshie called out. "Don't forget your bags." Whereupon I decided not to teach him a lesson after all, but to let him off for once. So, stepping over his servants and their bedrolls, I marched huffily into the spare stateroom.

Really, Prince Khooshie could be very childish, sometimes.

I did not linger long in the stateroom. As a seasoned traveler—salty, peppery, gingery, and sage—I knew how important it was to get ahead of the *canaille*. I wanted us to be first with our begging bowls when the privileges were being dished out. So before the rest of the passengers had finished grumbling in their quarters, I rushed Khooshie round the ship to make him known to everybody who counted, including the purser, the chief steward, our cabin steward, and particularly the captain at whose table we wished to sit.

At four pip emma, Khooshie withdrew, pooped, to his stateroom, while I ensconced myself in the first-class bar on A Deck. Only one detail remained—I had to make a splendid impression on the bar steward. I was able to do so in a remarkably short space of time. "I'm giving up drinking," I informed him after ordering my third whisky in eight minutes flat. "And in this endeavor I am bound to succeed, as I have had so much practice."

"Congratulations, sir."

"January the first, that's when I'm giving up."

"What year would that be, sir?"

"Next year, of course. Nineteen twenty-five."

"That's only four days away, sir."

"Oh, my God, is it? Still, I've made up my mind. It's to be my New Year's Resolution. This time I really mean it, bartender. When I say I'm giving up on January the first, I mean it." And to show that I meant it, I thumped the bar counter with a spare fist. "I mean it. And I'm going to keep you to that promise, bartender."

"You can rely on me, sir," he said, giving me a refill after I'd tapped the glass again with a badly-bitten fingernail.

"I have been repeatedly warned that one must be very careful with one's drinking in India, as one can become a terrible old soak otherwise."

"I believe so, sir. You're an American gentleman, are you, sir?"

"Certainly not. The fact that I was born and brought up in Beamington, Ontario, a town of sunbaked, frostcracked brick, splintering timber and brown grass, is totally irrelevant. I am British to the core."

"Of course. How silly of me."

I nodded and sipped thoughtfully as I looked around the empty bar. "Don't have many customers, do you?" I observed critically.

"Actually, sir, it usually takes the passengers a week or more even to *find* this bar, let alone patronize it."

"That's funny. I found it without any trouble."

"Yes, sir, I can believe that."

"I suppose," I said, sipping even more thoughtfully, "that as we're likely to see a great deal of each other, I should know your name."

"Bert, sir."

"Except," I added, "that I'm not likely to see a great deal of you, as I'm giving up drinking in four days time. So it's okay—don't bother giving me your name."

"Very well, sir."

Lordy-lord, I was feeling good. Even the bar steward commented on it. "You seem unusually happy, sir," he said, polishing a row of glasses. "People don't usually look too happy when they're going to India."

"You're right, I'm positively brimming. But then it's been a very difficult year, bartender, so any change would be an improvement."

"How's that, sir?"

"Only last May I was fleeing from Canada and reaching England at the lowest point in my fortunes. I've been fleeing countries for ten years, now, but this year was a record. I've had to flee not just one but two countries this year. Two countries in one year, would you believe it? I'm traveling with an Indian prince, you know."

The bar steward, unable to adjust to what appeared to be an abrupt change of topic, looked uncertain, and opened and closed his mouth; but he had no need to worry, it wasn't a *non sequitur*, I was just filling in a detail or two. "I saved his life, you know," I added.

"Are you a doctor, sir?"

"No, a pilot. He flopped into the Channel, and I fished him out. It was only after I had undunked him that I learned that he was no less than a prince. His father turned out to be one of the richest of all the rulers of the independent states of India. Who rewarded me," I concluded triumphantly, "by appointing me commander of his private air force."

"Well, I never," the bar steward said, breathing all over a glass.

"I think perhaps you'd better give me your name after all—it's still four days to my New Year's Resolution, and I suspect we're likely to spend quite a bit of them together."

"I expect so too, sir. It's Bert, sir."

"What is?"

"My name."

"Ah. Now there was just one problem about this air force, Mr. Bert. The problem was, why did the Maharajah want an air force? Was he intending, I wondered, to turn it against the supreme power?"

"God, sir?"

"Close—the British Government. I must confess—fill it up again, Mr. Bert—that as a loyal Brish subject I felt just a trifle guilty at the thought of creating five squadrons of fighters and bombers that might be used against the Brish Umpire. However, the staggeringly high salary that the Maharajah was offering quickly quashed any moral qualms—as money is apt to do—and I got down to organizing an air force with my usual flair, drive, and enthusiasm.

"Naturally," I continued, "this brought me into conflict with the government. They were already concerned about the political unrest that had been growing in India since the war. So while I was busy persuading myself that our private air force was merely a conceit on the part of the Maharajah of Jhamjarh, the government were convincing themselves that it was a weapon destined to be turned against the Raj. A battle of wills and other dirty tricks broke out between my growing organization and the government—am I talking too much, Mr. Bert?"

"Not at all, sir. By the way, Bert's my first name."

"My doctor maintains that the struggle has brought me to the brink of a nervous breakdown, one of the symptoms of which is that I can't stop talking, but that's nonsense. I'm the strong, silent type, the most reticent fellow this side of Devil's Island. Can't stop talking? Utter nonsense. Would you believe it?"

"Never."

"Funnily enough, though, now that the struggle is over and I'm barking on a long sea voyage which is supposed to be good therapy, I'm beginning to feel kinda jumpy—this despite the fact that my shoulders have been lifted off an enormous weight. You know, Mr. Bert, I can really talk to you. You really listen to a fellow. All too often in this day and age people don't listen to a fellow. Fill 'er up, will you." Mr. Bert and I went on chatting companionably for a while, until finally he nudged forward a pile of chits; so many, in fact, that I thought he was offering to play cards.

It was at that point that I suddenly noticed the two clocks that were clinging to the wall. They were both in agreement. It was seven-thirty. Good Lord, I'd been in the bar for hours. I'd only thirty minutes to bathe and dress for dinner.

So after an emotional farewell I departed, and wended my way back through the ship, along the carpeted passageway to Khooshie's suite. A lady and her son were on a reciprocal heading. "Mummy, why is that man walking that way?" whispered the little boy. "It must be getting rough," mummy said anxiously. "But Mummy—" "Hush, dear," mummy whispered back, recoiling and feeling behind her for the wall as I treated her to one of my charming smiles. Not having a titfer on, I tugged politely at my forelock instead—but not too hard, as I was getting quite concerned lately about my hair.

What with impressing the bar steward, and now pottering about my stateroom, bathing and sloshing scent about my person, and then having to adorn the lengthy form in soup and fish, I was late in reaching the dining room. Everybody else had been seated, and were already engaged in stilted tattle, the usual prelude to a long voyage.

The entrance to the ornate dining room appeared to have been designed with dramatic entrances in mind. As you entered through a wide glass doorway, you found yourself on an area shaped like a thrust stage, from which three wide steps led down to the polished dining floor. Moreover there was a great crystal chandelier in the middle of the golden rococo chamber which strongly favored the stage with its light. Consequently anyone with any presence at all was bound to attract attention, assuming there were no distractions, such as the grinding of icebergs along the hull. So naturally the moment I entered, everybody in the great lounge fell silent and stared, as I stood there shining and sparkling in my tux, pearl stud, and snowy hanky, my Brilliantined hair catching a thousand little lights from the chandelier—my hair was really plastered tonight. The subdued growl of chat subsided into a hush broken only by the crash of soup tureens from a far door, and the angry words issuing from an Art Deco grill in a bulkhead. "Whose is that noble form bathed in crystalline effulgence?" I could almost hear them saying—though visually they remained slackjawed and glasseyed.

To put them all at their ease so that they might not feel too inferior in my presence, I toned down my eminent expression and made a valiant attempt to look as ordinary as they; a laborious task given the vast expanse of my aristocratically equine frontispiece. Still, I succeeded. Barely thirty seconds kowtowed by before faces were averted en masse, and the buzz of conversation resumed, while the ice that invariably formed over social intercourse in British society melted like magic. In fact there was even a surge of inhibited tittering.

A senior steward materialized in front of me. "This way, sir," he murmured.

"What way is that?" I enquired, but laughed nicely into his Curzonish phiz to show that this was merely a particle of wit; to which he responded by leading me to the wrong table.

"Hold it," quoth I. "This ain't the captain's table."

"No, sir. Would you care to sit down, sir. We're a little behind schedule at the moment."

Tchk. Despite all my efforts to impress the company with Khooshie's importance, it appeared that we had not been selected to adorn the captain's table after all.

At ours, Khooshie was busily inhaling the vegetable soup. "You're late," he said reprovingly, delicately dabbing his cinnamon chin. "I was just about to eat your bread roll, Bartholomew. Incidentally, why were you walking in that funny fashion as you crossed the floor of this sumptuous saloon?"

"Motion of the ship, of course, foolish lad."

"But the boat is not moving."

" 'course it is. We sailed hours ago."

"You may have sailed but we haven't. The boat is not moving at all. It is still leaning against the harbor wall."

"Nonsense. It must be halfway across the Bay of Biscuits by now."

"There's been a delay," said a refined English gent at the far end of the table. "It's not sailing until some time this evening."

"Well, there you are, that explains it," I said, nodding approvingly at the company, as if they'd finally got it straight.

They stared back rather stupidly before resuming the communal slurp.

There were eight of us around the groaning board, a full complement on that first evening. The company included Hortensia Fitchmount, headmistress of a school in Simla, and the ship's medical officer, Dr. Simpson, a shy man who occasionally spoke about the ancient Persians. Next to him sat an Indian Civil Service administrator and his wife, both of whom were plainly upset at sharing the table with an Indian. They would continue to look affronted until they learned that Khooshie was the heir to one of the richer princely states, whereupon they condescended to fatlipped smiles.

The gentleman at the far side of the table who had with such evident amusement explained the sailing arrangements, was a Mr. Francis Postillion. He was about my age and handsome in a refined English way. Fair hair flopped over an intellectual brow. The ends of his straight hair frequently curled into his eyes, the resulting irritation making them a trifle bloodshot. Sometimes the ends of his hair caught in his eyelashes, causing the hair to twitch distractingly. He looked as if he belonged in an Oxford college, making erudite remarks and absent-mindedly hogging the port.

He too had joined the ship at the last moment, and claimed to have something to do with the Government of India. "I'm a dusty archivist," he told me later, so convincingly that I immediately suspected that he was something else entirely.

The eighth and final occupant of the table was an American journalist, Petronella Spencer.

As I continued to chat away, already the life and soul of the party, my eyes strayed to an adjoining table. I started. A large man in fancy dress was staring back at me with eyes like two chips of blue ice.

I nodded, but received only a contemptuous glower in

response before the beef-colored brute looked away. A typical staff man, I thought. As well as the ice chips embedded in his face, there was also a formidable nose and a large gray mustache of the type favored by senior army officers.

He growled at his wife, whose backless gown revealed a spine like a reinforcing rod. You could see its outline clearly through her powdery skin. He must have been rumbling about me, because his wife turned to stare in my direction.

"Who's that?" I asked Hortensia. "The uniformed thug at the end of the captain's table where I ought to be?"

Hortensia, whose long face held a look of permanent disdain—Khooshie later confided that at first he mistook her for my long-lost mother—replied severely that she could not tell, as she did not have eyes in the back of her head.

However, she obligingly cranked round to look. A moment later she turned back to take the horsewhip to me with her eyes. "If you mean the person in the gold lace, you must know who that is?" she said.

"Cinema usher? Swimming-pool attendant?"

"It's the Viceroy of India, of course," snapped the wife of the civil servant. "Field Marshal Lord Blount."

Blount, Blount. I looked back at the great man, and: "Now I remember," I said. "Of course. I knew him when he was just plain General Sir Hebrand Blount."

Actually I had never met that particular senior officer. I only knew of him. Aside from a skirmish or two in the Boer War, he had never commanded men in battle, a background that tended, I thought, to make senior officers all the more bloodthirsty. At the beginning of the Great War he was commandant of the Staff College, Camberwell. After the war he was made Chief of the Imperial General Staff, a reward, I believe, for his efforts in maintaining a steady supply of cannon fodder for the army in France. In the last year of the war, Britain's Prime Minister, Lloyd George, had become greatly alarmed at the way the army was gobbling up the youth of the country. He attempted to resist the spendthrift generals by holding back the country's last reserves of young men. Blount, along with his cronies Field Marshals Robertson and Haig, had led the resistance to this namby-pamby economy on the part of the 'frocks' and had succeeded in the end in feeding the last of the island's youth into the western front's martial mincing machine.

And now, apparently, he was governing India. Lovely.

"Imagine, having the Viceroy of India at the very next table," the ICS man's wife breathed.

"Say, I wonder if he'd give an interview," Mrs. Spencer said in her rich, resonant voice. Petronella Spencer was a tough-looking American with a scarlet slash of a mouth.

"Never mind him," Hortensia said. "What I want to know is, where's the ship's captain? He's supposed to be up there at the head of the table."

"I expect he's trying to get the ship to start," I contributed. "That's why there's a delay, see? I expect he's down in the engine room, cranking the engine."

"With a crank handle, do you suppose?" Mrs. Spencer enquired.

"That's ridiculous," the ICS man snorted. "You don't start ship engines with crank handles."

"Course not," said Mrs. Spencer. "They all have self-starters now."

Later, between courses, I turned back for another inspection of the august personage at the adjoining table, wondering if, once again, a senior officer was about to make life difficult for me. I can't say I much liked the look of Blount. He had a square face like a sandstone cliff from which sprouted the fierce vegetation of his peppery eyebrows, and an ample mustache. The mustache, mostly gray except for a yellowish stain or two, entirely filled in the area between his hooked nose and a mouth like the entrance to a piggy bank. Perched above the redoubtable beezer were light blue, penetrating eyes, all too plainly capable of harboring arrogant stares, as I had already discovered.

Sensing my scrutiny, which after all was coming from only a few feet away, he turned and treated me to another such stare.

Which caused me to abandon the physiognomical inventory in a hurry, and turn to the more rewarding sight of a strip of raw salmon on my plate.

"That's her, that's her," Khooshie said suddenly in an urgent undertone, and tugged uncouthly at my sleeve.

"Her who?"

"Her, her, the girl I was telling you about. Miss Golightly. At the table next to the gold pillar. The one I love."

"You've fallen for a gold pillar?"

"No, no, the girl, the girl."

Hortensia and Mrs. Spencer turned and looked in the appropriate direction.

"The one you met at the diplomatic shindig?" I asked.

"Yes. Don't stare—you'll embarrass her."

"She's just a child, surely."

"She's fifteen. Yes," he went on, going all mushy, "she is why I changed all my traveling arrangements. She is the one I love."

"You mean you're only on this ship because of her?" Mrs. Spencer asked.

"Oh, yes," Khooshie said. "Originally I intended to be going homeward in my father's yacht."

"His father's yacht," breathed the ICS man's wife to her husband. They darted hankering looks at each other.

"Gee, how romantic," Mrs. Spencer said, looking at the handsome lad in the perfect dinner jacket decorated with the diamond star and crimson ribbon of the Jhamjarh Order of Merit, which he had awarded himself an hour or so previously.

Meanwhile various waiters continued to pour various drinks into various glasses: hock, chablis, claret and Burgundy; and showing neither fear nor favor, I accepted all offerings, and continued to be the life and soul of the party, talking, among other subjects, of antagonists I had known and bested. "Among whom," I expounded, removing Khooshie's hand from my glass—he had capped it in a vain attempt to discourage a refill—"I can boast one sovereign and prime ministers galore."

"Prime Minister Galore?" Mrs. Spencer asked. "I know him well. He's from Tuscany."

"That's the one. And among others I can number—though I've never been particularly good at arithmetic—are several relatives, not excluding my parents, ministers of state, army instructors, orchestral conductors, dogs, parrots, and my very first battalion commander. Gosh, he really hated me, though in fact I was the most perfect soldier ever to plod the Western Front, a fearless, talented, obedient servant of God and temperance, who genuinely believed, poor sap, that he was fighting a crusade for liberty and democracy. It was this colonel who subsequently encouraged me to transfer from the army to the air force, where my chief antagonist was to be no less a personage than the Chief of Air Staff, whose particular resistance to this winged, pipped, striped and ribboned flyer—that's me, Petronella—had roots initially as tentative as the radicle of a bean, old bean, but which finally produced a plumule of California redwood proportions, and merely because every time I met him I tended to follow him around, opportuning him, treading on his heels, and breathing gin and advice all over his increasingly magenta countenance and...but enough about him. Let's talk about me. My next antagonist was—or was that the one before?—was Major Auchinflint, who behaved very vindictively toward me—I was a mere colonel by then, and, let me see, yes, there was that headmaster at Fallow Grammar School who—"

"Bartholomew," Khooshie hissed, wrenching at my tux. But like drinking from a spittoon, once started it was difficult to stop; though I must admit that even I was becoming aware, after I'd been prattling nonstop for half an hour, faster and faster, louder and louder, that I was in some danger of becoming garrulous. Everybody at my table had fallen silent, apart from Khooshie's hisses, and, indeed, so had everybody in the vicinity. All except the Viceroy. He had summoned a pair of aides to his table, and was now consulting them with an air of urgency.

So I stopped talking, to allow anyone who wished to continue the conversation, but nobody did, so I was forced to keep the party going by resuming my light, amusing discourse on notable antagonists. Until I became aware that someone was tapping me on the shoulder. It was one of the Viceroy's aides. He was standing by my chair, his face novocained with embarrassment.

"Sir? Sir? Excuse me," said the aide.

"What, what?"

"You are disturbing the Viceroy's party."

"Oh, is he giving a party? Why wasn't I invited?"

"You are causing a disturbance, sir," the young officer murmured. Aware that everybody in the entire dining room was listening, his cheeks were rigid with self-consciousness. "To begin with, you are speaking rather too loudly."

"Perhaps it only seems that way because everybody else in the room is so hushed," I explained patiently.

"His Excellency feels you are speaking in an undisciplined, not to say hectic manner."

"If you're not to say it, why are you saying it?"

"There's no need to get excited, sir," the aide said, but was interrupted by the voice of his master which sounded at least as loud as mine.

"For God's sake, Brownlee, don't stand there arguing. Get rid of him. And get his name. We're not putting up with this sort of nonsense on this ship."

I swiveled slowly in my seat and stared directly at the Viceroy. I was utterly dumbfounded. Get rid of him? Get his *name*? Just who did he think he was?

I just couldn't believe it, that even the boss of an entire subcontinent would say such a thing, and order about another passenger who, for all he knew, might even be quite a worthy sort of bloke.

I mean, I might have understood it if he had *known* that I was a disloyal scoundrel. But he was speaking in that fashion without even being aware of my immediate past. I tell you, I was utterly confounded and astounded and dumbfounded, and my lineaments mirrored these emotions. They must have, for the Viceroy's own face took aboard several additional emotions of its own, chief among them being a suffused rage that anyone would dare to stare at him in such an undisciplined manner.

His gritty sandstone face cracked and his mustache worked so violently that half of it disappeared up his nose. From several feet away I could plainly see his knuckles whitening around a crystal goblet.

His voice, however, was under sufficient control to avoid the scene that might have ensued had he actually bellowed. "Don't you dare stare at me like that," he said. No, it was not entirely under control. There was a distinct beat there, as if an aide was pounding him gently on the back to dislodge something in his craw. "Come here."

"Eh?"

"*Come here.*"

After a moment, more amazed than ever, I rose, just as the siren sounded three times and the ship gave a small lurch. No, honest, it was definitely the ship that lurched. I might have been guzzling alcohol in several different forms for the past fifty hours or so, but I would never demean myself in such posh company by actually lurching. In fact I crossed the gap between our two tables in so perfect a straight line that even Euclid would have applauded.

As I halted and stood in front of him, His Excellency stared at me as if I were something brown on the sole of his jackboots.

I stood there, determined not to fidget.

After a few hours the Field Marshal said in a low voice, "What's your name?"

"Bartholomew Bandy, sir."

"Are you drunk, Mr. Bandy?"

I was just about to reply when the ship lurched again. Or so I thought, but there was no corresponding movement on the part of the other passengers. Far from swaying in sympathy with the yawing motion, the other diners remained frozen, silent, and very nearly breathless.

"Yes, I think that's all I need to know," he said contemptuously. "Except that I shall be watching your conduct very closely from now on."

"All right," he added after a moment. "You may leave the room."

"Pardon?"

"You will leave the dining room," Field Marshal Lord Blount said.

I gaped all over again. I was being ordered out. Something that had not happened to me since I wet my short pants back in school. I was shocked almost into sobriety. Which was fortunate as it enabled me to think rather more coherently and allow me to weigh the two courses open to me: to defy the Viceroy and reseat myself, or to obey the order. I dismissed the first almost immediately. The penalty was likely to be severe. Even if the Viceroy did not order his aides to eject me forcibly, which would cause an indelible scandal, if I remained I would have to sit there as isolated as a ship with a yellow flag, pallid with humiliation, nerves in tumult, sweating with embarrassment, floored, grounded, stumped, and socially catatonic. Whereas the walk to the exit would be an agony. But at least some tatters of dignity might still cover my parts—assuming I managed to reach the door without staggering again.

As if to forecast this possibility, the ship lurched again, and the siren blasted, and the deck shifted. As I stood there for centuries I saw Khooshie staring at me and then breaking all records in his haste to disconnect his gaze. He looked away so quickly he must have risked ricking his neck. His face was a muddy pink.

So I bowed slightly to the Viceroy, and with as much dignity as one could stick in a gnat's arsehole, I turned and walked off across the polished floor which was now perceptibly in motion as the ship disconnected from the shore.

It was not an easy journey. I had to weave between rigid tablefuls of stonefaced diners, and gaping, whitecoated stewards. And so toward the glaring, semi-circular stage at the entrance, watched every step of the way by three hundred pairs of goggling optics, and in dead silence.

The walk was easily the worst in a life that had seen quite a few such spectacles. But it was better than sitting there for the rest of the meal—if I'd been allowed to. Anyway, by exercising the utmost self-control, and proceeding in the most cautious manner possible commensurate with actually getting anywhere, I managed to reach the three wide steps and to mount them without staggering.

I had reached my stateroom before I decided to totter against the bulkhead. At which point it occurred to me that perhaps I had better not wait until 1925, that perhaps I had better bring my New Year's Resolution forward a bit. I was beginning to suspect that I had been drinking just a little too much lately.

Skulking on the Boat Deck

A fter that ghastly scene enacted before every single first-class passenger on the ship, I decided to stay in bed for the next six weeks or however long it took to get to Bombay.

Khooshie agreed that this was an excellent idea. "It's all right for you," he stormed the morning after the public execution, "but I have been utterly humiliated. You have shown me up in front of the whole British Empire. I shall never be able to face myself again."

"I didn't realize I was talking so much."

"Talking so much?" He waved his arms as if gathering in the sheaves. "You were talking as if you had glossological diarrhea."

"Whatalogical diarrhea?" I croaked, noting that though I might not have much influence over the boy's affairs, I was having some effect on his vocabulary. That phrase of his was the sort that I might have employed in a linguistically self-indulgent moment.

"Not only that," he went on loudly, "You were talking as if you were hailing the masthead in a cyclone."

"Well, it wasn't my fault."

"Not your fault?" he shouted, his dark eyes with their pallisade of black eyelashes bulging under the pressure of his passion. "Not your fault? You were drunk. You were utterly helpless—if that's not your fault I don't know what is. You were disgustingly inebriated."

"Not disgusting, surely?"

"You were stinking with whiskies," Khooshie stormed, kicking a couple of servants aside. They did tend to litter the suite, there was no doubt about that. They seemed to have deposited their bedrolls everywhere, like elephant droppings.

The Maharajah's handsome son often flew into a temper, but it usually passed like a summer storm. There was a tender heart inside that narrow chest. If he felt that his passions were excessive or his words unjust he quickly made up for it, provided that this did not involve him in an actual apology, which, of course, would have been *lèse-majesté*. But this time it looked as if several hours were going to pass before I was forgiven.

"Well, you should have stopped me," I mumbled.

"Did I not try to, many times? Did I not keep whistling impotently through my teeth? But you just went on and on." And he went on and on about the manner of my discourse, and how I had completely ruined his chances with Mrs. Golightly.

"Miss Golightly, you mean."

"Mrs. Golightly!"

"I thought it was Miss Golightly you were interested in."

"It is, but it seems I cannot get to her without buttering her mother all over. And I was getting on so well with her, too."

"Mrs. Golightly?"

"Miss Golightly! But now I am having to pretend I am not with you—that I am not having the foggiest notion who you are. Which will not be easy," he added, subsiding somewhat, "when they see that we are living together."

Too unhappy even to remonstrate over the way he was characterizing our domestic arrangements, I cradled my head and rocked it carefully. "I wish I was dead," I moaned.

"A sentiment that seems to have been shared by a remarkable number of people," Khooshie snapped. "Really, Bartholomew, you are thirty-two years old, it is time you are pulling yourself together," he added, demonstrating his ability to command the language with authority one moment, and lose his idiomatic grip the next. "You are just too conspicuous to be in good taste, Bartholomew, that is what the trouble is. You are just too conspicuous."

My decision not to reappear in the dining room until we reached Asia was reinforced by the looks, nudges, comments, and titters that greeted me over the next couple of days from the entire passenger list, including the second-class people. "That's him, that's him," one woman whispered loudly, and I heard another describe how I had been frogmarched from the dining lounge by the Viceroy's bodyguard. One second-class passenger had personally seen me staggering helplessly about the deck. He just refused to remember that a storm was raging at the time.

It was also being said that I had lost my job as a result of my scandalous behavior with a Mrs. Golightly, and that it was the intention of the authorities to throw me off the ship at Malta and bundle me home in disgrace. This was not as unlikely as it sounded. Practically everybody with interests in India was dependent to some extent on the Imperial authority. Even clashing with a district resident in British India could have serious consequences, so to come into conflict with the government at its highest level, the King-Emperor's representative himself, was considered to be plain suicide.

It was hunger that finally overcame shame. As the ship ploughed deeper into the Atlantic, the bow battering the waves with roars of rage, and the air silver-plated with spray, my appetite, which over the past frantic months had been declining in inverse ratio to a dipsomaniacal consumption of alcohol, began to revive. I grew hungrier and hungrier. The midmorning broth and the late evening buffet which could be taken in solitude were simply not adequate. The cold blustery air increased my appetite still further. I was positively famished. Finally—the hell with it. Halfway across the Bay of Biscay I dressed for dinner and marched, arms swinging, back to the scene of my wigging before the world, and after only a mouthful or two of encouraging oxygen, I sauntered in as casually as the heaving deck would permit, looking as if I had as much right to be there as anybody. Before seating myself, I panned a defiant visage around the splendor, daring anyone to deny me my rights. By gad, if anyone stared back, I would give them the physiognomical works, all right.

Not a soul reacted to my reappearance. This was because there was hardly anyone there. The dining room was nearly deserted. The few passengers who had braved the marine undulations were too preoccupied with their queasiness even to remark my entrance.

The captain's table was totally deserted.

Even those passengers who had risked the odors of rich sauces and pork crackling did not look as if they would be tarrying much longer. They were sitting there clutching the table with ivory knuckles as their avoirdupois kept falling to zero, or rising rapidly until it reached half a ton, depending on whether the ship was sinking or rising. Their nerves were being further teased and shredded by the crash of crockery, the reverberating clash of upset utensils, and some chef-like vituperation.

At my table the only survivor was Hortensia, who observed that "Even the Viceroy and his wife are flat out with *mal de mer*."

"Sick, are they? Gosh, that's too bad." I said sympathetically as I thought of the Viceroy gagging in his bunk, with just enough strength left to raise his head and vomit over his best uniform.

Preserving that thought, I tucked into all seven courses of the evening meal, and even had an extra helping of suet pudding, the sight of me eating it causing the last of the diners to sideslip, cheeks bulging, to the exit.

We were deep into the Mediterranean before the January seas—it was now 1925—began to subside to a sullen heaving, and the dining room slowly regained its upper-crust population. Which, after an initial stare or two, paid no further attention to me.

The Viceroy paid no further attention either. He had dealt with me. If I was anything like the people he was used to dealing with, that was that. He would never hear from me again.

Though I might have derived some satisfaction from describing the Viceroy and his wife in a prejudiced sort of way, I'm afraid I had to admit that they were a not unimpressive couple. Lady Blount was a thin, tensely dignified woman in her late forties, her emotional hatches too thoroughly battened down by an upper-class upbringing to pose much of a danger. As for her husband, I could not deny that he cut quite a figure, especially when he wore his dress uniform with its masses of gold braid and its array of stars, orders, badges, and sashes. He might have looked even more imposing had the uniform been suspended from broader shoulders. To compensate for their narrowness, however, he increased steadily in width from the waistline down. British brasshats often seemed exceptionally wide in the haunch region, possibly because of their uniform jackets, whose style, in combination with the puffing-out effect of the cavalry breeches that many of them favored, made them look like harbor buoys.

To be completely fair, however, his paltry shoulders and fine, childbearing hips did not seem quite so out of proportion when draped in evening wear, or in the Harris tweed suits that he seemed particularly fond of. And there was no denying the authority built into the square Scots face; authority that was known to brook no slackness, opposition, or weakness of any kind in his inferiors. I felt that I would have to treat him very warily once we showed our hand in India; that is, when the Royal Jhamjarh Air Force became operational.

Because he was likely to be a particularly difficult adversary I proceeded to study Field Marshal Lord Blount and acquaint myself with his character, history, and routine...at least, that was the ostensible reason why I began to watch him with the dedication of an eagle scouting for its evening meal. I noted that once the ship was on an even keel again, his routine was quickly established. He and the missus were invariably the first to appear for breakfast each morning. They returned to their suite at eight-forty, to re-emerge promptly at ten o'clock for a stroll about the deck, awarding regal nods to those passengers who were worth acknowledging. At eleven, the two of them repaired to the first-class saloon, which was where the mid-morning soup was dished up. (They were still serving hot broth the day we arrived in Bombay.) At eleven-thirty, while the Vicereine returned to the suite for a spot of shut-eye, hubby occupied a roped-off section of the promenade deck, there to transact official business, his aides providing him with a steady supply of notes, briefs, *aides-memoire*, orders for people to be executed, etc.

At one pip emma came luncheon. Two to four p.m., siesta. Five-thirty, drinks in one of the first-class bars—the best one, not the cubby-hole on A Deck that I had discovered on my first day aboard, and to which I had never returned, except in spirit. There the Viceroy sat in state, receiving senior officers, first-class supplicants, and others. Once he even deigned to receive the ship's captain.

I noticed with vague disappointment that he attended few of the special events with which the ship's personnel plagued the rest of us, the games, dances, concerts, and recitals that might have provided an opportunity for reven—for further study. His only relaxation appeared to be the occasional game of bridge with his wife and their cronies, a General in the Indian Army and his wife. And he went to bed at a disgracefully early hour, never later than eleven.

As well as studying his routine, I searched for biographical material on him in the ship's library; but there was little except the entry in *Who's Who*; from which I learned that he had been born forty-seven years previously in Scotland and had made a good job of suppressing his lowland accent and adopting the thin, nasal speech of the English brasshat, and that his hobby was photography. I could have told *Who's Who* that myself. I had observed him diligently photographing everything in sight from the moment he marched aboard. During the stop at Marseilles he had not only gone ashore with his bellows camera but with a tripod as well. Plainly he took the hobby seriously. He seemed especially pleased with a feature of the camera that enabled him to set it, hurry in front of the lens, and snap his own photo as he stood smartly at the taffrail, or posed on the boat deck, shading his eyes as he scanned the horizon like stout Cortez.

And quite frequently he opened his photograph albums to the best people.

Among those so honored was Petronella Spencer, who had managed to obtain an interview with His Excellency via outrageous flattery. I asked her what his photographs were like, hoping to be told that they were really rotten; but she said that they were pretty good, considering, quite well composed, though the subject matter was kinda restricted: mostly views of the ship's superstructure, buildings of architectural interest, and self-portraits and pictures of his wife.

"No photographs of any human beings at all, eh?" I said.

That was the day the ship called at Port Said, gateway to the Suez Canal. Actually it didn't just call in but hung around for days, taking on fuel and water, and some Indian Army deserters in chains.

Though I had not so far disembarked at any port en route in case the ship left without me on purpose, I did go ashore at Port Said, even though I had already seen Egypt. Few other passengers followed the example. Whereas many of them had explored Marseilles and Valletta quite assiduously during the stopovers there, they refused to set foot in Egypt in case they met an Egyptian. They had a poor opinion of the 'Gyppies', regarding them as decadent and deceitful. Personally I thought that after a sojourn in first class, Egyptians would have made a nice change.

Postillion was one of the few passengers to join me on the gangway. "I thought that after being in Coventry for so long," he said in his upper-class drawl, "you might welcome a spot of company."

"Not particularly."

"I'll come anyway. Just having a quick shufti round Port Said, are you?"

"I was thinking of taking the day trips to Cairo, Memphis, and Sakhara."

"That's all right, I don't mind going there."

So we became tourists together; he quite liked Egypt; but he was not very appreciative of the marvellous sights. He complained that Memphis was dusty.

He was moderately enthusiastic about Cairo, though. He was keen on staying the night at Shepheard's Hotel, as he had heard so much about it. He changed his mind, though, when apprised of the tariff. "Six pounds for a single room?" he exclaimed. "The department certainly wouldn't wear that."

Postillion was not exactly the ideal traveling companion. Few of the sights of Ancient Egypt interested him. He was frank enough to confess that he had no use for culture. He'd had enough classical muck at school to last him until his civil-service pension. He was even less pleased when we got back to Port Said and a grinning pedlar sold him a packet of French postcards. The Arab had recommended them as being thoroughly worthwhile. "Very rude, sir, very smutty," he'd opined. But when Postillion opened the packet he found them to be, indeed, French postcards: views of the Place de la Concorde, Notre Dame, and the like, the only nude being a photograph of a Greek statue—male.

"Dashed depraved lot, the Egyptians," he said, attempting with a laugh to suggest that he appreciated the joke.

He continued to trail along even while I was visiting Simon Arzt, the famous outfitters, to purchase a solar topee. Thus protected, I set off to explore what little of Port Said was worth exploring.

Finally I turned to him, saying suddenly, "Keeping an eye on me, are you, Postillion?"

"What? My dear fellow, why on earth would I wish to do that?"

"I have the impression you've been doing so ever since you so hurriedly booked passage on the ship just hours after I did."

"Don't know what you're talking about, old man."

"In that case you won't mind if I go off on my own to meet somebody with a foreign accent," I said, moving off.

Thirty paces later as I headed along the sea front in the direction of Lake Menzaleh, he caught up.

"My dear chap, I'm merely keeping you company, that's all," he said. "I thought you could do with a friend."

"No. So either come clear or bugger off, Postillion."

His pale refined face turned pink. "You're very rude, Bandy, I must say," he said.

When I continued to stand there in the hot street gazing at him through a haze of flies, he said at length, "I don't know why you're being so suspicious."

Again I turned and walked off. Again he caught up, breathing hard. "Oh, all right," he said, angrily sweeping a hank out of his eyes. "You win."

"You are spying on me?"

"Yes, yes."

"For the Foreign Office?"

"For the Government, yes."

"That's better," I said, patting him approvingly on the back. "Now that wasn't so difficult, was it?"

As we walked along the sandy sea front he said irritably, "I don't know what they expected me to do, anyway. I'm not trained for this sort of thing. I was supposed to be going to India to evaluate certain intelligence information, not this cloak and dagger stuff. There's a suspicion the Russians are up to something, out there. . . . But when they heard you'd booked passage on the *Viceroy*, they rushed me onto it too, saying they couldn't spare anyone else, and as I was going out to India anyway. . .you're not really meeting a foreigner, are you?"

"I'm off to the red-lamp district."

He stopped dead. "I'm not going there," he said.

"Oh, come on, you'll enjoy it."

"I never paid for it in my life."

"I bet you never got it free, either. Oh, come on, Francis."

"Won't."

"It'll be a new experience."

"I don't like new experiences. I don't like any kind of experience. I'm an academic."

"Oh, come on."

In the end I managed to persuade him to accompany me to the red-lamp district, which was on the outskirts—or should that be outtrousers?—of town. There we drank thick Turkish coffee at a sidewalk cafe, cracked nuts, and watched old men puffing hubble-bubbles in the shade.

"You should have told me you were just sightseeing," Postillion said reprovingly.

Actually I was there for a purpose, which I carried out later, alone. I purchased a packet of pornography.

And I made sure the goods were genuine; I made sure of that before parting with a *piastre*. In fact the examination lasted twenty-five minutes before I was satisfied that I was in possession of the genuine articles: a dozen prints on ordinary photographic paper of plump Egyptian hoydens bent like crossbows over Birmingham beds, furcate negresses, succulent houris, collared studs with extraordinarily long, thin penises, and even a sample of rampant fauna, an aroused yet somehow disconsolate donkey.

These studies were not, of course, for my own consumption. Though I had advanced from the priggish trench excavated for me by a Christian upbringing, I still could not entirely approve of pornography, especially as the art was invariably deficient in imagination...though mind you, I did pick up a useful tip or two...no, the photos were for somebody else entirely.

Unfortunately I had still not managed to plant the pictures by the time we left Port Said, and the grubby packet was still on my person as the ship beat rhythmically down the Red Sea under an increasingly fierce sun. I was anxious to get rid of the incriminating material. After that scene in the dining room, being caught with filthy pictures would put me on the same level as Oscar Wilde or the Marquis de Sade's chiropodist. But

I had to maintain my hot hip pocket as a safety deposit. I did not dare leave them in the stateroom. The staff tended to nip in and out of the accommodation quite frequently, Hoovering, tidying, bedmaking, hairdressing, manicuring, or delivering drinks, meals, or remedies at all hours of the day or night. It would be just my luck if a steward found the pictures and took them straight to the captain, who was a Victorian *paterfamilias* with exceptionally narrow-minded eyes. He looked quite capable of putting me off the ship even if we were in the middle of the Red Sea.

Besides, I needed the pictures to be at hand when the opportunity arose. Which it hadn't, even by the time we reached Aden at the plug end of the Red Sea.

In the end, planting the filthy pictures on the Viceroy— which, of course, was the reason I had purchased them—as I reminded myself every time I shuffled through the collection to make sure they were all there—proved hopeless. The closest I ever came to his photograph album—into which I was hoping to slip the pack and augment His Excellency's collection with a few samples of extraneous material—was six feet. It was all very disappointing. Night after night I had lain in my luxury bunk, composing variations on the scene where the Viceroy's album is passed proudly to some influential friends of his. The friends, preferably including wives, are suppressing their yawns manfully—or in other cases, womanfully—as they turn page after page of cathedrals and ruined kirks, symmetrical gardens, Scottish crags, blurred shots of the Marseilles *vieux port*, seascapes, Valletta harbor, a sand dune, dhows, and numerous self-portraits. Producing a continuous stream of appreciative cooing noises, the friends turn yet another page—to reveal a clump of loose photos. These are assumed to be part of the Viceroy's collection, naturally. He hasn't had time to mount them. The friends—the men have influence at court, the women in society—pick up the photographs. They grow terribly still. The gentlemen's glasses steam up. Hurriedly they wipe them and restore them to humid beaks, and examine the photographs as if studying for a gynecological exam—or zoological, if the first picture is the one involving the donkey. Meanwhile the wives, resting their worthy bosoms on their spouses shoulders—one bosom per shoulder—are similarly transfixed. Thinking that the photograph has somehow slipped in by mistake—they're giving the Viceroy the benefit of the doubt, see?—they turn to the next picture, anticipating yet another shot of Kilmarnock Academy. But no, it's the one with the sepia trollop and the Egyptian weightlifters. . . .

But perhaps it was just as well that I failed to plant the photos on Field Marshal Lord Blount. With my luck, I would almost certainly have been caught, like the photos, in the act.

India!

B efore sailing for Bombay I had outfitted myself pretty thoroughly at Gieves of Old Bond Street, purchasing items essential for a sojourn in the East, such as calamine lotion for seared lips, talcum powder for sweat rash, salt tablets in the shape of Lot's wife, pith helmet, water wings for the monsoon, snakeproof underwear, pigsticking lance, and a fan for men. Also, hearing that there were no books in India, I had laid in a stock of reading material, including a history of the continent. From which I learned that India had been invaded pretty thoroughly over the centuries notably by the Aryans, Aryans being Persians of good family who, finding not much class in India, imported their own in the form of the rigid castes that Hindus were still stuck with: the Brahmin or priest class, *Kshatriyas*, the warriors and nobles to which the Maharajah belonged and who was therefore inferior to many of his own subjects, the *Vaisyas* or cultivators, the *Sudras* who did most of the labor, and the Untouchables, who had no caste at all.

Over the years, other invaders followed the Aryan example, including Sandy the Great and Tammy the Lame. Consequently the natives were pretty resigned to being subjugated long before our lot arrived.

Upon landing on Indian dust, the English immediately realized that it was time somebody ran the place properly. India certainly couldn't be left to a people who lived their lives as if they actually believed in God, and who refused to eat delicious bacon, ham, pork sausages, and so forth.

After taking over three-fifths of India, the British, as the English had then become, decided to call it a day, and allow the rest of the territory, in the form of several hundred kingdoms, to remain independent. Their rulers would owe ultimate allegiance to the Crown, but otherwise could govern their subjects as they pleased. If the princes ruled scandalously they were required to make sure that nobody heard about it, otherwise the paramount power would be forced to intervene. More than one rascally ruler had been overthrown when his autocracy became too extreme. The independent Muslim State of Khaliwar was the example we were most concerned with. Its Nawab, Sharif-ul-Khalil, had indulged in distinctly pro-German activities during the Great War. When he persisted in misbehaving himself, the British marched in and replaced him with a compliant weakling named Mohammed Farookhi.

Recently, though, my employer, the Maharajah of Jhamjarh, had come to suspect that Sharif had regained power in his state while maintaining Farookhi as a figurehead, and that Sharif had aggressive intentions toward Jhamjarh and the rest of India; but the Maharajah had found it impossible to convince anyone else of the danger except me (but then he was paying me such an enormous salary I would have believed anything he said).

To resume our history lesson, of the 500-odd independent states, some were almost as large as Persia, others were the size of a Persian carpet. Jhamjarh in Central India was one of the larger states, 50,000 square miles of low hills, irrigated plains, patches of desert, and tangle of jungle, with a population of about eight million. The royal lineage went back to the golden age of Hinduism at the start of the millenium when the kingdom was founded by Putta the Exalted, about whom it was said that snakes died when he bit them.

Jhamjarh was also one of the richer states, along with Baroda, Hyderabad, Gwalior, Kashmir, and Mysore. Some said that Jhamjarh was the richest state of all, though its value in money terms had never been computed. The national treasure filled a chamber thirty feet long. I knew this because one evening when he had nothing better to do, the Maharajah showed me to the *toshakhana*. Accompanied by the Hereditary Controller of the Treasury–who was paid a salary of eight rupees a month—about three bucks—he took me along to that strongroom. It was guarded by *chowkidars*, all of whom were sound asleep when we arrived. Though the state treasure was worth hundreds of millions of dollars, it was not a very impressive sight. For one thing, most of the loot was tucked away on shelves, and in chests, drawers, and cupboards. Also, because of the inadequate lighting in the windowless chamber—its exact location in the City Palace in Djelybad must, for obvious reasons, remain a secret—the treasure hardly gleamed. I had imagined an Aladdin's cave of flaring gold and squint-making diamonds, or a choc-a-bloc Monte Cristo equivalent. Instead there were shabby coffers and frayed trayfuls of precious stones that were less vivid than geological specimens in a museum. The rest of the Maharajah's family assets consisted of cabinets filled with necklaces, pendants, bracelets, coronets, eyebrows and fringes, jewelled and enameled weapons, rose-water basins, palm-leaf boxes, perfume bottles, and censers, and numerous chests of ancient coins. Perhaps with a few more lighted lamps it might have looked a dazzling abundance. But even the containers were difficult to appreciate despite being of unimaginable value: boxes, chests, caskets, trunks made of solid gold worked by craftsmen and studded with rubies, emeralds, sapphires, and so forth. Yet in that light they looked hardly more interesting than fire buckets or coal scuttles. About the only thing that made my heart beat fast with avarice was a diamond the size of a doorknob. The Maharajah let me hold it for a minute before insisting on replacing it in its special satin-lined box. "The trouble is," he said as we left the chamber, "that the treasure keeps increasing." And he went on to explain that his radiant capital was augmented generation by generation and rarely subtracted from. Whenever a queen or princess of Jhamjarh had passed on to the next existence, her possessions, precious gifts accumulated over a lifetime, went straight to the treasury, while her successor ordered a complete new outfit of gold and jewelry; which would ultimately end up in the *toshakhana* as well. "And I'm the only one who is allowed to spend the stuff or give it away."

"Oh, hard luck, sir."

"If only my people would ask for more," he said. Then looked at me sideways, realizing that I was joshing; whereupon he covered his mouth and giggled.

This morning he was attired in one of his ghastly calf-length coats. It looked as if it was made of curtain material. Thick, brocaded and purple, it was grabbing him by the throat at the top and abrading his knees at the bottom. A gold chain hung from the tight collar with a 2,000-year-old Hindu coin dangling from it. The coin was the size of your average hubcap. Perched atop his fuzzy gray hair was a purple velvet cap. Diamonds hung from his earlobes and sparkled on his knuckles.

All of which was useful in distracting attention from his face, which was so spectacularly ugly that even after living with it for fifty years he was still trying to hide from strangers by trying to retract the face into his collar like a tortoise, or partially cover it with a skinny hand. It certainly was a bizarre face. It was concave. His bulging brow, sharp cheeks, and Punch chin all sloped inward toward a small nose and a strange orange mouth, and moreover the skin was blotched and pockmarked.

I thought he was beautiful, because of his eyes. They more than made up for the catastrophe of his mug. They were large, misty black, and glorious in their depth and sensitivity, and contained no vanity or meanness. Which was not to say their owner could not be mischievous, or peevish, or even unjustly accusing; but nothing could alter the fact that when he was tranquil and you looked into his eyes you felt you were seeing straight into the universe of his soul.

He had the misfortune, he said, as we strolled along to Khooshie's new golf course in the City Palace grounds, to be an enlightened ruler. In his thirty-year reign he had built many temples and public buildings. He had also modernized and extended the State's railway system, raised the school leaving age to ten, and had reduced corruption in the public service until it was now merely prevalent rather than widespread. "And of course you have seen my concrete highway, which is running all the way from here to the bridge over the Bamm River—five whole miles of two-lane highway, with one lane in each direction," he added proudly.

"M'm."

"And under my rule the judicial system has become strong but utterly fair. Only the other day when a family forced a young woman to join her deceased husband on the funeral pyre, we made them pay for it. We fined them no fewer than thirty rupees."

"I bet that taught them a lesson."

"Indeed yes. It is a very serious offence now, you see, to incinerate women," the Maharajah explained. "Even Mrs. Golightly."

I was just about to ask what Mrs. Golightly had to do with it, when a golf ball came whizzing up and struck one of the Maharajah's servants.

"Fore," Khooshie called out from the distance.

Having been introduced to the game in England, the prince had ordered a nine-hole golf course to be built in the grounds of the City Palace. As a remarkable variety of buildings were scattered within the seven miles of palace wall, this had presented the Minister of Public Works with some problems, which he solved by grassing over a few roads, and demolishing the Palace guards' recreational facilities and the Alexandrian Fountains.

This morning Khooshie was playing with John Derby, one of our squadron commanders and my best friend.

Fair-faced, square-shouldered Derby, normally a coolly cynical bloke, seemed to be in rather a temper. "God damn it, Khooshie, you can't allow that," he was shouting, apparently referring to the activities of the prince's servants. Khooshie's ball, having bounced off the head of a member of the Maharajah's entourage, had rolled into the rough, and two of Khooshie's men were busily mowing the grass in that area.

They were still arguing as they drew level with us. "Oh, very well," Khooshie was saying irritably. "But it is very hard indeed to hit a ball when it is in all that grass."

"But that's the whole point of the game."

"How can it be the whole point of the game, to make things so difficult? Surely the whole point of the game is to hit the ball and go on hitting it until it falls into a hole. But how am I ever going to make it fall into a hole if I am not permitted to hit it freely?"

"But you're not making it fall into the hole even when you reach the green! One of your servants always rushes over and pops the ball down the hole for you!"

"They are only trying to be helpful."

"I notice they don't do the same thing for me, though." `

"Well, my goodness, of course not," Khooshie said with an indulgent laugh that was slightly spoiled by the irritable mood he was in this morning. "Why should I pay my servants to put your balls in the hole? Be reasonable, John."

Derby muttered, and wandered over, and said in an undertone, "I can put up with him clearing away all the undergrowth whenever he lands in the rough, and even with his habit of taking a free shot whenever he misses the ball, but I damn well draw the line at him putting a servant in every bunker so they can throw out his ball whenever it lands there."

In the meantime, Khooshie had gone marching up to the Maharajah. "Father," he said in a peremptory tone, "have you considered my invitation to Mrs. Golightly? I wish to invite her for a lengthy stay in the palace."

"Oh, dear," the Maharajah said, one hand strangling the other, "I do hope you will not insist, dear son. She is a terrible woman."

"Nonsense, pater. What is terrible about her?"

"Well, for one thing, she looks down on me, dear son."

"That is natural enough—she is a foot taller than you."

"Besides, I thought it was Miss Golightly that you were interested in, dear son."

"I have lost interest in the daughter—she is too immature. It is now Mrs. Golightly I wish to sleep with."

"I do not think that the lady in question would be entirely amenable to that arrangement, Khooshie," the Maharajah said unhappily. It was torture for him to deny anything to his son. "Besides, the priests are saying that it is high time that you are entering upon the period of continence before your marriage."

"Damn the priests," Khooshie shouted, thwacking the earth with his mushie, or whatever that club was called. "I cannot be expected to do without a woman for days on end, it is more than flesh and blood can bear." But it was obvious that he knew he would have to accept whatever it was the priests had decreed, however much he hooked his divots, sliced his birdies, or hacked at the green with his exalted putter.

Some days Khooshie could be almost as difficult as his father.

Sigga, Not in a Good Mood

For weeks I had been looking forward to the arrival of my senior medical officer, not least because she was also my fiancée. Sigridur Jonsdottir, M.D., was traveling on the Maharajah's private yacht along with the rear party of technicians, tradesmen, and the final batch of pilots and observers, and the ship was due to plonk anchor into the Gulf of Cambay sometime in April. I had been waiting eagerly for the Maharajah to inform me as to the precise time of arrival so that I could fly to the west coast in my private two-seater Bristol fighter, and welcome her to India, and bear her in triumph to the Haksar Palace.

When she finally arrived, though, the reunion was not noticeably successful, not least because I wasn't there.

Afterwards I suspected that the Maharajah had done it on purpose. He had taken a dislike to Sigridur in England when, in her forthright Icelandic way, she had grilled him on the tonnage, rigging, and performance of his steam yacht, and he had not known the answers. It had made him, he feared, look silly in the eyes of the English whose good opinion he craved (but which, because of his grotesquerie and superficial lack of dignity, was rarely forthcoming). In any event, he failed to inform me as to the ship's time of arrival. Instead he invited me to a banquet in my honor. Consequently, when she arrived at the end of the four-hour feast and was shown up, so was I.

Later, His Highness was full of apologies for failing to inform me that the yacht had arrived three days previously, though he rather spoiled his look of concern by turning away to snigger up his sleeve, the old bastard. Anyway, the result was that I was not there to meet her and she was forced to spend two days and three nights in a cramped railway carriage instead of two or three hours in my Bristol fighter. So that when she arrived and was escorted into the banqueting hall, shiny with heat and tacky with sweat, gritty with loco smoke and itchy with fleas, and found me reclining on silk cushions and being cooled by a giant fan as I dabbed fastidiously at Indian delicacies, she was not in the least appeased.

"Sigga," I cried amidst the Indian kerfuffle or *dhoom-dham*, and climbing to my feet with the help of a *Huzra* or two, "what a delightful surprise. I didn't expect you for days. Did you have a good journey? Gentlemen, this is my fiancée and our new medical officer, Sigridur Jonsdottir. Sigridur, this is... well, I can see you're a bit done-up and run down, so I won't introduce you to everybody, especially as there's hundreds of them, except perhaps I might introduce you to my personal staff. This is Iqbal, my senior secretary, and that's my tutor, I'm learning Hindi, you know, as much as one word per day, and this is Bin, he does my crosswords, and that's Haggi, he's in charge of my lemonade, and...but perhaps this isn't the moment for them, either. Yes, of course, I quite understand why you're unwilling to give me a kiss. You're embarrassed because you need a bath. No, no, don't apologize, I know how hot and smelly one can get in the tropics, though I'm quite used to it by now, I can keep wonderfully cool and fragrant. Anyway, my dear, I won't weary you with formalities just at the moment...why are you quivering that way, Sigga? Good Lord, you haven't got malaria already, have you? Iqbal, quick, fetch my personal physician."

As it turned out, she didn't have malaria or anything worse than angina, judging by her expression as she looked down at my get-up. To please the Maharajah I had allowed him to caparison me—a word usually applied to horses but, according to some malicious people, appropriate enough in my case—in eastern garb, complete with curly slippers. His Highness had been as pleased as a dairy cat when I acceded to his request that I go native, saying that he felt I was already becoming Indian in spirit if not in complexion. He'd had his *sirdars* dress me in a variety of colors that would have made Biblical Joseph go quite viridian with envy. I was wearing mint-green jodhpurs half-concealed under a long, falseteeth-pink coat trimmed with gold, an orange silk scarf, and a striped turban in the colors of a small African nation.

At first I had felt a touch self-conscious about the ensemble as the Maharajah took me by the hand and led me into the banqueting hall in the City Palace. However, I soon regained my composure. There was so much color there already that I did not stick out unduly. At least I didn't think so until Sigridur entered like a Wagnerian helmet. It was the way she stopped dead at the sight of my costume. By then I had convinced myself that I looked fine. The Maharajah had said I looked lovely, even. But Sigridur looked at me as if I were first on the bill in a low-class music hall. As her bright blue eyes swept over my garb I shriveled like a dick in an Icelandic fiord.

At first I rather resented being optically struck down in that fashion, and ascribed her attitude to provincialism. However, my reaction to her reaction proved to be quite unfair when, following her gaze, I looked down at myself and saw that her disgust was amply justified. Half the feast I had partaken of had skittered down my clothing. I was positively besmirched with comestibles.

The problem was that the material I was wearing had failed to conform to my form, but had bunched as a result of my being hunched on the cushion. Thus any food that was accidentally dropped on to the way to my inlet valve had tended to fall onto bulging folds of material instead of plopping straight onto the floor.

All the same, it wasn't my fault. This was my first eastern tuck-in, and I wasn't used to gormandizing without benefit of cutlery whilst seated crosslegged on cushions. To eat in the lotus position took a certain amount of practice. It was not easy for a beginner to avoid dropping the foodstuffs, especially as they were served in so many dishes. By the time Sigridur had strode in, lashing her thigh, twenty-eight brass dishes were scattered around me. I knew the precise number because I had an opportunity to count them while hanging my head in shame. The beaming brassware, incidentally, mostly contained rice. There was plain rice, rice with lentils, rice with spice, rice with apple, rice with gravy, and rice that seemed to have nothing in it until you chomped a mouthful, whereupon the inner linings of your throat burst into flame and quickly ate through several layers of tissue until finally the heat and smoke was allowed to escape through the back of the neck. There were also offerings of sweet dishes, but it was difficult to tell which they were, so that you were continuously proceeding from sweet to sour and sour to sweet, rissoles to sugar balls, coconut cakes to goat meat, or from chicken fritters to something that tasted like wine gums dipped in gravy browning. Moreover the food had to be eaten with your right hand while you craned forward from the crosslegged position. So really it was hardly surprising that some of the grub slopped onto your clothing.

But Sigridur was in no mood to make allowances for festal inexperience, and after one last look at my face which, as I discovered later to my chagrin was also somewhat smeared with sauces and dotted with rice, she turned and walked out with as much dignity as her travel-stained clothing would permit. Spurning my Haksar hospitality, she insisted on being taken straight to the aerodrome hospital.

After a bath and a rest she adopted a slightly better mood, and finally agreed to accept my excuse that I had not expected her until the following week. All the same, while agreeing that my failure to welcome her was not my fault, she reserved a certain amount of blame, kept it in reserve as it were, presumably for use as a backup reproach on the next occasion when I was at fault.

After she had seen the palace her refusal to take up residence therein was confirmed. She simply refused to wallow in luxury. Wallowing might be all right for effete Anglo-Saxons but Icelanders were made of sterner stuff. "If I am to be your medical officer," she said, "then it is my duty to be available to the men at all times."

"They'll like that. But—"

"No, I shall sleep here in this plain but wholesome hospital," she said in her amazingly good English. But then, Icelanders had to be good in some foreign tongue, as the rest of the world could hardly be expected to learn Icelandic.

"Good for you, Sigga," said John Derby.

"Still, darling," she went on, "you must not feel the slightest guilt at living in a palace while the men have to put up with these conditions."

"That's telling him, miss!" cried an envious groundling.

"But I've explained over and over that—"

"It's all right, we understand," Sigridur said, linking arms with two members of the underprivileged masses. "You go ahead and sleep between your silk sheets with a clear conscience, while the rest of us turn and toss ourselves in our crude bunks, eh, boys?"

(Her English was not, of course, *entirely* perfect.)

A Swank Mess

By the end of April the Royal Jhamjarh Air Force, five squadrons of fighter, bomber, and reconnaissance and transport aircraft, was seriously thinking of opening for business. The advance and main and the rear parties had finally settled down into their quarters, the men into their comfortable wooden huts on the aerodrome, and several of the officers into nearby Haksar Palace. Across the great, sprawling aerodrome, hangars billowed and bellowed as engines were run up, and workshops clanged, and gun alignment butts popped and stammered. The aerial firing and ground ranges were now nearly complete, and the practice bombing range had been fenced off with high barbed wire so that peasants and holy cows might not stray onto the targeted plain. We had initiated educational courses in a variety of subjects from navigation at night to Indian cultural taboos, and the classes were even being attended by a few earnest souls. We had even solved some of our supply problems. Now all we needed was an enemy, to justify all the expense.

The aerodrome was located in the flat plain eight miles east of Djelybad, the capital of the state. From the air, which was where I was to be found most mornings when I couldn't sleep—owing to having become a temperancer—the aerodrome looked thoroughly untidy. At the east end, the runway was little more than a few hundred yards of scraped landscape marked out with oil pots for night work, opposite a long, straggly line of open canvas hangars that housed the RJAF's hundred and thirty or so aircraft. Sprawling across the centre of the base were the prefabricated wooden mess halls, lecture hall and cinema, recreational facilities, ablutions, gymnasium, and the white concrete hospital where Sigridur had her surgery, consulting room, and living quarters. On the far western side of the complex were the accommodation huts for the men. (Because of the nature of the organization we had decided on a military rather than a civil hierarchy. After all, we might want to shoot somebody for desertion some day, and the men might object if they were civvies.)

Roland Mays, at fifty the oldest chap in the Air Force and by far the best-dressed—his blue-gray uniform was so disciplined as to resist the slightest temptation to wrinkle—was half-way through a tour of inspection in his capacity as Chief of Administration when I landed on the rude runway, back from a three-hour flight along the Khaliwar border eighty miles to the north. He was waiting for me as I taxied up to the dispersal area.

"Morning Deputy Supreme Air Lord Bandy."

"Morning, Roland. To the dark tower have you come?"

"If you mean the control tower, yes, I've inspected it," Mays said blandly, and retreating under the black umbrella that was being held for him by his umbrella boy. Obviously he had failed to grasp the poetic allusion. I should have saved it for Sylvius Hibbert, our Chief of Operations. He not only knew 20,000 long words, he was also well up on literary allusions...except that it would not have worked on him, as his name was not Roland.

Accompanied by various ground staff chiefies, we strolled along the line of hangars for the daily inspection. Some of the hangars, permanently open at both ends for maximum air circulation, contained as many as eight aircraft, and as I threaded through them, squeezing a coaming here and patting a crimson elevator there, I couldn't help gloating at the thought that I could decorate them in any color scheme I wished. That was something I had longed to do when flying the dung-colored RAF craft. And in fact I had already plastered some of the machines in tasteful colors.

Mays was looking at one of them now, and grumbling about all the red, blue, green, pink and purple paint. "You just don't have an artistic eye, Roland," I said airily, to which he replied that if *that* was artistry, then long live color-blindness.

"By the way," he went on, beginning to sound official, "I don't like to complain, but—"

"Garn, you love to complain, just like the rest of us."

Mays smiled, carefully removing a grain of sand that was despoiling his uniform. He enjoyed being joshed. It made him feel like one of the boys—which he definitely was not.

An Establishment man if ever there was one, Mays was a polished English gent with a plump, contented face complete with artistic dash of silver at the temples. He had been high up in the Paymaster General's office during the war, and might have gone on to a senior position in the City had it not been for his wife. The lady had developed a marked antipathy to the physical side of marriage (apart from a goodnight handshake) and Roland had been compelled, he said, to set up a mistress in the Bayswater district of London. His wife found out and promptly expelled him from their detached Tudor residence, while his father-in-law (naturally Roland had married the boss's daughter) proceeded to freeze him out of the firm.

After a while, though, Mrs. Mays decided she wanted him back. Roland declined her invitation to return to the guest bedroom, but the more he resisted the more determined she became to hang onto him. She even offered to submit to his revolting advances once a week provided he agreed never again to enter Bayswater except to pass through it on the Tube. When Roland persisted in his refusals, she pursued him all over London, even going so far as to create a scene in his club. To Roland Mays, a club was sacrosanct, as much a refuge from life as was Valhalla to a Viking. Unnerved, he fled to his standby club, but she tracked him down there as well, so that when my offer of a job came along he was desperate enough to accept a short-service commission until such time as his wife came to her senses and decided to make do with her Pomeranians.

Now, ten months later, he had settled contentedly into the life of a pukka sahib, his pleasure at being able to emboss the words *Haksar Palace* at the head of his notepaper moderated only by his regret that there were no decent clubs in the vicinity or, for that matter, on the entire subcontinent.

"It's that prime minister chap," he was saying as he completed his inspection and turned back to the staff car, his umbrella boy scuttling to keep up.

"The Dewan? What about him?"

"I'm just not getting anywhere with him. Can't you do something about it?"

"I thought I'd sorted him out. I told him that if he didn't cooperate with us, I would start to paw him all over."

"Paw him?"

"You know—pat him, hold his hand, drape an arm over his shoulder, that sort of thing. As a Brahmin, he hates to be touched by us low-caste whites."

"Oh, I see...anyway, the last batch of lorries reached Bombay docks weeks ago—the ones he volunteered to handle. But when I tackled him about it he said it wasn't the right time for it—his personal planets weren't in the right conjunction, or something. Them and their dashed planets."

"All right, I'll threaten to give him a kiss if he doesn't get moving. Anything else?"

"No, just the usual complaints," Mays said. "One of the men's huts is swarming with ants. They all want to go home."

"The ants?"

"The men. Some of the Bolshier ones are asking why they can't put up at the Haksar Palace like the officers."

"Damned cheek. They'll be wanting mirrors and chests of drawers next."

"They say they have to sleep twenty to a hut, while you have a bedroom the size of a Zeppelin shed all to yourself."

"What's wrong with that?"

"Well, nothing, but—"

"Anyway, I'm sure you can handle it."

Later, after a hard morning's work spent convincing the men that we had their best interests at heart and that we were making every effort to rid their barracks of ants as well as snakes and scorpions, Mays and I strolled up to the Haksar Palace for a nice lunch and our usual siesta.

The Maharajah owned five palaces. Three of them were rarely used, though they were kept fully staffed and maintained in case he felt like dropping in for a visit. He and Khooshie preferred to dwell for most of the year in the great walled City Palace in Djelybad.

The City Palace was notable enough, but mine was the more beautiful, "Well suited," as Hibbert was heard to murmur, "to Mr. Bandy's aspirations to grandeur."

Grand it was, though it was only the third largest of the palatial quintet. Until the aerodrome was built, it had stood solitary on the sandy plain for two hundred years, a breath-stealingly ornate masterpiece in sandstone. The long facade was encrusted with elaborately presented verandas and balconies, each a sculptor's work of art, and hundreds of ornamented pillars, the whole topped by ethereal cupolas, turrets, towers, and domes. The rest of this incarnadine glory was almost as elaborate and even more pleasing, for whereas the front faced only a crude road leading through a flummox of hummocks to the tumble of huts that was the mile-long 'drome, the rear verandas and balconies overlooked the famous Peacock Gardens which stretched down to the ferocious gash of the Bamm River.

As for the interior, its baroque corridors and niche-cooped sculptures of god, beasts, and god-beasts almost stunned one into unreality.

Architecturally, the palace was most noted for its domed Durbar Hall with its Persian tiling, pink marble, ancient Hindu sculpture, sumptuous printed silks, ivory fretwork, and ebony furniture, the whole climaxed by swirls of exquisitely carved balconies rising to a great glass dome that was cracked and fractured in only a few places, causing only minor floods over the mosaic floor during the monsoon season. And here I lived in splendor with my hundred and seventy-one servants and guards and my fifteen personal assistants. Gosh, it was a far cry from the days when I just had one measly batman, Smethurst.

Oh yes, and a few of my officers lived here too, including Mays, Hibbert, and squadron commanders Cot McNeil, a lanky Canadian, Bruce Shovell, an impertinent Aussie, Douglas Brashman, who had been a flying instructor with me at Gosport, and John Derby, the golfer.

They and a few others were relaxing in the enormous, tapestried mess lounge when I descended the staircase after my afternoon nap. And with them was Medical Officer Jonsdottir in her blue skirt and maidenly blue blouse.

She had still not consented to sleep at the palace, but at least she was now joining the other officers in the mess after work.

"Hello, darling," I said.

"Hello, sweetie."

"Not you, Shovell—I was addressing my fiancée."

"Oh, sorry, mate."

Sigridur laughed with the others and waved her glass. It was only then that I noticed they were all boozing like mad. At three p.m., too.

I beckoned to a white-coated waiter and rather ostentatiously ordered a cup of coffee.

After a while, Sigridur noticed that I was not my usual self—possibly because I was glaring goiterously from the far corner. She came over, perched on the arm of the chair, and gently tweaked my starboard earlobe. "What's the matter, *elska*?" She asked.

"Nothing."

"Come on, you can tell your doctor."

"Told you. 's'nothing."

"I suppose you hate to see us tippling when you can't."

"Well, it is only three in the afternoon."

"But they've all finished work for the day, Bandymin."

"All the same."

"Come on, *elska*, come and join us."

"Won't."

"Oh, come on," she said, tickling me. "One little drink won't do you any harm."

"Don't want."

After a moment she got up and sat in an adjoining chair, looking at me with troubled blue eyes. A few months ago that spirited girl would have given me hell for these naggy responses. Once, before she realized what a great man I was, she had treated me as if I were a routed, lame-witted hobbledehoy who was only just worth while saving. She had taken a fancy to me against her better judgement. But since her discovery that I really was, as I had claimed to be, one of the great air aces of the War and, subsequently, a splendid film actor and peerless Member of Parliament, she had become so respectful that even I found it hard to take—and I could take a fair amount of idolatry and stuff. I didn't want her to become as infuriating, dense, illogical, prejudiced, and interfering as she used to be, but damn it all, I rather missed her wild castigations and exuberance.

I stole a glance at her as she sat there with her soft, uncertain eyes; and the old heart quite flipped over with love; with greater love than ever, as I began to understand how basically vulnerable her position here really was. Glancing around to make sure nobody was looking I leaned over, and kissed her hand.

She smiled back, looking touchingly relieved.

By and by we joined the others at the round coffee table; but almost immediately the sight of all that ice-cold, whistle-wetting lager undid me again; and old Hibbert, aware of my problem, made it worse by apologizing for their perfectly natural spot of relaxation after a demanding day's training. "It's just arrived from Bombay," he said, gesturing at the hundred or so beer glasses on the round table. "We just thought we'd, you know, sample a bottle or two, to ensure that it had not perished...."

I grunted, avoiding Derby's eye—he was grinning at me as if he thought I actually envied them their sparkling libations—

and turned to shop-talk with Hibbert. I made a point of loudly sipping my coffee.

As a mimical remonstration it feel flat as an old glass of Guinness. The swine all continued to slosh the golden, thirst-quenching beverage into their swinish maws with every sign of enjoyment.

However, I did manage to discomfit Hibbert. After a first self-conscious sip he didn't touch his glass again for nearly half an hour.

Hibbert seemed to find my teetotalism a trial, even though he himself drank sparingly and was the driest man in the air force. Like the plains on which the air base was located, everything about Hibbert was sandy: his face, his voice, and the scalp showing through his thin, sandy hair. Even his manner was sandy: fine, smooth, and dry. He was a brilliant administrator, and had but one flaw: he couldn't help regarding me with respect. Somehow I had made a favorable impression on him when he was adjutant and I was CO of our Dolphin squadron, and he had still not quite managed to sort himself out. I don't know—what with his deference and Sigga's altered estimation, I was beginning to feel a bit defensive, almost as if, deep down, I suspected I was not as wonderful as they thought, and that they might discover this for themselves one of these days.

While Hibbert was often over-deferential, square-shoul-dered, cynical-faced John Derby, over there behind that dim-pled glass of scintillating suds, was often distinctly under-deferential. Like now. "Sure we can't tempt you, Bart?" he asked, holding up his glass so that the light shone from it in golden torrents.

"No, thanks," I said curtly, taking out my Mills bomb.

"Oh, come on, Chief," Bruce Shovell said loudly. "One perfect bleeding sparkling chilled glass of bloody marvellous cold-as-charity lager isn't going to turn you back into a souse."

"If it doesn't make any difference, there's not much point in drinking it then, is there?" I said snottily.

The Australian and the fresh-faced cynical Englishman sniggered at each other as I toyed with my Mills bomb, repeatedly yanking out the pin and then reinserting it.

"What is that?" Sigga asked.

"A practice grenade," somebody explained.

Actually it wasn't but I didn't want to worry them. It was perfectly safe. I'd been playing with it for a month now. A local *tahsildar* or tax collector had received the projectile as a gift, and he had brought it to me with a query as to what it was. I thought I had better confiscate it before he found out.

Ever since then I had been carrying it around and taking it out now and then to fiddle with it, to give my hands something to do, to distract them from their former occupation of clasping themselves around every available stein, goblet, mug, tankard, tumbler, or Toby jug. The feel of its pineapple texture in my palm was comforting.

After a while I realized that my presence was beginning to spread a wet blanket over the occasion. "You just don't understand," I said to the company in general. "I'm trying to start drinking again, but I just can't."

"Trying to start?" McNeil asked.

"I've been struggling to convince myself that I need to get back onto the booze, but can't summon the strength of will. Try as I might, I simply can't overcome this desire for total abstinence. I know it's weak, but there you are—I'm helplessly in the grip of temperance."

McNeil and Hibbert looked at each other.

"You ought to help me, you lot, instead of strengthening my resolve," I went on aggrievedly. "I need someone to convince me that drinking is the only way to halt this appalling decline. The fact is, I haven't had a good afternoon's sleep since I stopped, my nerves haven't been functioning properly, and I'm in danger of putting on weight." My voice cracked. "Can't you see how much I need help?" I cried.

Even Bruce was looking a mite uncertain. "What the bleeding hell is he talking about?" he enquired.

"I mean, if I don't get help soon, one day you'll find me lying here with a look of vacuous bliss on my face," I whined, "surrounded by temperance literature and unopened cases of *Wee Sleekit Cow'rin' Tim'rous Beastie Highland Cream*. Then you'll be sorry," I said with a catch in my voice, which obviously got them right there, judging by their expressions.

Which was when Sigridur finally pulled herself together.

Until now she had been overawed by my history, and rendered uncharacteristically reticent and shy by the overwhelmingly male company.

This time it was too much for her. She jumped up and cried, "Oh, stop talking such nonsense—and give me a kiss, you great horse-faced charlatan!" Whereupon she wrapped a powerful arm around my shoulders, hauled me upright, positioned my face, and pressed her gorgeously mushy lips firmly in place.

Finally she let me go, and I fell back into the armchair with a wheezing thump.

In the uproar that followed she looked around, her fair face flushed and shining, and from that moment was accepted as wholeheartedly in the mess as was possible in the circumstances. Until now, she had been treated politely enough, and indeed with some awe because of her spectacular scale. But there had been a reserve only natural in a situation that was surely unique among armed forces, the presence of a chief medical officer among a thousand men who was not only a woman but a positive Aphrodite. Now the exuberance of her satiric embrace quite melted the reserve and broke down much of the barrier of preconception as to how a young woman should deport herself in such surroundings. They would all be much more relaxed from now on with a person who could behave as spontaneously as they themselves. Good Lord, they now discovered, she was one of them after all, in spirit if not in form.

"My God, I hope he doesn't marry you so that I can," Derby said, looking at her with either impersonal admiration or gelid lust—with his good-looking but basically pessimistic face it as hard to tell which.

After a moment he said to the company in general, "Listen, I really must come to the defense of our esteemed brigadier. He wasn't always a beastly abstainer, you know. In the old days, Bandy would have been reeling about with the rest of us, with a drink in each hand and another on his head. Isn't that right, Hib?"

"Er, yes," Hibbert said, while I looked affrontedly at Derby, though in fact feeling grateful to him, realizing that out of friendship he was attempting to reduce the gap that must inevitably open up between an O.C. and his troops.

"Yes," John continued, "Bandy used to be quite a reasonable sort of chap—as drunken, debauched and dissolute as the rest of us. And look at him now."

"What's wrong with him?" Sigga cried, springing to my defense. She came over again and put a protective arm round my shoulders. "There is absolutely nothing wrong with him that a few drinks and some plastic surgery wouldn't fix."

It was quite a while before the mess recovered from that disgraceful comment. Everybody looked at me with evident enjoyment as I repeatedly pulled the pin from the Mills bomb and reinserted it just as repeatedly.

Finally I put it away with an air of decision. "Oh, very well," I said. "Far be it from me to interfere if you're determined to put out your lights and livers. I've no wish to be a wet blanket. Or should that be a dry blanket? Anyway, if you really want me to join you in alcoholic excess—"

"Of course, we wouldn't want to force you to overcome your desire for total abstinence," Derby said.

"No, no, it's all right. You've won."

"No, Bartholomew," Sigga said, picking up her cue from Derby and looking really concerned, "we don't want to influence you."

"Yeah, don't let us stop you being a lousy, mealymouthed temperance bastard," McNeil said warmly.

"You won't," I said. Then: "I mean...no, you've utterly convinced me. It's my duty to start drinking again."

"But—"

"No, it's too late now," I said firmly. "For weeks I've been helplessly in the grip of my willpower. But I see now that sacrifices must be made for the good of the Air Force, regardless of personal cost. Waiter!"

"Sir?"

"I'll have one of those lagers you have there."

"Sir."

"No, wait. I'll have all five of them," and a great cheer went up as I quaffed the first of the five glasses in hardly more than three swallows.

Somehow a full scale mess binge developed after that, and was still going on late into the evening, the high points of which were Douglas Brashman's famous ballet dance to the strains of Delibes played on the Victrola, and a hide and seek organized by those two inseparable and insouciant pilots, Fletcher and Carberry, commonly known as Fetch and Carry, which was not too successful, as nobody could ever find the person who was hiding in the Baroque caverns. One officer named Halbert Jones was still missing two days later.

As not infrequently happened during the dying stages of a mess binge the talk turned professional when Major Neale said, "You know, it might help a bit if we knew why we were practising gunnery and bombing, and what we were defending the aerodrome against."

Major Neale, who was in charge of the policing and defense of the base, was a dark-skinned, black-mustached former infantry officer. Though he had a ferocious sort of face, he was gentlemanly and genial in behavior. However, it was said that he could be inflexibly ruthless when armed action was necessary. Personally I was a bit scared of him, and always treated him with great respect.

I put my feet up and thought about it. Neale was right, of course. The uncertainty as to why we were here was not making it easy to concentrate on the training schedule.

A few months ago, I thought I knew. In London I had worked my brains to the bone to create this five-squadron air force for the state of Jhamjarh. The Maharajah had utterly convinced me that his neighbor, the state of Khaliwar, was also creating an air force, as well as a German-officered army, and was planning to attack. But by now we were beginning to wonder whether we were training to fight phantoms. It seemed so unlikely in this year of 1925 that a modern air force could be created without the outside world knowing about it. Certainly none of the Dewan's spies inside Khaliwar were providing acceptable proof that a Khaliwar Air Force existed.

Our own intelligence efforts were no better. While enquiries in Europe had established that the Fokker Werke of Schwerin had recently sold 200 fighters to a customer east of Suez, there was no sure evidence that the destination had been Khaliwar in particular or even India in general.

"I'd say that our top priority should be to find out once and for all whether there's anything to the rumors about a Khaliwar Air Force," Neale added, dislodging beads of beer from his mustache with a forefinger.

"How?"

"Aerial reconnaissance," Derby said promptly.

There was silence broken only by a drunken yowling from the Durbar Hall.

"After all, we have a fast plane already fitted out for photographic work."

"And I'm ready to fly it," Cot McNeil said.

"So am I."

"Me too."

"Out of the question, gentlemen," May said. "The Dewan has made it plain he won't countenance any flights over Khaliwar territory."

"But bloody hell, mate, how else are we to know what we're up against?" Bruce Shovell shouted.

"Right," said McNeil. "We sure as hell ain't getting any answers from the Dewan's office." The Dewan was responsible for Jhamjarh's intelligence service.

I stirred. They all watched as I took out my faithful grenade, removed the pin, and bit it. "I'm afraid we can't do anything without the Maharajah's say-so," I said.

"Then we won't tell him. Damn it, I don't see there's much risk. I could dart in and out of their territory long before they could catch a Bristol fighter," Derby appealed; but Mays, Hibbert, and I were all in agreement that we could not take any action that was counter to the ruler's wishes. He might dock our pay. "But I'll take it up with the Maharajah, next time I see him," I promised, focussing carefully on the Mills bomb, and being very, very careful to reinsert the pin. I'd had trouble before with Mills bombs, and I certainly wouldn't want anything to happen with this one, especially as the nearest exit was a good half mile away across the tapestried mess.

In My New Nightshirt

A day or two later there was another binge, and in the morning I was surprised to find myself in bed attired in my new nightshirt. I was surprised because I had been keeping the nightshirt for a special occasion, such as a weakening of Sigga's resolve, and because I couldn't remember inserting myself into it—the nightshirt, I'm talking about.

It was a beautiful garment. Made of finest lawn, it had been tailored for me by my personal *derzi*—though not without the difficulties and misunderstandings one associated with India. I had asked him to tailor me a Napoleon III nightshirt—you know, the design with the short, voluminous sleeves for admitting the maximum of fresh air in a fetid age, and a frilly Versailles collar—frilly in a thoroughly masculine style, of course. I'd had great difficulty in getting him to run me up a satisfactory garment, not least because he was a Muslim and familiar only with the pyjamas that his forebears had invented (from the Persian pay-jamah, pay = foot or leg, jamah = clothing).

Finally, however, he had managed to turn out an acceptable raiment, and this morning I was wearing it for the first time, and luxuriating in its rich tactility. Moving carefully so as not to disturb a minor headache, I snuggled deeper into the down, and gazed around contentedly at my vast bedroom with its painted ceiling—eight deities and some clouds. When first shown into this chamber, "And this, I take it, is where you exercise the cavalry?" I'd enquired. But then, nearly all the rooms were like this in the Haksar Palace.

I became aware that Iqbal, my number one servant, was in the bedhall, picking up my uniform from all parts of the parquetry. "Oh, Iqbal," I yawned, "what time is it?"

"Ten o'clock, Sahib."

"Good Lord, I appear to have slept in. Still, it's Saturday, after all...isn't it?"

"Approximately, Sahib. By the way, sir, I have sent urgently for the Dewan."

"You have? Why?"

"Last night you said it was urgent that you see him as soon as possible."

"I said that?"

"Yes, sir."

With a stab of guilt I realized that I must have summoned the Dewan during a certain squiffyness.

I groaned and sat up—and discovered that it was not a minor headache after all. And that I seemed to have lost my fingertips. Also, a pair of old underpants had recently resided in my mouth.

Carefully I lay back again—just as the prime minister appeared at the far end of the chamber.

"There is an emergency, Mr. Bandy?" cried he as he drew inexorably closer, his long mauve tunic flapping and his Brahmin features working overtime.

"There is? My land, what is it?" quoth I back, and starting to get out of bed, so agitated was I at the news, whatever the news was.

What stopped me from getting out of bed completely was that my legs had also gone numb.

"I don't know, Mr. Bandy," said the Dewan.

"There's an emergency and you don't know what it is?" I cried, massaging my limbs through the lawn material.

"You haven't told what the emergency is."

"How can I when you haven't told me yet?"

"Haven't told you what?"

"About the emergency."

"How can I tell you about the emergency?—it's you who is telling me about it."

"No, no, you are the one who is telling me," the Dewan explained.

I looked at him for a moment, then slowly cocooned myself again, and uttered a long-suffering sigh. And to think that initially I had formed quite a good impression of the Dewan. A bulky, fifty-year-old Brahmin with a pair of enormous purple eyes embedded in fat, he had been highly respectful toward me—at first. Recently, though, his attitude had changed. Gone was the esteem from the pluperfect purple plum eyes. And though he had an excellent command of English, now he invariably managed to misunderstand me. I suspected he was doing it on purpose to discombobulate me, because he resented what he saw as my undue influence on the Maharajah, not to mention the fact that I was being paid a bit more than him—his official salary being 700 rupees a year, while mine came to about 750,000.

The change in the Dewan was not the only transformation I was to recognize in India. I was to discover that the reality of people is as tenuous as that of overall perception. Nobody was as he seemed, nor seemed as he was. But then, what more appropriate place than India to make such a discovery, whose Hinduism was based as much on a conviction that the world was a false impression on the mind as upon the ideal of negation, of kindly indifference to human needs.

None on these thoughts fled through my head as I gazed indulgently at the Prime Minister and said, "I see. This emergency—another of your misunderstandings, is it?"

"Misunderstandings? I don't understand, Mr. Bandy," he said, refusing once again to use my official title in the hope that his abstention would encourage the Maharajah to demote me. "Last night I was deeply involved in an important consultation with His Highness, and the next thing that happens is that a messenger has arrived in a great state of perturbation with a request for my immediate presence. Naturally I assume that the abrupt summons must be the result of an emergency involving our beloved Jhamjarh, and I come forthwith, not more than eleven hours later. So what, pray, is this supreme emergency that will justify dragging me away from urgent affairs of state?"

"You are being so critical this morning, complaining of my taking you away from important meetings," I said slowly and with dignity, "that I'm not sure I want to tell you now."

The Dewan continued to stare down at me with disrespectful eyes—which, given their gibbous volume, could contain a great deal of disrespect. Meanwhile I was racking my brains, trying to remember why I had requested his presence.

Ah!

"Ah," I said loudly, winced, and resumed at a lower volume. "It's this, Dewan Sahib. I should like to address the State Council as soon as possible on a matter of great importance; that is, on the subject of obtaining reliable information re the situation in Khaliwar."

"There is no situation in Khaliwar," he said with great dignity. "My spies report that nothing whatsoever is happening there."

"As we are charged with the aerial defense of Jhamjarh, Dewan," I said, "we should like to confirm that for ourselves."

"You are saying that you do not trust the Maharajah's information?" he asked eagerly, in the hope that he could quote me as being critical of the ruler.

"I have nothing but affection and respect for His Highness," I responded, covering my ass like mad. "It is your lack of information we're talking about, Dewan Sahib. We cannot do our jobs properly unless we know, even if only approximately, what we are facing...if anything," I added, still covering.

The argument continued to bounce back and forth, until I suddenly realized that my nether limbs were still immobilized. That I was paralyzed.

"Oh, my God," I said.

"What?"

"It's my legs."

"What about your legs?"

"I can't move them."

"That is most unfortunate," the Dewan said.

"Iqbal."

"Sahib?"

"Fetch my personal physician, will you?"

"Something is wrong, sir?"

"I can't move, Iqbal. I'm paralyzed for life."

"That is a great tragedy," the Dewan said, endeavoring to fill the bowl of his face with concern. "Once upon a time my uncle was paralyzed. They thought he was dead, and they incinerated him."

"Oh, but that is terrible, sir, terrible. I will fetch Dr. Lal at once, sir, at once," Iqbal exclaimed, feigning great agitation—though being a Hindu, his philosophy forbade him from caring what happened to anyone.

He promptly ordered an orderly to fetch the doctor, meanwhile fussing around the bed quite convincingly, tucking in a sheet here, untucking it there, and smoothing the fifteen silk pillows with his dark hands, until the doctor arrived.

So far, Dr. Lal had proved to be quite good with potions, incantations, and quinine tablets. On this occasion, however, his ministrations, which mostly consisted of a series of tuts, were inefficacious. Paralysis of the limbs was plainly beyond his competence or even his understanding. The best he could manage was to draw down a sheet for a timid inspection of the southern end of my ankle-length nightshirt.

Oh, God, how I wished that my fiancée, Dr. Sigridur Jonsdottir, M.D., was here to provide a second opinion. Not that Dr. Lal seemed willing to provide even a first opinion, so reluctant was he to venture into that difficult area so feared by doctors of having to commit themselves to a diagnosis.

Another thought stapped me vitals: now I would never be able to make love to Sigridur. After being kept waiting for months, too. It wasn't fair. I had become bedridden and chaste at the same time. And me only thirty-two years old.

"What exactly is the matter, Brigadier Sahib?" Dr. Lal asked anxiously.

"I told you—I'm paralyzed."

"Where, sir? How?"

"My legs—they feel—" my voice caught—"as if they're in a cast."

"But that is natural, surely? Your legs are bound to have the same caste as the rest of you."

"Cast, man, cast, not caste."

"Except, of course, that you white chaps have no caste at all, or at best a very low one, and that applies also to your legs," Dr. Lal said, gaining confidence. "That is what makes things so very difficult for Indian medicos such as myself when we are having to treat you British. We Brahmins are not supposed to touch people of a lower caste, which, of course, means practically everybody. For a doctor, that can sometimes make things quite difficult, quite difficult."

"But damn it, I'm a fighting man—that makes me a *Kshatriya*, doesn't it? That's high caste."

"Not high enough, I'm afraid," Dr. Lal said, retreating another step.

"Well, dammit, at least test my feet reflex."

"I tell you I am not touching your feet. If I did I would have to spend the rest of the month purifying myself."

"You don't have to use your hands," I shouted. "Use a pen or something!"

"You want me to autograph your feet?"

"I'm telling you to do the reflex test! You're a doctor, you must know about that. Stroke something down my soles, to see if...." My voice broke. "To see if there's any pedal motivity."

"You want me to fetch your bicycle?" Dr. Lal asked uncertainly. His English comprehension sometimes deserted him at critical moments.

Finally, however, he understood, and, ensuring that there was no actual physical contact, he ran one of his pens—there were several of them pinned to his dhoti, all different colors—he used the puce one—down the soles of my feet.

The feet twitched a bit, indicating that there was still hope that they might regain their usefulness, provided prompt surgical action was undertaken—as I suggested to Lal.

"It is true that I have a *Chirurgiae Baccalaureum*," mused

he, distastefully disposing of his puce pen in my lemonade glass, "but I have not done any cutting since the Black Hole of Calcutta, practically. So it might be better if you brought in a somewhat more experienced surgeon. I recommend my brother-in-law. He—"

"Excuse me," said Iqbal, "but I think I know what the trouble is, Brigadier Sahib."

"You?" Lal said scornfully. "You are a layman. How would a low person like you know such a thing?"

"I am thinking that your personal *derzi* has made yet another mistake, Brigadier Sahib. Perhaps because as a Muslim he is used to sewing the legs of pyjamas."

"What?"

"He has sewn the bottom part of the garment as if it were pyjamas—you have both legs in the same half. That, I think, is why you are having difficulty in moving your nether limbs."

After a moment I leaned up and covered my southern sector. "I knew that," I said.

"Of course, Sahib."

"I was just testing Dr. Lal's competence, that's all," I said, and giving Lal a look to suggest that he had not received very high marks.

When Sigga heard all about it—"You're drinking too much," she said. "It's high time you cut down, Bartholomew."

The State Council

When Sigridur heard that I was driving to the City Palace to lobby the members of the state council, she invited herself along. "While you are bullying the Government," she said, "I shall attend the ladies in the *zenana*."

It was a glorious day for the eight-mile drive. Good Lord, how often had I longed for conditions like these during 1924 in raindrenched London. I positively gloried in this high, naked-as-Prometheus sun that wore not so much as a scrap of cloudy raiment, and this northeast breeze, lightly baked and done to a turn by its caressing passage over Ganges plain and Deccan tabletop. If this was the dreaded Indian Hot Weather that the civil servants had talked about aboard ship, then I was all for it. Unless one stood out in the open for a defiant period, one hardly even sweated.

Sigga was glowing with happiness that day, at having a day off from all the sore throats and ingrowing toenails, and was full of compliments. "You look beautiful, Bartholomew," she said, pressing her shoulder against me, and crunching several of my bones with her powerful hand.

"M'kew," I said. I was wearing a dazzling palm-beach suit instead of my blue uniform. "And you look quite good, too."

"Thank you, *elska*," she said, smoothing down her wrinkled air-force skirt and blouse, and went on to talk about the plight of the women she was about to visit, and confessed herself appalled at the conditions that even members of the royal household lived in. Many of the women in the *zenana*, as well as being medically neglected, had never received so much as an hour for formal education, were totally illiterate, and were without skills of any kind. They did not even have hobbies or occupations to while away the murderous hours. Only the children in the *zenana* were given any sort of tuition to make them aware of, if not fitted for, the outside world.

Some of the women, she said, had never seen a man, and had not seen the outside world for years. "They do not even allow the Hindu doctor to see them," she told me. "He has to reach through a curtain to feel them."

"Are they always sure it's the doctor?"

"And that's it," Sigga said, ignoring my interjection. "No physical examination, no tests, specimens, anything. We must do something, Bartholomew. It is bad enough being confined in purdah all their lives, but to be isolated without proper care or medical attention, and with nothing worthwhile to think about, it is terrible. No wonder they spend so much time quarreling over trivialities. There are also some extremely debilitating sexual customs."

"Really? What?" I asked. But despite my air of indifference, she refused to say what the customs were, except that they were concerned with the upbringing of the children.

Within days of her arrival in India, she had become a constant visitor at the *zenana*, the isolated wing of the City Palace where a hundred women with ties to the royal family were secluded, or, as Sigridur put it, imprisoned. And there she was beginning to turn heads with seditious ideas about the rights of women to expose their faces shamelessly in public, and to learn the multiplication table.

As we drove in through the great palace gates, I was amazed all over again at the scale of the Maharajah's principal residence. It took up literally half the city, an enormous aggregation of buildings embraced by seven miles of wall thirty feet high and twenty feet thick, walls that had held off the beseiging Mogul emperor Humatune for two years back in 1530–

something, before the inevitable traitor opened the gates to the Mogul hordes.

Unlike the Haksar Palace, this one did not exactly qualify as a fine architectural entity. Many of the buildings within the miles of wall were beautiful enough, but disharmonious— ancient Hindu classicism clashing with Edwardian Pomposity. The stout walls had a terrible job holding them together stylistically: the palace proper with the *zenana* wing, the Tent Building with the vast stables, the barracks, the temples, and the garage built to house the Maharajah's thirty automobiles, and the gardens, croquet lawns, tennis courts, polo ground, park, elephant compound, camel enclosure....

The palace proper was one of the most astonishing buildings in India, and, given the competition of such places as the temples of Khajuraho, that was saying something. The entire front of the building was carved. Not a square foot of sandstone had been left in peace. There were over a thousand sculptures and *bas-relief* of gods and beasts worked into the facade, many of them engaged in acts of lovemaking that were as complicated as they were shameless—shameless because each and every copulation had an audience of men, women, dogs, and other interested bystanders. While the flat roof of the building supported a tower that poked a good sixty feet into the breeze, and which looked rather suggestive to me, though I couldn't confirm my suspicions as it was partially obscured by so many fancy cupolas.

As for the interior of the building, it contained the usual magnificence: brilliant frescos, ornate alcoves, galleries of silk and silver.

The hall where the State Council meetings were held was located in this building. It adjoined the ruler's private quarters, if any quarters of his could be considered private—he was pestered by priests, courtiers, family, officials, and supplicants from morning 'til night, and could really only be assured of peace and quiet while reading the Shastras, or when meditating between the hours of four and six in the morning.

As I was not a member of the Council, I had to wait until other state business was accounted for. Finally summoned, I entered with my briefcase—which contained an apple and a jam sandwich in case I got peckish on the way home to my palace—and I salaamed toward the *gadi*, and noted that for once Khooshie was in attendance. I hoped this meant that he was again taking his responsibilities seriously.

I had to squint every time I looked at the prince. He was attired in a dazzling golden coat with a high collar as he sat cross-legged next to the throne. He wiggled his fingers and smiled at me; but then hurriedly adjusted his expression, as if he felt that the friendly gesture had been unseemly.

The Maharajah merely inclined his head. He was wearing an *achkan* in cornflower blue, with a matching turban. Two enormous rubies glowed in the blue material of the turban. In the darkish, shuttered chamber, they looked like malevolent eyes, in contrast to the real eyes below, which were deep, dark, and utterly beautiful, portholes onto the seascape of his soul.

As a European accustomed to such odd practices as sitting on pieces of wood, I was offered a chair. The rest of them being seated cross-legged on cushions, I declined, and to show that I was as good as them any day, I chose a nice gold cushion and embedded my nates therein.

After a ceremony of tea and sweetmeats served in little silver dishes, the meeting, chaired—cushioned?—by the Dewan got down to the item on the agenda that was of indirect interest to the deputy commander of the air force. This was the weekly talk, delivered by General Pertab, on the reorganization of the Jhamjarh Army.

Pertab, who was Minister of Police and Defense as well as commander-in-chief of the army, was a tiny man of about fifty years, with fuzzy gray hair up to the tree line of his bald brown dome. He favored pince-nez, spoke with a thin, reedy tone that was so hard to listen to that it was an effort to isolate what he was saying from the way he was saying it. You tended to squirm at the voice rather than absorb the communication. Thus, some time elapsed before I was able to take in the fact that he had doubled the size of the Jhamjarh Army practically overnight.

We congratulated him most heartily, and, "Thank you very

much," he said. "And the best of it is, there has been no need to take on any more men."

There was a further round of congratulation from the others, but all I could say was, "Eh?"

"Except, of course, for the general staff," he added. "The reorganization necessitated a fairly considerable increase in the size of the general staff. But as far as our two divisions were concerned, all that was needed was to divide them up. So now we have four divisions in the army."

"That is very impressive," said the Minister responsible for Justice and Nautch Girls. "Jolly good, Pertab, jolly good."

"It's wonderful, my dear Pertab," the Dewan said warmly. "You have doubled the size of the army, and all without any increase in the budget." He turned his purple plum eyes on me. "It is a pity that the other arm of the defense forces cannot be equally concerned with economy."

I waved away a few hundred flies—there seemed to be more of them than usual today in the palace—and said haltingly, "Uh, have I got this straight, General: you've created two new divisions by splitting up your two existing divisions?"

"That is correct, Mr...Brigadier...uh...."

"But you haven't taken on any more men?"

"That is the beauty of it, you see," Pertab said didactically, removing his glasses with a flourish, and smiling to reveal his tooth. "Apart from increasing the size of the general staff it has all been accomplished quite painlessly, financially speaking." And he turned to look at a statue of Siva, perhaps under the impression that it was the Maharajah. Without his glasses his eyesight was not too reliable. "It has allowed me to find employment for two major-generals, Your Highness," he informed the statue.

"It is wonderful. Congratulations all over again," the Dewan said.

"Perhaps," Khooshie suggested, winking at me, "we could split the general staff as well. That way we could have two general staffs instead of just one."

"That also is a wonderful idea," said the Minister of Justice and Nautch Girls a little doubtfully, though he continued to bob sycophantically at the prince.

The Maharajah stirred. This was so unusual that everybody turned to look at him. "Well, I hope that this expansion of the army means that the money I put into it will achieve something, for once," he said; and went on to complain that however much money he sank into the army, that was exactly what happened—it sank. The *lakhs* of rupees seldom seemed to transform themselves into new hardware, new facilities, or even new boots for the mainly barefoot militia. The Maharajah added that on the occasion of the last visit of the ruler of Kolhapur, the army had managed to get off only fifteen shots of a nineteen-gun salute. Upon being asked for an explanation, the officer in charge had explained that his field guns had run short of powder.

"The Air Force is costing a terrible lot of money too," His Highness added.

"Exactly," said the Dewan, looking at me triumphantly.

"But," the ruler added, "at least we are seeing results." Whereupon the Dewan had the cheek to nod at me again sharply as if the ruler had added a further criticism.

"Why is it," the Maharajah said, turning to the C-in-C, "that we are always so short of bullets, for instance, that on maneuvers the men are only allowed to shout, 'bang-bang' when they are aiming their rifles?"

General Pertab glanced angrily at his aide-de-camp who was standing in the background. The aide came forward. "The general cannot answer," the aide said. "He is too offended."

The Maharajah was immediately concerned. Apparently it was a serious matter when the C-in-C was offended. "Of course, we know it is not your fault, my dear Pertab," he said hurriedly. "We are not blaming you in the least. We know that you have been terribly busy at the staff college, taking a course in Sanskrit Phonology. All the same," he added, "the shortage of ammunition is surely a serious matter. The Maharajah of Kolhapur was very put out at losing part of the official salute, I can tell you, very put out indeed. He has not entirely forgiven me for giving him only a fifteen-gun salute," he said, slashing at a fly with his ceremonial yak-tail fly whisk.

While he was speaking, another officer had entered. After a hiss of whispers he handed General Pertab's aide a message. The aide scanned the message, hesitated, then with a quick glance at the ruler, handed it to his master.

Pertab read the message, glanced up at the aide, read it again, and rather casually placed it under his army cap.

Khooshie must have been watching this byplay with some interest as well, for he now said, "What is the message, Uncle?"

"Oh, it is nothing—nothing to worry about. It is army business."

His evasive manner increased Khooshie's interest. "May I see it?" he asked, giving me a wink as if to say, isn't this fun?

Pertab looked flustered. He glanced worriedly at the Dewan. "Goodness me," he said, "it's just a minor matter, my dear Khooshie—much too insignificant to take up time at a Council meeting."

Khooshie persisted, mainly out of boredom and mischief; he hadn't noticed the mysterious glances passing back and forth between the C-in-C, his aide, and the officer who had handed in the message. "But surely it must be of some significance, Uncle, for it to have been brought into the Council meeting in the first place?" Khooshie said, glancing at me to see if he was creating a good impression. "Let us hear what it is all about, please."

Again Pertab glanced at the Dewan before replying somewhat irritably, "One of our officers has been found dead at the border, that is all."

I caught the Maharajah's eye. He roused himself, turned, and smiled ingratiatingly at the C-in-C. "May I?" he asked, holding out his delicate brown hand.

The aide brought the message to the Maharajah. He read it, his smile fading.

Finally he said quietly, "He was tortured and killed?"

"Yes, your Highness."

"And thrown from Khaliwar over the border for us to find?"

Beside him, Khooshie had ceased to loll, and his eyes sharpened.

"What it is all about, Pertab?" the Maharajah asked; and when no immediate response was forthcoming: "I am serious, Pertab. I am wanting to know all about this."

Pertab gestured angrily at his aide. The aide hesitated, then said, "Some days ago a Khaliwar patrol attacked some of our men. Two of our men were killed, Your Highness, three were injured, and one—this officer—was captured."

There was a silence, until the Dewan started to whistle in a preoccupied sort of way and to pick at the sleeve of his mauve silk gown.

"This happened some days ago?"

"Yes, Your Highness."

"Why was I not told?"

The aide failed to answer, and to my chagrin the ruler failed to pursue that line of questioning. Instead: "You are telling me that we were attacked by Khaliwar in our own state, that we had several casualties, and one of our officers was captured, then tortured and thrown back to us as if he were...some trash they were throwing out?" The aide hung his head. "And I was told nothing about this?"

Khooshie jumped to his feet, fists clenched, eyes afire, and started to shout at the officers.

The Maharajah finally managed to restrain him with placating motions and appealing looks, while the aide said shakily, "We didn't want to worry you, Your Highness. It was just another border incident."

"Another? Another? How many have there been?"

"Only two, Your Highness," the aide said, he in his turn darting appealing looks at his superior. "There were hardly any casualties the first time."

Half an hour later, the Council meeting had arrived at the conclusion that the object of the first border incident was to take prisoners and presumably interrogate them for military information, but that the more recent irruption into Jhamjarh territory was a distinct gesture of disdain and hostility—

"Because we did nothing about the first incident," Khooshie shouted.

This time he was not going to be hushed. "Throwing back the body of this officer in this...this brutal way, it is as if they are saying, 'We know you will not have the courage to do anything about this either,' " he raged, seething his way up and down the chamber.

But the Dewan, who had had suspiciously little to say about the affair until now, seemed determined to justify the Khaliwarian contempt. "I am sure that General Pertab will be taking precautions from now on," he said, smiling encouragingly at the C-in-C, "to ensure that such an incident does not recur."

Khooshie halted, hands on hips. "How?" he shouted. "By pulling our men away from the border, I suppose?" But he was again gently hushed by his father, though the old man was looking equally troubled.

"Well," said the Dewan blandly, "if there are no more items on the agenda...?"

"No more items?" I said. "Of course there are, sir. These incidents, along with other signs, like the assassination attempts on Prince Khooshie in London, show that Khaliwar is as aggressive as ever. You can't ignore things like that. Or the possibility that they are building up a modern army and air force."

"My dear Mr. Bandy," the Dewan said with great amusement, "can you seriously believe that a modern air force could be tucked away inside Khaliwar without anybody, including the Paramount Power, knowing about it?"

"Well, it's...it's possible. Khaliwar is quite a wild sort of country—"

"I have a hundred spies inside Khaliwar," the Dewan interrupted. "And not one of them has been able to find a single piece of evidence to support this absurd notion. I mean," he ended, looking around as if inviting the others to look equally incredulous, scornful, and amused.

"We can offer a method of finding out once and for all whether we have anything to fear from Khaliwar's armed forces," I persisted. "We have a fast airplane equipped for taking aerial photographs." I took a deep breath. "Accordingly I am asking formal permission to make photographic reconnaissance flights over Khaliwar."

They reacted as if the latest incident at the border had not occurred at all. There was a chorus of protests, followed by a noisy discussion, the gist of which was that it would be foolish to risk "further antagonizing" Khaliwar, just when good relations were being restored between the two independent states.

"Further antagonizing?" I said, open-mouthed.

"We have obviously very much upset Khaliwar by our failure to respond to their first border incident," said a minister nervously. "We must be much more careful in future, that is all...that is my opinion."

"Exactly," the Dewan said. "We have upset our good neighbor to the north quite enough as it is." He then proceeded to counterattack on another front by reminding the ruler that if he fought a war and caused fatalities, he would be defying several dozen Hindu precepts, and risking his future existences. Presumably the Maharajah had no wish to interrupt his progress toward union with the godhead by coming back as a dung beetle. The Dewan maintained that even if it were true that Khaliwar was contemplating armed aggression—and he was not prepared to admit that such was the case—but even if it were true, that was all the more reason why Jhamjarh should not arm itself to the teeth, which could only make things worse. It might infuriate Sharif-ul-Khalil. The Dewan was not prepared to admit that Sharif was the real ruler of Khaliwar, but if he was he would be greatly upset to discover that Jhamjarh was prepared to defend itself, and he might attack in order to eliminate this threat. The Dewan kept pointing out that Indian history proved conclusively that Hindus were no match for Muslims. "If we fight, we might get hurt," he explained patiently. And besides, what was the point? Hindus were devout followers of *maya*, the belief that the world is unreal and illusory. What would it *really* matter, he pointed out, if Sharif, or Farookhi, or whoever was in charge, conquered Jhamjarh—or even the whole of India? A defeat would not affect the Maharajah's progress toward Brahman in the slightest.

No, it would be best if Jhamjarh continued to establish itself as being weak and defenseless. This would demonstrate to Khaliwar that they had absolutely nothing to fear from Jhamjarh. Accordingly, the Dewan suggested, would it not be a good idea to disband the air force? And, to establish conclusively that Jhamjarh believed in peace, might it not be a good idea for the army to make some unilateral disarmament gesture as well, say an offer to get rid of its tank? "Oh, what a wonderful idea," the Dewan exclaimed, applauding his own proposal. "We inform His Highness the Nawab of Khaliwar that we have scrapped our entire armored division. If that does not utterly convince them that Jhamjarh believes in peace, then I am toasted teacake."

Studious, gray-haired General Pertab was not prepared to go that far along the path of appeasement, but was otherwise quite ready to take up a submissive posture. He enjoyed a tranquil life interrupted only twice a year by the winter exercises and the spring march-past. So he too was inclined to urge the ruler to avoid action that might upset the ruler of Khaliwar.

"So," the Dewan said complacently, "If I might summarize the sentiments of the State Council meeting, we all agree that it would be a great mistake to carry out these photographic adventures at this juncture. His Highness suspects that any hostile action on our part is exactly what Sharif-ul-Khalil is looking for—an excuse to attack us."

"I agree entirely, Dewan Sahib," said General Pertab, removing his gold pince-nez and breathing on them—presumably to cloud the glass, for he made no attempt to polish the lens. "No doubt the commander of the Air Force is anxious to justify the immense sums that are being expended on his air force by undertaking dangerous adventures of this sort, but in my professional opinion the consequences could be fatal."

"Sir, we could be in and out of their skies long before they even got close enough to identify us," I said despairingly.

The Dewan pounced. "As we are the only ones in the whole of Central India with aircraft," he said contemptuously, "it would hardly be necessary for them to get close to identify us. No, gentlemen, we have upset our good neighbor to the north quite enough as it is. This proposal of Mr. Bandy's to invade the territory of a fellow princely state is infamous, quite infamous in my opinion," he said, and his cousin, the Minister of Public Works nodded vigorously, as did his brother-in-law the Minister of Justice and Nautch Girls.

I looked hopefully at the Maharajah, but apart from a slight tremor of his *chowrie*, I received not even a helpless smile from him, but merely a preoccupied look as if he wished he were in some other palace. As for Khooshie, he merely snorted, and turned and walked out, and half an hour later was taking part quite happily in a polo match against the 51st Lancers, leaving me to trudge worriedly back to the Rolls, to discover that somebody had let the air out of all the tires—probably one of the Dewan's spies.

Looking Gloomy

The apathy, skepticism, fear, and downright opposition to self-defense utterly permeated the Maharajah's court. At every council meeting, now, there were arguments in favor, not of strengthening the state in the face of Khaliwarian provocation, but of weakening it in order to avoid antagonizing Sharif-ul-Khalil, or Mohammed Farookhi, or whoever the hell was in charge up there. So it was hardly surprising that the Maharajah's resolve was weakening fast. It had been a struggle for him to accept a strong defensive posture in the first place. A warlike stance was hard to reconcile with religious genuflection. He could end up thoroughly knotted. The idea of combat clashed with his deepest beliefs in Brahman of which every soul, Muslim included, was a part. The soul of the Universe that was Brahman required the conviction that any attempt to kill another was also an attempt to kill Brahman. There was no greater sin than that.

"But don't Hindus occasionally kill each other?" I queried.

"Of course, my dear Mr. Bandy. We have entire tribes born and brought up to commit robbery and murder," he said proudly. "Our belief in the sacredness of life is nonetheless sincere, and any lapse from the tenets of Brahmanism is cause for the greatest regret."

"But, Your Highness, the purpose of your army and air force

isn't to kill others, but to deter others from attempting to kill you."

His deep black eyes, the only beautiful feature of his person from his caved-in face to his veiny shins widened as he stared at me with enormous admiration. "But of course," he squealed. "That is true. We would not dream of using them to attack anyone else. Yes, yes, what a wonderful discovery!"

"Well, there you are, then, sir. They're purely defensive arms. And the stronger you make them, the less likely are you to be attacked."

The Maharajah capered, ecstatic; and almost immediately slumped onto his *gadi* with a negative head shake. "But," he said, "the Dewan says that with such strength comes the temptation to use it."

"I can't see your army ever wanting to do that," I said, recollecting the last Jhamjarh army maneuvers.

Even Khooshie was now wavering in his conviction that Khaliwar had aggressive intentions. As attackless weeks flowed by, his diminishing resolve was crucial. It was he who had stiffened the ruler's sinews in the first place, convincing his father that it was his duty to defend his people even if this meant sacrificing a few Brahman points. But Khooshie was now more interested in polo than in national security. The Maharajah had given him seventy polo ponies for his nineteenth birthday, and appointed him captain of the number one team.

British attitudes were not dissimilar, if RAF opinion was anything to go by. Learning that the sole RAF base in the entire area was the one at Charanwad, halfway between the northern boundary of Khaliwar and the imperial capital at New Delhi, I wangled an invitation from their senior officer, Wing Commander Troughton. This was not too difficult as there was already much curiosity about the RJAF in RAF circles.

Our exchange of letters was cordial enough, but by the time we reached the RAF aerodrome they had received a full report on me from the Air Ministry in London. Consequently the reception in the mess was so dead as to be practically putrid.

The fact that I had brought along several former RAF pilots eased the tension only a little.

After a stiff dinner, Troughton referred to the idea that Khaliwar might attack a fellow independent state as being utterly preposterous, while the possibility of the Khaliwar Army being turned against British India was ludicrous. He personally had met the Nawab, old Mohammed Farookhi, and had found him to be a jolly good sort with as much harm in him as a field mouse. But even if Farookhi had been a second Alexander, had we never heard of the British and Indian armies, not to mention the Royal Air Force, which was a match for any opponent in the world?

John Derby looked up at the ceiling fans as they sluggishly stirred the post-prandial smoke, and said, "You regard your six Bristol fighters, two Avro trainers and a Harry Tate as being a match for anybody, do you, sir?"

The wing commander flushed noticeably, quite an achievement as he was already a purplish red to match all the Burgundy he had been drinking, and said, "I assure you—Derby, is it?—that in an emergency we could have the rest of the squadron back from Iraq in no time at all." He was clearly put-out that Derby had taken an inventory of his strength.

"The Khaliwar Army," mused the RAF adjutant. "Ever seen it?"

"No."

"Well, I have," he said, happily aware that everybody in the mess was listening intently. "Green turbans and Ross rifles, that's about all it amounts to. I was in their capital only a few weeks ago. Watched a battalion exercise. Absolute shambles. No, take my word for it, they wouldn't stand a chance against the Gurkhas, Sikhs, or Scottish Borderers."

"And the war will be over by Christmas," John Derby said.

As the significance of that reference to one of the more fatuous statements of the Great War sank in, the party turned as lively as a bear den in the depths of winter.

In The Mango Grove

Despite an autocratic situation that easily could have produced a tyrant, the Maharajah was a good deal closer to his people than any Western leader could ever be. The Jhamjarians loved him—because he was there to be loved. The Indian psyche seemed to need human as well as mythic gods. They would have adored their ruler even if he had regularly tortured them in relays, and exercised a *droit de seigneur* over their daughters, sons, and goats. In the case of our Maharajah, the affection in which he was held was reasonable. No supplicant with a request, grievance, or appeal was ever turned away from the City Palace without obtaining an audience with the ruler, though there might be a wait of a few days.

Not content with being palatially accessible to his eight million subjects, the Maharajah sallied forth across the State twice a year to meet those of his subjects who didn't have the means to make the journey to Djelybad. With him on these jaunts to outlying villages went an amazing expedition numbering upwards of a thousand men and at least a dozen women, including his adoptive mother and her attendants, and three dancing girls. In the fantastic procession were red and gold elephants, ivory, black, maroon, and Mignonette Rolls Royce cars, *gharis* and *palka-gharis* for the purdah'd ladies, buses for the nobles, officials, servants, jesters, and astrologers, and tongas, carts, and motor lorries for the lesser breeds. For security there were lines of glittering lancers on horseback, resplendent in scarlet and gold. And there were vehicles filled with hundreds of assorted tents, to be set up in different parts of the jungled, sugar-caned, betel-leafed, rice-sodden, hill-slashed State.

I made one of these trips soon after Sigga's arrival in Jhamjarh, Khooshie having invited me to accompany him in his favorite Rolls Royce, the one with the washbasin in the back. I was entranced by the splendor of the occasion. The procession that wound out of the narrow, blindingly white streets of Djelybad was fully two miles long, shuffling and creaking to the rhythm of the Royal Jhamjarh Military Band which played out-of-tune and arhythmic versions of Great War songs such as *Pack Up Your Troubles*. Actually there were two bands, the other being the Royal Judiciary and Medical Department Orchestra, comprising drums, pipes, and a portable harmonium.

Several elephants had also been brought along in case Khooshie felt like indulging in a tiger shoot when we reached the jungly area. How I wished it were possible to take photographs in color, then. The elephants were gorgeous, carrying about a quarter ton of exquisitely-worked silverware in the form of anklets, harness, and frontlets laced over crinkly foreheads, and a silver framework for the scarlet and gold *howdahs*. The elephants had even been carpeted: fine Indian rugs laid over their backs. The mahouts were also caparisoned in the same blazing colors.

It still amazed me how bright the colors were in India compared with the no-less-hot Middle East where practically everything seemed bleached.

Khooshie's pleasure in the pachyderm splurge quickly diminished, however, when he found that the crinkly beasts tended to slow the procession. In Europe he had developed a taste for fast cars, and was not too pleased to find his Rolls Royce reduced to a speed of one point seven miles per hour. So on the second day the elephants were sent home in disgrace. "Perhaps I will make do with a spot of pig-sticking," he said.

The evening of the first day of the tour was one that I was to treasure in memory. It was when I first saw the blossoming of the Maharajah's canvas city, the tents being set up whenever the expedition reached a new region of Jhamjarh. As well as for accommodation, the tents served as living and dining quarters, and as storerooms, bathhouses, garages, stables, armories, and for formal receptions. As they rippled toward heaven, hauled by thin, gleaming *Sudras*, I was filled with wonder. I'd heard that Indians had a gift for tent design, but the ones that grew from the coarse ground that day were breathtakingly lovely, dazzling in their elaborate designs and colors, open-sided *shamianas* and other fluttering masterpieces of fine fabrics, with Mysore silk touches in reds, greens, yellows, and cobalt blue, tasseled, pelmeted, brocaded, beflagged, and ornamented and embellished to a degree undreamed of by Barnum, Bailey, and Lady Astor. They were of all sizes, from pup to big top, and the throne room was the finest of the lot, an enormous fabric sculpture in the shape of a partially completed pagoda, Persian carpeted, lined inside with flowing silks, and containing the *gadi* and its ivory, mauve, and gold canopy.

This was where the handouts to the villagers were made in the form of advice, comfort, and mediation. And also coin of the realm, for the Maharajah liked to dole out small sums to all who requested it. There were surprisingly few spontaneous requests. It was quite touching the way the citizens, who for the most part lived on a nickel a day, had to be egged to beg, to be prodded into asking for a few annas. Even before the handout they were gazing up at the ruler with eyes full of shyness and adoration. Afterwards they'd have washed his feet with their tongues had the honor been permitted.

While the Maharajah's biannual tour lasted for several days, I remained just long enough to wonder at the joy and affection with which the autocrat and his son were greeted. They were received at every village with horns, tom-toms, and idolatry. Even Khooshie was adored, though he paid scant attention to the multitudes.

But then Khooshie was not in a very good mood these days. Even the outrage at the border had failed to rouse him beyond an initial burst of indignation. Now all he had to say about the matter was that in reality it was the Khaliwarians who had failed. "They attempted to humiliate us. Obviously they have failed—we do not feel the least humiliated."

"But it was a gesture of the most vile contempt," I stormed.

"You don't understand, Bartholomew," he said patiently. "There can be no humiliation if we do not feel it."

"God!"

"Exactly," Khooshie said, obviously pleased with my progress. "*Now* you're beginning to understand."

Khooshie seemed to be more interested in sex than in the safety of his independent state. "It's all right for you," I remembered him saying on the first night of the biannual expedition when I visited him in his elaborate crimson tent. "You have Sigga, but I have nobody to love." And a tear formed at the corner of his left eye, crept down a long black eyelash, and plopped noisily onto an illustrated copy of the *Kama Sutra*.

I gestured toward the three dancing girls who were huddled in the corner of his inflamed quarters, jingling and giggling. "I suppose they're just here to wash the dishes," I snorted. The girls, who had tiny brass bells sewn to their pantaloons, giggled harder than ever while peeking at us through their fingers.

"They are here only to dance," he muttered.

"Oh, sure."

"It's true," he shouted angrily, just as four musicians entered. "They are to sing and dance until I fall asleep, that is all." And he went on to snort that he would have no more fun and games with girls from now on, because the Dewan, the priests, and his adoptive mother had decreed that no Nautch girls were to be permitted the honor of his bed until after he was decently married. The Rani had said that at his age he should long since have settled down. At this very moment, he said, she was negotiating for a bride of the correct caste and lineage, and who was from a family entitled to nineteen guns. "I tell you," Khooshie confided, gazing gloomily at the prettiest of the three girls, who giggled and hid her face behind her raised arm, and blushed under her pigment, "they're taking so long about getting me a bride that I'm becoming pretty bloody frustrated." And to show how anglicized he had become he said it again. "Pretty bloody frustrated."

If he was, it was probably for the first time in the life of that handsome boy with the dainty chin, the dinky nose, and two lots of spiky black eyelashes that had sent European women into a trance of envy.

I gathered that throughout his childhood and adolescence he had struck the thousand palace attendants all of a heap as well; though such was the uncritical adoration accorded the hereditary rulers that they would still have pampered and worshipped the boy had he been a cross between Quasimodo and Merrick, the Elephant Man. That he wasn't ugly still caused his father great wonderment. "How could such a beautiful boy have sprung from my loin chops," the hideous old chap had wondered at me one morning.

All his life, Khooshie had been petted, pampered, and indulged to an extent remarkable even by the indulgent Indian standards. He had always been given everything he wanted, and constantly watched over. That he wasn't now the brat of brats was a tribute more to his own faint restraint rather than his father's sense of proportion. It was his rebellion against the overcoddling that had saved him from becoming a Caligula, as had happened to some heirs and rulers of princely India. Quite often he had gone into hiding to escape the smothering attendants. "My favorite hidey-hole was that sixty foot monument in the middle of the palace roof," he told me one day. "They never did manage to find me when I hid in there...at least," he added, his brow clouding, "I don't think they knew...but of course it's possible that they did know, and were just pretending not to find me...." His face fell. The possibility had only just occurred to him, years later.

"I never hear much about your mother," I asked him, "when did she die, Khooshie?"

"Which one? Father had five or six wives at one time."

"Did he? Anyway, I mean your real mother."

"I never had a real mother."

"Surely you must have had a real mother."

"If I did, I never knew which wife it was, because they all

treated me as if I were their son. Why, did you have a real mother?"

I thought about it for a moment, then: "I'm not sure." I said.

This was the first time I'd learned that the ruler had had more than one wife in his youth. It appeared that he had given up that sort of thing when the priests, to his relief, gave him permission to cease copulating for the good of the state; whereupon all five wives had vanished into the *zenana*, where four of them had subsequently died of enteric fever, and the fifth had been killed in a quarrel.

The pampering of Khooshie had included a steady supply, from the very moment of puberty, of dancing and steam-cleaned servant girls. In fact, listening to his reminiscences, one got the impression that half the court had been standing by, waiting with bated breath for his testicles to descend, so that they could treat him to his first mistress. "But that's all finished now," he sighed, with the air of a redundant Casanova.

"Anyway, Bartholomew," he added over a further sigh, and gesturing at the tinkling concubines, "you can have them if you want." And he departed, adopting a posture that suggested he was auditioning for the part of Forlorn in *The Pilgrim's Progress*.

It was the next morning that the paranormality began. After a breakfast of stickly orange drink and even stickier cakes in the fluttering breakfast tent, I picked up my camera and ambled along to the throne tent to watch for a while as eager, awed Jhamjarians carted, tonga'd, bicycled, dragged, or limped up from all points of the compass for their share of the regal dispensations. I watched, standing beside the ivory-coated Dewan, making penetrating observations the while. "Funny, I always thought everybody in India wore turbans," I observed penetratingly. "But out of the hundred people standing over there, only seventeen have turbans. The rest are wearing Gandhi titfers, Punjab caps, pith helmets, fezzes, or old underwear."

I also asked various intelligent questions like, what was everybody saying.

"At the moment His Highness is reproving a money lender

for charging more than the usual eighty percent interest," the Dewan replied. "But mostly they are bringing His Highness their quarrels with their neighbors, and asking him to judge who is in the right."

"Ah."

"By the way, Mr. Bandy, I have arranged to introduce you to a Sadhu."

"You have? Why?"

"You were expressing much curiosity about the lives of the holy men of India," he replied.

"I was?"

"Oh, yes, great curiosity. You were most interested in their intuitive conviction of the oneness of diverse phenomena as apprehended in the semi-bifurcation of divinity."

"Well, I...I remember asking you about the Indian rope trick."

"Exactly. So if you will come with me to the village, I will take you to one of the most amazing of all Sadhus," he said, following this up with so many respectful gestures that I was compelled, like a thistledown in a meadow breeze, to head in the direction of his salaams.

Still, that was okay with me, as it was a fine day for a walk. Also, though I had already been pestered by a million holy men, I had not yet visited a typical Indian village.

The village was only a quarter mile away, with the usual Untouchable community on the outskirts. (Untouchables were not allowed into village or town, and mostly lived their crushed lives hoping from a distance.) To reach the village we walked over noisy bristles, gray-green cover masquerading as grass, and through a stand of cotton trees that were bare of leaves but burning with crimson flowers like so many warning flares.

The settlement was most uninteresting. It was hardly more than a clutter of whitewashed mud, with a bazaar on what was presumably Main Street. The bazaar comprised a number of open stalls, most of them selling brassware or rice, or rice in brassware. They were not doing much business. The place was almost deserted, most of the inhabitants having gone to goggle at the tent city. The most active residents were the kites as they dived for scraps. The humans sat listlessly under black umbrellas in the dusty, flywhining street, or in the shade of their whitewashed abodes. Many were old—old men of thirty, and women even older.

They stared uncomprehendingly at the aristocratic bulging-eyed Brahmin in the beautifully cut ivory coat buttoned to the throat, and at the balding Westerner with the face suggesting that he should be wearing a saddle rather than ducks and a bush shirt.

There seemed to me more animals in the village than people: the inevitable wandering cows, one of them comically gawping from someone's open window—the bugger had actually strolled into the house—monkeys skittering over roofs and walls; glassy-eyed dogs. I cringed from dogs. So many of them looked diseased.

Three boys and two girls, looking bright and intelligent enough, though greatly undernourished, followed us for a few paces then lost interest as the Dewan led the way to a mango grove on the far side of the village. And there, bare, crosslegged, heels embedded in meatless thighs, sat the promised Sadhu.

India, of course, was famous for its holy types who drifted up and down the country, living on the charity of others, free not only from any obligation to earn a living but even from the bonds of caste. In return for a few coins they were supposed to sell you an insight or two into Hindu philosophy. Some of them painted themselves in earthy pigments, but this one, a horrible old sod, naked except for a coin purse round his dangles, was covered in ash, as if he'd just been raked from a campfire. Glaring menacingly, he held out his hands. "Alms," he sang.

"Arms? You already have two."

"Money." He was actually holding out both hands as if expecting a positive shower of largesse.

I had already given to at least a hundred thousand beggars, whether they called themselves holy men or not, so I kept my hands in the pockets of my white ducks. "If I give you money I won't get a word of thanks," I said. "And if I don't, you'll spit at me." Anticipating such a reaction I moved back a pace. "So why should I give you a bean, Dean?"

The old fiend continued to scare me with those eyes of his, which were set in a head like a roasted nut. A long spittoon-yellow beard wisped down to his bare belly button.

"The more you give to the holy man," the Dewan said with amused contempt for my ignorance, "the more do you build up credit in the next world. So it is written."

"And I know who wrote it—the first man to think up the racket."

The Dewan treated me to a supercilious look from his great bulging eyes, turned and walked off as if it was he who'd been insulted, not the bag of bones squatting in front of me.

"Friend of yours, is he?" I asked, jerking my thumb after the departing premier. "Your agent, perhaps?"

His voice was high-pitched and sing-song, but it could employ good English. "It is the *chela* who is my agent," he sang. "It is he who obtains money for me. I do not soil my hands with such matters."

"You were holding out your hands for it just a few minutes ago."

"My *chela* is not here."

I had been a little curious as to how the naked Sadhus managed to survive in the heat of summer Madras or the cold of Himalayan winter. So I asked him how.

"I have no need of clothes," he replied. "They are of this world."

"So is money, but you seem eager enough for it."

Slowly the lips in his wizened malevolent face parted to reveal a full set of teeth—all of them rotten. And he cackled with laughter.

I was so startled that I recoiled.

"You are an angry man," he squealed.

"I'm not in the least angry."

"Your brow is not dented with ire, nor is the surface of the pond of your mind flurried, but you have been angry for too long."

"Bollocks."

He chortled harder still. "For five rupees I will help you to tranquility, to understand the world, and comprehend that the universe of the trillion stars is no more than a thought. I will teach you all knowledge and understanding if you wish."

"Sure," I said, glancing at my watch. "I've a couple of minutes to spare."

He rocked back on his heels, still laughing to himself. "To start with," he said at length, "you wish to see the Indian rope trick?"

"You can make a rope rise by itself? Go on, then."

"No."

"You won't?"

"Yes."

"Yes you will, or yes you won't?"

"I will and I won't."

"What does that mean?"

"I would tell you if you were capable of understanding," the Sadhu said in his unnatural sing-song.

"Don't tell me, show me. Prove you can make a rope go up by itself."

He gestured dismissively. "That is nothing. I can make a man, my *chela*, climb the rope and disappear from sight."

"Oh, sure. And I'm Daisy Dublin, Queen of the May. You don't even have your *chela* handy," I pointed out.

"Admittedly, making my *chela* climb is the hard part," he said, looking at me with a strangely derisive smile.

"Especially when he's not available. And the hard part for me," I said heartily, "is to believe that you're not an old fraud."

"In Brahman, Mr. Bandy, we are all frauds, all falsely representing ourselves in such terms of reality as the conviction that to see is to believe, to believe is to see, and to see is to see. Whereas the only truth is that to believe is to believe."

"You got me there, pal. Can't answer that."

"It is not answers you should be seeking, Mr. Bandy," he said after clearing his throat and in the process creating a sound like a hippo emerging from six feet of sewage. "What you should be seeking is defenselessness."

"I happen to be in the business of defense, old boy."

"The defenselessness of ultimate humility, which will give you the way into the garden of faith. Clearing your mind of the conviction of what is real is the first small step."

"That's crazy. Real is real, and there's not two ways about it. This boot is real, this nice warm air is real, being demonstrably oxygen and nitrogen, where's the uncertainty in that?"

The bright emnity had returned to his eyes in their dusty sockets. "Perhaps later you will be worth talking to, Mr. Bandy," he said. "Perhaps later." And he dislodged his heels from his thighs and prepared to stand, his movements causing the stink from him to become more evident than ever. Then he called on his *chela* to help him up; who came forward to oblige and to give me rather a surprise, as I hadn't noticed him until then, even though he seemed to have come forward from directly in front of me rather, for instance, than from behind, where I might have had an excuse for failing to see him. It was just a shade disturbing.

Just a shade.

My Bedchamber

Sigridur had decided to move into the Haksar Palace after all. Though she still expressed disdain for the decadent luxury that seemed to suit me so well, it was getting too hot to trudge from the aerodrome to the palace twice a day. The fact that she had woken up to find a snake in her hospital room had had nothing whatsoever to do with her decision, she said.

Upon my return from the biannual expedition I went straight to her room, eager to recount the events of the day; but though it was eleven pip emma, she was not in her room.

She was in mine.

"Oh, Sigga," I breathed, flinging off my clothes.

"Now just hold on thar one goldarn minute," she said in a poor imitation of Cot McNeil's accent. "I only came in to talk."

"Fine. Now we've talked—let's go, eh?"

"I only got into bed to make myself comfy while I was waiting."

She was sitting up in bed in a plain cotton nightdress, not nearly as nice as mine but with contents much superior. Though the neckline was modest her bust utterly failed to cooperate. She was having difficulty deciding how to handle it, so to speak. If she leaned forward her bosom got exposed, but if she leaned back it got outlined, neither of which postures seemed likely to abash the cad I quite plainly intended to become.

"No, I mean it, Bandy," she said severely as I reduced myself to a pair of socks and dived in beside her. "I am here because I have so much to tell you."

"So have I. Give us a kiss."

"Stop that. I am in no mood."

"Oh, Sigga, you're so lovely. I don't deserve this."

"You're not getting it. Bartholomew, I need money," she said, dodging out of bed and creating a fragrant breeze as she headed toward my wallet. It was on the floor, along with my trousers. "I have just come from a girl of eleven who is to be married tomorrow. You are to stop the marriage immediately."

"What?"

"You must stop the ceremony. She is tiny. It is impossible."

"She can't be eleven—it's not allowed until they're fourteen."

"And I suppose that means that the whole abominable practice of child marriage has been utterly wiped out? I assure you that girls as young as nine are still being married, frequently to lascivious old men in the civil services," she said, wrenching currency out of my pants. "I am paying back the dowry—it is only a few hundred rupees—to save this little girl, at least."

Preoccupied with her story she got back into bed. As she did so I was treated to even more of her munificent curvature; whereupon the dank sheet arose as if a wee tent pole was being assembled for a miniature biannual expedition; though I was careful to hide it. If my pulchritudinous inamorata perceived it in her present mood she was quite likely to deal the offending member a sharp lateral blow with the heel of the hand, an effective and reasonably safe procedure sometimes adopted in extreme cases by no-nonsense nurses.

"I tell you, Bartholomew," she went on, leaning back and solving the bosom problem by crossing her arms over it, "it is terrible, the lives they live here, the women and children, the abominable practices, the religious fervor of people who seem to think that being under the protection of their triad of gods they can drink thick, polluted water with impunity, eat sweets covered in flies, and so forth. And, oh, the way they treat the poor animals, the cows they reverence as devotedly as they starve them. I just don't know where to begin in getting these Indians to pull themselves together."

She was safe enough, now. A sharp lateral blow was no longer necessary.

Now she was telling me about her trip to the new Djelybad hospital that afternoon. There she had examined a girl of five whose parents had offered her to the gods in hopes of future favors. She had been handed over to the temple women for instruction in the arts of singing and dancing, but it was the priest who had done the most instructing. The child had reached hospital with a crushed pelvis and internal injuries.

"And do you know, I even heard a priest teaching some children that the world is purely an illusion, and that only unreality is real," she said indignantly. "I mean, what a frightful thing to tell innocent children."

"Funny you should say that. Recently I met a Sadhu, who—"

"I mean, it could mark a child for life, hearing things like that."

"M'm," I said, leaning back on the pillows, and looked with mixed feelings at this innocent, loving beauty with the cheekbones that molded her face with just the right touch of artistry, the mixture composed almost equally of frustration and affection over her seemingly low desire quotient and her concern for the wellbeing of others even when they didn't want their wellbeing seen to.

Becoming aware of my rueful scrutiny, she turned and gazed back at me. As she looked into my eyes her expression changed, and started to melt. A flush tinted her face, her lips parted, connected for a moment by a silver strand of saliva.

She put her arms around me and kissed. Oh, my God, this was it, at last.

"Oh, Sigga...darling..."

"Ouch."

"Wot?"

"There's something hard down here."

She reached down; and brought up the Mills bomb.

"What's this doing here?"

"I wondered where it had gotten to," I said thickly as I ceased lapping at her creamy shoulder to accept the grenade. "I misplaced it the night of that first binge." And I leaned over, and chucked it under the bed.

She was hauling off her nightgown! Oh, lummy! Panting, heart thumping like billy-ho, I tore off my socks.

As I did so I discovered that the pin of the grenade was still in my hand.

The ring was on the third finger of my left hand.

In a flash, I realized what had happened. I had removed and reinserted the pin so many times that I had weakened its hold on the hole it was supposed to be inserted into. So that when I chucked the thing under the bed, out of the way, the pin had slipped out.

"Oh...my...God," I said, just as the Mills bomb went off.

We were heaved at least three feet into the air, still wrapped in each other's arms.

However, we soon thumped back onto the bed, saved from injury by the thick mattress, but half-deafened by the bang, half-blinded by the flash, and coughing through the fumes, as smoke billowed up from the bed.

We were still lying there, bare, in each other's arms when half a dozen officers burst into the bedroom and came racing down its considerable length.

They halted and gaped at the smouldering bedclothes.

"I say," Mays said; and, "Wow," said Bruce Shovell as he gazed in awe and admiration at my smoldering kip. And again: "Wow."

His Highness

When I walked into the operations building after a morning spent in formation flying with one of the Snipe squadrons, it was to learn that the Maharajah had arrived.

"He's been waiting for more than two hours," Hibbert whispered as we looked in at the skinny little man. He was sitting motionless in the visitor's chair in my office.

Today he was wearing just a simple white dhoti and a white cap. His eyes were sightless, only his lips were moving.

I went in and spoke to him. When he failed to answer I stood there for a moment massaging my brow where the leather flying helmet had left a crease in my forehead. I didn't know whether to shake him awake or not. He seemed to be reciting some words over and over, silently, his eyes open and seemingly focused on a point very much further than the far wall of the office; and it seemed to me that Christ might have had eyes like that when he thought things over in the wilderness.

They quite stapped me in the vitals, those eyes did. I felt I was in the unpresence of a man who had detoured into a different world.

Becoming aware of my presence, he broke off. The next moment he was slashing at my face with a weapon.

I recoiled, staring at him stupidly, thinking I'd committed some offence by overhearing his silent words. His weapon was really frightening, too: a length of cruelly-twisted wire with a leather piece at the end, studded with razor-sharp stones. But then I realized that it was only his diamond-studded fly whisk. He was keeping the flies off my face.

"Sorry to have kept you waiting, sir," I said, retreating behind my desk.

"Oh, that is quite all right, Mr. Bandy," he said huskily. "I am used to waiting."

"Uh. . .would it be impolite to ask what that was you were saying over and over, sir?"

"They were Sanskrit words, Mr. Bandy," he said, his orange lips twisting into a smile. "They are the words of a prayer called the *Gayatri*."

"What do the words mean?"

"It is three thousand years old, and it says that our meditations should be on the glorious light, which should illuminate our minds."

"You're on pretty good terms with God, aren't you, Maharajah Sahib?"

He tittered, but his lined, sunken face was expressionless again when he removed his hand. "No, Mr. Bandy," he said in his high, unlubricated voice. "No such luck, I'm afraid." And then he started to talk about the weather. He knew that Britons always talked first about the weather before getting down the rest of the bad news.

"The Indian Hot Weather is late this year," he observed, again hiding behind his fleshless brown hand. "Usually by now it is roasting hot."

"You mean this isn't the hot weather?"

"Oh, dear me, no," he said, and actually dared to show his face for a moment, to show how amused he was.

Deciding that the conventions had been sufficiently observed, he continued, "Anyway, what I am coming to see you about, Mr. Bandy, is to thank you for your exhausting report on the situation re Khaliwar."

"You mean exhaustive report, don't you?"

"Do I? Yes, perhaps I do. . .it was a wonderful report, Mr. Bandy. I really don't see how you had the time to write so many pages. Anyway, I am most pleased, Mr. Bandy. I am so glad that you agree that we have nothing to fear from Khaliwar and that Khooshie is quite safe."

"Hang on a mo, Your Highness. I don't remember saying anything about Khooshie in the report. And I certainly didn't say definitely that we had nothing to fear from Khaliwar."

"Of course," he said apologetically, "I only got as far as page ninety...."

"You see, sir, the whole point of the report was to say that defensive measures were vital, if—"

"Yes, yes," he said twitchily. "I know that Khaliwar has been provoking us like mad, never missing an opportunity to put us in our place, raiding into our state, and then blaming it on us for not defending our border properly, and so on and so forth. But everything is fine now. There have been nothing but smiles and goodwill messages from Mohammed Farookhi for ages, now."

"This sudden switch on their part from potshots to hearts and flowers—shouldn't we ask ourselves why the sudden change, sir?"

"No, no, no, we don't want to ask any questions at all, Mr. Bandy, it is so nice and peaceful now."

"Sir, I really do think we should make an effort to find out exactly what is going on there."

"The Dewan assures me that there is nothing going on, Mr. Bandy," he said agitatedly. "Please don't worry about it."

"Sir, at the very least we should confirm whether or not they have an air force."

Suddenly flaring with anger he started shouting at me, so agitatedly, in fact, that his guards came running into the office, clawing at themselves in an effort to find their weapons, before being waved out again by the Maharajah. "You are still wanting to make dangerous reconnaissance flights," he said, beating time to his ire with his fly whisk. "But I absolutely forbid it. We must not anger them, they are bad enough even when they are in a good mood. No, no, I tell you our policy must remain one of peace and love," he said, whacking the desk as if he wished it were my botty. "Especially now that they are being so friendly, with this invitation from Lampur Kalat."

"Invitation to where?"

"I have just told you. Really, Mr. Bandy, you are becoming most, most...I am talking about Lampur Kalat, their capital. But you know all this, so why are you looking so blank? The Dewan has told you all about it."

"All about what?"

"The trip to Lampur Kalat."

"What trip?"

"The one to Lampur Kalat! Really, Mr. Bandy—"

He stopped as I sat up. "You're not thinking of going, are you, sir?" I asked.

"No, no, of course not. What an absurd idea," he said withdrawing a tin of Farrah's Original Harrogate Toffee from a fold of his Chanderi muslin dhoti, opening it with distinctly trembling hands, selecting a square of toffee, and popping it between his queer orange lips.

"I should think not," I said.

"It is Khooshie who is going."

"What?"

"The Dewan informed you two days ago."

"Informed me what, what?"

"About the invitation to Khooshie to be a guest of the Nawab for a few days," the Maharajah said, dribbling toffee juice.

"Well, obviously," I said, feeling an obscure anxiety—you could never be sure that what Indians seemed to be saying was what they were actually saying, or what they were actually saying was what they were thinking—"it's quite out of the question, isn't it. Especially after the way they tried to bump him off in London."

"Oh, no, that could not have been them, Mr. Bandy. They have reformed. No, no, I really do not see any reason why he should not accept, if only for the good of his health," he said, wiping juice off the shelf of his chin with a handkerchief.

"Good of his health?"

"The Nawab is offering all sorts of wonderful distractions," he replied hurriedly. A nerve in his hollow cheek was twitching, and his very eyes looked haggard.

"I see," I murmured uncomprehendingly. "Anyway, whatever the inducements, Your Highness," I said, "you know it's out of the question for your son to go to Khaliwar. He'd be safer checking a tiger's tonsils than accepting an invitation from them."

"You don't understand," the Maharajah said. "He has already gone."

"He...*what*?"

"He has already gone to Lampur Kalat."

Perspiration soaked my shirt and trousers.

"He's already gone?"

"Dear me, yes. He left this morning. Let me see—he is traveling in a dozen or so motor-cars. He is not, of course, traveling in all the motor-cars, he is riding in just one of them. The others are filled with servants and his bodyguard, and luggage, gifts for the Nawab, and so forth—"

"Your Highness."

"Yes, Mr. Bandy. What?"

"When exactly did he leave?"

"Oh, before eight o'clock this morning, Mr. Bandy."

"He's taken the main road north?"

"Yes, the main road."

I looked at my watch; and felt my intestines slump badly. It was nearly half past one.

"He will be in Khaliwar by now," the Maharajah said. Affected by my expression, his own had greatly deteriorated, and his skin had taken on a frightful yellow hue.

"If he is," I said unsteadily, "you won't see him again. At least, not until they've got what they want from you."

His bony hands were tearing at each other. "You cannot know that, Mr. Bandy," he panted. "You cannot."

"I wasn't sure before," I said, reaching into the commode for the field telephone which was connected to the tent where my airplane was hangared, "but I am now, Your Highness. I am now."

Twenty minutes later, flying flat out in my Bristol fighter, I reached the main road that scored up the centre of Jhamjarh from Djelybad to the Khaliwar border and beyond. And there I turned north, bumping along in the warm air at 800 feet. And in seconds the Bamm bridge appeared, looking absurdly fragile as it carried the road across the Bamm River gorge.

As Khooshie had elected to travel by car rather than train, this was the route he must have taken. It was the fastest north-south highway in the state. Not that that was saying much. In the whole of Jhamjarh, there were only two routes running north and south, the other being little better than a cart track.

This one was oiled gravel for much of its length. It even had a concrete surface for the five-mile stretch between the capital and the Bamm River, concreted because the Maharajah was particularly proud of his steel bridge over the Bamm, and liked to show it off to visiting dignitaries as an example of the progressive policies of his independent state—the concrete surface being the other example.

Actually he owned two steel bridges, the one I was staring down at now, and the railway bridge twenty miles further west, which slashed across this same gorge.

Usually the sight of the Bamm road bridge was quite comforting. If blown, it could bring any invasion from the north to a dead stop. For though the bridge was less than a couple of hundred feet long and the river, at this time of year barely deep enough to swirl away the dead bodies that Indians were inclined to chuck into the water courses, the gorge under the steel feet was far too deep to negotiate in any other way.

Today, though, as I flew the big, stiff fighter northward along the road, I was not the least comforted. I was feeling too mad at the prince, his father, and all his advisors.

When I had finally grasped what the Maharajah was saying back there in the bedchamber, I had sat quite paralyzed for what seemed like seconds on end, and when he asserted that I had been told all about the invitation to Lampur Kalat days ago, I had gaped wider than ever. "I was not," I'd panted. "Nobody told me anything. Who told me? Nobody said a word. He's already gone? Oh, my God."

"The Dewan told you. He did not tell you?"

"No, no, no! Good God, sir, how could you let him—after their attempts to obviate him in London?"

The Maharajah thought for a moment, then: "I am sure that is not the correct usage of the word obviate..."

He was trembling all over, and his brown creased face had turned jaundice yellow. "I thought you knew all about it," he said, attempting to get to his feet, but failing, enervated by my shock. "I must admit I was surprised that you had nothing to say on the matter. But now I understand. Really, it was most negligent of the Dewan. I will have to speak to him about it at his earliest convenience, I promise you." And he went on to explain that he had received a message from the Nawab of Khaliwar stating that relations between their two states would be greatly enhanced if Prince Khooshie were to pay an official visit. "A formal, three-day visit, they said. And they hinted that a refusal would greatly worsen our relations."

He went on to admit, in a voice strangled and squeaky, that he'd had doubts about the wisdom of such a visit, but that Khooshie had insisted on going, and had thrown a tantrum when the Maharajah argued. In the end he had been forced, he said, to agree.

I could visualize that scene, all right. The Maharajah was quite incapable of denying anything to his son. His love for the prince was practically idolatrous. On one occasion I had actually seen him throw himself at the boy's feet in gratitude for some concession. On another occasion he had wept tears of joy when Khooshie impulsively embraced him. A smile from Khooshie could gild the day for the Maharajah, a critical or complaining word could cast him into the darkest depression.

Given the excessive indulgence that had surrounded the boy since birth, it was hardly surprising that the lad was used to getting his own way. On this occasion he was particularly keen to get it because along with the official invitation from Mohammed Farookhi, he had received an unofficial message in which the Nawab had hinted that a particularly inventive orgy might be laid on for the prince's benefit involving three of Farookhi's own daughters, plus some interesting mechanical devices from Japan.

Khooshie had grown used to being indulged sexually as well as in every other respect, and if anything, his interest in sexual reinforcement had sharpened since his year in Europe. But upon his return home he had faced nothing but frustration because of the court tradition that if the *Yuveraj* had not married by the age of nineteen he must remain celibate until he was. Servant girls, concubines, and nautch girls must all be denied him until after he was decently married. Unused to self-control, he had become increasingly fretful, as I had seen, healthy activity on the polo field, pig-sticking, and tiger-hunting from the back of an elephant having proved to be inadequate substitutes.

The sly invitation from Lampur Kalat—whose spies had presumably reported Khooshie's frustrations—had proved tempting enough to overrule all other considerations of common sense and parental distress. He had gone to the court priests and insisted that their moratorium on sexual activity applied only at the Jhamjarh court, and not when he was away from home. After abortive consultations with several Brahmins, one was finally located who was willing to sanction this interpretation.

I would never understand Indians, never. I could hardly believe that the Maharajah could take indulgence to such lengths that he would allow the boy to put himself in danger purely to avoid a scene, when he was aware that the indulgence could be fatal. That the Maharajah had been aware of the danger seemed to be confirmed by his visit to the Haksar Palace. It was a subconscious appeal to me to translate his own misgivings into an action he couldn't take himself. But he had almost certainly left it too late.

Halfway to the border, now, and still following the gray line of the road as it jogged and darted between the fuzzy green fields of north-central Jhamjarh.

I unstuck my eyes from the traffic only to massage them under the goggles, or to summarize the flickering needles on the Bristol's wooden instrument panel. The coolant temperature was high. No point in burning out the valves for an extra

5 m.p.h. I reduced engine revs, and dropped my hand onto the radiator shutter control; but it was already fully open.

In other circumstances such a flight in this big biplane with its powerful V12 engine would have been a pleasure. It was not often that one could wear just a shirt, slacks, and brown leather shoes in the cockpit. The air, plucking importunately at the blue air-force material, was caressing. But the awareness that the prince's life and my salary were at stake rather spoiled the occasion.

I continued to inventory the road's contents as the airplane thumped over the warm, uneven air. The highway was remarkably busy considering the total absence of motorized traffic. A main artery connecting a thousand scrimpy villages, it was packed with traffic: one string of camels so far, many herds of goats, the odd wandering cow. And the omnipresent buffalo carts and their drivers, goatherds, and camel goaders. And women carrying merchandise on their heads, costumes vividly colored, brilliant reds and yellows and blues. And peasants, peasants, peasants everywhere, on their way to field or friend or market stall. If Khooshie's retinue had been forced to negotiate such a jam, surely, surely it must have been slowed repeatedly.

Unfortunately, the humble peasants invariably cleared out of the way whenever automobiles approached.

I kept hoping to find the convoy parking behind a mile of goats or camels, or better still, overturned in the ditch. No such luck. It was six hours now since they had set out. They were almost certainly across the border by now. And if the Khaliwarians had any sense, the nineteen-year-old prince would be seized the moment he passed their guard hut, his captors rejoicing at the coup of managing to entice the Maharajah's son into their territory with such ridiculous ease.

Damn, damn, damn fools.

On and on droned the Bristol, bumping over the warm, roller-coasting air alongside the road. I was keeping a few hundred feet sunward, cutting across bends and curves only when I could do so without losing sight of the traffic. Which was thinning now as the border neared. Gaps of as much as three inches were appearing between the carts, beasts, and pedestrians.

Perhaps a dozen miles to the frontier, now. Few independent states bothered to demarcate their territories, but Khaliwar was an exception, presumably because it felt it had something worth stealing, like a secret or two.

Still no sign of the twelve automobiles, not even a forlorn breakdown by the roadside. Which was infuriating. There should have been at least one breakdown. Cars simply didn't make journeys in this country without conking out at least once. It was in the manual. But Khooshie and company had negotiated the imperfect surface at least this far without a single mishap.

Below the wavering wings the landscape had turned scrubby and jungly. And suddenly the road was bare of native traffic. There were few villages this close to the border. As if the peasants knew something we did not....

Still no sign of the Maharajah's big, beautiful bloody cars. Well, what did I expect, it was six and a half hours since they had set out and it was only seventy miles or so from the Bamm River to the border, seventy-five from the outskirts of Djelybad. Indian progress tended to be leisurely, but hardly leisurely enough that their average speed would be less than about twelve miles an hour.

Finding it harder to observe the road as it wound through the tousled landscape, I throttled back, leaden-bellied. With only four or five miles to go, I glided, hopeless, downward. The air, eddying past the inadequate windscreen, grew warmer, and the bumps in the air grew more violent. I thrust up the goggles for a clearer view as I hung over the side, vaguely recognizing the terrain. I had flown along the northern border once before out of curiosity, to see what Khaliwar looked like. Now I recollected that the road crossed the border through a narrow pass.

And there it was, dead ahead, that gap in the hills. So that was that. I was too late. They were over the line.

Yes, and there was Khaliwar's pretentious frontier post, a

wooden box, a striped pole over the road, and a flagpole, the Khaliwar flag hanging innocently limp. (Ironically, while peaceable Jhamjarh's flag boasted two bloodthirsty hatchets crossed on a green ground, the Khaliwar flag was a tranquil crescent moon.) The road I'd been trailing gouged a couple of hundred yards into the pass before curving to the left and disappearing from sight.

Careful to avoid invading their territory, I pushed the stick over to turn back, and increased power slightly to maintain a height of about 300 feet. A stiffness had been built into the Bristol fighter's controls to strengthen it for steep dives and violent evasions. Even at reduced power, it still took a fair amount of force to work the ailerons, as I was doing now. (They say you can always tell a Bristol fighter pilot by his bulging biceps.) As the scrubby landscape revolved in front of the nose, I wondered dismally what I was going to do now.

The cars appeared, above the nose.

My God. They were still in Jhamjarh territory, if only just.

As I banked, bloated with relief, and the road spoked into view once more, the cars reappeared, as they emerged from a tangle of dusty trees: nine, ten, eleven, yes, all twelve of them, the dozen luxury automobiles, dusting along at a good twenty miles an hour.

I had relaxed my concentration on the road for less than a minute in order to study the frontier post, and in those seconds I had missed the convoy as it wormed through the skinny trees.

The trouble was that in those seconds they had come appreciably closer to the border.

At the moment I was too relieved to do much except loll the napper over the coaming and beam down at the glorious view as it canted and swiveled, the airplane droning quietly, its big propeller turning hardly faster than a Dutch windmill. Now I could see Khooshie in the leading car, an open-topped Rolls Royce with stainless steel panels. These caught the sun and perforated my retina with black dots. So did the jewels in his turban as he waved. I waved back vigorously, swamped with relief.

Most of the following cars were gray with dust so that it was impossible to tell their original color. The second, third and fourth were crammed with members of the Prince's bodyguard in their red and gold uniforms.

I snatched a glance at the clock in the instrument panel. Eleven minutes past three. So they must have been held up en route after all.

Now it was time for the final obstruction: me. So I dived and started waving and waggling the wings, pouring just enough power into the Falcon engine to stay a hundred feet up. Hollering absurdly, I gestured, pushing forward against the wind with the palm of my free hand to indicate that they should halt. They waved back; and continued on.

I stared in disbelief. They were not only carrying on toward the border, they seemed to be accelerating as if they thought I was urging them on. What the turd was the matter with them? Couldn't they recognize urgent stop signs when they saw them? But they seemed to think I was spurring them on. Or entertaining them. For when I nearly ran into the hill at the entrance to the Khaliwar pass and had to snatch at the controls, they waved harder than ever, and one or two of them even stood up in their car for a better view of my amusing antics.

They were now only about a couple of hundred yards from the border.

That wasn't the worst of it. Not only were they about to enter Khaliwar, so was I. In fact I was now well inside the forbidden territory. My gyrations had carried me deep into the gap beyond the striped frontier pole. The Bristol fighter was droning down the gorge, well beyond the border post where half a dozen people in colorful gowns stood waiting, presumably a reception committee.

I was invading Khaliwar. And I could not immediately rectify the situation because the aircraft was below the top of the narrow pass, bouncing along at a leisurely eighty miles an hour with not near enough power to zoom up out of the way. And there was certainly not enough room to turn.

The heat from the rock below was causing the aircraft to

gavotte. I slammed on power. The engine spluttered. For a heartfailing second I thought I'd drowned it.

The engine gulped, then bellowed angrily, the sound beating back from the rocky sides of the pass. Slowly the machine gained height, receiving unenthusiastic support from the baked air.

The way was horribly narrow, the road at the bottom of the pass keeping a dry meandering watercourse company. However, it was quite a short dash through the hills. After only a few hundred feet the road gouged left into more open country. I gripped the joystick ring and forced it sideways and back a little. The big machine wobbled to the left, bouncing violently in the waves of heat from the rocks below. Then I was round the corner, and out of sight of the small, harmless reception party at the border post.

Which brought me in sight of a very much larger and considerably more harmful reception party which was waiting just round the corner.

I almost ran into them, I was that low. I had a sudden shocking impression of orderly groups of men in uniform, a yellow and black flag, and armored cars, before they were whizzing past under the wings. Then I was climbing, and staring wildly back over the stabilizer.

No, I hadn't been seeing things. An army unit, at least a company in strength, was sitting there at the end of the pass, spread all along the road and up the hillside—armored cars belching blue smoke, with small triangular flags fluttering from their masts, and the perforated barrels of heavy-machine guns at forty-five degree angles. And clumps of soldiery here and there.

Perhaps as many as two hundred green-and-black-turbaned heads were turned in my direction, plainly taken by surprise as the hefty biplane came belting round the corner at almost zero feet, flying straight at them. Then it was up and over, up the hillside, over the top, engine screaming in the hard defile, and then vanishing in a suncatching flash.

I'd surprised the army just as they were about to surprise the

convoy of guests as it puttered round the same corner in twelve fancy automobiles.

This was the real reception party, not the innocent-looking group at the border post.

Seconds after frightening the daylights out of them, and myself, I was up and over the low hill, and down again to the messy Jhamjarh countryside. And obtaining an apoplectic view of the dusty automobiles as they continued to head for the respectable Khaliwar reception committee and the ambush beyond.

Desperate, I climbed a hundred feet and looked frantically for a flat stretch of ground to land on, ahead of the column. There was no flat ground. A few trees, including *champak* with faded green blossoms, a slash of thorny bushes, patches of raw earth, thrusts of gritty gray rock. Not even the road was suitable for an emergency landing. It was wiggly, too narrow.

I banked the machine smartly over the pack of cars and gestured violently again, pushing the wind, go back, go back. If anything, the stupid cars went faster.

Now as furious at Khooshie's doltishness as I was anxious for his safety, I looked over the ground for some way to dive on him so dangerously close that he would have no alternative but to stop. But the terrain made this impossible. There seemed to be no way to stop the stupid, stubborn, undisciplined fool—

Unless I could show him what was in store.

Without further thought, I dived, pulled out, lashed at the rudder bar, hauled back the stick, and did a flick roll to bring me head on to the pass, a lightning horizontal spin. On full power I hurtled over the nice, polite reception party near the guard pole—half a dozen dark faces starring up—and up the pass I flew again, the road twisting low underneath. The machine bouncing violently in billows of hot air, caused me to bite my tongue. The metallic taste of blood infuriated me all the more. At the same time I wondered if this would entitle me to put up another wound stripe.

The road started to curve. I turned with it on rudder. A second later the army reception party reappeared. This time they were slightly better prepared. Warned of my approach by the noise beating back and forth in the rocky channel, a machine gunner on an armored car opened up.

I dipped the nose to bring a target into the line of fire. The ring sight embraced and then rapidly enlarged a squad of men in light brown uniforms. I pressed the lever in the middle of the ring grip of the joystick.

As my single Vickers gun was not loaded, naturally nothing happened. I was just indulging in a spot of practice. And encouraging them to shoot at me, the more wildly the better.

To this end I circled round again as fast as possible, and dived on them again. This time a good many soldiers obliged, popping off with machine-guns and rifles, some of them, the ones scattered up the hillsides, actually firing downward, aiming into the cockpit.

For a moment I was quite happy to be shot at, as this produced a great deal of noise in the geologically confined space. However, my enthusiasm diminished somewhat when, on my next dive and zoom, the whole lot joined in and a heavy machine gun got the range. Holes appeared in the wings. And just as I was noticing this, a bullet struck the cockpit bar that secured the butt of the Vickers. Even in the dazzling sunlight that was flooding the interior of the cockpit, the flash as the slug struck the bar was bright. Ragged metal flowered. Christ, Christ, explosive ammo. Simultaneously, part of the coaming shredded. That was either another bullet or a ricochet.

I hadn't believed for a minute that they could get that close. It said a hell of a lot about the Khaliwar army training. And frightened me so much I broke off the dive and zoom campaign and climbed away at full throttle; though my excuse for doing so was to look back across the state line to see if the idiots in the fancy cars had finally got the point.

It seemed so. All eleven cars had halted—barely fifty feet from the border post. Some of the occupants were gawping up at me, others were staring down the gorge. They must have heard the clatter of gunfire. It would be enormously amplified by the hills. Also there was light blue gunsmoke rising into the air at the far end of the pass.

Now that it seemed to be all over with, I was greatly relieved at the thought that I would not have to face that murderous fire again. I had gotten out of the habit of being shot at. My nerves weren't as good as they used to be. I was shaking, admitting to excitement but suspecting that it was blue funk.

No, I wasn't going near that company of sharpshooters again. They were far too skilled at their trade.

But a moment later I saw I would have to. Lorryloads of troops and armored cars were appearing at the far end of the pass. And now they were starting toward the frontier post—and, of course, toward Khooshie and company.

Though my splitarsing had halted the Jhamjarh convoy, they were just sitting there, gaping at the advancing troops, making no effort to turn around in the road and go home again.

What else was there to do? I banked yet again into the gorge, too disgusted even to swear. At reduced throttle to give the army time to get out of the way, I dipped down to within a few feet of the road, following its wiggles on rudder and keeping the leading vehicle, an armored car, within the ring sight. At our combined speed it enlarged rapidly in the sight.

I couldn't see the driver. Presumably he was behind those slits at the front of the car. But I could see the machine gunner at the top of the ungainly-looking vehicle. He was not firing at me. He was too busy having fits as the aircraft with its menacing wingspread of forty feet came blasting toward him over the hot ground.

It was now up to the driver, as I had little room to maneuver laterally. I was hoping that he would pull off the road before we met. I was forcing myself to stay down until the very last second, though it took some effort of will to do so.

There he went. He was not turning off the road, but slamming on the brakes, which proved to be just as effective from my point of view. The lorry behind screeched into him, and the two vehicles then slewed.

Just as I thought I'd finished work for the day, there was a jarring impact that kicked my right foot off the rudder pedal, and when I tried to replace it, there came a searing pain.

A minute later I was back over the line, and, to distract

myself from the leg, I peered down at Khooshie once more; and saw that he and his mob had finally got the point. The sight of army vehicles racing toward them along the gorge had provided the necessary stimulus. The cars were all maneuvering frantically through clouds of dust in their eagerness to turn and go back the way they'd come.

Finally they got themselves sorted out, and headed back toward Djelybad. They had taken so long about it that it was just as well that the armored cars and troop transports had jammed themselves in the gorge. It was highly unlikely that the Khaliwarians would have respected the frontier.

The Prince managed to get home fairly smartly, albeit in a bad temper at missing all the Japanese love aids. As for me, it was not until I reached Sigga's small hospital that I learned that a bullet had gone clear through the calf muscle of my right leg, and that a sausage of white tissue was hanging out; but that otherwise there was no damage.

Trying to Look Grateful

"I have decided to become an actor," Khooshie announced, sitting on my bed, "as the weather is becoming too hot for pig sticking."

"I see," said I. Actually I could hardly see a thing as the enormous bedroom was so dark. The tall, ornate slits pretending to be windows were blocked by carved sandalwood screens which had been put up the moment the Indian Hot Weather arrived. Thus the chamber was illuminated only by chinks of light. Nevertheless the chinks were intense enough to enable me to see objects as distant as five or six feet.

"It is a pity you missed the play last night," the prince continued, leaning on his forearm. Fearing that he might lean on my leg as well, I moved it away from his scented form. He was chewing betel nuts. "A theatrical troupe from Poona. Father put me in complete charge of the arrangements, overseeing the erection of the stage in the Ganesh Hall, and organizing a wonderful orchestra—three musicians, not counting the Minister of Public Works, who graciously consented to play the triangle during one of the intervals."

"Gee, I wish I'd been there," I said. I was, of course, lying. I had attended a Hindu play shortly after my arrival in India. It had no beginning or middle, or, so far as I knew, no end, as it was still going on when I left at two in the morning.

It had also contained much embarrassing improvisation—

111

mimed representations of the procreative act, or worse. And I'd thought that it was only us Westerners who had sex on the brain.

"I appeared as a Thespian in the seventh act," Khooshie said. "I was excellent. The other actors said so."

"M'm. By the way, did I ever tell you I was once an actor myself?" I said.

"So I have decided to put on another play," Khooshie said, ignoring the interruption. "And I shall play all the parts except for the female impersonations."

"I shall certainly look forward to that, Prince," I said, "as soon as my leg mends next January."

In a characteristic burst of discontent, the nineteen-year-old continued, "We should have a proper theatre in Djelybad. Every time there is a visiting troupe we have to go to all this trouble of building a stage, and putting up the curtain, and a footlight. Lots of other salute states have their own theatres, why should not we?"

I agreed, and a silence fell. It was broken by yet another change in his mood. This time it was one of irritation. "Once again you have saved my life, Bartholomew," he snapped. "I have been told to say thank you very much."

"You're welcome."

"Of course I am welcome. I am always welcome."

"M'm."

He lay back on the bed and clasped his hands behind is gleaming black hair. "By the way," he said, "I have decided that I am no longer interested in aviation." And he cracked another nut between his front teeth.

"Oh."

"There is simply too much extraneous information involved." he said, wiping juice off his chin with my sheet. "It is not good for the memory to be clogged up with extraneous detail such as the morse code. The memory should be kept clear of petty detail. It is the principles, the strategies, the grand designs that are important, not all this rot about how clouds are formed or how a plane is rigged."

"M'm."

"Accordingly," he said grandly, "I have decided to relinquish the position of Commander of the Air Force. So that will be your title from now on."

"Oh? You're promoting me?"

"I suppose so."

"So I'll be getting a raise, then?"

"A raise?" he corrected. "Certainly not. We are paying you quite enough as it is."

"Yahbut a promotion isn't a promotion without a raise—rise."

"In that case it is not a promotion, but merely an amendment to your title."

"Huh."

After a moment he became restless, rose from the bed, and went for a short walk. He disappeared into the darkness, cracking nuts. After he'd covered about a quarter mile, he returned and said sharply, "You truly allowed yourself to be shot?"

"To be shot *at*, anyway."

"In order to alert me to the danger?" he asked out of the hot gloom.

"Well, yes."

"This repeated rescuing of me," he said. "I hope you are not going to make a habit of it, Bartholomew."

"I'll try not to."

"It is putting me in a deuced awkward spot, you know. It is forcing me to feel grateful. I have never needed to feel grateful before, Bartholomew. The experience is unsettling."

"Sorry."

"That's all right," he said, cheering up slightly. "No need to apologize. It's just that I wouldn't want this constant saving of my life to affect our friendship, Bartholomew."

"No, I wouldn't want that either," I said.

I was to have four visitors that day, the next being Dr. Jonsdottir, who gave me a warm kiss, then promptly blinded me by throwing open the nearest shutter, admitting an oblong of ferocious sunlight into the bedroom.

As she changed the dressing on my leg she started lobbying

me again about the women of India. This time it was about a girl named Ganeshbala. Ganeshbala had proved to be a brilliant scholar, and the Maharajah had sponsored her further education in Europe for three years.

Unfortunately, as soon as she returned home, Ganeshbala had been dumped straight back into the *zenana*. "And purdah is destroying her, Bartholomew," Sigga said, briskly tying the bandage far too tight. "The other women have been tormenting her ever since she walked in on leather shoes. Imagine, shoes made from holy mother cow! She has no friends, they won't let her wear the Western clothes she brought back. She is desperate. Worst of all, she says, she is never alone. She has tried to kill herself."

"What can I do about it?"

"I wish you to speak to his nibs and get her out of there," Sigga ordered; and went on to say that she would have pestered the Maharajah herself, but he had refused to see her, or even to admit her to his part of the City Palace.

"Well, there's a good reason for that, Sigga. You see, he can't stand you."

"What nonsense."

"'t isn't. He thinks you're crass, insensitive, rude, tactless, and your voice hurts his ears."

"No," Sigga said, shaking her head with an air of utter certainty. "You've got it wrong, dear. That's *you* he's talking about."

"Course it isn't."

"'t'is. You fit the description perfectly. I mean," she hissed, a safety pin between her teeth, "nobody is more tactful than I am."

"*Everybody* is more tactful than you."

After a moment we laughed simultaneously, and she leaned over to give me a hug. Which was exceedingly pleasant as she was wearing very little except dark blue pantaloons and a layer or two of light blue silk, with a filmy headdress over her golden curls; and she smelled as if she'd just done the hundred yards in a bath of eau de Cologne.

But when I started to explore the material she drew back. "No, Bartholomew," she said. "There's no time for that."

"When will you have time?" I asked, reaching eagerly for my diary. "How about tonight? Can you fit me in at around ten p.m.?" But she began to talk again about bloody Ganeshbala.

She just missed the opportunity to tell the Maharajah about Ganeshbala herself, for he arrived barely two minutes after she left. Though His Highness preferred to swathe himself in a simple dhoti and sandals, his subjects greatly enjoyed the sight of him in his jewels and finest array; which, having just come from a public function, was how he was attired that afternoon. He wore a splendid golden gown and multi-colored turban, both drenched in baubles.

"Are you there, Mr. Bandy?" he enquired, feeling his way through the semi-darkness. One of the servants had closed the shutter the moment that Sigga departed.

"Yes. Over here, sir," I sang out; and, after the civilities: "You sound gloomy, Your Highness," I observed. Suddenly apprehensive that he had brought bad news—come to think of it, he almost *always* had bad news—my heart grew unruly. "Is anything wrong?"

"Everything is wrong," he sighed, and lapsed into a long silence. "But enough about me," he said at length arranging himself on the visitor's cushion, and after cogitating for another few weeks he said suddenly: "I am a reformed character, Mr. Bandy."

"Oh, yes?"

"I see now that I have been just a little too indulgent with Khooshie." He gestured helplessly. "It's just that whenever I look at him, it is as if all my willpowers are draining away, you see. I am quite helpless with awe, that one as ugly as I could have produced so beautiful a person. We have a saying in Jhamjarh: *Punnamna naraka trayate tat putr.* It means, roughly, *Having a son rescues a man from hell.*"

I nodded gloomily in the darkness.

"But I see I could have lost him by being so kind. No, not

kind, stroke out that word. I could have lost him by having no courage."

"But now it is different. I will see that he is taken in hand. The priests are being very kind, they are saying that it is prolonged contact with the West that has made such a terrible mess of Khooshie. But, no, I am still taking all the blame. From now on I will see that he behaves himself."

The Maharajah then took another few days off for meditation, rocking back and forth on the yellow cushion. Though it was dark, somehow I could see his deep black eyes glowing, as if phosphorescent.

Suddenly in a different squeak of voice he said, "I am not at all fond of the Viceroy, Mr. Bandy."

"Viceroy of India? Oh, aren't you?"

"Yes, I like him a lot."

"*Really?*"

"You don't like him?"

"No."

"Neither do I. I do not like him in the least. He is so sure about everything. He is quite convinced, for example, that everything he sees, smells, touches, and so forth, is utterly real. Do you know, Mr. Bandy," the Maharajah squealed incredulously, "he might look at the walls of this bedroom for example, and rap them with his knuckles and he would say, 'These walls are utterly real.' "

"The fool."

"He is a stupid man."

"Yes."

"But I am not the least afraid of him."

"No."

"You are not afraid of him either?"

"Yes, I am."

"You are? You are afraid of him too? So am I! You really are?" he cried, bouncing excitedly on the yellow visitor's cushion. "So am I. I am scared of him, he is so cold and calculating. And his wife is even more toffee-nosed—though I shouldn't say that."

"Why not?"

"Because I like toffee. I have often observed, you know, Mr. Bandy, that there is really only one thing wrong with Englishmen in India and that is Englishwomen in India. They are looking down on us Indians all the time...what is the point of this discourse, please?"

"You are distinctly wary of the Viceroy?"

"No, now I remember. The point is that very many British officials are jolly good chaps, even some district commissioners, very hard-working and genuinely caring for India, and so forth. But this Lord Blount has no warmth or anything else." His speech was now so agitated that saliva was positively raining down his Punch chin. "But I will tell you right now, Mr. Bandy, while I am still feeling so unreserved, that I am wishing I had never created this air force of ours. It is causing so much trouble."

"What's wrong, Your Highness?"

"Ah. You have noticed my anxiety and my furrowed brow. That is very perceptive of you," he said, wiping his chin on his golden sleeve. "I have been summoned to New Delhi," he added abruptly.

"Oh, dear."

"And so have you."

"Oh, God."

"I fear we are to receive a thorough wigging, Mr. Bandy, over the incident at the border. Mohammed Farookhi has complained to Government about your invasion of Khaliwar. They are telling the Viceroy that their territorial integrity has been utterly flouted."

"Goldarn nerve."

"Oh, I agree utterly, considering that they were waiting to pounce on my son the moment he crossed the border. But they will not believe us. They have been entertaining suspicions about us ever since we started the air force, and after all, we cannot deny that you did actually invade their independent state."

"When do we have to go to Delhi?"

"Immediately. Tomorrow."

But then he heaved himself out of his dejection and his

cushion and clenched his fist and slashed at the air with it. "Well, I will not go," he cried. "Sucks to him, so there! I mean, who is he to order me to be reporting to him on the double? I have a lineage of two thousand years. Mine is bigger than his any day."

But a moment later he was trembling again. He sat back on the cushion as if his legs had lost their strength. "If there is one thing I am hating, Mr. Bandy," he whimpered, "it is arguments and black looks, and being given a thorough wigging."

"Sir, you're not part of British India. Do you really have to obey the summons?" I asked. I was hoping he would defy the Government, because if he didn't go, I wouldn't have to go either.

For a moment I thought I was going to be allowed to remain in bed; but then he cried, "I shall go, but I shall inform him that I will not be insulted! I will tell him to his very face!"

But a moment later, despairingly: "Unfortunately I have no excuse. The astrologer has said that it is a perfect time for me to travel. So I shall have to go."

And finally, drawing himself up, and glaring at me as if it were all my fault: "But I will not be polite to him," he cried. "I shall be utterly reserved, dignified, and chilly as anything. I shall not make the usual abject apologies, I shall just stand there, looking ill-done-to. That will teach him a lesson, don't you worry."

"But do I have to go as well?" I whined.

"Yes, we must leave immediately, I am afraid," the Maharajah said, demonstrating how it should be done by leaving immediately.

I lay there, lightly perspiring, feeling as if several lead sinkers were attached to my stomach.

I don't know. With the growing uncertainty about life that seemed to be smothering me these days, I seemed to be suffering from mettle fatigue, my grit was turning into funk, my derring-do into derring-don't. Throughout my life I had been able to face antagonists *sans peur et sans reproche*; but the kind of decay that I associated with effete liberalism— overcompensating for the other fellow's point of view—

seemed to have settled in. I dreaded another confrontation with the all-powerful Viceroy.

My final visitor of the day was, to my faint, preoccupied surprise, Hibbert again. He had been to see me on routine matters that morning. He came gliding down the bedroom in his blue summer uniform—how did *he* always manage to emerge creaseless from an airplane cockpit while *I* looked like a caterpillar—and murmured, "Hello?"

"Over here, Hib."

He came over and ran into the bed. "Hello," he said again. "How are you feeling, Bart?"

"Terrible. There's a chair against the wall over there, Hib."

"I'll stand if you don't mind, sir," he said, sounding either stilted or ill-at-ease. "Are you really feeling terrible?" he asked.

"Yes. I have to go to New Delhi," I said, and told him about it.

He didn't seem to be taking the ghastly news as seriously as he should. He just kept murmuring, nodding, and taking deep breaths.

Finally: "It's about John Derby, Bart," he said.

"What about him?"

"He's gone on a photo reconnaissance flight over Khaliwar."

"Oh, Lord, that's all I need," I said, cravenly fearful about the effect this might have on the coming interview with the Viceroy. Then, raising my voice: "Who said he could do that? We've no authority for that. You shouldn't have let him go, Hibbert—the Maharajah has expressly forbidden it."

"He had no authority. He and Dave Simpson just loaded up with film and maximum fuel, and took off."

"When?"

"This morning, while I was with you."

"Shite."

"He said they couldn't hide a whole aerodrome and an entire air force. He swore he would find out where they were by midday. And, well, that's it."

"And did he find it—the Khaliwar air force?" Hibbert remained silent. "Well? What does he say?"

"He isn't back, Bart," Hibbert said. "He's more than four hours overdue."

"Four? Four hours? God damn it, why didn't you tell me sooner?" I shouted, jumping out of bed. But then, growing dizzy, I had to sit on the edge of the bed, supporting my head in both hands.

"I didn't want to bother you, Bart, until I was sure. After all, you're..." He gestured at the bed. "I've mounted an air search on our side of the border."

"He might have crash-landed somewhere...."

"Yes, it's possible," Hibbert said, and went on to describe the system he was employing to search for the missing aircraft between the aerodrome and the border.

"But not over. We can't go into Khaliwar, Hib."

"No. The pilots have strict instructions not to cross the line."

"I'll try," I said wretchedly, "but I'm quite sure the Maharajah won't let us look for him inside Khaliwar."

"No," Hibbert said; and, after a moment: "I'm sorry, Bart."

"There's still a chance. It's only four hours."

"Yes, of course," Hibbert said out of the gloom, and trying really hard to sound optimistic.

Limping Along

Determined not to respond with obsequious speed to the Viceroy's peremptory summons, the Maharajah announced that he would not set off for New Delhi until he was good and ready. He then lay awake all night, worrying about being late for his appointment on the following Monday afternoon.

Like many independent states, Jhamjarh had its own railway, though, like Khaliwar, it was privileged to use a gauge similar to that of the system that served British India. Thus when we reached the main Bombay to Delhi line late in the morning, it was a simple matter to attach the Maharajah's private coach onto the Delhi Express.

Though luxurious, the Maharajah's mobile quarters were not particularly comfortable. The coach was furnished in the Victoria style, and even had a prickly horsehair chaise-longue. Moreover, the Indian Hot Weather was now fully upon us, but the only cooling system was made up of musky breezes through the window blinds. As the ornate private coach shimmied up Central India, the temperature of the interior reached 110 degrees.

"If it's like this in May, what must it be like by midsummer?" I enquired.

The Maharajah was not listening. He had been sitting motionless for hour after hour by an open window. While I was titrating enough brine to keep a cow in salt for a year, he hardly perspired. The only sheen came from his fathomless eyes.

As we chuffed into Shampur railway station, which was about halfway to our destination, even the percussion of the crowd outside failed to flam paradiddle on the old man's trance. I doubt if he was even aware of a station platform seething with strident bundle-bearing citizenry, men in white, women in colors marvelously bright. So I took it all in for both of us. I watched, fascinated, as men and women, children and goats, surged toward the train as it squealed to a halt, and a competition of shoving and elbowing was arranged. Women ululated, children howled, goats scoffed and taunted. There was not a porter or ticket collector or stationmaster in sight to control the crush. Soon, passengers were oozing and bulging from every train doorway and window, and some men even attempted to clamber onto the roof of the royal coach, until the Maharajah's servants kicked them off. The roofs of the public coaches were soon matted with humanity, who seemed to enjoy barbecuing themselves under the solar coals.

Yet when the rush was over and the train fit to bust, the numbers left on the platform seemed scarcely to have diminished. Many of the families seemed to be living there permanently, judging by their barricades and bundles, and their hissing spirit stoves.

The train sat in Shampur for two hours in the sweat-trickling heat. Finally and without any apparent assistance or encouragement from the station staff—if there was a staff—the train suddenly jerked violently, hooted, hissed, howled, and started off backwards.

However, in no time at all, the driver realized that he was heading back to Bombay, whereupon the train underwent another convulsion and started off in the right direction.

As our swaying coach gathered speed, a blessed breeze billowed through the windows, bringing with it not just a little relief from the swelter but wafts of that exciting, undefinable smell of India...except that, having said that, one was immediately tempted to define it as a mixture of spice, sandalwood, eucalyptus, harsh Secunderabad tobacco, human and bullock dung, and a certain *je ne sais quoi*.

"Makes you wonder how Western countries must smell to Indians," I remarked to the Maharajah who had returned from the dead. "How did England smell to you, sir, when you first went there?"

"Wet macs, soot, and twenty Woodbines," he replied, and looked pleased with himself when I smiled as widely as the heat would permit.

The journey to Delhi went smoothly enough, apart from the rocking, jolting, and bumping, two days' tedium, and painful thoughts about John Derby—I kept wondering if I should have defied the Maharajah and the government and mounted a full-scale search over Khaliwar. To distract myself from a sort of suspended grief I spent much of the journey at an open window, gawping and ruminating. Impressions of India tended to come in bursts. You were either being visually numbed by monotony, or overstimulated by human chaos. One moment we would be traveling at fifteen miles an hour through greenery, through a surprisingly lush landscape considering that it had not been watered for six months, the next you were in a featureless plain with an elephant silhouetted on a pink horizon. Then clattering through a community of crumbling houses and yelling children, hands outstretched along the track. Next an entirely different, lacerated vegetation looking as if it would never revive, no matter how drenching the coming monsoon. Ending in a road and a level crossing, and a pack of dangerous dogs.

And then, dreaded Delhi.

Though the temperature in New Delhi could reach three figures in the month of May, it was a mere eighty degrees as the Bombay express pulled into the new city's grand railway terminus. There the Maharajah was met, with much formality and Hindi chatter, by a friend of his, the ruler of another princely state. This man, tubby as a spoiled dog, with an aversion to non-Indians, owned a palace right next to the

Viceregal residence which he occupied for at least four days per year when the Chamber of Princes was in session. This was where my Maharajah was to stay.

"I tried to persuade him to invite you, too," the Maharajah said apologetically, "but he didn't like the look of you."

"Why not?"

"You reminded him of Lord Curzon."

So I had to make do with the reception from a government official named Hornby who, in honor of the occasion, had dyed his face yellow. It clashed horribly with Delhi's brick red soil. Too many gin slings or chota pegs, I thought.

"I'm to look after you during your stay in New Delhi," Hornby explained as we drove in a government car—a really cheap, rattly affair—to the Ritz Hotel.

As we chatted he kept glancing at my walking stick. Finally he politely probed for the reason I was limping so heavily.

It was the opening I had been looking for. Fixing his citron phiz with basilisk survey, I replied, not quite untruthfully, that it had something to do with the incident that had led to the loss of one of my squadron commanders.

"Oh, I say, that's terrible. Was he...I mean, is he...?"

"He's been missing for four days, now."

"That's terrible," Hornby said again, obviously knowing nothing about it; which was all I wished to know. Khaliwar, quick enough to raise a diplomatic ruckus about my irruption into their territory, had not yet complained about Derby's aerial trespass. I didn't know whether that was a good sign or not.

The hotel I was driven to was by no means up to the standard of its London namesake where I had once stayed with dearest Katherine. It was not even in the best part of town, but was some distance down the Grand Trunk Road that wiggled dustily for 2,000 miles from Calcutta to the North-West Frontier. The hotel had not been painted or refurbished since the Coronation Durbar.

Inside, half the lamps had failed. The light that remained was considerably subdued by flyspecks. The rush matting on the floor was as worn as the desk clerk's features.

"Not exactly the Ritz, is it?" I said to him.

"Oh, yes, sir, this is the Ritz. You are in the right hotel, all right."

"You think so?"

"Oh yes. Mr. Hornby himself made the booking," the clerk said, bowing quickly toward my official, who, catching my eye, had the grace to look embarrassed.

"Sorry about this, old man," he whispered as I tripped along to my room—literally, as the matting was so uneven. "But this is where they said I was to install you."

"Put him in the worst accommodation you can find, is that it?"

"There are worse hotels than this," he replied, sounding as if he were trying hard to think of one, while he busied himself frowning at my luggage. The Maharajah had arrived with three trunks, four suitcases, and five tea crates. but it seemed that one suitcase was good enough for me. "I don't understand what's going on, sir, but I gather you're not particularly in their good books, you or your employer," he added. "They aren't even giving your man a gun salute."

"He won't like that."

"That seems to be the general idea. Blotted the old copy-book, has he?"

Mr. Hornby seemed sympathetic enough despite his color. His eyes were yellowed by booze, his face by malaria, and his mustache by tobacco. He had a habit of drawing strands of it into his mouth and chewing on them for a while before smoothing them back into place.

He didn't behave like a senior official, though he certainly seemed old enough. He looked like the sort of person who, after a few drinks, would ask how old you thought he was. I sincerely hoped he wouldn't. He looked sixty, but was probably half that age.

When I asked him when we were to see the Viceroy he replied that the Maharajah was booked for four that afternoon, but an exact time had not been arranged for my interview. "I'm supposed to keep an eye on you until then," he blurted before hastily modifying the expression. "That is to

say, I'm supposed to look after you and see to your needs
until. . . ." His voice petered out as he realized that his amendment had come too late. "I have arranged for a carriage after
lunch to show you around the capital," he added hopelessly.

"That's very good of you, Mr. Hornby," I said, wondering
why they were going to all this trouble to keep me amused. "A
carriage, eh? Coach and horses?"

"Actually it's a *tonga*. Pony trap, really."

"Well," I said, "I guess I should be grateful it's not a
tumbril."

As we clopped around the spacious new city thrown up by Sir
Edward Lutyens, he pointed out the sights dutifully but
with little personal interest. "That's Parliament House," he
coughed, gesturing with his cigarette at an enormous round
building which had 40,000 pillars and a silly dome. And, a few
minutes later: "That's where you'll be seeing His Excellency,"
he said, pointing through a great width of ornamental railing
and gatery. Far beyond the gates was a long, low palace that
disappeared on both sides into the trees. "And I gather that's
where your Maharajah is staying," he added, pointing to a
mausoleum-like joint further along the street.

A moment later he was commenting that he should like to
have known a little more about us. "I must say it's very
awkward, knowing you and your boss are in everybody's black
books, and I'm the only one who doesn't know why," he said.
"I mean, what exactly have you done, to be treated this way?"

"What way?"

"This way. Your Maharajah not being put up in Government
House, and so forth, and being met at the station by somebody
like me. I mean," he added hurriedly, "not that I'm not
unimportant, because I am—not unimportant. Even so, I must
admit I was pretty amazed when they told me that I was to
greet a Maharajah and an air-force general on behalf of his
excellency, especially as it was only yesterday that they were
pulling out all the stops for the ruler of Khaliwar."

"Mohammed Farookhi? He was here?"

"The Nawab of Khaliwar, that's right. He's still here. They

put on a splendid show for him when he arrived. Brass bands, guard of honor, gun salute, gifts, the lot."

"Do you happen to know why he's in town?" I asked, fanning away a cloud of flies. Even Hornby's foul cigarette—he was smoking a dried lavatory brush—could not keep away the insects.

"It's just a three-day state visit, I understand. Exchange of gifts, speech or two, tea with the vicereine, that sort of thing."

"Treating him right royally, are they?"

"Definitely. There's even talk of a knighthood for him."

"I hope my Marahajah doesn't hear about it," I said.

"Don't see how he can fail to, old man, what with all the pomp, cocktail parties, and the like. Don't know why they're making so much fuss over him, personally. He looks, well. . .a bit decadent, if you ask me. But I suppose they have to repay his hospitality. The Viceroy and company aren't long back from a visit to Khaliwar, you see."

"The Viceroy actually visited Khaliwar? When was this?"

"Few weeks ago. Everybody was very impressed with Farookhi's hospitality. Even I was invited. My word, you should have seen the gifts some of the chaps brought back," he added enviously. "And I believe. . . ." He cleared his throat, blushed, and looked away. "I heard some members of our party were fixed up with dancing girls while they were there."

"Is that right?"

"All I got, though, was a tin of biscuits."

He lit another cigarette with some difficulty—the smelly wind kept blowing out the match flame.

"Did you see any aircraft while you were there?"

"H'm? In Khaliwar? No," he said, melancholy now. "We did see their army, though. And by Jove, that was an experience. You never saw such a farce."

"Farce?"

"They held a march-past for our benefit. Utter shambles. We'd a hard time keeping our faces straight, I can tell you. One of our chaps, Major Barr-Nunn, swore some of them had flintlocks."

We were now skirting Old Delhi where, Troy-like, half a

dozen civilizations had flowered and gone to seed. I saw nothing, took in nothing, I was so interested in what Hornby was saying. He was chattering away as if I were a psychoanalyst, confirming that not only was most of the RAF unavailable for emergencies—so was the army. Almost every unit within hundreds of miles had been sent to the North-West Frontier to deal with the troubles that were so much a part of that incendiary region.

While I was still feeling a little dazed by the heat and the implications, he stopped gossiping and said apologetically, "If you don't mind, old man, I'd better not say any more. I do have this tendency to say either too much or too little. That's how I lost my job as SDO in the Punjab, actually.

"God, though, I loved that job," he said, sucking wistfully at the wet remains of his cigarette. "I was only a twenty-four year old Sub-Division Officer barely a year out of England, and they gave me a whacking great slice of the Punjab to govern. The DC was a three-day journey away and I was responsible for a hundred miles of territory along the Indus. I was in complete charge of hospitals, the police, schools—I was magistrate and civil judge, jail superintendant, head of Land Revenue. My word was law to hundreds of thousands of men, women, and children. God, I loved those people. They treated you with reverence—reverence toward me, if you please." He laughed. "But they had pride, and some of the *Tumandars* and *Zaildars* were noble men. I learned Urdu and Punjabi in order to serve them better, and a bit of Jhatki as well. If I was arbitrating in their disputes I wanted to understand what they were talking about in their own language. And if I was trying somebody for murder, or—or for some of the awful crimes you can come across in this country, I wanted to make sure that the punishment was just."

I was beginning to feel quite an affection for old Hornby. I asked him if he'd had a wife out there, or similar company.

"No, I was entirely alone. Saw a white man perhaps every three or four months. It suited me just fine, you know. If I'd gone into India Office I'd've had to go to work in a top hat and striped trousers. Out there—" he gestured roughly northward with his thick, nicotine-stained fingers, "I worked in shirt sleeves, and dined without socks. My best friend at home was a sheep."

At that moment I was gazing out of the *tonga* at a variety of beasts on the road from Old Delhi—goats, long-haired Tibetan horses, bullocks, yaks, and a camel reclining in the brick-red dust. These last words of his restored my attention.

"Your best friend was a sheep?" I asked uneasily. Well, after all, he had confessed to wifelessness.

"Yes." He coughed between cigarettes. "It was a gift from a Baluchi chieftain. I was supposed to eat it, but it looked so like my Aunt Prudence I just didn't have the heart. So I just let it wander around the compound, and I'd talk to it occasionally."

A cotton-swathed corpse passed us on the other side of the road. It was supported by four young men with no calf muscles. As I watched, they set it down by the side of the road. The flimsy quartet then wandered off. Not for long though, I hoped, in this heat.

Our *tonga* driver, who was proceeding slowly so that the flies could keep up with us, edged around the carelessly-clad corpse.

"What time is it?" Hornby asked. He didn't appear to notice any of the horrid things that were going on all around us.

"Four o'clock."

"Bit early," Hornby muttered, cupping his hand round a flaring match.

"Bit early for what?"

"He said to have you back at the hotel no sooner than four-thirty."

"The Viceroy said?"

"No. Chap called Postillion."

"Francis Postillion?"

"You know him?"

I explained; and: "So he's on the Viceroy's staff, is he?"

Apparently four o'clock was yardarm time for Hornby. After politely offering me a nip, he had one himself from a hip flask. "Personally," he said, leaning over confidentially, "we all think he's in the Secret Service."

"M'm." I sat there in the *tonga*, jouncing and cogitating.

At length: "He said you were to have me back at the hotel no sooner than four-thirty? Were those his actual words?"

"That's right. So you'd be available when the Viceroy was ready for you."

"But then shouldn't he have said no *later* than four-thirty?"

"Beg pardon, old man?"

"You said he told you to have me back at the hotel no *sooner* than four-thirty."

Hornby opened his mouth, but it remained hung open for so long that several flies hurried up.

He clopped it shut again. "That's right," he said wonderingly, and taking several strands of his mustache into his mouth. "He did say that.

"H'm," he added. "Peculiar."

When I entered the hotel room, so many thoughts were wheeling and colliding in my head that a couple of minutes elapsed before I realized I had a funny feeling.

I stood in the middle of the floor and looked around. Nothing seemed to have changed. The flies were still butting the window, the ceiling fan turned just as wearily, and the bed was unflawed except at the edge where I had sat down to remove my shoes and socks and allow the air to caress my bunions. My suitcase still lay on the luggage stand beside the chest of drawers with the measled mirror.

I opened the suitcase. It was empty.

My God. Somebody had stolen my undies.

Then I remembered that a servant had put the contents away. This was confirmed when I sidestepped to the dresser. Yes, the drawers were in the drawers, and the shirts and socks. And my favorite pyjamas, the red Cossack ones with the black embroidery.

My expensive toilet equipment, then. I padded through into the slatternly bathroom; but nothing had been interfered with. The silver-backed brushes and comb and shaving equipment were neatly arranged on the shelf above the porcelain basin.

The level in the eau de Cologne bottle seemed to be the same, the bar of soap unsullied.

So obviously one's sixth sense was sending mischievous signals. I would have to have a word with it after dinner.

As it turned out, there would be no time for dinner. A messenger arrived from Government House soon after with the information that my appointment with the Viceroy had been set for nine o'clock that night.

A strange and rather ominous hour, it seemed to me. It made my other appointment, the one with the Maharajah, urgent enough for me to forego dinner. So I went straight to his pal's palace to find out how his talk with the Viceroy had gone that afternoon.

As soon as I saw the old man I knew that it had not gone at all well. Every few minutes, tears of mortification were springing from his eyes. And he kept bare-footing up and down the palace reception room, slashing at the pillars with his fly whisk—the ceremonial one, studded with cruel diamonds.

"They have been insulting me continuously all afternoon," he wept, stamping his bare foot.

From the moment he stepped off the train he had been greeted with the absolute minimum of ceremony. He had been met by an inferior official. There had been no guard of honor. No arrangements had been made for the nineteen-gun salute to which he was entitled. He had been curtly addressed by the Viceroy's aide-de-camp. He had been granted an insultingly short interview. There was to be no cocktail party for him. "I have not even been invited to tea by the Vicereine," he cried, his squeaky voice sending shivers down to my tail. "I have always had afternoon tea with the Vicereine. I have always dreaded it, but it is a tradition, and they have utterly flouted it," he cried, whacking another pillar, an action which was quite remarkably violent for him. All his life he had disciplined himself to resist aggressive impulses. "And he has actually upbraided me in the presence of others," he said, weeping enough tears of mortification to set back his soul's progress by several centuries. "He has deliberately humiliated me."

Abruptly he sat on a cushion and covered his face with his hands and moaned and rocked. I tried to console him by cussing the Viceroy for all I was worth, but what worried me most was a growing suspicion from what the Maharajah was saying—or not saying—that he had been unable to resist the Viceregal intimidation. That he had given in.

There were three ranks of rulers in independent India: those of some hundreds of tiny states who could claim no treaty rights or law-making independence; those with partial executive independence; and a few who had complete legislative and administrative independence, with a perfect right to their own armed forces. Both Jhamjarh and Khaliwar came under this third rank, and the Maharajah had repeatedly reminded himself on the train that no Government or any imperial office, India, Colonial, or Commonwealth, had control over him. He and his family had ruled Jhamjarh long before the Moghul dynasties. So the British were not going to tell *him* what to do. And he had reminded me at least twice that he was not afraid to assert himself, as witness his dismissal, many months previously, of a British Political Agent who had displeased him, "Because the fellow had such terribly bad breath, Mr. Bandy."

But that afternoon, the Viceroy had threatened him with the British Army, and it was clear that he had caved in.

"He actually threatened to send in troops?"

"Yes, yes, unless I stopped all this nonsense, as he put it," he said in his screechy voice, his eyes in that ruined face looking not the least spiritual.

"Surely there'd be a terrific stink about it if he did?"

"That is all very well—people could stink all they liked, but that would not do me much good once they had marched in and taken over my administration, as he said he would do."

"I thought you were determined to face up to him, sir. And I think you would have won, because right now he hasn't got much of an army to march in."

"How can you be so stupid?" he stormed. "If only a lance-corporal marched in I would be overthrown, if he represented the Raj!"

A moment later he was covering his face with a purple sleeve and moaning through it. "It was unbearable," he wept. "He would not believe me when I said over and over that I had no intention of threatening the British. He simply will not see that perhaps it is Khaliwar we are worried about, that it is Khaliwar who should be on the mat, not us. But he won't listen. Proof, he says. Where is the proof? And the trouble is, he is right. Where is the proof, Mr. Bandy, where is your proof?"

"Sir, what about their troops hiding behind a rock, ready to pounce on Khooshie?"

"Mohammed Farookhi has told His Excellency that it was only a welcoming party," he cried, beginning to redirect his anger onto me. "They told him that they wanted to give the boy a nice surprise—and you spoiled it!" The accusations he was passing on from the Khaliwarians via the Viceroy were now being transmogrified into his own condemnations. "I see now that it is your fault that I have been treated as if I were a, an Untouchable!" And as the memory of the afternoon's interview flooded back, he broke down and wept again, in an agony of humiliation, so that it was some time before he could round on me again. "If you had not been so very quick and efficient in forming my air force, all this would never have happened," he shouted, his eyes emitting flashes of lightning and raindrops. He turned indignantly and started out across the marble floor in his bare feet.

But a moment later, after glancing at me once or twice from the exit as I stood there gazing interestedly at the floor, he came back, and his next words were as calm as a rock pool. He had disconnected himself. "No, no, forget what I am saying, Mr. Bandy," he said, and actually reached out with his skinny hand to touch mine, regardless of the fact that my hand was bare. "You have been a wonderful, loyal person, quite uncondescending, and everything. So please forget what I am saying, Mr. Bandy, and when the Viceroy slings you in jug, as he is promising to do, don't you worry, I shall come and visit you whenever I am in New Delhi, don't you worry."

"Gee, thanks," I said.

Leaving Government House

At nine o'clock that night I was shown into an ante-room on the first floor of Government House. An hour and ten minutes later I was still waiting.

This was most annoying, as I had taken particular care to be there on time. Though the great building was only two palaces away on the same avenue as the Maharajah's digs, I had given myself extra time for the tuxedo'd stroll. Which was just as well, for when I reached the wrought-iron barricade I found that there was still a considerable distance to limp between the gates and the thousand-pillared building whose wings disappeared into parkland. I had to accelerate from a stroll to a lurching march, leg hurting like hell, and even then I was only just in time. It was he who was late.

The Viceroy, it appeared, was entertaining a distinguished visitor at dinner. The fact that this was the Nawab of Khaliwar, His Highness Mohammed Farookhi, did not exactly smooth the corrugated brow. In a way, though, it was quite flattering. They seemed to be going to a lot of trouble to put me in my place and emphasize the suzerain favoritism. I was certain it was being done on purpose. It was hardly likely that my interview just happened to clash with this latest gesture of friendship toward the state that they believed to be one of the most loyal of all the six hundred native realms. That the staff had also placed me within aural range of the Viceroy's speech in fulsome praise of Khaliwar's moderation seemed to strengthen the assumption of a plot to douse me in the icy waters of their disapprobation. The state dining room was only a few dozen feet from where I was seated.

For over an hour I was allowed to enjoy the sounds of diplomatic revelry: the clink of gold cutlery, the tinkle of cut glass, the ladylike laughter and the manlike rumbling.

After a while, finding that the old nates were becoming a trifle numb, I arose, limped out of the ante-room, making an effort not to click the cane too loudly on the parquetry and marquetry, and after a short walk, managed to reach the entrance to the state dining room without being challenged, though there were literally thousands of *chowkidars* and servants all over the place.

In the entrance there were a pair of decorative pillars. From behind one of them I obtained quite a comprehensive view of the interior, and it was a splendid scene that greeted my nutbrown peepers: dazzling silver candlesticks, massed banks of flowers, sparkling crystal, and hosts of diplomats in black and gold, infantry officers in scarlet and rifle green, and numerous flunkeys who were the most gorgeously uniformed of the lot. There were also a few civil servants in white ties and tails.

As for the Viceroy at the center of the head table, he looked particularly fine in his star-spangled get-up. Some trick of the light or luminous foolery made his flared face with its hooked beezer and flourishing mustache seem almost handsome. Strangely, there were no women present. Either they had withdrawn after the speeches or had not been present in the first place. Wives and children usually migrated to the hills as soon as the Indian Hot Weather arrived. They were probably all in Simla, the most favored hill station. But if the wives had taken to the hills, where had the ladylike laughter come from? Probably from the guest of honor. As I stood there at the entrance, pressed against the gilt pillar as if trying to become a caryatid, and dribbling a bit at the sight of the leftovers—I had not eaten since breakfast on the train—I gazed at Mohammed Farookhi with more than routine curiosity. I had been hearing some deliciously vile gossip about him. He was said to be a gormandizer of rare foods, such as the private parts of dangerous animals. He was said to have the finest collection of antique sex aids east of Istanbul, and to have separate harems for boys, girls, and grown women of fifteen. Most of the independent rulers of India were decent enough chaps trying to do their best for their peoples, provided it was not too inconvenient. Only a dozen or so took excessive advantage of their autocratic position. The ruler, actual or otherwise, of Khaliwar was considered to be the worst, notorious for his cruelty and Claudian excesses. So I was delighted to get a good view of my first monster of depravity.

To my disappointment, he looked quite ordinary: a man of fifty or so with a fat, glistening face the color of treacle tart, attired in an ivory coat transversely slashed by a cerulean sash, and bearing a star made up of diamonds that flicked colored lights in all directions. On his head was an indigo turban hung with a hundred pearls, or possibly even fewer. As I gawped I even saw him smile, as he leaned over to listen to another head-table guest.

As I gazed pruriently upon his visage, it began to waver. Good God, I was about to faint. For a moment I thought it was Farookhi's evil influence, or the effect of hunger. But it was only the heat. The temperature in the room, augmented by several thousand candles, was causing the Nawab's face to melt and wander.

When I flagged back to the ante-room it was to find Francis Postillion in urgent consultation with a servant and two stout Punjabi soldiers in ceremonial uniforms.

"Where the devil have you been?" he enquired when he saw me, after dismissing the others with a flick of a pampered hand. He had obviously not been attending the chinfest along the corridor as he was attired in dinner jacket rather than tails. "My dear chap, you can't go wandering around Government House as if you'd come to unplug the lavatories."

"Hello, Postillion. Fancy meeting you here."

"Nothing fancy about it," said he in a surly fashion. "I work here."

He took a deep breath to calm himself, and raised a hand to smooth a wrinkle or two from his high brow.

"You've Brilliantined your hair, Francis," I observed. His once unruly crop was glued fast to his bony cranium.

"What? Yes. His Excellency told me he didn't want floppy hair on his staff," he muttered.

"Well, Bandy," he went on, "you've really done it this time, haven't you? Attacking an unarmed reception committee is surely a record in outrageous behaviour, even for you."

"That's what happened, is it?"

"If you have a more interesting version," Postillion said, moving gracefully to a pedestaled vase and examining it with interest, "I'm perfectly willing to listen."

"I'll save it for the Viceroy."

"As you wish." He treated me to a cold look from that refined face of his. "But it might be worth your while telling me first. *I* might be inclined to listen."

"Meaning Blount won't?" I asked, sitting in the best arm-chair, laying my cane aside, and lighting my pipe. "That sounds like a criticism of the boss, Francis."

He was still examining the vase. "God, I hate beautiful things, don't you?" he said. "All this artistic muck the world is so full of. If I had my way, I'd order thirty lashes for anyone who showed the slightest sign of producing a work of art."

"Oh, all right, " I said as if he'd just persuaded me, "I'll tell you." And I proceeded to give him my version of what had happened at the Khaliwar border, concluding with the words, "But presumably you've confirmed this by questioning Khooshie and his team?"

He was now examining a Constable landscape. He was peering at it closely and contemptuously, as if suspecting that it might be genuine. "I gather the attitude on high is that any Jhamjarh witness would have to be considered unreliable," he said.

"Whereas a Khaliwar witness should be believed unhesitatingly?" I asked. I shook my head. "You know, Francis, the longer I live, the more I wonder at the propensity of people to cut the truth dead when they don't want to meet it," I said, emptying the blackened embers of my pipe into a very large ashtray. The ashtray, of intricately etched brass, was of a most generous size, being at least three feet wide and supported on a carved tripod.

"Do you honestly believe Khaliwar is harboring warlike intentions, or are you only trying to justify your job?" he asked. "My dear fellow, it's so absurd. It's just not possible to build up a modern army and air force these days without our knowing about it. I mean, dammit, they wouldn't dare even to try."

"I bet that's what George the Third said," I said, rapping my pipe on the edge of the giant ashtray after evicting the dottle.

As the Meerschaum rang on the ornamental brass, Postillion started, turned, and looked horrifed when he saw the neat little pile of incinerated shreds of Skipper John's Fine Old Shag Cut on the intricate brasswork. "Good God, Bandy, you can't do that," he exclaimed. "That table's fourteenth century!"

"Oh, a table, is it? Anyway, what do you care? It's art, isn't it?"

"Yes, I know it's a beastly antique, but Lady Blount's very proud of it, and she'd blame me."

"Well, I'm sure if she did, you'd blame me."

"Yes, that's true," he said, calming. "After your latest example of moral turpitude, she'd have no difficulty believing anything of you," he added; and before I could find out what he meant, a young officer in dress uniform appeared to summon us into the presence.

The regal office at the front of the great wide building—Viceroys and Maharajahs alike seemed to go in for grandiose construction—was a sumptuously furnished and exquisitely decorated room with a thousand books under glass and no fewer than three tigerskin rugs.

And there the great man sat, looking like Judge Jeffreys after a heavy loss at backgammon.

He was ensconced behind his desk as I walked in (leaning heavily on my stick in the hope that this would elicit sympathy), and he was sweating, presumably after all that hard work putting away seven courses and a reservoir-full of hock, Moselle, Burgundy, port, and brandy.

As I approached he attempted to hypnotize me with an ophidian glare but I was too preoccupied by the fact that there was nowhere for me to sit. The entire area in front of the desk had been cleared of furniture, possibly to make way for a firing squad.

Presumably the chairlessness was premeditated. The only seat in the vicinity was near the bookcase, but it had been bagged by Postillion. You could tell because he had his hand on the back of the chair, ready to sit the moment the Viceroy gave him permission to do so.

Against the far wall there was a matching pair of heavily padded Indian seats with carved backs, but I could hardly route-march all that way and sit down. Besides, that would have placed me behind His Excellency, and, well, there was no point in upsetting him. All the same, the prospect of standing before him like a truant was not calculated to put me at my ease.

However, there was nothing else for it. A timid soul, I just didn't have the nerve to saunter to the far wall and sit thirty feet behind the great man in his magnificent diplomatic uniform with the masses of medals and gold braid, I would just have to try and look relaxed, and stand there as if I really preferred standing.

He continued to stare at me for quite a while after I had braked to a halt at his vast desk. If his stare was meant to soften me up before the offensive, it worked perfectly. I was having trouble keeping my breathing as relaxed as my posture. In order to distract my lungs from a tendency to pant with fear, I looked over the desk, but there wasn't much to see, except for a silver inkwell and pen set, and a leather-backed blotting pad. There wasn't even a telephone on the desk.

On the blotting pad, only one word disturbed the virgin surface. I found this rather curious. How could just one word

of whatever document had been blotted have been repro-
duced on the white absorbent material? Why not the whole
sentence, or at least a wet phrase? But of course it was possible
that he had not been blotting a whole letter, memo, death
warrant, or whatever; perhaps he had only managed to write
one word, gotten stuck, and blotted it while waiting for
further inspiration.

Fortunately the Viceroy was continuing to hector me optically, which gave me plenty of time to study the word and
determine which one it was. This was not too easy, as it was
upside down from my point of view. And also, of course, back
to front. *Y-r-e-t-u-a-r-f-l*, it read. *Lfrautery?* That wasn't a word,
surely?

Thinking that perhaps I had the sequence wrong, I tilted my
head and yawed slightly to port in order to obtain a better
view. When this twisting motion threatened to unbalance me I
placed a sweaty palm on the shiny desk for support. But the
word still came out as *lfrautery*. I was pretty certain that even
the fussiest lexicographer would not tip his hat to such a
word...though that was by no means certain, given that even
the shortest Oxford dictionary was jammed with words like
fenugreek, tragopan, and stramineous.

Getting quite interested in the problem, I leaned further
over the desk for a still closer look; and immediately perceived
that a certain amount of distortion had occurred when the
word was blotted. The first letter was quite smudgy. Could
that be an "f" rather than a "t"? Ffrautery—that sounded a
touch more plausible. Wait! I'd misread that letter u, it being
upside down. My eye had failed to reinvert it. It wasn't a "u", it
was an "*n*". So that made it *ffrantery*.

Unfortunately that didn't seem to get me anywhere either,
though it was now beginning to look more like a word born in
England, a country full of odd spellings and pronunciations.
But why was there a comma in front of *ffrantery?* Ah! Possibly
the comma belonged to the previous word...no, it really did
look as if it were part of *ffrantery*...*unless* it was the inky
remains of a letter—which, coming in front of a couple of
consonants, was almost certainly a vowel. A, e, i, o or u?

Offrantery? Iffrantery? Uffrantery? Affrantery? But this procedure was becoming inefficient. It was obvious that I should eliminate the possibility that there was such a word. So I straightened up and glanced around for a dictionary, and as luck would have it there was a fine bookcase against the wall only a few feet away. It had leaded glass doors, behind which were numerous weighty tomes, one of which might be a dictionary. But in glancing in that direction I caught the eye of Francis Postillion. For a moment my own traveled onward in search of enlightenment, but then darted back to Postillion's. He was looking queer. His normally pale aesthetic face was engorged, and faint hissing sounds, just audible over the tense silence, were issuing from his nostrils in bursts, almost as if he were trying to suppress an incipient hysteria. Upon catching my eye for a second time a look of panic, almost of terror, overcame his normally well-schooled visage. He wrenched his face aside, while the effort to suppress whatever it was that was bothering him was now causing giant beads of perspiration to burst from his lofty brow.

In the microsecond before he looked away, he had darted a look at the Viceroy; which drew my own attention back to that august personage as he sat behind his splendid desk; and I could not resist a start at the sight of his inflamed face, whose accusatory glare had now been replaced by one of stupefied rage.

It was at that moment that his vocal cords came out of anesthesia. He demonstrated that this was so by shouting at the top of his voice, "Stand up straight, man! How dare, how *dare* you present yourself to me in that, that deformed posture, that, that insolent—How bloody dare you come before me like that!"

"It was that word there on your blotting paper," I explained, leaning over again to point to the word in question. "I was trying to see what it was.

"You know how it is, Your Excellency," I continued when he failed to reply immediately, and wrinkling my nose a little to suggest that we were not unalike, that in an idle moment he had probably done just the same sort of thing, "when you're waiting for somebody to turn up, you tend to read whatever's available—the advertisements in the Toronto Street Railway Company cars, the small print on your tobacco tin, somebody's newspaper—you know how it is. I was just curious about that word there," I said. "It looks like the word *effrautery*, but I don't—"

He actually attempted to swipe my hand aside as once again I pointed to the mystery word, so totally in an uproar was he. The physical effort to restrain himself was quite evident. He was even starting to pant, and his eyes to bulge—a dangerous development, I thought, as they were already halfway out of their sockets.

"It's not that I wanted to be nosey or anything," I went on, his contribution to the conversation having temporarily dried up. "I mean, I'm not in the habit of reading people's letters even when they're the right way up. But when you see just one word right in the middle of an otherwise virgin blotter, it's just too tempting for—"

"Shut up! Shut up!" he screamed. "I'll have you arrested, I'll have you arrested for—" He looked round wildly for whatever excuse to arrest me might be lying around. And he continued to scream at me for a good two minutes, before breathlessness again intervened.

Finally, realizing that perhaps he was not behaving with the coolness and dignity expected of the King's supreme representative abroad, he sat down again. (I forgot to mention that two minutes ago he had jumped to his feet so smartly that his fourteen or fifteen rows of medal ribbons jingled like Santa Claus's sleigh.) The descent back into his chair was almost as violent, though, causing his fiery face to wobble, while his normally tight mouth issued fresh quantities of pants.

Some time elapsed before he had recovered sufficiently to get down to business. Meanwhile the smart young officer was twitching his smart mustache, while Postillion had now graduated to a series of deep, slightly shuddery breaths in an effort to resupply his lungs.

Announcing that as the facts were too well established to necessitate discussion, the Viceroy announced that he did not intend to review the situation. He then proceeded to review it. "You have blatantly violated the territory of a loyal and trustworthy independent state with whom we have a particularly sensitive relationship," he blared, his diamond blue eyes struggling to decide whether to look ferocious or contemptuous. "Fortunately His Highness the Nawab had graciously consented to accept our personal apologies; but that does not moderate the seriousness with which His Majesty's Government regards this incident." He paused, glaring with the viciousness of a wolverine. "I take it you do not deny that on the afternoon of Monday May the eleventh you personally invaded Khaliwar territory, and dived your aircraft repeatedly onto the assembled representatives of the Khaliwar government in an aggressive, dangerous, and threatening manner?"

I pursed my lips as I reviewed the accusation for flaws and exaggerations—causing his face to writhe so frenziedly that half his mustache seemed to disappear up his nose—before I finally conceded that it was accurate.

"Well, yes, that's true," I responded. "But—"

"But nothing! The facts are incontrovertible. And I have no wish to listen to excuses."

"But," I repeated, glancing at Postillion. But the secret agent's suppressed giggles, which had raised him slightly in my estimation, suggesting that there was a human being under that coldly negative personality, had plainly exhausted him, leaving him limp, pale, sweating, and apparently inattentive, for he didn't even seem to be listening any more.

"Silence!" said the Viceroy. "I do not intend to discuss the situation with you, with a man of your record of defiance and insubordination. I have not called you in for a discussion about this incident, but to give you your orders with regard to your so-called Royal Jhamjarh Air Force."

"My air force? What about it?"

"Under no imaginable circumstances has an independent state the right to an air force. Especially—"

"I understand there are no treaties or agreements prohibiting a salute state from forming an air f—"

"Silence! Will you be silent, sir? Interrupt me once more and

I shall have you arrested. Is that understood? *Is that under-stood?*"

"Yes, sir."

"Very well, then," he said, visibly trembling with rage. "We understand that you have five squadrons of aircraft already operating from a base near Djelybad, with bombing and gunnery ground targets in almost continuous use. Correct?"

"Yes."

"By God, you could hardly answer otherwise considering the evidence of your nefarious activities at our disposal, as well as of your treasonous and morally depraved conduct—"

"Sir, has the Maharajah not repeatedly assured you that the air force was never meant to threaten the authority of Great Britain in—"

"You have not had leave to speak," he said, screaming all over again, and pounding the desk so violently with his hairy fist that even his young aide looked a bit dismayed, and glanced appealingly at Postillion for some sort of intervention. But Francis was so exhausted by his struggles that he had actually sat down uninvited.

With a plainly superhuman effort, His Excellency controlled himself, though one of his hands was trembling so noticeably that he hid it from sight. He also decided that his inkwell was a more rewarding sight than me, for he addressed it for the next couple of minutes or so. "You are not here," he said unsteadily, "to attempt any justification for your actions. You are here to receive your orders. Which are, that you will hand over your air force to us within seven days. Seven days from today's date."

"Hand over my air force?" I said incredulously.

"Within seven days from midday today! Or—as I have already informed your Maharajah—I shall take action. If you have not complied with my orders by midday on Monday May twenty-fifth, I shall take over the entire civil and military administration of Jhamjarh. And I assure you," he added, finally wrenching his eyes out of the inkwell, and clenching his large fists, which had as much hair on them as a pair of sporrans, "that if you force me to such an extremity, I will also have you imprisoned on a number of serious charges. Is that clear? Is that clear?!"

"Well, yes, it's clear enough," I faltered.

"As soon as arrangements can be made, Postillion here will make his way to your base near Djelybad to ensure that my orders are carried out. You will spend the next few days liaising with him over the arrangements for handing over your entire fleet of aircraft to the Royal Air Force.

"That will be the first stage in the handing-over procedure. The second stage will take place next Monday when the aircraft are formally handed over. Your own pilots will fly the aircraft to RAF Station Charanwad.

"Finally," he said, staring up at me, "I should inform you, Bandy, that you are being left in command only in order to expedite these arrangements, otherwise I should have had you incarcerated immediately in reponse to this latest example of your gross and disloyal behavior. And I assure you I have the power to do so, and to keep you in jail as long as I wish.

"That is all," he said.

I turned to go, a bit crushed. But not crushed enough, it seemed, for almost immediately he added, "Wait. There is another matter that should be brought to everyone's attention."

When I turned back to his shining, fallow desk, he was busily opening a drawer. And drawing out a packet.

Oh, dear God.

Now I understood why Hornby had been keeping me busy that afternoon: to enable them to search my room, presumably in the hope of finding incriminating evidence of some sort— papers, perhaps, indicating that I was in the pay of the Bolsheviks, or that I was a paid-up anarchist or Freemason.

Instead, they had found the filthy pictures.

Aboard ship, failing to dispose of the photos, I had tucked them into a pocket of my suitcase, intending to throw them overboard one dark night. At least I think that was what I intended, but either there were no dark nights for the rest of the voyage, or else I had not been quite ready to part with them. Initially I had found them quite gripping, though not particularly erotic. If that was typical pornography I'd considered it a bit disappointing, most of the photos being decidedly clinical and lacking in imagination...except for the one of the dusky sportswoman who seemed to be rowing a skiff, except that those were not exactly oars that she was gripping...where was I? Yes. Anyway, I had genuine intentions of getting rid of the packet, but had failed to do so, and had, in fact, forgotten that they were in the suitcase when I packed it for the New Delhi trip. With ghastly consequences, for it was now quite plain that the Viceroy was convinced that I was not only a filthy traitor but a collector of traitorous filth.

Indeed, he said so. After removing the packet from the desk drawer with thumb and forefinger, as if handling a used diaper, he tossed it onto the polished desk with the words, "It seems you are not only a blusterer and a disloyal subject, but the sort of person who obtains his degenerate satisfaction from such filth.

"Well, I see no reason why I should encourage this sort of thing," he concluded, "and accordingly, this material is to be confiscated and destroyed." And, using a pen, he pushed the packet back into the drawer. "Now—*get out*."

And the worst of it was, I couldn't tell him the truth—that I hadn't purchased the photographs for myself at all—I had bought them for him.

PART II

In My Red Pyjamas

I awoke to find the bed rocking violently from side to side. In a trice I had flung myself over the side, and was scrambling under the bed. Plainly we were in the middle of an earthquake. I'd been dreaming of Haksar Palace. It was swaying as the earth betrayed it. Lovingly moulded plaster falling from the ceilings in ragged lumps to crash and explode in white dust on swirly floors. Balconies disconnecting from golden walls, pillars being sued for non-support, minarets crumbling, domes imploding.

The din of destruction was awful. Somebody was screaming. Fissures wide as canyons opening up—brown bodies teetering, then pitching, howling, into molten depths. Thoughts raced, a million miniature flashes of lighting surrounded by wildly staring eyes, and ears like aphrodisiac roots, and bald patch and receding hairline. Calculation: my four-poster was located say fifteen feet from the outside wall—which might conveniently collapse outward, enabling me to escape through a choking aperture. At least I wasn't in pain yet, apart from my leg which I'd hurt throwing myself from bed, unlike some poor devil nearby, the one uttering that chalk-squeak-on-blackboard, eardrum-lacerating screech....It wasn't a poor devil. It was train wheels, grinding.

I arose and climbed back into my berth in the Maharajah's private coach, glancing around to make sure that nobody had seen me fling myself into the fluff, dust, spiders, and oxydized copper coins beneath. Being observed, however, was hardly likely, as there was room in my sleeping quarters for little more than me and a tube of toothpaste.

With sleep-numbed fingertips, I fumbled for my watch. It was either twenty-five past one, or nearly ten past five. To clear up the controversy I stared out the window. The sun god had his flashlight out and was searching for something behind the distant hills. So it was either twenty-five past one or nearly ten past five in the morning.

I lay back on the pillow, feeling, to translate from the Icelandic, like death painted on a wall. And by and by became aware that we were grinding slowly into another main-line station.

The name of the station slid into view: Shampur. That was the one where we had been stuck for hours on the way to New Delhi. And again the platform was packed, even this early in the morning. Men, women, and children, wrapped in white like victims of a major disaster laid out for identification.

As the sun arose, so did they, and a Hindu hullabaloo. They proceeded to relieve themselves unashamedly, and went on to unwrap horrid food with unwashed fingers, and to eat fly sandwiches, or to pump up stoves, or pray and shout, or patch up quarrels or weave new ones.

Slowly, slowly, a hush descended again as the day brightened and the heat descended. By six a.m. it was well into three Fahrenheit figures. I felt like wet pastry.

The heat had been almost unbearable since long before we left the capital on the previous day. The fact that the Maharajah's private coach had been standing in the sun for over an hour had not exactly improved the situation, and I was in a sodden mood by the time Mr. Chatterjee of the Indian State Railways appeared and grovelingly enquired of the Maharajah if the train could now proceed from New Delhi Railway station, as it was already several hours late.

"You mean you've been waiting for His Highness to give you permission to leave?" I asked incredulously.

"But of course," Mr. Chatterjee said, spreading his nicely-manicured hands as if I'd asked rather a silly question.

Mr. Chatterjee was a Eurasian, which, had he not subsequently proved so detestable, might have aroused my sympathy, for Anglo-Indians were looked down upon by Anglos and Indians alike. He was attired in railway uniform, five of his brass buttons sported the emblem of the ISR company, and the sixth that of the Hyderabad Contingent Cavalry. His attitude suggested that he was somebody important. In fact he was a station master, en route to his wayside empire halfway along the line to Bombay, which happened to be Shampur station.

In New Delhi, as the Maharajah was too depressed to quarrel, I considered it my duty to substitute for him. "We've been baking here in the sun for over an hour," I accused.

"Oh, dear," Mr. Chatterjee said sympathetically.

"If you had to ask our permission, why didn't you do so an hour ago?"

"But sir," said Mr. Chatterjee with a patient expression on his suety face, "you are not the only one who has been waiting. We, too, have been waiting patiently at the other end of the train for His Highness to give us permission to depart."

"But we didn't know you were waiting," I shouted.

"I can't help that," said Mr. Chatterjee, looking curiously at the Maharajah as he sat on the horsehair sofa, buried up to the neck in dejection. "You ought to know by now that it is customary for train staff to ask important persons for permission to leave."

I opened my mouth to shout at him again, but then clopped it shut. I was beginning to understand that Indians were not quite as subservient to western logic as we were. Besides, if I continued to argue we'd be further delayed, as well as being done to a turn by the sun.

Nevertheless I could not resist a parting shot. "But surely," I said with wounding sarcasm, "you have a schedule that you're supposed to stick to, if only approximately—say, leaving within a day or two of the scheduled time?" But he wasn't the least wounded. He remained as bland as lard. Worse, he remained in the coach to argue the point, so I ended up delaying the train all the more.

Also, I'm certain that he tried to upset me further by requesting the locomotive engineer to pull away from the station with maximum acceleration, for the tug, when we finally set off, was violent. Moreover the jerks multiplied as they were transmitted along the train. Our coach, being at the rear, received the worst of the jangling impact. It was enough to pitch me off my feet straight into the paneling that separated the lounge from the kitchen. My pate cracked the woodwork. I ended up in a heap.

However, this enabled me to study the inlay work of the paneling with a closeness and concentration that had not hitherto been practicable, the subtlety of the inlaid design being fully comprehensible, it seemed, only from a prone position. It showed a devoted female attendant helping her master, the god Rama, to insert himself into his wife Sita, thus demonstrating that even in matters of sex, Indians tended to be a trifle passive.

Meanwhile, throughout the entire previous day, the Maharajah had been sunk in fetid humiliation. Used to fuss and flourish whenever he visited British India, and delighting in his nineteen guns—only two less than those of the ruler of Hyderabad—the unprecedented snub had reduced him to a near catatonic state. Though based on the frontiers of mysticism, he had lived all his life in supreme authority over millions of subjects. To be treated in this disdainful fashion was proving to be almost as painful physiologically as mentally. He was sick with shock. He had sat up all the previous night, motionless except for an oscillation caused by the train's hypnotic motion, his dhoti'd figure as sunken, it seemed, as his face, his great deep eyes flipped over on their spiritual gimbals to enable him to stare into the obverse of reality.

I made no attempt to entice him back, not being too keen on reality myself just at the moment, at the thought of surrendering my air force and my future.

That weedy, inconsistent, generous, toffee-gobbling, lova-

ble man with the fantastic eyes. From then on I'd only one
desire: to make the Viceroy pay for that humiliation.

Now it was eight o'clock the next morning, and the train was
baking in the Shampur station. Three blinking hours it had
been standing there, by now, protected from the sun only by a
bit of station overhang and by the window screens and
shutters.

In the coach the heat was intense, making it impossible to do
anything but soak in a hot bunk, mindless, too enervated even
to bemoan the loss of my job and perhaps my last chance to
make something of myself and achieve the fame and fortune
that I thought my soul desired.

After three hours sweat-squelching in there, I could no
longer stand my own sodden ruminations. It was pointless
even to think constructively. I had no idea what I was going to
do once I got back to Djelybad, other than upset as many
people as possible with the bad news. But I just couldn't lie
here, cascading pints of distilled Orangeaid, unable to come to
any conclusion while I was traveling between challenge and
response, ultimatum and reaction, crisis and resolution, halfway between the high diving board and the chlorine. I just
couldn't stand the inactivity any more, despite the heat. So I
forced myself from the mattress, and headed for the exit in
search of air and distraction, attired in my red Cossack pyjamas with the embroidered pocket, and a pair of Arabian
Nights slippers. And in these feverish garments I stepped out
onto the station platform.

I was almost flung back into the train by the heat. Incredibly
it was even hotter outside than within. The noise was infinitely
worse. Chattering folk jammed every square inch of platform,
hundreds slept in the shade, looking like mortuary inmates,
their forms covered in white, only their bare feet showing;
others sat patiently, staring at sempiternity; others milled
about the platforms, gabbling in Hindi, Marathi, Urdu,
Gujarati, and fourteen million other dialects. Spirit stoves
hissed, cooking pots steamed as individuals, whole families,
entire tribes, prepared meals, those with spare annas purchas-

ing snacks from the vendors, who, drifting restlessly through the throng, were selling sticky sweets and mulch. Other vendors sold water, carrying separate containers, one supply for Hindus, the other for Muslims, advertising the fact with their cries of *Hindi pani! Musselman pani!*

Families unable to crowd into shade, crouched under umbrellas, some such shades so perforated that they let in almost as much brightness as if they were not there. Pi-dogs with countable ribs wandered warily on the outskirts of the mob, packs of children shuffled up and down the train, looking hopefully at doorways. A swarm of them buzzed and shrilled around me the moment I stepped out, but soon gave up when they saw that I had no money on me, my Cossack pyjamas having only one pocket, and that obviously containing only a nipple.

Otherwise nobody paid much attention to me. It was quite common for Europeans to step off the train later in the evenings or in the mornings in their night attire, to buy *char* from the tea vendors, to stretch their legs on track or platform, or simply to visit other first-class compartments in the corridorless trains.

As I stood there like a wilting tulip, squinting round at the chaos in hopes of finding someone to hit, Mr. Chatterjee obligingly appeared, sashaying through the throng. He was shouting up at the peasants on the roof and waving his arms. When he drew close I clobbered him with a loud, imperialistic voice, demanding to know the reason for yet another extraordinarily long delay.

"Why isn't the train moving?" I shouted.

"Because it is standing still, sir," he replied with a smile that made ample allowance for my wits, which had plainly been dulled by the heat.

"Of course it's standing still—it's been standing still since the beginning of May, practically. What I want to know is why. Is there a hold up on the line, or something?"

"Oh, golly, no, everything is hunky-dory, sir."

"Then why aren't you moving?"

"But I am moving, sir. Only this minute I have been moving

the entire length of the platform." But then enlightenment widened his beady eyes. "Oh, wait, wait," he cried—appropriately enough, I thought. "Perhaps you are meaning to ask why is the *train* not moving? Oh, dear me, what an amusing misunderstanding occasionally arises between peoples." He chuckled and shook his head.

After several minutes of this sort of thing, I finally snapped. And that was when I made my mistake—behaving like every other imperialist in the country—and shouted that if he wasn't careful I would complain about him to the railway company.

Whereupon he asked quite imperturbably if I wished to enter an official complaint in the Official Complaints book; and that was when I made my second mistake. I shouted that I did so wish.

"Very good, sir," he said with an obsequious bow. "Please follow me." And he proceeded to lead the way through the crush and into the station building, down a long, tiled corridor, then a left turn, a right turn, and into a large wooden waiting room containing a jungle of thin brown arms, women entirely covered in brilliant reds and yellows, and approximately four thousand subdued children. Chatterjee threaded his way across the room toward an opening in the wall named Station Master.

A moment later I was in this office, whose window overlooked the dusty square at the rear of the station. And there I slashed an ill-tempered complaint in the Official Complaint Book, and was about to sign it and give my name and address, when I paused.

"Look here," I said, "there's no point in getting you into trouble unnecessarily."

"Oh, that's all right, sir."

"Whajamean, it's all right—don't you mind having a blot on your record?"

"Oh, dear, have you gone and made a blot on the record?"

"I mean," I said through clenched teeth—there must have been dust in my mouth for a gritty crunching could be heard—"I don't want to affect your career."

"How would that happen, sir?"

I closed my eyes and swayed a bit. Then said quietly but with some pressure, "By reporting you to your superiors."

"Oh, don't worry about that, sir," he said. "They never ask to see the Complaints Book anyway."

I looked out the window. At the far side of the tawny square there were two furrows in the weeds. I suspected that this indicated the presence of a railway track. It was probably a siding—for shunting blustering Europeans onto, perhaps.

After a while I said with closed eyes, "Look, Mr. Chatterjee—is there no simple explanation at all as to why the train is waiting for so long?"

"Oh, yes, sir. We are waiting for the next train from Bombay to pass through. But perhaps there has been a misunderstanding. Perhaps it, too, is waiting at another station for *us* to pass through."

"I see. I see. I see. Well, can you at least give me a rough idea as to when we'll be leaving? Today? Tomorrow? Father's Day? The autumnal equinox?"

"Oh, but it has already left."

"What has?"

"Your train, sir. It has already left."

"What?"

"It has already left, your train. That is what I was moving along the platform for, you see. I was signaling the train driver to start thinking about proceeding."

I stared at Chatterjee. He gave me a warm smile.

"While we were making our way through the station buildings," I said quietly, "my train left?"

"Dear me, yes. It has departed five minutes ago, at least. Did you not hear the whistle, sir, as we were proceeding along the corridor, the one with all the lovely tiles from your wonderful English tile manufacturers?"

"God, I hate you," I said as I ran out in my clammy jammies.

I pelted onward across the hall, along the passageways which were remarkably dim considering the intensity of the light outside, along the central corridor, the one with all the lovely tiles, and out into the open, almost tripping over a couple of dozen families as I skidded to a halt, staring in dread at the trainless track.

I looked around, praying that on my way back I had taken a wrong turn and arrived at the wrong platform, and that the train was waiting elsewhere. But the only other train in the vicinity was a rusty shunting engine on a weedy siding.

I had been left behind. Stranded three hundred miles from home, without clothes, identification, or an anna to my name.

Shampur Station

I didn't mind so much being caught out of doors in night attire. After all, I was as well-dressed in pyjamas as most Indians were in their Sunday-go-to-meeting togs. What alarmed me was being bereft of pelf. I had only recently come through a sticky patch when I'd had to exist on two quid a week, which had not been enough for three meals a day. I must still have been suffering the after-effects because I almost panicked, standing there in the middle of a station platform surrounded by clamoring Asians, one in particular who kept plucking at my ruby raiment and offering steaming tea from a battered tin utensil, and whining, "*Tahsa char, sahib, garumi-garum*." "Can't you see I haven't any bloody money," I finally snapped.

With a convulsive effort, a deep breath of hot, malodorous atmosphere, and a ripple of cheek muscles to hold down fear, I turned and stormed back in the direction of the station master's office with the intention of extracting Mr. Chatterjee's teeth one by one with a pair of glazing nippers, and then swishing out his mouth with ice water. As I slippered toward the far waiting hall, I glimpsed three burly Europeans, but I was too upset for a detailed appearance to register. I was aware through a blood-red haze only that they looked stolid, foreign in the sense of not being Anglo-Saxon, and that their heads were shaved. Then I was past them, elbows swinging, and it

was some minutes before the slightly comforting thought
occurred that if the worst came to the worst I could always
approach the coot-bald threesome for help. They could hardly
refuse a fellow Westerner a small sum to tide him over until the
next main-line train arrived.

I reached the waiting hall off which Chatterjee had his
office. I saw him immediately. He was standing at the counter
of the left-luggage office, chatting to a couple of turbaned
chums. I headed toward him. But I had to climb over several
dozen families, and the resulting squawk attracted his attention. He disappeared like magic.

One moment he was there, talking earnestly to the turbans,
and the next he had vanished into torrid air. By the time I
reached the counter of his left-luggage office there was nothing left but luggage: two tin trunks, three cheap suitcases, and a
parcel.

"Where'd he go, where'd the bastard go?"

The two turbans grinned uncomprehendingly, and then half
a dozen urchins were upon me, plucking at my pyjamas and
holding out their hands and screeching, though where they
expected me to store coinage or mintage I don't know.

To get away from the crowd and give myself a chance to
think, I hurried out the rear entrance into the square. The heat
sandbagged me. Rising from the ocher earth, it was visible as
writhing gauze.

Beyond the square there was nothing but open countryside,
the monotony broken only by a road which, commencing at
the square, headed roughly for a distant seashore. As it turned
out, the seashore wasn't. It was a mirage.

The inflexible sun burned down. I had to slit my eyes to the
thickness of a razor blade to tolerate the light. My curly
slippers were smoldering. I retreated deeper under the awning
of the station, wondering what to do.

"Does anyone speak English?"

Three naked holy men sat cross-legged with their backs to
the wall. They were shining with yellow axle grease. All three
of them grinned and held out their hands, and regarded me

with neither increased nor decreased interest when I pulled out the breast pocket of my pyjamas to show I was skint.

A line of women in bright red and orange gowns were seated on a bench. I looked toward them distractedly. Empty black eyes peered back through gaps in the bright material. One of them adjusted her gown to hide her bulging midriff bare.

I remembered the three white men. I was just about to turn back into the station in search of them when the faint sound of an engine drew my attention to the road that ended in the station square. In the distance glass flashed. A vehicle of some sort. I waited.

When first glimpsed it had seemed to be no further than a couple of hundred yards away, but minutes elapsed before it came bouncing into the square at high speed, an open car of an unfamiliar foreign make.

Decelerating noisily through the gears, the driver swung the vehicle around and brought it to a halt in front of the station just ten feet from where I was wilting, raising a cloud of dust like a destroyer putting down a smokescreen. The brakes squealed. The engine died. Several hundred children hemmed it in.

The driver, a European with solar topee and dark glasses vaulted over the side of the car with an ease betokening great physical fitness, and an idiotic disregard for the climate. The suntanned thighs under his khaki shorts were ostentatiously muscular.

From a distance he seemed to be hardly out of his teens, but as he approached, he grew older, until he was practically middle-aged by the time he reached me. Actually he was about my age. The illusion of youth was polished off completely when he removed his sun glasses to reveal eyes of the color and hardness of tungsten steel, underlined for emphasis by sun wrinkles.

His lips, upturned at the corners as if commencing a smile, only slightly made up for the general rigor of his appearance.

After glancing around carefully, he lowered his voice and said something that I didn't quite understand, as it was in German.

"Ha?" I enquired. I used to employ the Canadian "Eh?" but had recently adopted the Icelandic ejaculation.

"*Sind Sie ein neuer Flugzeugführer?*"

When I continued to look blank, he muttered under his breath, meanwhile shielding his eyes from my pyjamas. The morning sun, beating on my ensemble, was creating something of a glare.

Stabbing at me with a forefinger that looked as if it could have been used to drill masonry, he said loudly, "Russky peelot, *ja?*"

Peelot. Sounded like the Russian word for aviator. Russky. Was he asking if I was a Russian? But why would he assume I was Russian, let alone a pilot?

Could it be my jammies? I referred to them as my Cossack pyjamas merely in fun because, baggy in the leg, buttoned at the shoulder, and black-sash-belted, they had something of a Cossack look. In fact, when Sigga first saw me attired in this outfit, she had commenced a slow handclap and a yo-heave-ho, plainly expecting me to initiate a Slavonic caper.

But why would he jump from *Russian* to *pilot?*

Say what you like about me, but my reflexes were still instant, and I could still think at lightning speed in a genuine emergency. In no time at all I worked it out that he must have been expecting a Russian pilot, and that my pyjamas would appear to be a confirmation that at least he had the right nationality.

So, "Yah," I said, straightening up and deepening my voice as if auditioning for the Red Army Choir, "*Ich* Russky."

"*Wo sind die andere?*"

"HA?"

"*Ich haben verstanden es drei oder vier fleugzeugführer ware.*"

I responded with a helpless shrug of my expression.

Whereupon he sighed, and bringing his handsome, sun-tanned face close to mine he bawled in English with insulting slowness and an American accent, "And I don't suppose you speak English either, you dumb bastard?"

"English? Yes, I speak."

"Ach. A wonder. And you're one of the Russian pilots, right?"

This was it. I took a deep, inconspicuous breath. "You are from Khaliwar?" I asked.

"Of course. Where are the others?"

My God. It was true. The Khaliwar Air Force existed.

"Well?" he prompted sharply.

"Vot others?"

"I'm supposed to pick up three of you."

Three. The three shaven-headed types I'd passed on the way to giving Mr. Chatterjee a piece of my mind.

I spread my arms. "I do not understand." I said. "How can there be three of me? There is only vun of me."

"Three Russky pilots. We heard from Bombay that three Russian pilots were on the train." He stared at me fixedly.

I managed to keep cool, quite an accomplishment considering it must have been at least 130 degrees in the shade. And I shrugged, Russian style, i.e., adopting a contracting posture as if I were a slug that had just been speared by a knitting needle.

He looked away resignedly. "Another foul-up, I guess," he said. "Whenever you Russians are involved there's always a God-damn foul-up."

"And you Germans are so efficient? Is how you won the war?"

He flushed under his tan. "Well, at least we beat you figgen Russians," he said.

Then he suddenly grinned; so infectiously that I couldn't help responding in kind.

His amusement didn't last long. He drew himself up. "Permit me to introduce myself. Heinrich Strand, Oberstleutnant. And you are?"

"Vot?"

"Your name."

Good Lord, what was my name?

"Ivan," I said.

After a moment: "Well, that's a good start," he said, and waited.

"Zmeev!" I found myself forcing out the surname. The

shout startled so...
bullock defecated in...R STATION

Zmeev was a doctor...
where I had worked after...
think Zmeev would mind if I bu...

scattered guiltily. A nearby
of Moscow hospital
by Trotsky. I didn't
name.

"Ivan Fyodorevitch Zmeev," I...
verisimilitude.

He bowed easily, then: "Well, I guess it You know, for
we might as well get going." He looked aroun... body else,
luggage?" he asked.   ...re's you

Luggage. That was it, then. I might get away with ...
but being baggageless as well. . . .   ...as,

To postpone the inevitable I croaked in a ridiculous accent, "*Pazhalsta*, you say you are speaking to Bombay. Why did not telephone to here, to this railway station, to find out situation?"

"There's no line, that's why."

I began to hope again. And with hope came the stirrings of improvisation. I could not hope to convince him that I was a Russian traveler unless I had luggage. So where did one obtain luggage? Easy—in the left-luggage office.

"Well, come on, Dismayev, or whatever your name is," Strand said good-humoredly. "It's too goddamn hot to hang around."

"Yah, dah, I get luggage," I croaked, and turned and fought my way through the crowd that had gathered around the dusty car. The peasants had been listening as appreciatively as if we were strolling players.

In seconds I was back in the waiting hall with its long, flimsy benches jammed with even flimsier travelers.

I braked to a halt. Damn! The roll-type shutters of the left-luggage office were down.

I started forward again, tripping over a bundle of sticks, and trod on somebody's foot. His yelp was hardly audible over the human clatter. I grabbed the handle of the shutter and wrenched. It was firmly locked.

When I had followed Mr. Chatterjee along the short passage that led to his office, I'd noticed a door in the right-hand wall.

to the left-luggage office. I

It was almost certainl ..r was a cheap wooden affair
darted into the shade of yellow. After a quick
colored a most pasmaster's office door a few feet away,
glance toward mmed it into the yellow door.
I raised my f finished swearing—I'd forgotten I was
As soon ot boots—and I'd used my hurt leg, too—I
wearing der instead.
used m dwork cracked noisily but held. However, another
T proved successful. The door splintered open and
sh ked against the inner wall. And there was the luggage I
d espied whilst attempting to resume social intercourse with
Mr. Chatterjee—the tin trunks, parcels, and so forth. They
were crowded together on the wooden racks. The rest of the
office was empty. Perhaps these facilities were only for Europeans.

I snatched up the nearest suitcase, in a hurry to leave before
the break-and-entry attracted Mr. Chatterjee's attention.
However, I was not in such a rush as to be satisfied with just
any piece of luggage. The one I'd seized was cheap and nasty,
and the locks had broken. The bulging lid was held down by
coarse twine. It seemed to me that if I was going to steal an
item of luggage it might as well be the best. So I returned the
cheap suitcase and took the large leather one. It was scuffed
and damaged, but it was certainly the best piece available.

I rushed out, but shut the door as quietly as possible, hoping
that Mr. Chatterjee would not notice the mashed woodwork
round the lock, the flakes of yellow paint on the floor, the
dangling hinge, and the three-foot crack in the top panel. Then
hastened across the waiting hall, expecting to be challenged at
any moment.

Strand was stretching, easing stiffened muscles. "Here is
luggage," I rasped, and flung the case into the back seat, and
myself into the front.

I had made it. I had luggage.

Strand was lighting a cigarette. He stared at me over the
burning match. In the sunlight the flame was invisible. "You
are traveling without a hat?" he asked evenly. "In this sun?"

I patted the top of my head. He was right. Already I could feel myself getting sunstroke, and I'd only been in the open for thirty seconds.

"Was stolen," I gruffed.

"It's a three or four-hour trip, bo. You will never survive without one."

"No?"

"And going around in that," he added, gesturing with amused disdain at my crimson garb. "Is that what the well-dressed Moujik is wearing this season? They look more like pyjamas to me."

"Do they really?"

His cigarette cannot have tasted good, for he examined the burning end disgustedly, then disposed of the cigarette with a flick and click; and walked to the rear of the car. There he opened the trunk and brought out a grubby pith helmet. He skimmed it over to me. "There, put that on," he said.

"Is very good of you," I said, trying it on. The pith helmet was grimy and too small for me, but it kept off the worst of the sun.

Unexpectedly, Strand laughed at the sight of the hat perched high on my napper. The physiognomical rearrangement emphasized his wrinkles, but greatly improved his normally stony mazard. (Mazard, that was another of Hibbert's hardly used, real-steal words, a strained alternative to the word 'face'—so why didn't he just say face, for gosh sakes?) "If a camel wore a hat, that's exactly what it would look like," Strand chortled.

I was about to retort, when I realized that he was leaning into the back seat of the car—to examine the label on the suitcase.

Oh, no. Just when I had nearly made it.

I had already given him my name. When he read an entirely different name on the label. . . .

Blast.

He was peering closely at the label.

And then climbing behind the wheel of the car as if everything was hunky-dory.

I stared ahead across the folded-down windscreen. After a moment I strained around, leaned over the back seat and looked at the label.

The owner's name was in Cyrillic script. Strand had not been able to read the unfamiliar letters.

For a moment I felt weak with relief. Until it occurred to me that the luggage must have belonged to the Russian pilots that he had expected to meet. They could discover the loss of their luggage at any moment and come running. They must already be keeping a lookout for Strand. At any moment they were likely to appear and catch sight of the car in the square. They would certainly assume that it was their transport.

Therefore I had better get going pretty damn soon.

"Well, I'm ready," I said, squinching deeper into the passenger seat. If I could get away now, many hours would elapse before the Russians were able, in the absence of telegraph or telephone facilities here, to contact their employers and alert them to the fact that Strand had picked up an imposter. By then I should have accumulated quite a bit of information.

"Let's go," I said, one eye on God and the other on the station, and trying not to reveal my increasing agitation.

Infuriatingly, Strand merely looked at me stolidly. "Suddenly, you are in a hurry?" he said provocatively.

"I have been waiting here for hours."

"I was thinking of taking tea in the station."

"No, no, I've had some—it's awful."

Strand hesitated, tapping the steering wheel with nicotine-stained fingers. "It is a long drive," he said.

"All the more reason to get going," I said. My crimson pyjamas were sopping.

All of a sudden the bastard was in no hurry to leave, and I didn't dare urge him on. He would almost certainly delay all the more, if not out of suspicion then out of sheer cussedness. I'd met men like him before, the kind who were determined to dominate you with their personalities.

Now he was reaching for a flask. Not just one flask but two, one filled with cognac and the larger with Evian water.

As I sweated and swore in sopping silence, he swigged from

both. He was about to replace them under his seat, hesitated, then held them out.

"You want?"

"No, no, no."

I was desperate for both, but even more desperate to get going before the Russians appeared. If I watered my own throat, Strand would wait until I had finished. That could take ten seconds.

Unfortunately I had responded rather more agitatedly than was wise. Moving more slowly than ever, he put away the flasks, then placed both hands on the wheel, and whistled a bit. I could have slaughtered him there and then.

Now he was twisting his broad shoulderblades this way and that as if to loosen them after the long drive.

Now the swine was rubbing the back of his neck with his hand, removing his topee for a moment to do so, exposing a brier patch of cropped blond hair.

The Russians were going to burst out of the station at any moment, I knew it. Even if they had not been alerted by the missing suitcase, they were bound to check every few minutes to see if their transport had arrived. It was astonishing that they hadn't already investigated.

When they appeared it would take only a few seconds to establish that I was an imposter. And I would have lost a splendid opportunity to rectify the scarcity of intelligence information—which might just possibly make all the difference to the future of the RJAF and my job.

Oh, God. Now Strand was taking out a handkerchief to mop his wrinkled brow before carefully replacing his topee. And asking what aircraft I had flown in Russia.

"What?"

"Airplane, airplane. What airplane did you fly in Russia?"

It was getting worse and worse. Now he was asking me to name a Russian aircraft type when I had not the slightest knowledge of any Russian machines whatsoever.

"Ah. Ah," I said. "In fact, Heinrich," I began, wondering what I was going to say, "in fact...I was with Russian detachment with British forces in France. I was in Royal Fleeing Corps."

"English air force?"

"Is where I learn such good English."

He frowned. "I fought on the Western Front. I never heard of any Russky pilots with the English."

"Oh, yes, yes," I said, dripping. "Just small group of us with British—until Revolution," I added, inspired; though what I was being inspired about I'd no idea.

He opened his mouth to question me further, when there came a welcome distraction: a hullabaloo from the station entrance behind us.

Except that the distraction proved to be even worse than the situation being distracted from, because when I twisted round I saw the three Russian brutes forcing their way urgently through the mob at the entrance, their movements, expressions, and general attitudes distinctly agitated. And with them was Mr. Chatterjee.

I couldn't help it. I'd been screaming internally at Strand, ordering him to leave forthwith. I finally did it aloud. "Come on, come," I bellowed at him as if he were a mile away rather than eleven inches. "Let's go, let's go, quick, quick, quick!"

And he was so startled—he went. Down went his foot onto the starter, off went the handbrake, down and up went the accelerator and clutch pedals, and off we went. With a neck-wrenching jolt the big open car sped across the square toward the road or glorified bullock track.

I looked back, eyes wide as coal holes. The Russians were elbowing their way through the crowd, flinging the children aside in their desperation to clear the station entrance. Even as I watched they were through, and starting after the car.

They were waving their arms and shouting. They could clearly be heard.

I stared at Strand. Surely he must have heard the shouting. He had. He twisted in his seat and looked back—just as the rear view vanished in the dust that billowed up from our wheels.

"What was that?" he shouted over the noise of the engine.

"Nothing," I croaked. "Just the usual." And left it to him to work out what the usual was.

So he drove on, while I slumped down in the front seat in my pyjamas, quite burned out with relief and exhaustion.

A Fuzzy View

Three hours later we turned off the road which led to Lampur Kalat, and took to a secondary road that charged headlong into the mountains. And forty minutes later we reached the head of the Ujipatan valley, deep in darkest Khaliwar.

Blaring a yawn, Strand brought the car to a halt in the shade of a giant slab of rock shaped like a molar, and switched off. As the drumming of the engine and the wind hiss died, the silence boxed our ears.

"What? What is it?" I asked, languid in the swelter.

"Unlike you camels," Strand said, reaching for one of the flasks, "I need a drink now and then."

As he swished out his mouth and spat neatly into the dust, he regarded me speculatively. "You know," he drawled, "you're not much like the other Russians in the outfit."

"*Pazhalsta*, and you are more like an American than a German."

"I went to school over there. What English squadron were you with?"

I gave him the number of my old Dolphin squadron, and riposted with, "So you have many Russians in your Khaliwar Air Force?"

"A few. Talking about the Khaliwar Air Force, where did you sign on with them, Ivan?"

"Oh, recruited in usual way," I said, and trying to keep him off the subject of me: "I guess they signed you up in Germany, yes?"

Hopeless. He doled out information as if it were chloroform, just enough to keep me somnolent, not enough to cause complications. "*Ja*. And you?"

"*Da*, they signed me up, too. But what made you leave the Fatherland, Heinrich?"

He must have felt it was safe enough to answer that question for he became quite garrulous—two whole sentences. "Life is pretty bad in Germany just now," he said, shielding his eyes. The light was painful, even in shade. "Riots, inflation, Hitler."

"What is hitler?"

"By the way, Ivan, where'd you go to live after you left the British air force?"

"Oh, here and there," I said, gazing down the shimmering valley. "What very big valley," I continued. "How much is it to far end?" Christ, now I was asking geography questions.

"Fifteen kilometres. What do you mean, here and there? You must have settled somewhere."

It was getting like a duel. Phrase books at ten paces. I opened my mouth to allow another quibble to escape, but he forestalled me.

"How come you didn't go back to Russia?" he asked, scoring me with his steely eyes.

As I stood there with billows of heat striking the underside of my pith helmet and unrolling into my dry mouth, I practically stripped my mental gears in an effort to work it out. As a Russian in the RAF what would I have done? I would certainly not have gone back to Russia unless I was a Bolshevik sympathizer. He was trying to trap me into revealing that I was a communist, that was it.

From clues scattered along the wayside during the car journey from Shampur, I knew that Strand was not a red. I was quite certain about that. And whatever Khaliwar's feelings about the Raj, or whatever excesses and debaucheries the Nawab of Khaliwar had been involved in, nobody had even hinted that the rulers of Khaliwar had communist sympathies.

In fact, as Muslims, they would be particularly hostile to the concepts of Marxism.

I concluded that the safest course was to follow the truth as closely as possible. So: "I vent to England," I said. "And is vere I was recruited by Khaliwar agent, after proving I hated Bolsheviks like poisons." Like poisons, for God's sake. Steady, Bandy.

But Strand seemed satisfied. He relaxed noticeably, and proferred the flask with a friendly smile.

I peered inside. "There's only a little left," I said. "We should save?"

"Drink."

The couple of mouthfuls were warm, but at least they unstuck my tongue from its roof. Handing back the flask, I plucked at my pyjamas, trying to separate the crimson material from moist skin. It came away with a rasping sound. "If that is the last of water, we should get a move on," I suggested.

"No need, pal," he said. "We are already there."

I stared at him, then around the ragged rocks, then down the stifling valley. At the far end, ten miles away, the scene was topsy-turvy: the sky was at the foot of the hills, and the hills were floating in the air.

"Vat?" I enquired.

He gestured into the visible heat and the yellow ocher shimmer before us. "This is it," he said. "The air base and the headquarters of Sharif-ul-Khalil, ruler of Khaliwar," he said.

I stared, slitting my eyes. Wiping sweat from the sockets with a dank red sleeve, I looked again.

No wonder people had such difficulty in believing in the existence of the Khaliwar Air Force. I was staring straight at it, and still couldn't see it.

Actually it was another five miles' drive to the air base proper. Nevertheless, even allowing for the heat distortions and illusions, I felt I should have been able to notice something. But until we reached the checkpoint on the valley road, all I perceived was light brown sand, ditto hillside, scrubby undergrowth, and vague shapes that could have been anything.

The checkpoint—a road barrier, camouflaged huts, high barbed wire across the entire valley floor—was manned by natives of a much more impressive physique than I had encountered so far in India. And in place of the rather resigned expression that seemed to film so many Hindu eyes, the eyes here were hard as cinnabar.

Worse, the men looked disturbingly competent as they went about their duties in their casual but practical uniforms: sand colored blouses cinctured at the waist with a leather belt, the blouses worn outside dark brown trousers. From each belt hung a bayonet, a pair of pouches, water bottle, and, in the case of the officer, a holstered pistol.

Sometimes an army's professionalism can be gauged quite accurately by the quality of its footwear. If that was the case here, the Khaliwar Army could be formidable, for their boots were excellent, uniformly strait-laced to the knee, so that they could be cut away efficiently in case of injury to the lower limb.

At that point, further observations were postponed, for the officer was now studying me as carefully as I had been studying his men. He was a Caucasian—perhaps literally so. An epaulet-ted, brutal-looking swine he was, too. If he *was* Russian, and he spoke to me, I was done for right there and then—again perhaps literally, for he looked quite capable of killing first and asking questions afterwards. Even Strand was treating him warily.

Fortunately he dealt only with my Jerry escort.

As we passed through the checkpoint whose barbed wire entanglements stretched right across the entire quarter-mile-wide valley—God knows how I was going to get out of here again—and continued along the valley road, I found it very interesting indeed that Russians as well as Germans were being employed by Sharif-ul-Khalil. German officers and NCOs made sense, they were excellent organizers, but why Russians? I wondered if that particular specimen back there at the check-point had served with Kolchak's White Russian forces in Siberia during the civil war....

I suddenly realized that we were driving parallel to an aircraft runway.

It was only seventy yards away, yet I had failed to see it until this moment. It was nearly invisible as everything else in this hazy, blazing valley; the oiled gravel was the same color as the baked slopes. Even the edges had been blurred, made indistinct with scatterings of stones and low, artful undergrowth. Very clever. Almost invisible from the air.

As if my powers of observation weren't sufficiently negligent, we were past the first of the thirty or more hangars before I realized what they were. Just as we at the Djelybad aerodrome had erected hangars that were open at front and rear for maximum air circulation and protection from the sun, so had they; but theirs were superbly camouflaged as well, to ensure outlines such as nature in a slovenly moment might have created. Each hangar was packed with aircraft—fighters, two-seaters, vast bombers.

Well, I had located the Khaliwar Air Force, all right.

As if to leave no room for doubt, there was a roaring of aero engines, and a moment later a pair of two-seaters appeared, taking off more or less in formation.

They were only a few feet above the runway, and dipping dangerously toward it as if unwilling to abandon the hot, safe earth, engines at full power, straining for height in the roasting air.

"They must have some special job on," Strand said over the combined noise of car and aero engines. "Now that the hot weather is here, most of the flying is done in the early morning and in the evening."

As the two-seaters—Halberstadts—bellowed past seventy yards away, the racket, amplified by the rocky slopes on each side, made nosey questions impossible, so I just watched. Half a mile down the valley the aircraft were still wavering at only fifty feet. I remembered that we had entered the valley over a rocky ridge that was high above the valley floor, so I expected to see the aircraft dismantling themselves among the boulders up there. But somehow they managed to clear the ridge with quite a few inches to spare.

After rubbing my heat-seared eyes for a moment I looked around again and said, "I suppose administration buildings and such are at the far end of valley."

"No, they are here."

I looked around again, but turned blankly to Strand.

"In the caves," he said.

"Caves?"

"You have not noticed the caves?" he asked, driving slowly through a gap in a rough stone wall, and parking in its shade. After switching off, he gestured in a lordly fashion at the hillside, as if he had personally taken out an option on it.

The hillside, steep and perhaps two hundred feet high, was drilled full of holes. Dozens of cave mouths or tunnel openings gaped over the valley at various levels, from runway level to within forty feet or so of the top of the slope. Discreetly cut, winding, sharp-bended paths connected them.

"You live in there—inside the hill?"

"Whites at this end, native the far end," Strand said, gesturing further down the valley. "There are hundreds of men in there right this moment. Flying and ground staff, officers and men, some working, some sleeping. We work most of the night and in the early mornings and evenings."

"Hundreds?"

"They are not just caves. It is almost a city in there. Many of the passages criss-cross. Also there are numerous caverns and other excavated spaces."

"Well, I'll be..." I said, almost inaudibly.

The Khaliwar hills at the northern edge of the Deccan, the plateau that stretched south to the tip of the Indian peninsula proper, had proved to be readily tunnelable long before Sharif-ul-Khalil added his secretive contribution in the nineteen-twenties. While even the great Himalayas had at one time been underwater, here the land had been dry since the first cooling of the globe (according to Professor E.K. Bowells of Yale University, who was there at the time and had made notes), and had formed itself into granite intersected by crystaline formations. In the Ujipatan valley, the granite-base hillsides contained laminated quartz, feldspar, and mica, which had proved fairly safe to tunnel into even though the first burrowers had only the rudest idea of mining engineering. When their tunnels intersected it was usually the result of chance, while it was nature that deserved the credit for most of the caverns and many other wider sections, these having been formed by eccentric underground rivers long before ancient humans contributed to the aeration.

The earliest miners were thought to have been primitive tribes whose motivation may have been religious, their effort to release the earth god Dyhishwasha from his bondage. In the tenth century an improved and modernized cave system formed the then Hindu kingdom of Khaliwar's chief defensive line against the Sultan Mahmud of Ghazni who, the moment he ascended the throne of the Amir of Sabuktigin, had begun a holy war against all non-Muslims. Presumably the Hindus survived, for centuries later the caves were still forming a defence network against the invading Moghuls. For perhaps three thousand years, invaders from the north had been following this route in their attempts to break through into the rich, tropical south. But toward the end of the sixteenth century, King Lokendra Singh was faced by yet another onslaught from the north, this one from the most formidable of all the Moghuls, Akbar the Great.

Akbar was victorious and rooted Lokendra out of the caves. The population of the kingdom of Khaliwar promptly converted to Islam, and the state had remained staunchly Muslim ever since.

Lokendra having been hacked to bits and his entrails festooned about the place in a manner that the soothsayers declared to be unlucky, the caves remained unoccupied, except by a few unsuperstitious snakes, until late 1919. Two years after he was sacked by the British, Sharif-ul-Khalil, backed by the Nawab and his treasury, commenced the mining, electrification, and sanitary work to convert the caves into luxury accommodation, subterranean division. The work had only recently been completed, Strand said, though most of the personnel of the Khaliwar Air Force had been in residence for some months.

"Also," he added, "there are communications centres, armories, cinemas, and brothels, one each for officers and men."

"Everyone has his own brothel?"

"Wise guy. Also a hospital, firing range, small arms, library, canteens, radio room, telephone exchange, ammo dump—you name it, we have it."

"Sauna? Turkish bath?"

"No, we don't have them. But there are quarters for Sharif-ul-Khalil and his staff like something out of the Arabian Nights."

We were toiling up the slope to one of the caves, and I was so busy wincing as the stony ground mashed my feet through the curly slippers that I was late in reacting.

"Sharif? He's here?"

"Just moved in, ready for *der Tag*. Know what that means?"

"No?"

"Good. By the way," he said, halting at a cave mouth, "Bartholomew Bendy—of the Jhamjarh Air Force."

I stopped breathing for an hour or two. As I had been panting in the heat, the respiratory hiatus presumably confirmed his suspicions.

He knew who I was. He'd been toying with me all this time.

I breathed out, and shook my face to dislodge a shower of sweat. And I was just about to issue an unconvincing denial and then hit him with a rock, when he added, "I wondered if you had met him when you were with the British."

"Ah," I said feebly. "You mean *that* Bendy."

"You've met him, then?" Strand asked, turning sharply.

"*Ach so, ja*, vot a great men he vos," I said. Realizing that I had lapsed into the wrong accent, I reverted to a tone of Slav melancholy. "So tolerant, modest, reticent as day is lonk," I reminisced. "So brilliant, tactful, considerate—"

"*Ja?* What does he look like?"

"You don't know?"

"I'm on the planning staff, we've been putting together a dossier on him, but the descriptions of our agents in Jhamjarh don't add up, and we've no photos yet. Can you give us a description?"

"Of course. He is tall, dark, handsome—"

"Funny. We heard he looked like a Tibetan yak."

I glared at Strand before recollecting myself—or not recollecting myself. "I may be mistaken," I muttered. "Is lonk time ago." Then, to change the subject: "So? You are on the planning staff. Must be wery interestink work."

Strand regarded me discontentedly as if he were used to Russians but was finding it increasingly difficult to make allowances for them.

He replied ominously, "Listen, bo, when you meet Panyushkin, you'll have to answer questions a lot better than you've been doing with me." And he turned and walked into the cave, leaving me staring after him fearfully, wondering who Panyushkin was, and why I should have to answer his questions.

With so much to absorb in so brief a period, not least the idea of a subterranean air force, I'd had no time to consider what I was going to do once I had Trojan-horsed into the organization. But as I hobbled after Strand in my curly slippers and swiped baggage, I made a mental note to escape from the valley before I met this Mr. Panyushkin or any other Russian. I might be able to convince the Heinies that I was a Melancholy Slav, but the first Russky I met would give me away the moment I essayed their lovely, introspective tongue.

Five minutes later, after grimacing down a long erratic tunnel, past several caverns, and across two underground crossroads and a Y junction, we reached part of the living accommodation, deep in the cool hillside. Basically it was a wider section of the passageway, lit by loops of naked light bulbs. Numerous cots were ranged along one wall, each with its own utilitarian cupboard and bedside table. Just two of the beds were occupied—pilots who had been on all-night duty.

"Grab a spare bed," Strand ordered, "and get yourself organized, okay? Like getting into something more conventional," he added, looking distastefully at my soggy costume. "They'll never let you into the mess wearing that."

"The mess? Is that where we are going?"

His response was to look at his watch. "There's a lot to do and we haven't much time. Usually there's a four-day induction period, issuing kit, identity papers, and so on, but that has to be speeded up, now."

"Why now?"

"Why? You should be able to work that out," he said, in a way that decided me to get the hell out of here immediately without bothering with any more intelligence information.

Announcing that he was changing into uniform, Strand disappeared in the direction of his own quarters, further up the tunnel. The moment he was out of sight, I flung the suitcase onto a spare bed, and tore it open, praying that I had stolen suitable clothing.

The lid flew up to reveal a set of long, woollen underwear, yellowed at the crotch.

Wonderful. Just what I needed in the 130-degree heat outside.

There was also a pair of fur-backed gloves, woollen vests, a cloth cap, and a waist-girdled caftan of a thickness for keeping out Siberian gales.

Stupid Russians! What sort of a climate did they think India had? Furious at their lack of consideration for my needs, I flung the heavy clothing aside. And saw that the next items were several pairs of thick woolen socks.

But then to my relief, two long-sleeved white shirts appeared. Grayish shirt, rather, coarse and execrably haberdashed, but at least they would provide some protection from the sun. And on second thoughts the woolen socks might come in handy, too. I would have a lot of walking to do.

These handkerchiefs might come in useful as well, to cover the old nape during the hot pursuit. And, ah, there was a pair of gray trousers.

Best of all, tucked down the side of the suitcase, was a pair of brown boots. A typical Russian product, they appeared to have been fashioned from a superior brand of cardboard, but they were certainly better than the slippers I was wearing.

Hurriedly I flung myself into an alleged white shirt, the gray trousers, woolen socks, and brown boots, rejecting the cloth cap in favor of the borrowed pith helmet.

Anticipating that it would take Strand at least a quarter hour to wash off the sweat and grime of the journey and change into uniform, I turned to leave.

Whereupon he emerged from the oblong gloom. "This way, Ivan," he said, smiling and gaily gesturing. The fact that he was gaily gesturing with a Lüger pistol ensured that I entered into the spirit of it.

"Oh, it's that way, is it?" I said, smiling just as falsely; and noting with relief that he had merely been holding the weapon preparatory to slipping it into the holster at his waist. But good Lord, he must have changed into his uniform with its wings and medal ribbons at lightning speed to have reappeared so promptly. Almost, the suspicious swine, as if he hadn't trusted me to wait for him.

"You were quick," I glowered.

"I see you were even quicker," he said.

On the way to the mess he ordered me to wait for a moment while he detoured down a short passage and into a space which, judging by the sounds emerging from it, was a telephone exchange. I'd noticed that there were telephone lines draped along many of the passageways. But once again I had time only to walk along to the next intersection, study the signpost, and return to where I was supposed to wait, before he returned.

The signs had been no help at all. The one pointing left said IVCC. The one pointing right said VCC. The other two were equally cryptic. None of them pointed to the outside world. I didn't know which way to turn.

For a moment I thought of overpowering Strand anyway, and seeing if I could retrace our progress into the earth. However, I decided against this, as he looked stronger than me.

After a depressingly long walk, which, for all I knew, could be taking us even deeper into the hillside, we reached a large and lofty chamber smelling of stale cigarettes, damp, and curry, which I took to be an aircrew mess. It was divided by a wooden partition with a wide doorway. In one half there were trestle tables and benches, a dining area. It was brightly lighted and the tables were covered with scrupulously clean cloths— though a frighteningly large black spider was strolling across one of them.

On the other side of the partition was the mess proper. The floor had been concreted, and there were several utilitarian armchairs, coffee tables, ashtrays, and a pair of mismatched sofas. Lines of droopy lamps had been stapled to the ceiling. A dull red Indian carpet completed the decor. The total effect was to make the accommodation look more dismal than ever. But at least it was gloriously cool after the crematorium weather outside.

There were about a dozen officers in the mess, talking excitedly. I looked them over, trying to determine if any of them were Russians, but they were all dressed in the two-tone Khaliwar uniform with scimitars on their shoulder boards, but no insignia to denote nationality. I failed to hear Russian speech, but that was hardly surprising. The low, hard ceiling tended to scramble the conversation. But it wasn't just the unabsorbent surroundings that were dishing up distortion. I'd felt it almost from the moment I entered the valley: tension. In our travels through the caves we had passed quite a few uniformed men, and there had been a distinct agitation to their manner and conversational exchanges. By the time we reached the mess it had communicated itself to me. My heart was trying to beat its way out of my throat.

Now here it was again: excitement, urgency, anticipation. Everybody seemed to be talking faster than usual, some almost breathlessly. It made me more jittery than ever. I feared that it had something to do with me.

Apparently not. When Strand and I appeared, we received a scrutiny that seemed no keener than normal. One or two of the pilots waved or nodded respectfully at Strand, and the ones that looked at me turned away after a natural interval to resume their bright-eyed chatter.

I suspected that everybody in the caves had received some vital news that afternoon.

Strand now led the way to the dining part of the cavern. He settled himself at one of the tables and clapped his hands for service. I sat opposite him, feeling thoroughly weak-kneed and lily-livered, trying, not very successfully, to convince myself that I was bound to get away sooner or later.

An Indian mess attendant in a white jacket appeared from nowhere, to serve us an afternoon snack of unleavened bread, cheese, a bowl of fruit, and a large tin pot of tea with the milk already mixed into it.

As I poured a third mugful for myself within half a minute, Strand leaned over. "Try the goat cheese," he suggested. "It's a Khaliwar specialty—tastes goddamn awful."

He sounded tense, and was making no attempt to eat or drink. He was staring at me unblinkingly.

"What, what?" I said nervously; then, to change the subject—changing it from what I'd no idea—I said, "Tell me, Heinrich, what is all the excitement?"

"Excitement?"

"Everybody so jumpy."

A muscle in his cheek was twitching like a cliché. He looked around. "I guess," he said slowly, "they've been told that there's only a few more days to go."

"Before what?"

"Perhaps my superior officer will tell you."

"Yes?"

"Behind you," Strand said, rising.

"Eh?" I twisted around; and started. An exceedingly crude-looking fellow with vast shoulders and huge hairy fists decorated with red hairs was standing just two feet away.

As he was Strand's superior, and Strand was, I gathered, a far from junior officer on the staff, that made it incumbent upon me to stand up as well. Which I did. This respectful gesture enabled me to study the top of the newcomer's head, as he was only about five feet tall. He was also about five feet wide, and smelled of *fin de siècle* perspiration.

And he was Russian.

I knew it even before Strand introduced him, and before I noticed the ostentatious red stars on his shoulder boards.

"Allow me to introduce Mr. Panyushkin," Strand said quietly, and waited for my response.

It was not long in coming. "Oh, shit," I said.

After a moment, Strand came stiffly to attention, and rapped out a report in German. The newcomer nodded casually and replied in the same language.

Strand seemed tense in his presence, though he had not struck me as being the type to be overly impressed by authority. But perhaps Panyushkin was exceptionally senior. The stars on the shoulder-boards of his muscle-strained Khaliwar uniform were ostentatious enough.

So far he had not spoken. He was too busy staring at me through puffy eyes that looked like the tips of ice picks. And I had an idea that among the many mistakes I was certain to have made in passing myself off as a new recruit was an exceedingly bad political mistake.

This was just about to be confirmed. "A short time ago," Strand said harshly, "I informed Comrade Panyushkin that I had reason to believe you were an imposter, a spy."

"*Comrade* Panyushkin?" I said as my heart took the elevator into the basement.

"You have spent all day convincing me that you were anti-communist," Strand shouted, first in German, then in English. "Saying how much you hated the Bolsheviks! So you are not even a competent spy! It seems your superiors were not aware that everyone of us in the Khaliwar armed forces is an activist in the glorious cause of world communism!" He turned to Panyushkin and again brought his heels together. "He was not aware, Comrade Commander," he bellowed, again in German and English, "that here we are all dedicated to the sacred cause of Marxism!"

"Well, it was your fault," I said angrily. "You deliberately led me to believe you were White Russians. I mean, whatja-expect?"

Still Panyushkin said nothing; though his presence could be felt all right, as if he were radiating a tangible malevolence. He had not taken his eyes off me for a second, though, which was as unsettling as his baleful emanation.

He continued to stare at me with his icy eyes for a good ten seconds—actually it was a bad ten seconds—before addressing Strand in German, yet still without taking his eyes off me.

"You are to say something to the Comrade Commander in Russian," Strand said harshly.

"Certainly," I said. "*Ees agnyah daf polymya.*" The nearest equivalent in English to which was, "Out of the frying pan, into the fire," which seemed a reasonably appropriate test piece in the circumstances.

To my surprise, Panyushkin did not immediately dismiss me as a fraud. He now spoke for the first time in a voice like a hinge in Dracula's bedroom. "What part of Soviet Union are you from?" he asked.

"Moskva."

Slowly he relaxed, and a grim smile darkened his heavy, unforgiving face. "*Nyet,*" he said, shaking his head without taking his eyes off me. This caused them to swivel in a way that at any other time might have amused me. "*Kak vas zavoot?*"

"Ivan Smeev."

He smacked me in the face with an open hand, and calmly repeated the question.

"Captain Carruthers."

He tested it on his tongue. "Capt'yin Car'yuthers. . .English?"

"Canadian," I said; and, when his massive fist tightened as if he thought I was not being sufficiently cooperative: "Canada, Canada," I said hurriedly.

"Who sent you?"

"I'm an officer in the Jhamjarh Air Force."

"Ah," he said expansively, straightening his buffalo shoulders, aware that he had a rapt audience. The same awareness made him step back a foot or so, so that I could no longer loom over him.

As everybody in the mess next door crowded in the door-way to see what was going on, Panyushkin turned and spoke harshly to Strand.

My legs started to shake. I sat down and picked up my mug. There was still an inch of tea in it.

Before I could sip it was knocked from my hand. Strand was standing in front of me, shouting, his face inflamed.

"Get up!" he screamed, and when I failed to do so, he wrenched out his sidearm and viciously snicked off the safety catch. "Get up," he shouted again, "when you are speaking to Comrade Panyushkin!" So I thought I'd better get to my feet again, whatever my legs thought about it.

Panyushkin took over again. "What have you done with the Red Army pilots?" he demanded in Russian.

"Nothing. I—"

"How did you know they were arriving at Shampur? Who told you? Who is the informer?"

"Nobody. I—"

"You killed the pilots! That is how you have the suitcase!"

"Not at all. Your men are still there, as far as I know."

I seemed to be enraging him more and more. He had moved close again and was shouting straight up my nose. "Who sent you to spy? Or was it sabotage? Who told you about our arrangements at Shampur? Somebody in Bombay?" he bel-lowed; and, when I merely gazed down at him: "Well, we shall find out soon enough, you bourgeois parasite!" he said, and shouted into the darkness behind him.

Immediately three Siberian psychopaths in Khaliwar uni-forms with red-banded flat caps rushed into the chamber and surrounded me, bringing their bayoneted rifles dangerously close. On a further order from Panyushkin they seized me and held me firm.

"I will give you one more chance," Panyushkin screamed, reaching up to seize me by the hair, knocking my silly pith helmet off in the process. "How did you know about our arrangements at Shampur?"

"I didn't," I said. "And if you don't mind, I'm losing quite enough hair as it is, without—"

That was as far as I got before Panyushkin drew back his fist with the red hairs on it, and pistoned me in the side of the head, projecting me some distance down the tunnel, but unfortunately not far enough to give me a head start in an escape attempt. After which it was the guards' turn.

Looking the Worse for Wear

When I had confided to Strand, in an effort to convince him of my anti-communist credentials (as it turned out a somewhat unavailing enterprise), about my sojourns in three Bolshevik prisons, little did I know that I would find myself in another so soon afterwards.

In a way, this one, deep inside the hillside of Ujipatan valley, was the most alarming of the lot. It was in a cavern, and the cells were individual cages bolted to the floor, three of them, separated from each other by fluttering darkness. Each cell was about five feet square, and seven feet tall, the approximate height of the cavern. The cells looked home-made: welded out of odd lengths of angle iron and the like. They had probably been knocked together in one of the workshops along the runway. But though crudely fashioned, the cages were strong enough to withstand anything except a bulldozer or a hacksaw, and sensible precautions were taken to ensure that no other means of escape were possible. The steel-barred door was never opened without at least two guards being present, one to unlock the door and the other to stand well back with leveled rifle in case the prisoner made an unwise move.

Only two of the cages were now occupied. Last night the one nearest mine had contained a drunken German, but after a night of growling and snorting he had been hauled away by a couple of guards after being slapped around by a Russian officer. His cage was now empty. Because of the inadequate lighting it was impossible to see into the far cage. I had whispered loudly once or twice but the occupant must have been sleeping for he failed to respond. In fact he was so still I feared he was dead, until a moan and a groan escaped him in the middle of the night. I assumed it was the middle of the night, but for all I knew it could have been broad daylight outside.

Upon first surveying my ferrous kingdom I perceived that the only furniture was a slop pail, unlidded and therefore somewhat malodorous and hospitable to flies. The pail was emptied once a day by Untouchables, or sweepers as they were called. There was no bed. You slept on the rocky floor within the severe limits of the metal framework. Except that sleep had so far proved a bit difficult as the floor was so sharp. It would have provided a fine training ground for a fakir.

The culinary regime was almost as unsatisfying as the morphean arrangements. After a day of nothing to eat I received a small bowl of weevils and rice, and an earthenware jar that had been used to catch the drips from the ceiling, judging by the flavor of the water in it.

Neither I nor the other prisoner partook of luncheon—or supper, or breakfast, or whatever it was—I because I was not yet hungry enough, and he because he was either too sleepy or too indisposed to apply for his rations.

On the next favorable occasion I called out to the other prisoner in Russian, and this time received a reply. It did me no good, for the words, working their way through a filter of groans, sounded German. I was just about to enquire if he knew any French when the guard, who had apparently been waiting for an excuse to do so, rushed into the chamber and, thrusting his rifle butt through the bars, attempted to use me as a mortar to his pestle. Failing, he spat, and shouted at me to remain silent.

Deciding to try again later, I peered hard across the intervening empty cell, hoping at least to find out what the other jailbird looked like, but it was useless. The cavern was lit by a single bulb which dangled from a staple in the jagged ceiling.

As the walls were gray or dark brown and lacking in reflective quality, this did not provide a great deal of illumination.

The shortage of light and lack of creature comforts did little to raise the old morale. I didn't know, but I had a suspicion that I was not going to get out of this mess so easily. The Kresty Prison in Petrograd had been ghastly enough, what with the stink and the screaming voices, and the Peter and Paul Fortress had been oppressive in its cold and silence, but at least I could comfort myself with the thought that some day I would be released, as I was a perfectly legitimate prisoner-of-war, captured during a perfectly legitimate military battle. But here the situation was rather different. The only likely release was of the kind that Comrade Panyushkin was offering via a bullet in the back of the head. The worst of it was that, unless the Khaliwarians themselves informed the world, nobody might ever know what had happened to me. One moment I had been fuming in the Maharajah's private coach, and the next I had melted into hot air. Unless strenuous efforts were made to investigate my disappearance—and I couldn't see the government trying too hard—there was little hope of rescue. In the unlikely event that I was traced to this valley—and the Ujipatan was only one of many valleys south of the Vindhya Mountains which stretched for 800 miles from the Arabian Sea to the Bay of Bengal—they would need an army to fight their way in. And what then? Which of the hundreds of caves was I in? Lud, I didn't even know that myself.

So far I had been interrogated twice. It could have been worse, I suppose. The same urgency in the atmosphere previously noted seemed to have affected Panyushkin as well. He simply didn't have the time to employ the usual long-term methods of obtaining information from prisoners. There was no patience in him. So he made do with the old-fashioned techniques, threats, beatings, and the like, which I must confess were effective enough. A willingness to have my hide damaged in the cause was not part of my Jhamjarh contract. Nor did I feel that I suited a stiff upper lip. My face was stiff enough as it was. It was all very well for heroes in John Buchan spy stories—I had read his *The Three Hostages* on the ship—to put up with all that torture nonsense, but darn it, I had a low pain threshold. I didn't mind other people's blood, but the sight of my own made me feel quite faint. On the other hand, I had enough experience by now to know that if the information was dragged out of a fellow too easily, it was likely to create doubt or skepticism on the part of the interrogator as to the veracity of the confession; in which case he was likely to redouble his efforts. Thus I would suffer more in the long run than if I held out to the last from the first.

In the end, I thought I calculated it reasonably well. After a couple of hours of biffs and bangs and rude questions, I told them about three-quarters of what they wanted to know, presenting myself as a Jhamjarh mercenary who was in it only for the money. Which was so true that it sounded convincing. Then, under additional pressure from Panyushkin, mainly a threat to aerate my brainbox there and then with a dum-dum, I presented him with what would seem to be the balance of the information at my disposal. I was careful, however, not to enlighten him as to my true status. I informed him merely that I was a senior pilot.

"When will your air force be fully operational?" he demanded.

"Officially by the middle of this month, Comrade," I whined.

Plainly, Khaliwar's intelligence system was a good deal more efficient than Jhamjarh's, for I could see that he had already obtained this information.

This did not stop him from carrying on with the bullying, however. "Don't you comrade me, you stinking Western materialist bourgeois reactionary," he bellowed. (I may have put in one too many nouns or adjectives here.)

"Yes, Comrade," I said cringingly. Stinking, that was a good one. He himself smelled at least as bad as I did. Though in his case it was hardly surprising. In place of the sloppy but climactically sensible Khaliwar uniform he had changed into a heavy black outfit buttoned tightly to the throat. Perhaps it was out of nostalgia for the good old days when as a commissar he could kill anyone he wished. He even had the insignia: large red stars on his sleeve, glowing bloodily against the dark material.

His jaw was almost as massive as his fist but much better shaved. His eyes were tiny but scary enough, very similar to those of his Asian guards, the optical comparison being possible because three of those guards, slovenly and pitiless, were helping him to gather information.

Also present at the interrogations were Strand and a chilly German gentleman named Senger, who turned out to be my opposite number, the Khaliwar Air Force commander, though he was still subordinate to Panyushkin. He gave the impression of being a hard, disciplined communist, a breed that was rapidly rising internationally from the fires of the Russian Revolution. I was glad that he was there mainly as an observer. He looked sharper and more intelligent than the commissar. He might have asked the right questions. Panyushkin tended to render the interrogation inefficient by using his knuckles as punctuation marks.

The Russian's habit of grinding his face into mine was even worse than his hairy fists. He seemed to think that closer inspection of my face might bring the details more clearly into focus. How familiar that man was, the Bolshevik commissar, brutal propagandist and political disciplinarian of the Red Army. The Whites along whom I had fought in the Civil War had regarded that breed with especial loathing, and had bumped them off whenever they got the chance.

Fortunately Panyushkin was not one of the intelligent ones. He made the mistake of letting me know that he was in a hurry, which greatly helped me to stick it out. "It is a pity I do not have more time to find out all you know," he said in his ill-educated Russian. (That was another gratuitous advantage: he knew German but no English, so he either had to question me in Russian and then act as his own translator for Senger's benefit, or get Strand to translate my English into German. Either way it slowed the proceedings, and gave me more time to drag my confessional feet.) "Still, you will be useful to confirm what I already know." His face was so close I could count the ginger bristles on his massive chin. Also a few bubbles of froth mixed with black specks. "That is why—so far—you are only bleeding in one or two places, Captain Carruthers. You have saved yourself—for the time being—by telling the truth."

He leaned even closer. His breath made me wish I was wearing a yashmak. "So I advise you to go on confirming what we know. Because if once I catch you out in a lie it will be the pistol, not the fist. You understand?"

"Yes, Comrade."

"Right, then," he said, and to my relief, stepped back, to wander about his personal torture chamber for a few moments before turning to me again with hands on hips. "Now tell me, Comrade Dungheap, what in your opinion is the state of morale in your air force?"

I knew the Bolshevik mentality well enough to answer this untruthfully without risking a bullet. (At least I hoped it was untruthful.) "They will not fight hard, Comrade, I don't think. They are all in it only for the money, you see."

"That is good," Panyushkin said, looking satisfied. "It is exactly as we understand the situation. The decadent Western hyenas who are interested solely in material advantage will collapse the moment they are attacked by the disciplined forces of Marxism-Leninism."

"You really intend to attack?" I asked.

In reply he seized me by the hair and breathed noxiously into my face. He had been eating dead rats. "You are being sensible and cooperative so far, Comrade Carruthers," he said menacingly. "Don't spoil it."

"Sorry, Comrade," I said. And after a final glare, he let go my poor old hair.

Senger spoke, then nodded faintly at Strand. Strand intoned, "The comrade colonel suspects that there is more to be learned from you than he at first thought."

My heart missed a beat, possibly even two beats. *Damn. Damn.* I should never have asked that question. It seemed to have indicated to Senger that I was thinking for myself.

Senger spoke again. Strand was about to translate when

Panyushkin interrupted rudely and with a sneer, as if he felt
that the air force commander's questions weren't up to much.
"The comrade colonel wishes to know about your commander, Bendy," he said, and turned away to indicate his
boredom.

"Of course, Comrade," I said quickly, Strand translating
almost simultaneously. "I will tell you everything I know."

"First, what is the general opinion of him?"

"The men do not have a high opinion of him, Comrade
Colonel."

Senger continued to question me through Strand, sharply
and to the point, and even asked for any personal estimation of
Brigadier Bendy; to which I replied that it seemed to me that
the man was hollowed out.

"Hollowed out? What does that mean?"

"To begin with, he is spending much of his time in bed
instead of attending to his duties."

Panyushkin said roughly, "We know all this," but Senger and
Strand glanced at each other as if they already knew that I was
a moper, drone, and loafer. Which rather upset me, for some
reason.

"I still do not understand what you mean, hollowed out,"
Senger said coldly.

I pretended to think about it—until I realized that I really
was thinking about it. What did I mean? Hollowed out.
Scooped out. Like a used grapefruit? "Perhaps," I said faintly,
continuing in English, eyes becoming unfocused, "the war did
more to him than he thought...destroyed his faith in authority, and religion, and everything..."

Panyushkin began to bawl rudely. "Comrade Senger," he
said, "there is no point to this line of questioning. The Dewan
of Jhamjarh has already told us all we need to know about this
fool Bendy—"

He stopped dead as he realized that Strand was translating
this interjection into English from sheer force of habit.

He glared at Strand, then proceeded to lambast him in a
fashion insulting enough to bring a flush to the other's tanned
cheeks.

It seemed that the commissar had not meant his words to be translated; to have given away the information that Jhamjarh's prime minister was spying for Khaliwar.

Back in the cell I had enough consciousness left to congratulate myself that the beatings had not been entirely in vain, but that I had learned something in return. Not just that the Dewan was betraying his master, but that an attack on Jhamjarh might be imminent. That must account for the atmosphere of excitement that pervaded the caves.

I was still thinking about it when I actually fell asleep on the uneven rock floor. At least I think I slept, though it seemed that only a few seconds passed before the cage door was screeching open again, and once again I was having my hands bound.

I felt so weary, with buzzing brain and eye sockets used as molds for molten lead, that I was hardly conscious of even the direction we took.

But I woke up pretty fast when I found I'd been summoned into the presence of Sharif-ul-Khalil, the real ruler of Khaliwar.

His reception room was a large cavern illuminated by dozens of naked light bulbs suspended in clusters like Spanish onions. And as the rock walls in this particular part of the underground system were a light gray, this abundant light was further amplified so that you could actually make out a few details.

The most interesting detail was the chair at the far end of the cavern. It was made of wood and had a vaguely ecclesiastical look. It was draped in glowing swathes of red and blue silk, and softened with brilliant, tasseled cushions. A gold canopy had been rigged over the chair, which was plainly intended to serve as a temporary throne. Under it was a dais hammered together from lengths of unplaned timber and covered with colored cloths and a lavish rug.

A few white officers, including Panyushkin and Senger, with Strand off to one side, were present. Much closer to the throne and its occupant were several Indians in the shades-of-brown uniform worn by both army and air-force officers. They were all wearing the graceful green and black turbans that distinguished them from their foreign allies. They were standing close to the dais and talking in undertones. Occasionally one or other of them would glance at the Germans and Russians in a gleaming sort of way as if to say, look, we are privileged to stand much closer to our lord than you.

I gazed, hypnotized, at the figure on the throne, and indeed he was a compelling sight: black-whiskered, and with eyes that seemed somnolent or apathetic, until he raised their heavy lids. Instantly they became incandescent, piercing. He was attired in a splendid dark blue robe with white and gold embroidery. On his head was a tall turban of blue and white cloth ablaze with precious stones and loops of pearl. Just visible under the robe were white silk trousers and gold slippers, which at the moment were stretched out and perched on a dark blue cushion. A stark naked sword hung from his jeweled belt.

As for his manner as he looked over his respectful court, it was so self-consciously regal that I half expected him to break into song, something from *Chu Chin Chow*, perhaps.

When I was first shoved into the cavern he treated me to a quick glance, then ignored me for the next few minutes while he conferred in undertones with a member of his Indian staff. Which gave me plenty of time to study that face of his, and come to the conclusion that I had better behave as sycophantically as the rest of them. Sharif looked quite capable of sparing my executioner his exertions by taking his place. Even from the length of the cavern I was sure I could detect in his eye the sort of expression you would expect from a famished falcon. One could not assert that he emanated evil, but on the other hand he was certainly not dear old grandad, not with those bleak, hooded eyes and that scimitar of a beak. Even in repose his posture was one of poised aggression, as if he were at 2,000 feet and had just espied an obese bunny.

At last he was gesturing in my direction. I hurriedly adopted a humble posture.

He spoke. One of the guards gave me a shove. I stumbled forward. With my hands bound behind me, I only just managed to remain upright.

Advance, friend, and be recognized, I thought idiotically.

The dais was high enough that, even seated, Sharif was able to look down on me; which he did with a cold indifference that was as unflattering as it was welcome. My God, I was determined not to rile this man.

It seemed that apart from his own tongue, he had no other language but English, for it was that language he directed toward Panyushkin. "This is the dog who pretended to be a newly-arrived Russian pilot?" he enquired.

Panyushkin waited alertly while Strand translated this. "That is so, Your Highness," he said huskily; and cleared his throat quite nervously.

Sharif continued to address Panyushkin. Strand was much too inferior an officer to be looked at directly. "And you have obtained a confession from him?"

"Yes, we have all the information from him that we need at the moment."

"I could offer the services of my own torturers if you wished," Sharif said with a graceful gesture. Gold rings encircled several of his fingers. "They are perhaps more adept than your people."

Fortunately nothing came of this suggestion; at least not immediately. Instead, there was a further exchange between Sharif and Panyushkin before the ruler turned his head and exposed me to the full force of that dark, cruel face. A wild pig with a splinter up its arse might have looked kindlier.

Even then he did not address me directly. "He is not badly hurt," he observed. "How long did it take him to cooperate?"

"He confessed inside two hours, sir," Strand translated.

Sharif's beard stirred, as if his lip were curling. "But then this is not a man in front of me," he sneered. "It is a mangy dog that cringes at a glance."

"That is so, Your Highness."

"Then as a dog, should he not be closer to the earth? Should he not be on all four paws?"

There was a momentary hesitation before Panyushkin barked. A moment later I was seized and forced to the floor, which, I now perceived, was roughly concreted. And when I failed to adopt a posture to their liking, a boot collided with my ribs; and one of the guards gestured fiercely.

The Khaliwarians laughed excessively. The German officers smiled dutifully and looked away.

Now Sharif was scowling. "Does the Englishman not resent being called a mangy dog?" he said, louder. "You have no pride, Englishman? Well, speak."

"Sticks and stones may break my bones, but words will never harm me," I said.

He stared. "What does that mean?" he demanded. "What is this, 'Words will never harm me?' I do not see the sense in it. If I tell the guards to pluck out your eyes, are not those words harmful?"

"Gosh, I never thought of that, Your Highness," I said, looking really impressed by his logic...which, now I came to think of it, made a certain amount of sense.

His attitude to me became plainer still. The longer he gazed upon my cringing figure the profounder his contempt. "What is your position?" he asked suddenly.

"I'm on hands and knees, Your Highness."

"Your position in this air force of yours," he hissed.

"I'm a sort of insignificant flight leader."

He picked his nose, regarding me thoughtfully the while. "If such as you is a leader," he said, molding a ball of olfactory material between thumb and forefinger, "then I do not think we have much to worry about.

"But tell me," he went on, flicking his thumb and forefinger apart, "what do you think I should do with you, Englishman?"

"I am at your mercy, Your Highness. By the way, I don't suppose it matters, but actually I'm a Canadian. I haven't quite perfected my phoney English accent yet, that's why you—"

He wasn't listening. "Should I kill you now," he mused, "or should I keep you alive for another four days, so that you may die in the knowledge that all your friends in this air force of yours will be joining you in hell...?"

He didn't appear to expect a response, so I kept quiet—externally, at least. Inside, I was in turmoil, as I tried to work out what day this was. Tuesday? Wednesday? Thursday? Four days, he'd said—to his offensive? Of course it must be. Four days. Four days.

I was so preoccupied with a useless tangle of thoughts—four days from when?—how did you count our days underground without a watch?—that I hardly heard Sharif when he said with a look of revulsion that I hoped was simulated, "I do not know whether to yawn or to spew in the presence of this cur. Take him away. Take him away."

For the fourth time—fifth?—sixth? I was thrust back into the cage, unbound, and hurled against the far bars. The iron doors squeaked shut, two of the guards departed, while the third loitered at the ragged entrance to the cavern. In the dim light I could just make him out as he propped his rifle against the wall and fiddled with a tobacco tin.

How I longed, how I longed to get at him, and escape with the news. I felt as if every capillary in my body was about to burst with frustration.

A match flared. As the cigarette he was about to smoke was barely an inch long he tilted his head while he lit up, so as not to set fire to the hairs in his nostrils. Once the butt was satisfactorily alight, he stood there puffing for a moment before settling himself on a stool, and leaning his back carefully against the sharp rock wall.

Four days, four days. We had left New Delhi on Tuesday, May 12. Shampur station, early the next morning, May 13. But how long ago was that? It seemed a very long time since I'd hopped into Strand's car in my pyjamas...

In the ceiling, the solitary light bulb flickered and dimmed, then brightened again. Far down the passageway outside, somebody shouted. The sudden metallic echoless sound seemed to amplify the silence that usually prevailed in the cliffside quarters.

I stood there for ages, gripping the crude bars, desperate to know whether it was night or day. Unless I knew, I could not even plan on a time of escape. It would be pretty ridiculous if I managed to get out of the caves only to find that it was midday, and that the valley was thronged with armed guards. But even the temperature was no help. The heat of the valley did not penetrate this deep into the hillside, nor any morning breeze. Thermally, there was nothing to go on. The heavy humidity in here never seemed to alter.

Well, then, I would just have to escape and risk broad daylight. But how? Without the key or a hacksaw there was no way out. How did they manage it in pictures? Easy. The hero always managed to overpower the jailer by getting a strangle-hold on him, then reaching through the bars for the convenient keys. But perhaps Panyushkin had seen those silent films, for his jailers had been briefed very carefully, it seemed, to deny the prisoner an advantage. For instance, when I was being returned to the cell and when my hands were being untied, at least one guard kept his distance and his rifle leveled until I was safely hemmed in with scrap iron. Similarly when the rice and water was being dished out, a guard remained well clear, with weapon at the ready.

Even if I managed to grab one of the jailers as a hostage, I had no confidence that those Siberians would respect the life of a captured comrade. I'd met men like these in Trotsky's Red Army. They didn't have much respect for human life. They were quite capable of shooting a pal if he got in the way. It seemed that my only hope was that in time they would grow careless. But what with the anticipation of action, the excite-ment, the tension in the air caused by the preparations for the coming offensive, they were not likely to relax before it was too late. I mean, look at the guard sitting over there, smoking his third cigarette butt in twenty minutes, his flat eastern Siberian face a blur in the sour, humid air. Though I was securely locked away in a five-foot cage, yet still he remained on guard. Stupid brute, sitting there struggling to keep his current cigarette alight. Presumably the tobacco wasn't wrapped in the right brand of toilet paper.

Even as I stood there glaring at him, he got up from the stool and dropped the remains of his cigarette on the floor. He then bent his knees, rudely discharged, and ambled out of the cavern. A moment later he returned for his rifle.

The moment his footsteps receded, a voice hissed out of the gloom.

The voice came again. "I said, do you speak English?"

I thought for a moment. "Yes," I said.

"That's marvelous," the voice whispered, not very distinctly. "I've been waiting hours for this. Who are you? Are you German?"

"Canadian."

"Canadian?" There was a deathly silence, then: "Jesus. It's not. I don't believe...it can't be."

"It is. 's'me. Hello, Derby."

"It's pronounced Darby...you should know that by now...."

"Why didn't you speak up before, when you had the chance?"

"I did."

"You mean that time you mumbled something? I thought it was a foreign language. And you're still mumbling."

Silence, then: "I got beaten up. I seem to have lost some teeth."

It was my turn to be silent. "I'm sorry," I said at length. "But by God, I'm glad to see you again, John. Not that I can see you, of course. I thought you were dead."

"Once or twice I wished I was. Have you met Pan whatsisname? But for God's sake, Bart, how did you get here?"

"I'll save it for when you're feeling stronger," I said, beginning to feel a stir of hope now that I had someone to share my hopelessness.

The next two or three minutes were taken up with whispered exchanges interspersed with pleas from each other to speak less loudly, in case the guards heard us.

"I just can't say how glad I am to find you alive, John. A true friend...."

"Let's not get maudlin, old man. Let me tell you what happened," he said; and proceeded to do so; to describe how he had taken off that fateful morning and crossed unobserved into Khaliwar; and how he and his observer, Simpson, had flown back and forth across the state for over three hours in an effort to find any trace of an enemy aerodrome, or any hint of air activity; without success.

It had not occurred to him to overfly this northern part of the state as it was such unlikely terrain for air operations, being for the most part rocky and rugged, with some quite high, jagged hills. "But presumably that's why they picked it," he whispered.

Then suddenly he spotted part of the Khaliwar army. And how. It was a considerable force of armored cars and lorry-drawn field guns. Derby had dived on the long, dust-enveloped column, and Simpson had managed to take at least a dozen pictures from as low as 300 feet. Better still, they had determined the column's destination. It was a huge staging area in the foothills, sixty miles north of Lampur Kalat. The area had been packed with troops and vehicles and great dumps of fuel and/or ammunition. There Simpson exposed another dozen plates.

"Sixty miles north of Lampur Kalat, did you say? You mean south, surely—ready for an attack on Jhamjarh."

"I don't mean south, I said north," Derby hissed, sounding as if he'd just come from the dentist.

At which we both fell silent for a moment as we considered the implications.

"My God, they're going into British India as well," I breathed.

"That's the conclusion I've come to, since," Derby said.

"Anyway, go on."

"Well, anyway...we were so busy gloating we didn't see the Fokkers until it was too late."

"Shades of the Western Front, eh? So you found the Khaliwar Air Force as well. Damn good work, John."

"Didn't do us much good, did it? First we knew we'd located their air force was when they started shooting at us from all directions.

"We didn't stand a chance. We were down less than two minutes later, riddled from skid to gudgeon."

"You got down all right?"

"We pancaked about a mile from the staging area, so it only

took them a few minutes to reach us—a party of Russians, with Pan-usedskin."

"You couldn't make a run for it?"

"I was dazed by the crash, and Simpson was hurt. I couldn't leave him lying there. I wanted to make sure he got medical attention."

"How badly injured was Simpson?"

"In the crash? His leg was broken." He paused. "They killed him."

"What?"

"The Russians. They couldn't be bothered carrying him all the way back to the camp."

"Killed him?"

"Before I knew what was happening. Shot him in the head."

"The Bolsheviks."

"I gather that's what they were. Yes."

Somewhere along the passage outside, quarreling voices were heard. I assumed that the sound was coming from the 'guardroom', a scooped-out hollow in the wall, about twenty feet along the passage.

We listened. The voices grew louder. Then the quarrel abruptly ceased.

After a while I said, "I'm beginning to think it's at least as much a Russian as it is a Khaliwar plot."

John must have been thinking about it too, for he whispered, "I suppose there could be a lot in it for the Soviets if they backed Khaliwar, and Khaliwar succeeded."

"Even if they didn't, the damage to British interests and prestige would suit them fine."

"What chance do you think they have, Bart?"

"Well, from what I heard in New Delhi—"

"You've been there? When?"

"I'll tell you later. But I learned that most of the British and Indian armies are on the North-West Frontier, hundreds of miles away, and nearly all of the RAF has been detached to Iraq."

"We already knew that."

"Anyway, the thing is, we're just about the only fighting force between here and the Himalayas.

"I'd say," I added, feeling queerly detached about it, "that they've a good chance of conquering half the country before the Government can do anything about it."

Underexposed

A n age of indeterminate duration went by. Periodically we whispered, plotted, abandoned hope, revived. How to get out of the ground. Or even simply how to get out of our five-foot cages. We decided on an elaborate scheme where one of us would distract the guards while the other—it was all nonsense. We planned on attacking the guards simultaneously when they took us out together for interrogation, but of course they never did.

On the far side of the cavern one guard or another sat on the stool, smoking or grumbling, occasionally relieving himself where he sat, which did nothing to improve the atmosphere in the cavern. Panyushkin looked in just once, wrinkled his nose, and went out again. Strand had disappeared entirely.

At snatched moments we whispered, otherwise tried to get comfortable on the sharp floor. I could stretch out fully in the cell only by lying diagonally. The ground was sharp and greasy, but I slept fitfully between stabs of worry. "What the hell does it matter what time it is?" Derby hissed at one point. "But I don't know when to fall asleep," I complained, "or when to take my afternoon nap."

After that, another endless period passed, a day and a night or what? Despair set in. We stopped whispering even when the guard was out of the cavern. John moaned in his sleep. I asked a guard to tell us what day it was. He fixed his gaze and his bayonet. I decided to snub him from then on.

Funnily enough, though I had recently been whacked in various other parts of the head and body, it was my leg that hurt most of all, the one that had been punctured over the frontier post. The muscle felt hot under the grimy bandage. Sigridur had taken exceptional care to keep the wound clean, and apart from the discomfort it had caused me remarkably little trouble ever since. Now it was hurting again. I was concerned that it might become infected, though I don't know why I bothered to be concerned. After all, according to Sharif, I had only four days to go. Three days. Two days?

We thought that today might be Friday, May 15 ("It's my day off tomorrow," Derby said). But we could easily have underestimated the time by ten, twenty, even thirty hours. The meals were no help. We felt sure that they missed one whole day. We quarreled over whether two meals had been served within thirty minutes. Perhaps Panyushkin was practising for when he went back to the Lubyanka.

Then the day of our execution arrived.

We became aware of a loud authoritative voice far down the passage. A couple of minutes later, Strand entered at the head of a squad of Russian soldiers.

Our hands were bound. We were uncaged.

"Is this it?" I asked.

Strand wouldn't look me in the eye. A bad sign. Instead he barked an order. Our arms were gripped and we were dragged to the exit quickly, as if the soldiers were in a hurry to get it over with.

One of the soldiers in the brown and brown Khaliwar garb looked fifty years old. His face was a field of stubble. He had a large growth on his face like a third cheek.

We stumbled along one rocky corridor after another. The passageway narrowed so that the man with the lump and his buddy had to let go and push me forward from behind. Four soldiers shoved past to lead the way. They seemed to be treating us a little more considerately than had the flat-faced sub-humans in the prison. Perhaps, knowing what was coming, they felt that there was no point in adding to our discomfort.

As we veered into another rock corridor, I turned to the elderly peasant with the growth. "Listen, Uncle, that lump on your face, you should get it removed," I said in Russian. The words seemed to scare him, or perhaps it was because he had been addressed. He jerked back, and disappeared from sight. "Shut up," Strand said. He seemed tenser than ever, as we crunched and stumbled through the earth.

"What time is it?"

After a moment he answered curtly, "Four o'clock. Now keep quiet."

True to Bolshevik tradition, I thought, they had come for us at four in the morning when the tide of the human spirit was out.

With Lüger in hand, Strand and his Russian squad crunched onward, half of them lurching along ahead, in case we were tempted to dart round some convenient corner, and the other half behind, in case we decided not to go after all.

The way grew spacious and a faint draft stirred the sour, humid air. We stumbled over a narrow railway track, like a coal-mine railway. It led past a series of excavated areas that were filled with boxes of ammunition and explosives. Squarish 100 kg. bombs, hundreds of boxes of machine-gun belts, boxes with German markings. Entrenching tools, portable winches, rockets, flares, coils of wire. It was a busy bright area. Half a dozen laborers were loading stores onto small rail trucks, others pushing the trucks ahead of us to the outside.

The tunnel widened still further. There was room to walk alongside the rail lines.

"You're going to shoot a couple of prisoners?" I asked. "Funny, I always thought German officers were honorable."

"You are not prisoners, you are spies. Spies are shot."

"This man here, he isn't a spy. He was shot down. He's a normal prisoner. You didn't used to do this on the Western Front."

The unflattering tone of voice I was using made no impression, "I have my orders," he said coldly.

"What does Panyushkin hope to gain?" I began, but he shouted for silence, and a moment later we were in the open air.

It was dark. The atmosphere was like exhaled breath.

The pleasure of being out in the open again almost outweighed the dread. The stars were unbelievable. They seemed to be just a few hundred feet up hanging brilliant in the Prussian blue sky. Gold dust from a hidden moon had been sprinkled on a distant ridge.

The whole valley was a pointillist composition of electric light, shaded lights all along the single runway for dotted miles, pricks of light from canvas structures, slashes of light silhouetting items of machinery that reared up in the distance, splashes of light smoothing the surfaces of airplanes inside hangars. At four in the morning the entire valley seemed to be vibrating with urgent activity.

We were being escorted from either side, nails digging into our biceps. We were halted. Oil lamps were being lighted. Each was bright enough to illuminate the rocks around us for half a dozen yards. Strand gestured us forward again. As we trudged over the rocky ground. I kept looking up and down the valley and listening. Clanging sounds from yellow canvas, generators roaring distantly, aero engines intermittently. (How my heart lurched at the thought of airplanes ready for take-off.) Tiny distant figures flicked now and then in front of streaks of light. A vehicle of some sort traveling slowly along the runway. Another, loaded with boxes and anonymous metal, heaving and groaning down the valley road which was now behind us. We were in the rough area between road and runway.

I caught Derby's eye. In the available light it looked desperately appealing, imploring me to think of something. But our hands were tied, our arms gripped tight. The best I could offer was a smile, wry as the end of a dream.

We reached our grave.

It had already been prepared, in what appeared to be the valley graveyard. The oblong looked neat and capacious, as if dug by machinery rather than your everyday sexton. It was easily big enough for us both.

"Halt."

I was having difficulty in breathing. I couldn't inflate my lungs properly.

It was all very well telling yourself that you'd be glad to be out of it, but resignation was easier said than done, resolution was sicklied oe'r with the pale cast of vacillation.

It just wasn't fair. The Maharajah was paying me a quarter million dollars a year, and I'd hardly had a chance to enjoy a bean. And what a sordid end...not even a prayer in my heart. All that had been suffocated in the mud of Flanders and under the weight of evidence of an unjust war.

Strand was holding my arm and drawing us, Derby and I, together. For what purpose I had no idea or interest. I was already half out of my body in the hot dark, dancing in the hot, washed-out air fifty million feet up....

"Are you *listening?*"

Strand's voice, faint, but growing a little stronger.

"Are you listening? In a moment I am going to yell at you."

He was holding my right arm and Derby's left, and hissing at us both. Derby mumbled. "They won't know what I'm saying, the Russians. Do not understand?"

We were dumb.

"Listen, listen, I'm trying to save you," Strand said.

In the lamplit darkness the slovenly guards were muttering, lighting cigarettes, nudging each other in that simple Russian way I remembered from 1919. They were twenty or thirty feet away.

Strand, looking every inch the arrogant Hun, stepped back and with fury in his voice shouted, "You are to lie down in the grave! I will pretend to shoot you! I will shoot into the ground. You must pretend you are dead, understand?!"

We gaped. He stepped forward and slapped Derby's face. The crack of his hand was very loud in the still night air. "Idiots! I am saving your lives!"

Some of the Russians began to approach. Strand waved them away. "Pigdogs," he screamed, beside himself, it seemed, with fury. "Lie still, whatever happens! Now get in, get in!"

With hammering ventricles I sat on the edge of the grave

then slipped in. I fell. My hands were still tied. I cried out in the dark, thumped to the stony bottom. A moment later Derby slithered down on the top of me.

Five seconds later came the crack of a pistol, as Strand fired into the grave.

Receiving the bullet was like the sledgehammer blow. I felt the shock in the rock. A moment later there was another shot and another thump and earth tremor. I felt Derby start violently and for a second I though it had been a terrible, heartless joke. "Oh, Jesus, please," Derby whispered, and then he was trying to stifle, as I was, an inclination to pant with terror.

Something wet dripped onto my face. Blood. Derby had been hit. No, it was sweat. Sweat, or perhaps he was dribbling.

The silence after the shots was deep. It seemed to go for a long time. My arm was twisted up behind me. It hurt. My face hurt. My leg hurt. Derby weighed forty tons.

We ceased to breath as voices grew loud, five feet overhead. There was a pause. When we heard the voices again, they were further off.

A shovel clinked. "Oh, no," Derby said; but fortunately he continued to lie still. Nothing happened. No shower of stones descended, just shouted orders. Strand's voice.

Derby's ear was only three inches from my mouth. I spoke. "I think I'm going to sneeze," I said.

Sweating Like Mad

Four hours later it was searing daylight and we were huddled above a gully in the shade of a rock slab, waiting for a lift back to civilization.

It was eight a.m. and already a scorcher. Even through caked and slitted eyes the sunlight pierced to the back of the head. The air seemed to have no oxygen in it. Worse, the insect life was vigorous. Though we were miles from anywhere, the flies had found us and were trying to get at the moisture in our mouths, or shelter from the heat in our earholes.

The rock we had our backs against was throwing the blackest shadow since de Sade, its radiation making scorch marks in us like careless ironing. Though we had been supplied with water, after the trip across the valley we were parched as potter wasps. Derby, still in his bloodstained lightweight flying overalls looked even worse than I felt, and I felt terrible. My leg ached and burned, my head had recently been borrowed by a rugger team and returned in deplorable condition. And this was only the start of a two hundred and twenty mile journey home.

After our recent experiences, I was so corroded with the body's emergency chemicals that it had taken an idiot spell for me to understand why Strand had helped us to escape, when it was he who had gotten me imprisoned in the first place. In fact, I still hadn't grasped it. I made a mental note to ask him to explain it again when he arrived—if he arrived—to pick us up at the agreed spot, over there by the rickety bridge over the gully. The bridge, the only landmark for miles in the semi-desert, was where he had told us to wait for him. We were a hundred yards up the gully from the bridge, hidden.

"And you understand how to get out of the valley?" he'd said. "Across the runway here, and up the hillside. You'll find the path near the top that will take you out past the valley guards. They don't know about it—the path is known only to a criminal tribe."

"Criminal?"

"There will be no trouble from them. They are in the army now. Sharif killed all the women and children, and rounded up the men." He thrust a cluster of water bottles at us. "You will need these. It will be hours before I can join you. And don't get lost. I will not be able to hang around waiting for you."

Well, that part wasn't too hard to understand. Now, four hours later John and I were huddled in the shade of a rock off the road but with a clear view of the stretch that led to the Ujipatan valley, including the small wooden bridge over the gully.

To distract myself from my own aches and pains, I fell to studying Derby to see how he was bearing up. His face was badly bruised and he had lost two of his front teeth. He was not going to be too happy when he examined his face in the mirror. His high, square shoulders and unemphatic good looks and his expression of perpetual skepticism had attracted many a female glance. Now with that crenelated mouth the cynical smile might not have quite as much effect...though where women were concerned, who knew? They might even get an extra thrill from imagining being bitten by those fractured incisors.

"Damn glad you've survived, John," I mumbled through a crack in my lips.

"When you all thought I'd gone west, I suppose there were scenes of grief in the mess?"

"Yes, I'm sure there were."

"You weren't grieving with the rest of them?"

"No, I was having a cup of tea. John?"

"What?"

"We still don't know what day it is, or when the attack—"

Without warning, a giant biplane whistled overhead, just a few hundred feet up.

"Look out—get down."

Two minutes later, another Gotha bomber hissed overhead, propellers loafing. And a minute later, a third.

We stared after them, shielding painful eyes.

"Gothas."

"Yes."

"Coming in to land."

The great biplanes swept onward into the Ujipatan valley, engines muted.

"Do you get the feeling," I asked, "that all hell's about to break loose?"

"I certainly do."

The whirring of the three giant Gotha bombers faded, to be replaced by a distant grumbling. Cautiously we peered around our rugged rock, along the road into the valley. At first we could see nothing except flashes of light and clouds of gray dust boiling into faded sky. Then shapeless blobs appeared. They seemed to be riding along at an altitude of ten or twelve feet above the road in the shimmering heat. Slowly they touched down, transforming themselves into lorries with flashing windscreens.

A few minutes later they reached the little bridge, our rendezvous point, and drummed and rumbled over it. We counted twenty-two big trucks, some canvas covered, the others open, loaded with boxes, crates, drums, and bales.

"Supplies moving forward."

"That's the third bunch of trucks we've seen in two hours."

Huddled under the rock, we watched the vehicles dissolve slowly into the khaki terrain. The dust hung in the air. Overhead, buzzards hovered like waiters.

We fell silent. We waited. It grew hotter still, which hardly seemed possible.

A few feet away a group of boulders had gathered together

to form a pleasing composition. A movement from that direction caught our attention. A snake appeared, waved its tiny head in the air for a few seconds. It started to wriggle toward us.

Derby uttered a muffled cry, picked up a rock and threw it. The snake hurriedly changed direction, and disappeared under a stone.

"It was just a little snake," I said with an amused croak. "Only a few inches long, for God's sake."

"Oh, yes? You haven't learned much, then. It was a krait."

"What's that?"

"Only the deadliest snake of all in this snake-infested realm, that's all. One nip and you're dead in ninety seconds."

"Oh," I said faintly. And, to teach him a lesson for using that tone: "I think I saw one under the rock we're leaning against."

Strand turned up in the tourer about half an hour later, just as we were coming to the conclusion that a bite from the krait might be preferable to dying from heat and dehydration. We had already drunk our supply of water even though we knew it was foolish to assume that Strand would turn up before the buzzards started to take an interest in us.

"Hurry," Strand shouted as we panted up to the open-top car—which actually had its top up, at the moment. "There is a headquarters unit on the road just a mile back. Get in, get in."

"You got here only just in time," I croaked as I bagged the front seat. "I'm half-baked." But though John agreed readily enough, Strand was too worried about the headquarters unit to answer. He accelerated carefully through the gears, splitting his attention between the potholes, the temperature gauge, and the rear-view mirror....

After three miles or so of sweltering travel we reached Khaliwar's main north-south highway, and turned left.

Left? "This is north, isn't it?" I shouted over the noise of the engine.

"Yes."

"But Jhamjarh is south."

Strand shouted back that in the entire state of Khaliwar,

only two roads ran south: the main road, the one we were on at present, which struck through the capital, Lampur Kalat, and continued down to Jhamjarh, and an inferior road to the east which wandered south toward the Parbati River. The latter, he said, was our best choice.

"Why?" Derby asked in a hostile way. He had not forgiven Strand that slap in the face, even though he recognized there had been nothing personal in it; that his German saviour had merely been trying to impress the firing party.

"Because just about the whole goddam Khaliwar Army will be on the main road," Strand shouted.

"They really are intending to attack?" I asked. Even now I couldn't quite believe it.

"Tomorrow."

"Tomorrow?"

"Five in the morning."

"They're attacking at five a.m.?"

Derby and I looked at each other starkly.

After a moment Derby shouted, "That still doesn't explain why the hell we're going north instead of south."

Strand explained patiently, as if he should not have needed to do so, that Sharif was already moving troops and supplies both north and south along the main road. It would be utterly impossible to maneuver past the endless columns. Moreover, even if the alarm had not been raised about our escape from the Ujipatan valley, we were certain to be challenged repeatedly by the military police to explain our presence on a road cleared exclusively for army vehicles.

Panyushkin, he said, was certain to discover soon enough that Strand had flown the coop. Knowing that Strand was familiar with many of the details of the coming offensive, he would take urgent measures to stop him before he crossed the Jhamjarh border. By traveling north initially and then east to the other road, we might buy ourselves two or three hours before we were located.

"In that case," Derby said, "why don't we head west, toward the Ujipatan valley? They wouldn't expect that either."

His sarcasm was lost on Strand, who thought Derby was merely being stupid.

A few minutes later we caught up with the supply trucks that had passed us half an hour previously. As the road was narrow and the ground on either side unsuitable for overtaking we were forced to crawl along behind the convoy, swaddled in blankets of dust.

"Wait a minute," Derby said suddenly, lisping through his broken teeth. "Why are these lorries going north instead of south? They're trying to throw Panyushkin off the track as well, are they?"

"You still don't seem to understand the situation," Strand said wearily. "Tomorrow's offensive isn't just against Jhamjarh. There's two divisions scheduled to jump off for British India at five o'clock tomorrow—with New Delhi as the objective."

Derby sagged back against the seat, staring at the back of Strand's neck. "I don't believe it," he muttered.

The dust from the trucks ahead seemed to thicken. After a few minutes of sandblasting, Strand fell back. It made little difference. We continued to be smothered in dust. Moreover, the car engine was overheating.

Finally he pulled off the road and nudged the car behind a stand of trees where it would not be seen from the road. He switched off.

As the car hissed away, Derby said, "Well, this isn't a very good start for the journey, is it? One lot of lorries blocking us ahead, and another lot coming up behind."

"Just a few kilometers ahead we shall be turning off this road," Strand said. "So we might as well wait until they clear out of the way."

The sun burned down. Some vultures came over to take a speculative look at us. An entomological scout noted our position then flew off to inform the other flies.

"Why are you doing this, Heinrich?" I asked after a moment. "Helping us get away." And when he didn't answer immediately: "What's turned you against your communist chums?"

"My communist chums? They are no chums of mine, chum."

"They're not?"

"I hate those commie bastards as much as you do, Captain Carruthers."

"Captain who?" Derby enquired from the back.

"But damn it, it was because you discovered I was anti-communist that you denounced me," I said indignantly.

"Who's Captain Carruthers?"

"When you said how much you hated the commies," Strand said, "I thought Panyushkin had put you up to it. That it was another of his goddamn tricks. He was already pretty suspicious of me. I thought you were a plant and he was using you to trap me."

"Let me get this straight," I said. "While I was trying to convince you I was a dedicated White Russian—which I wasn't—wasn't Russian, that is—I was putting my foot in it—thinking you were White as well—which you are. But that you were pretending to be Red. But you thought I was really Red, getting you to admit you were White—which you—"

"Never mind that," Derby said truculently. "What I want to know is, where does Captain Carruthers come in?"

Strand was busy lighting up. Derby glowered more than ever when Strand failed to offer him a cigarette. "It was only after I had denounced you," Strand said, "that I realized you really did hate the commies.

"So now," he continued, inhaling savagely, "you're wondering why I joined up in the first place if I hated them so much, *ja*? Well, it's simple enough—I didn't know about communism then, and about people like Panyushkin, and his ideas about turning Germany into a Soviet republic. I needed the money, and Sharif and his boys were offering one hell of a lot of it. And I wanted to go on flying until the German air force got going again. I thought it would be a real vacation out here, with flying as a bonus, *ja*? So I made like I was one of them. I think they were not convinced, but they needed experienced flyers, especially somebody like me with staff experience." He stared broodingly at his cigarette tip. The smoke from it was inscribing a vertical blue line in the starved atmosphere. "But I had to be real careful of Panyushkin—make sure I attended every one of his goddamn lectures on Marxism, and sound gung-ho for Lenin. But all the time, Jesus, I was crazy to get home again, away from that crazy bastard Sharif and his Russian masters. He doesn't know that's what they are, of course. He really believes that when he takes over India, they'll let him keep it."

"You really think he can beat the British Empire?" Derby asked scornfully, temporarily forgetting about Captain Carruthers.

"Listen," Strand said, turning so sharply to face Derby that drops of sweat sprayed from his face, "Sharif has been planning this for seven years, just waiting for the right moment. He's studied the American War of Independence, and believes there are many similarities in the situation. And he believes—and I think he's goddamn right—that he'll get one hell of a lot of help from his fellow Muslims the moment he can show he's got the British on the run. And in my opinion, buddy," he ended, raising his voice so that, half a mile away, a pair of buzzards rose in alarm from a heap of something, "that will happen one minute after he hits British territory."

He paused to run a hand over his bristly blond hair to scratch the crown vigorously. "And let me tell you what he's got to do it with. He's got four divisions of troops trained by Prussian officers and NCOs. I've seen them exercising. They're good. They've learned to move. *Jesus* have they learned to move. They make our offensive in 1918 look like a tortoise race. And they can concentrate fire-power like nobody's ever seen before. And they have all the latest equipment—French communications, Swedish eighty-eight mil LFGs, Italian self-ranging mortars, fast armored cars designed and made specially for them in America. Six thousand vehicles of one kind or another he's got, so that no Khalil doughboy needs to march more than ten paces. In short, they have a small army, but it's mobile like you've never seen before. Now tell me, *buddy*—what've you got?"

When Derby merely squirmed and scowled, I said, "Well, let's see. There's Hamish McQuarry of the Fifty-first with his deadly sporran...but he's on the North-West Frontier at the moment...Jesus, Heinrich, they really do have all that, tucked away in the hills back there?"

"Not in the hills any more," he replied. "Half of their army's on the move right this minute, and the other half is already in place, in staging areas."

I was about to ask urgent questions, but was interrupted by a derisive snort from Derby. "Ridiculous," he lisped. "So they're well-armed. But what's four divisions against a whole empire?"

Strand replied with such superior scorn that Derby almost broke the rest of his teeth in his anger. "How long did it take your empire to defeat a handful of Boer farmers?" he asked. "Three years, *ja*? And the Boers had little more than rifles—not like Khaliwar's dozens of field guns, scores of mortars, hundreds of machine-guns, thousands of trucks adapted specially to this climate, three regiments of armored cars, two hundred fifty aircraft—"

"Two hundred and fifty?" That was me. "That many, eh? And the army really knows how to use this stuff?"

"I don't see why Sharif can't take India," Strand said, calming down. "And he could make it real hard for the British to get a foothold again, assuming that a disillusioned India would let them. They only rule now because Congress, the princes, and the populace think they're invincible. Or at least pretend to think it. They—"

He stopped. A mile along the road lazy dust was rising: the 'headquarters unit.' Strand carefully extinguished his cigarette.

As the column of trucks strained by, I watched with considerably augmented interest, noting with a shock that the dozen or so vehicles were traveling at least as fast as our touring car. And that while all the trucks seemed to have the same basic design, they were varied in shape or length, as if each had a different function—one a command post, perhaps, another a mobile fuel dump. At least three of them had long aerials whipping about.

"My god, they're wireless-equipped."

"So are his aircraft," Strand whispered, seemingly quite

proud about it as if it were his armed forces we were talking about.

"Really?"

In no time at all the convoy had disappeared into its own dust cloud. A disturbed silence fell.

"What was that unit, exactly?" Derby asked. Even he sounded subdued, shaken by the air of efficiency with which the column had been going about its business.

"I am saying no more," Strand said, lighting another cigarette.

"Why not?" I asked.

"I must have something to bargain with."

"How d'you mean?"

Strand treated me to a hard grin. "You don't think I'm taking these risks for nothing, do you? Just because I hate the commies?" He pursed out a feather of smoke, then added a couple of smoke rings. "I'm going home. And for that I need money."

"Oh, I see." I twitched as sweat streamed down my back. "You'll tell us about their plans in return for your passage home."

"In return for a lot more than that, Captain Carruthers," Strand said.

"That's not Captain Carruthers," Derby said scornfully. "That's Bartholomew Bendy."

Strand was staring. "You are Bendy? The commander of...?"

"That's him," Derby said. "That's Bendy."

"Whatjamean, Bendy?" I said. "You know perfectly well it's Bandy."

"Oh, all right," Derby said, "if you want to be pernickety."

"You are really General Bendy?" Strand asked, with rather unflattering incredulity.

After a moment he began to laugh. "Panyushkin had the commander of the enemy air force in his hands and did not know it? *Mein Gott....*"

"Yes, of course," he went on, starting the engine, but still gazing at me wonderingly. "I thought there was something about you...Well, Herr General, your air force is the one factor that has most worried Sharif-ul-Khalil and his command."

"I guess it would."

"Which is why his number one priority is to wipe it out," he said as undramatically as if he were offering a recipe for treacle tart.

After a moment I said carefully, "And as you were on the planning staff, you know exactly how he proposes to accomplish this."

"Right," he smiled. "But don't worry, Herr General, I will give all the details to your Maharajah as soon as he has given me enough money to get back to Germany, and a little extra, perhaps, to live in a little comfort, *ja?*"

He backed the car slowly and carefully out of the trees.

"I quite understand," I replied, my voice wobbling as the car bumped painfully over the ground on its way back to the road. "You are taking great risks for us, and you might not be safe from Panyushkin until you are out of the country."

"You are very understanding, General."

"Well, I appreciate that you must have something in the bank. But could—" I stopped as the car bounced back onto the road. "Could you at least give us a rough idea of what's in store for us?"

Strand thought about it for a moment as he accelerated northward, for our journey south. "Well, I'll tell you just one thing," he said, "so you'll understand that there is an urgency about getting back to your aerodrome in time. And that is that your air base is to receive special treatment one hour before the general offensive against Jhamjarh and British India. And I don't just mean it's going to be bombed to hell."

He paused to mop his head and neck. The streaming sweat was drawing pink lines in the dust on his face. "Take my word for it, Herr Bendy," he concluded, "if you don't get back in time, every one of your men will be dead. By six o'clock tomorrow, you will have no air force left."

Me in a Cloud of Dust

At first, Derby and I were not particularly worried. We were now well on our way and it was still only eleven ack emma. That gave us the rest of the day to get back to Djelybad, which was now only about 130 miles away. We were maintaining a good average speed, about thirty miles an hour, judging by Strand's map. And this alternate route down the east side of Khaliwar was not as bad as we'd feared. Part of it was little better than a series of potholes and concrete-hard grooves strung together with ox buns and donkey droppings, but long stretches were nearly as good as the main road south. We felt confident that we would be back in plenty of time to take precautions against an aerial strafe or bombing, or whatever it was they had planned for us.

The other traffic on the road seemed to be our worst problem. As we neared the Parbati River the villages proliferated, and there was increasing competition for road space. Had the peasants insisted on their rights, we would hardly have reached the Jhamjarh border by August bank holiday. Fortunately they had been trained to clear out of the way whenever Brahmins or white gods like us appeared. As soon as they heard or saw our motor car they whacked their beasts frantically off the road. Which was just as well, as Strand's system was to drive at the highest possible speed with the horn blaring.

At noon we reached the river, which at that time of year was hardly more than a trickle of diarrhea. There we halted near the cracked bank to top-up the tank with fuel from the two-gallon cans strapped to the back of the car. We also unpacked the bread, goat cheese, and fruit that Strand had stowed. But the cheese had melted into a rarebit, and anyway we had little appetite after all that bouncing and swaying under a sun that rendered even the fabric top of the car too hot to touch. All we could bear to eat was the fruit. And although Strand had loaded gallons of water, the supply was diminishing at an alarming rate. Finally he suggested rationing. We were to allow ourselves just one cupful per hour until we reached a safe supply. He refused to consider making a purchase from the *pani-wallahs* in the numerous villages in the area, distrusting the purity of the water at this time of year. He was also unwilling to enter a village in case we encountered a policeman or official who could contact the capital. It was highly unlikely that communications had been established with these remote villages but Strand was not inclined to chance it.

After reviving the car with water, fuel, and shade, we gathered round Strand's map for an idea as to what sort of terrain we would face from now on. The map indicated that there was a jungle about four miles ahead which looked as if it might extend right to the Jhamjarh border. This heartened Derby and I, as a jungle, we thought, would protect us from the sun. We were both getting badly sunburned though we'd hardly been out in the open for more than a few seconds at a time.

The notion that jungle cover might soon be needed came just as we had finished reloading the car and were about to start off again. Derby suddenly looked up.

"What?"

"Didn't you hear it?"

We listened. The faint drone of an aircraft diminished, then strengthened.

To evade the sun we had thrust the car deep into a tangle of *dhatura* trees. It was just as well, for two minutes later the airplane, a two-seater Halberstadt familiar from wartime days, flew low overhead. It was obviously following our rutted road.

The Khaliwar insignia, a black Sanskrit cross like four broken arms against a green ground, was disturbingly clear against the brown camouflage.

"Perhaps it's just a training flight," I hazarded.

"No. They are looking for us," Strand said.

We stared up through the *dhatura* trees with their white, bell-shaped flowers, as the machine continued on, until it melted into a slice of optical illusion.

In the hard stillness came a pattering sound—sweat from Derby's battered face, dripping onto a fat leaf. "God," he muttered, "I'll never complain about English weather again."

Silence resumed, thick and oppressive. Though the vegetation overhead seemed comprehensive, yet the sunlight still slashed through, burning the backs of necks.

Strand looked grim. "Panyushkin must have gotten on to me already," he said.

"'s'alright," Derby said, scornful of Strand's anxiety, "we'll soon be hidden in the jungle."

Strand glanced at him as if he were an idiot, and ordered us curtly into the car.

A couple of minutes later we were back on the yellow road, pushing a way through a heat that felt almost solid.

The light, too, was torture. I would have given two hours' water ration for a pair of sunglasses.

We reached the jungle unobserved. It began as an increasing density of sabre-toothed shrubbery, then a series of tatty palmyra palms, and then, suddenly, there was complete cover, a canopy courtesy of close-packed mango trees. "We should be all right now, all the way to the border," Derby said defiantly, as if saying it would make it so. He had hardly finished speaking when the two-seater, whose engine noise must have been muffled by the vegetation, flew overhead at the perfect moment—from their point of view—as we were crossing a glade.

The Halberstadt flew on, following the road. Strand accelerated back under cover.

"Do you think they saw us?"

He didn't answer, but drove faster than ever, concentrating

on keeping the wheels out of the cart grooves embedded in the road. Meanwhile I looked around at the jungle in a disillusioned way. This was not what I had envisaged. I had read about the Indian jungle in the Kipling stories, and had imagined it to be a lush and leafy abundance through which humorous animals peered and squinted, as in Henri Rousseau paintings. The actuality was a distinct let-down. We were hurtling through a miserable affair of arthritic trees, hummocks and rises of gray grass, the occasional toddy palm, masses of seemingly dead bamboo-like fields of elephantiasis-stricken corn, and various other items of sunblasted woodwork. There was some wildlife, but mostly it was filthy monkeys. The jungle was emaciated, and looked as if even a monsoon deluge would never revive it.

Moreover, it didn't even provide decent cover. We were out in open patches almost as often as we were in shade. At one point, ten minutes after entering the jungle, we found ourselves in the open for nearly half a mile, over a field of yellow grass, before regaining the next turmoil of trees.

We waited tensely for any evidence that the Halberstadt had seen us, but nothing had happened by the time we were forced to slow behind a trudge of *vaisyas* with bundles on their heads.

"He can't have seen us," Derby said.

Strand was too unhappy to snort derisively or even to sound his horn. He waited for the farmers to move off the road of their own accord. As for me, I was busy putting myself in the position of the observer up there. If I were him I would have been surveying every yard of the road as the pilot flew alongside it. I would not have missed a large black touring car on a jaundice-yellow track. And having spotted it, I would not have given the game away by reacting, like coming back for a second look. I would have continued to fly onward as if nothing had happened.

What then? "Did you say they have radios?" I shouted over the whine of the engine as Strand accelerated again.

Strand glanced at me, then turned back to the road. "Yes. Every observation machine and bomber in the fleet has a morse transmitter and receiver," he said, "and even some of the single-seat Fokkers."

"So he can contact Ujipatan valley?" I asked, pointing upward.

"Not from here. The range is too great."

"He didn't see us," Derby said. "I'm sure of it."

"But he can contact other aircraft?" I asked.

"Within thirty miles, *ja*. And they can pass it on to Ujipatan."

"*Merde*."

"I think so, too," Strand said.

And we were right. The Halberstadt returned twenty minutes later with the hired help: two red and green DVIIs, reflecting wicked sunlight as they banked onto their wingtips. And naturally they arrived while we were in the open.

Perhaps they were inexperienced, or perhaps they were Russians. They attacked incompetently, from the side instead of lining up with the road. They might also have achieved a little more if they had taken advantage of the sun, even if it was nearly overhead. As it was, Strand had plenty of opportunity to take rudimentary avoiding action by braking sharply and then speeding up.

It was enough to throw the enemy pilots. The first sprayed the ground far ahead of us. The second missed so completely that we couldn't even see where the bullets had gone, though some of them were tracer.

Then we were back under the trees, the sun taking flash photos of us through the dusty foliage.

Another open space appeared all too soon, but as it was only a hundred yards' stretch with a palisade of bamboo on the far side, Strand did not hesitate. We were in the open for only half a minute. Nothing happened. Either the fighters had no time to dive on us, or their reflexes were sluggish.

But after another mile, when the jungle opened up again, we were faced with a fairly considerable stretch of yellow track, a quarter mile of it. Moreover the track was almost straight.

Strand stamped on the brake pedal. The car shuddered to a stop, out in the open. The engine stalled.

As Strand tried to start it again, Derby bawled, "Hurry up, hurry, they're coming." And he continued to shout and bounce up and down, until I shouted to him not to be a back-seat driver.

We had an impression of aircraft darting about in the dazzling, burning sky, and a rising engine note. Any moment I expected a meteoric shower of lead or steel or tracer or explosive ammo. The car gasped and blustered, a sitting target. God, the Khaliwar Air Force was slow. We seemed to have been in the open for minutes.

I started to get out and push, when the engine caught. Strand managed to reverse back under cover just before an airplane flashed close overhead, popping and bellowing. Bullets gnawed and chewed on the road, sending up dinky dust clouds. Sliced bamboo rained.

Strand continued to grind the car in reverse deep into the trees before stopping with a neckjolt, and switching off.

As the thrumming died and the aircraft rasped frustratedly above the trees, there came a massed screaming of parrots. Hundreds and hundreds of them, angrily flapping, bright green parrots, tenors, sopranos, basses, castrati, all squawking and hollering, alarmed or indignant at the disturbance of racketing tappets and blaring exhausts from above and ground level.

They were all hopping mad. And they were not the least placated when Spandau guns stuttered over the howling of engines, and bullets slashed at distant foliage. Expecting to be stitched, we flung ourselves from the car and dove into the undergrowth, forgetting about snakes.

Several additional strafing runs were made before we realized that the enemy were shooting into the trees three or four hundred feet away, at the point where we had backed into the jungle.

By and by the shooting stopped, and the aircraft went back on patrol, droning, droning. At the jungle edge, grit hovered, imprisoned by bars of sunlight.

"Well, what now?" John burst out; and, when I looked at

Strand: "Well, you're the senior officer—why don't *you* make a decision now and then?"

"This is Strand's operation, John. I'm just here to salute."

"Yes, you seem to be dodging quite a bit of responsibility lately," he replied, mumbling, and hiding his face in the map.

Strand, dabbing a sweat-blistered forehead with an already dripping handkerchief, watched me surreptitiously as if wondering how I would react to this criticism by a subordinate.

The only action I took was to gaze at John thoughtfully as he sat there under a eucalyptus, with his head in a map, his entire form black with sweat and annoyance. I had often envied John his successful post-war treatment. During the war he had suffered as much as anyone in seeing nearly every one of his friends killed or maimed. One of them, his cousin and boyhood hero, had been sacrificed just twenty-four hours before the Armistice. But he seemed to have exorcised the devils that tormented so many men of imagination. He had resorted to solitude rather than psychoanalysis. After the war he had lived alone in a hut on Vancouver Island for eighteen months, gradually overcoming the fury and depression. "Nobody is that helpless in the grip of fate or psychic hurt," he said once. "We're all ultimately in charge of our own lives, whatever the dream-dissectors say." Which words, recollected once or twice over the past few months, had made me annoyed at my own failure to permit time to heal the injury.

I had come to admire Derby's strength of character. But since coming to India, he seemed to have gone downhill at a rate of knots and, since our escape, the deterioration seemed to have accelerated. The situation was the opposite to what one would have expected. John, inheritor of that English quality, partly a matter of humor in adversity, which had seen his countrymen through crisis and calamity for centuries, should have become a tower of strength by now; while Strand, in command and under pressure, should have turned arrogant and intolerant, but instead was becoming more brave, dependable and human every minute. It was all very disappointing. One liked to have one's prejudices confirmed.

An incident that occurred a few minutes later did little to restore John to his former proportions. While Strand and I were crouching at the edge of the jungle, surveying the open spaces ahead through field glasses and trying to decide how to get across it in safety, a tiger wandered up.

The first I knew of it was when we were on our way back to the car, stumbling over jungle debris, and Strand suddenly gripped my arm with a hand like a tourniquet.

"Stand still."

I followed his gaze. A tiger was standing on its hind legs, peering into the car.

Aircraft snarled overhead, ceaselessly circling, invisible in the stabbing sky. The tiger, though, was silent.

Derby, in the car, was pressing himself backward, his face bloodless. This, in combination with the bruising, made him look as if he had died last Christmas.

His eyes were alive enough, though, even if his voice was a trifle feeble as it said:

"Help."

The tiger had its gigantic front paws on the side of the car, and was peering in at Derby a little short-sightedly, blinking its big yellow eyes.

"Don't move," Strand hissed across to Derby. "Just stare at it. If it is not a man-eater, it will leave sooner or later."

"Thanks very much," Derby whimpered, sweat raining onto his chest.

The tiger, which, stretched up like that, looked at least ten feet long, not counting the twitching tail, had seen us; yet it turned back for another inspection of Derby, who must have been emanating one hell of a stink of delicious fear and sweat, enough to whet the appetite of even the most replete example of the species *Panthera tigris*. And Strand, the only one who had brought along any equipment at all, did not have a weapon to hand. So there was nothing we could do but watch and wait.

The magnificent orange beast, stripes rippling over its muscles, continued to stare at cowering Derby. Its nose was twitching—possibly a little fastidiously because Derby, as he admitted later, was smelling badly, apparently not just with sweat and fear. As it shifted a paw, its claws grinded loudly over one of the fuel cans.

I looked around for a stick or some sort of missile. Fortunately it was not needed, for after a while the tiger, treating Derby to a final, perhaps rather wistful glance, contracted itself back onto all fours, and then turned and wandered off until it was swallowed up by dusty olive vegetation.

While Strand, reminded that there were hazards other than Fokkers, dug out his Lüger and strapped it on, Derby gibbered for a solid five minutes. "My God, my God," he kept saying, "did you see it? Fifteen feet long if it was an inch."

"Ten, anyway."

"It wasn't bloody looming over you like the Savoy Hill mast! I tell you it was fifteen feet long, with teeth..."

"Yes, but wasn't it a beauty?" I said admiringly.

Derby was too shaken even to glare. The tiger's eyes had quite unnerved him. As we drove slowly forward to the edge of the jungle, he slumped back and sat limp as a rag doll, looking shrunken and sodden.

We managed to cross the next stretch of open country uninjured if not unscathed, thanks to Strand, who drove like a demon over the rutted track.

For a moment I thought the worst experience was going to be the heat. For the past half hour I had been protected from the sun inside a relatively cool womb of jungle. Now as we roared into the open, the heat smote me like a sandbag, and the sweat threatened to drown my eyeballs.

I would not have believed it possible that the white hot sky could radiate with such smothering devotion. The light alone was so intense that we couldn't even scan the hellish heavens for imminent danger. It permitted only slitted eyes, and I could see nothing but swirling dots and optical thistledown.

The enemy didn't catch up with us until we were fifty yards from cover on the far side, and only one of the fighters managed to loose off a few shots from its twin machine-guns. They were, however, competently aimed, for once. We never actually saw the airplane, but the proof that it was there was a bang and a shower of glass, accompanied by the howl of its engine and a tardy popping sound just audible over the thump-thump-thump of our bottoming suspension system.

Then we were under blessed cover again, and Strand was slowing for a quick review of the damage; which turned out to be a few holes in the top, and a shattered windscreen.

We felt that we had gotten off lightly. But: "They're getting in some practice," Strand said. "They'll be ready for us next time."

Next time was only five or six miles further on, where the road wound up a hillside. This time, venturing into the open did not seem too great a risk. There was no straight stretch, and the track curved around the hill.

Strand, refusing all offers to spell him at the wheel, drove as fast as he dared, while Derby and I tried to keep a lookout for diving aircraft. This was almost impossible in the wildly bouncing vehicle, and the first attack was unanticipated. A green Fokker came in from the side, firing continuously. He broke off, almost ploughing into the hillside. The next pilot dived and zoomed on us, but was able to loose off just a few rounds. The third took his place almost immediately but failed to get his sights on us before we skidded around a corner. For a second or two he was actually below us, blasting down a shallow ravine before pulling up in that remarkable way of the Fokker DVII. Even in this heat it could still climb at a forty-five-degree angle. We could see right down into his cockpit. He had odd socks.

A holy cow saved us on the next open stretch of road. It almost made one believe in holiness.

Pursued by fighters, we heeled into a bend and encountered a cow, wandering in the middle of the road. Beyond it were half a dozen peasants wrapped in mutton cloth. They were women, following a cart laden with the kind of market produce that made you avert your eyes.

Strand stamped on the brakes, and the wheels locked and skidded in the dirt. He lost control, the car went shooting off the road, and bounced violently down a steep slope, lashing down bushes and sending up a bow wave of loose stones.

Simultaneously the leading fighter opened fire with explosive ammunition, raking the part of the road that we would have been occupying had it not been for the cow.

We reached the bottom of the slope unscathed, but feeling as if we'd been processed in one of those new-fangled washing machines that Eaton's were selling back home—to find ourselves back on the same road, and traveling along a stretch that we had already negotiated, which seemed decidedly redundant. That was how we knew that the bullets had raked the road just ahead of us. We drove past the evidence: splotches of scarlet on white cloth, and a disemboweled cow.

The agony of that incident was that we couldn't stop to find out if the two fallen figures were dead or injured. Other peasants were gathering around the casualties. If we had joined them, Strand believed, the Fokkers would have fired into the lot of us.

The jungle ended completely while we were still miles from the border. And to worsen the situation, the road ran more or less straight over the flattest, obstruction-free plain we had yet encountered.

The sun having dipped to a more obliging angle, we were now able to see the opposition clearly. There were no fewer than eight aircraft up there, two observation machines and six fighters. Even as we counted, another pair of Fokkers flew up and joined the wheeling throng. As they did so, two others peeled off, presumably heading for home at the end of the day shift.

With that sort of devotion to duty, the chances of our charging successfully across miles of wide open country seemed pretty weedy.

We huddled under the final instalment of jungle, sheltered by tall palmyra and hanging gardens of creeper. Around us, monkeys were discussing us and parrots scolding us, oblivious of the heat which to us seemed worse than ever. I should not have believed it possible for humans to survive in such heat, even in a hammock and surrounded by electric fans, blocks of ice, and a platoon of *punkah wallahs*.

Impersonating a zombie, I helped Strand to cool the engine before it dried up and burned out, to refill the tank from the fuel cans, and to pick out shards of glass from the windscreen.

John, who was suffering the worst from the heat was writhing on a blanket, too exhausted to sleep, too peevish and feverish to eat. His irritation was not the least soothed when Strand, chores completed, announced that he must rest, and promptly fell asleep in about half a minute. "Look at him lying there with his mouth open," John hissed. "Swine."

"We'd be dead if it wasn't for him."

"Exactly. If he hadn't interfered we wouldn't have had to go through all this. And another thing: what right has he to sleep when I can't?" He suddenly picked up a long black centipede. "I'll teach him," he said, and I was only just in time to prevent him from dropping the centipede into Strand's mouth.

Perhaps John was hungry. "We still have a long way to go, John," I said, proferring a hunk of elastic bread and an open tin of mixed meat and veg. It was available because I myself had rejected it a few minutes previously.

"Don't want it."

"Come on, eat a bit."

"Stop looming over me! You're spattering me with sweat."

"You must eat something, John."

"Not hungry."

"Come on, down the little red lane."

"Up your little red lane."

"You must keep up your strength."

"Why?"

"If you eat your vegetables," I said averting my eyes from the slimy contents of the tin, "maybe Strand will let you have a nice juicy mango." But he turned his face to the wall, or rather to a peepul tree.

So I lay back as well, wondering if I would have the energy to sit up again. I felt as if my clothes had just been picked out of a hot tub and fed through a mangle, with me in them.

Like Derby, I found it impossible to rest under the torrid pressure and the menacing drone of aircraft, circling, circling. In the last few minutes the engine note seemed to have deepened, turning into a growling baritone. So now I was having aural hallucinations as well. It sounded as if they had a whole squadron up there. As I squinted upward I caught a glimpse of one of the airplanes in a gap in the branch-cluttered canopy. In the second that it appeared and disappeared, it looked enormous. I assumed I was back to optical illusions again.

The position of that airplane suggested that they knew where we were to within one or two hundred feet. I wondered uneasily what they were planning now. Presumably they were tapping out dits and dahs to each other on their morse keys and listening to ideas and suggestions on their earphones as to how to liquidate us. By now they must be frantic, not just to prevent us from getting through with Strand's presumably vital information, but to repay us for the frustration and discomfort that they, too, must be suffering in this smothering temperature.

Their dedication to the task of killing us, the intensity of their efforts, and the disruption it must be causing to their plans for the morrow, made me very much aware that Strand's information must be very important indeed. They were tiring out numerous pilots who ought to have been resting, ready for tomorrow's offensive. They were also wearing out dozens of aircraft and taking the risk that our side might be alerted by this desperate aerial activity. I mean, listen to them up there. It sounded as if there was an armada above the trees.

They were certainly not going to these lengths merely to stop us from warning of an impending attack, when it must already be obvious from their troop movements that an attack was coming.

I made up my mind. I crawled over to Strand and shook him. He came instantly awake.

"*Ja*, what is it?"

"Strand, I must know now what your information is."

He groaned, rubbed his eyes, and groaned again. "Oh, you bastard, you woke me up for that?"

"It is important, Heinrich."

"Why now, anyway?" he mumbled.

"What if you're killed? The information will die with you."

"Cheerful bastard...but don't worry," he said, reviving and stretching, "I do not intend to die."

"Damn it, Heinrich, you'll get your money, even if I have to pay it myself. But I must know."

Strand stood up. He had cut off the long trousers of his uniform at the thigh. The shorts made him look more ragged than ever. As for his tunic, it was so saturated it adhered to him like a gouda rind. And though his voice remained cheerful his square face was haggard as a theatre curtain. "I'm sorry," he began, just as the first bomb was released, "but I shall tell you only after your Maharajah has promised me the mon—"

That was when we heard the thin, whistling sound. A second later the bomb exploded fifty feet away with a bang that, collected by a thousand leaves, amplified itself into the ending of the world. And then another crash and flash of fire, even closer.

We were saved because we were lying flat. Even so, the shock waves, loaded with dust and branches, stink bugs, monkey limbs and green feathers, almost rolled us over the ground like barrels.

Instinctively, as another sequence of bombs whistled down, I covered my head. Interesting how such danger invariably inspires the protection of the head and face rather than, for instance, the groin—rather putting the idea of man's preoccupation with sex in its place and suggesting that, deep down, a man values his mug rather than his mentule. Though I admit that I might have drawn up my knees at the same time as I was shielding the old frontispiece—I don't remember.

Another four explosions followed, then several more, at varying distances. Fragments of trees pelted down, the sunbeams slanting through the jungle grew blue and dense, dust turned into solid pillars. The air beat on our ears.

More bombs, more explosions, more bombs, sometimes bursting in pairs, almost simultaneously. One crashed so close that I was lifted inches off the ground. I was grinding my face into the dirt, now, fingers in ears and mouth open to lessen the risk of burst eardrums. Thoughts were coming thick and fast as well, including the realization that the giant aircraft I had glimpsed through the leaves had not been an optical distortion after all. It really had been a large aircraft. A bomber. Almost certainly a Gotha. I could see it plainly on the screen of memory, and couldn't understand how I could ever have doubted my senses. I should have perceived it and allowed the warning message to get through.

Bombs continued to cascade into the jungle. Tiny fires flickered in the rolling dust, monkeys screamed and hurled themselves prodigious distances through lacerated tree tops. Cordite smoke swirled, hugging the trees. Unseen engines groaned and howled, the hot earth under us drummed and thumped and something fell on me, beating me between the shoulder blades.

The onslaught went on and on, some bombs falling quite far away, others close enough to whip at our wet, stinking clothes. And then it all died down as abruptly as it had begun; to be replaced, after a minute or two, by the resumed droning of circling aircraft.

Slowly we leaned up, dazed and half-concussed, a miraculously unharmed trio. Flames crackled somewhere in the jungle. White smoke drifted, wraithlike, bright green parrots flew dementedly. One of them hit a branch and dropped to the ground like a shot duck. There was another lying just two feet from me. It was the parrot that had thumped onto my back.

I caught Strand's eye. "They must have brought up the Gothas," he said.

He came to a decision. It did not cause him much satisfaction, that was obvious.

"Perhaps I had better tell you," he said.

"What?"

"I will tell you what I know of their plans."

I was slow, dazed by the din. "The details you were going to sell to the Maharajah?"

"I guess there's always a possibility that I shall not live, once we are in the open," he said, dusting himself down with a convincing air of nonchalance. "So I will tell you now. I will trust you to see that I am paid, *ja*? If I make it."

"Yes."

He walked unsteadily to the car, which, purely fortuitously, had been left in just enough of a hollow to protect it from blast, and reached into the glove compartment. Taking out an army-type notebook with attached pencil, he scribbled briefly. On his way back he staggered slightly, as if his balance had been affected by the bombing.

"If I don't make it," he said, holding out a scrap of paper, "You'll send the money to my mother in Dresden, *ja*?"

"Well...all right."

"I want two thousand. English pounds."

"All right."

"The way things are back there, she could do with the money. Okay?"

"Okay."

"Okay." He glanced at Derby, but John didn't seem to be taking much interest. He was staring sullenly at the dead parrot. "Well...Sharif and Panyushkin have a pretty realistic picture of what they have to face over the next few weeks, and most of it doesn't lose them one minute of sleep. They know the British Army is scattered all over hell and gone, and most of the air force isn't even in the country, let alone ready to fight.

"That leaves only the Jhamjarh Air Force. And that's the only thing that worries them."

Derby started nervously as a *koel* bird uttered its rising screech; and started again when I started coughing. Patches of burning jungle were smouldering my lungs.

"So you're their number one target. They know you're the only outfit that can cause them any trouble at all."

"I hope you don't expect to be paid just for that." Derby said.

"No," Strand said, equably enough. "What I'm selling you is this: Sharif has been secretly infiltrating men into Jhamjarh for weeks. They should all be in place by now, ready for their big moment before dawn tomorrow."

I sat up, staring, but Derby persisted in petulance. "That's still not worth two thousand," he mumbled.

"How about this? The infiltrators are former criminal tribesmen who've been specially trained by the Khaliwar Army for commando-style operations. We've been referring to them as the dacoits." He paused to light a cigarette—though how he could bear to draw more smoke into his lungs I don't know. The jungle was burning all around us in small, fiery patches. The blue smoke was growing thicker every minute. "They have two objectives tomorrow. The dacoits who are hiding out in Djelybad are to storm the City Palace at four tomorrow morning. The Maharajah and his son are to be taken alive if possible, but it doesn't matter if they're bumped off. My own feeling is that the dacoits won't even try to take them alive.

"The main force, several hundred of them if everything's gone according to plan, are to storm your air base from the west—operating out of Daja."

"Daja?" Derby and I looked at each other. "The village just west of the aerodrome?"

"Three kilometres west," Strand said, coughing.

"It was used by lepers," Derby said. "But it's deserted now. I've flown over it often enough. It—"

"Believe me, it won't be deserted by tonight, bo. It'll be packed with dacoits. And their orders are pretty simple. Everybody on the air base is to be killed, without exception. No wounded, no prisoners, nothing." He looked at me squarely. "Tell me, General, what chance do you think they have of succeeding?"

I didn't need to ponder that question. "If there's hundreds of these infiltrators, the men won't stand a chance, unless we warn them. Even then..." And I thought of Sigridur in the base hospital.

"That's Sharif's assessment, too," Strand said. "But just to make sure, your air base is also to be bombed.

"The surprise attack is planned for not later than four a.m. The bombing attack is to come at five. And Sharif doesn't care if the dacoits are still down there, slaughtering everybody—he just wants to make sure.

"Naturally the dacoits don't know they're to be bombed as well. Sharif hasn't told them. They're expendable," Strand said, wiping the sweat off his face, but smearing it with grime in the process. He took up his solar topee and planted it firmly on his cropped head, and continued as calmly as if he were giving us a weather forecast, "I will tell you a few other details, including what I know about the attack on the City Palace—I was involved mainly in planning the destruction of your air force— but that's the important information. I think it will not be an exaggeration to say that unless you can warn your friends in time, and your Maharajah, they'll all be dead by breakfast tomorrow.

"And as I said, they're going for British India as well, at the same time. I think they'll have New Delhi inside a week."

Looking Hot and Bothered

At eight o'clock that evening we were out in the open again, driving ahead of an extravagance of dust, and expecting a convergence of bullets.

Before starting out, Strand had explained what he would try to do. After studying the terrain ahead for as far as the field glasses would reach, he had concluded that lateral evasion might just be possible, provided we gave him precise warnings. The ground on either side of the road seemed firm enough to accept the car wheels, its surface packed hard by months of unrelieved sun, only mildly pimpled here and there with rocks and dabs of vegetation. If he could zigzag on and off the road at the right moment, he said, we might just manage to survive the next few miles until we reached the border.

Of course we all knew that we could hardly avoid being aerated. Even Russian pilots could not keep missing a clumsy touring car while it bumped over a flat landscape, whether we zigzagged or not. But the only alternative was to skulk in the jungle until all hope of reaching Djelybad in time had gone.

Accordingly, sapped by heat, enfeebled by dehydration, enervated by fear and desperation, we tore from cover into a still ferocious sun.

After the smoke and jungle gloom it took our eyes a mile to adjust to the glare of evening. Whereupon we confirmed that the enemy had indeed been reinforced. Circling slowly at 1,000 feet were two white Gotha bombers, giant biplanes with deep-voiced engines sandwiched between a fantastic spread of wings.

Fortunately they had already attacked us in the jungle, so their racks and bays were empty. The danger would come from the Fokkers. And there were no fewer than a dozen of them up there, green as parrots. Slow to react to our abrupt dart into the open, they now came tumbling down the sky in a snarling competition to see who could get at us first, while the great Gothas remained in ringside seats. But the fighters were overeager, and got in each other's way. Two of them nearly collided, and we had covered another half mile before they got back into position.

At which moment Derby and I simultaneously hollered, "Now!" and Strand wrenched at the wheel. The lead Fokker fired at the same moment. Puffs of dust, tiny sparks, and whizzing gravel erupted from the dirt road, and the following aircraft fired at the same spot, though by then we were twenty feet off to one side, the car wheels drumming over the flat, flinty ground, and lashing through thorn bushes.

The other Fokkers in the queue had no chance to adjust before they were roaring past, ten feet up, their bareheaded pilots plainly visible above the squarish fuselages of those marvelous machines.

It took them all of two minutes to circle round again and line up behind us once more; and again, just before they fired, Derby yelled, and Strand skidded the car off the road at a good sixty miles an hour and in a huge cloud of orange dust which helped further to frustrate the enemy pilots. And once again the aircraft bringing up the rear failed to adjust to the situation before they overshot.

On their next attempt to pepper us, Strand varied his tactics by weaving the car from side to side. This raised an enormous cloud of dust from the verges behind which we must have hidden quite effectively, for no bullets came anywhere near us that time. Looking back from the S-bending car we could see the orange dust billowing high into the torrid air and hanging there.

Meanwhile the bombers confirmed that their assets had been disposed of by making no attempt to line up on us. They had unloaded everything into the jungle. The best they could manage now was to loose off occasional bursts of machine-gun fire from their turrets, but they were much too high for accurate shooting, and showed no inclination to come lower.

It couldn't last, of course. Belatedly the pilots began to anticipate the zigs and zags. Bullets struck the car with increasing frequency. Some of the bullets were explosive and made chung-ing noises. Still, half the distance to the border had been covered, and not one of us had yet been hit.

Strand was driving masterfully, veering on and off the road, wiggling from side to side, charging over the fields and dodging boulders. Unfortunately not all of them. The car hit a rock. The car began to squeal and vibrate. I bit my lip. Blood mixed with grit to form a metallic paste.

Behind, dust billowed. A biplane flashed through the orange cloud. Another, deciding on a new point of view, came in from the side. A disorderly line of spurts leaped over the ground, but the slugs gave up just before they reached the target. As the Fokker blasted overhead it very nearly collided with one of its brothers that was coming in from the rear. That was their second near-collision. Third time lucky, perhaps.

The white bombers continued to circle in the oven of the sky, observing, and the fighters to dive and zoom without much effect, and I actually began to believe that we might make it, that any second now they would run out of ammunition or we would reach the trees on the Jhamjarh side. And then one of their explosive bullets ignited the fuel cans strapped to the back of the car.

We had failed to anticipate that disaster. It had not occurred to any of us to ditch the spare fuel before setting off again. We realized our mistake quickly enough now, though, when the petrol whumped into a mass of flame, a great yellow glare of fire. The expanding gases blew Derby into the front seat.

It was fortunate that we were traveling at top speed when the cans exploded. The ball of fire which might otherwise have engulfed us was fanned backward by the rushing air. By the time it was ready to devour us, we were already throwing ourselves out of the vehicle.

There was another whoosh and boom as the last of the fuel exploded. Black smoke mixed with orange dust unrolled. We were enveloped in fumes and grit. Still staggering after leaving the car, I fell, striking my head against a rock. Derby was down, coughing and retching. He was feebly brushing himself. Strand was sprawled several feet away. He raised his head as a pair of Fokkers roared overhead, low enough to produce eddies in the smoke and dust.

As the gritty blizzard thinned and calmed, and another fighter roared overhead, I looked around dizzily. There was no cover for miles.

"Play possum—stay down," I croaked at the others. "Stay down."

They got the point, and lay still; which was just as well, for one after the other, the dozen aircraft flew in a way that suggested they were studying our prone figures for signs of life.

A minute later came the deep, booming unsynchronized beat of Gotha engines. The giant bombers, too, were taking a good look at our sprawled corpses beside the burning car. At least, I hoped that was how they were seeing us.

It was a wasted hope. Machine-gun fire erupted. Sand jumped about. Small stones, twinkling in the low sun, danced wildly around us. I had one ear to the ground. I could hear the earth thudding and squeaking.

Another storm of bullets churned up the hot ground. One struck a rock and, distorted, howled off into the distance with a thrilling sound.

Discolored dust, smoke from the blazing tourer, orange grit, fresh orange sandy dust from the stitching bullets enveloped us—mercifully taking time to settle. The smoke from the fiery car was funneling straight up.

"Anyone hurt?" I asked.

"No."

"No."

"Here they come again."

Snarling engines, sounding louder, softer, louder, as the

pilots maneuvered for their potshots, while the bombers continued to study the situation. And I had a sudden intuition that Panyushkin was in one of those bombers, and that is was he who had given the order to kick us when we were down.

I didn't actually see the aircraft, of course. I had my eyes shut so tight I felt grit grinding between the lids. The skin over my head, body, legs, felt as if it were crawling, cringing, as if every square inch of it was expecting to be favored with the awful impact of a bullet. On the Western Front I'd heard the sound of bullets striking mortal flesh. It was a dreadful, unmistakable sound, a wet, splintering smack that still punctuated my nightmares now and then.

The next spray of bullets, some of them explosive judging by the chirping sounds they made as they struck the ground around us, seemed to come closer than ever, tilling the orange earth around, behind, before, between us, lashing it into a drumming storm of grit, sand, pebbles—slugs spitting off some larger surfaces, whining off others.

Another respite. "Anyone hurt?"

"No."

"If you get me off, God," Derby was saying over and over, "I promise I'll be good, I promise, I promise."

My own flesh was screaming as well, anticipating that splintering smack, as I heard the Fokkers lining up for yet another attack. They were desperate to get us. We would have to survive another run. Would they stop at three? Three was a good number. Surely as none of us had moved during the previous strafes they would give up and go home to their sausages and sauerkraut, or borscht and black bread. It wouldn't be pork sausages—Muslims didn't eat pork. Except the pilots wouldn't be Muslims, would they? Unless that was an entry requirement. You had to be Muslim as well as communist. And what was it Hindus didn't eat? Beef, obviously. No wonder they were on such good terms with God. There were so few material distractions for Hindus, such as food, clothing, ballroom dancing, etc.

Here they came. The popping of the machine-guns grew loud. The earth under my ear thudded and squeaked. The vibration as the slugs bit and excavated made my head judder. I could feel the side of my head lifting a millimetre repeatedly under the thousand little impacts.

Something plucking at my leg. Oh. My. God. A snake. Taking cover from the attack. A krait. I had one and a half minutes to live.

I started to count. Eighty seconds to live. Seventy seconds. The rasping of aircraft continued. Sixty seconds. Fifty. Ridiculous to be more fearful of the clean bite of a snake rather than the mangling impact of a bullet. But there you are, nobody was completely rational in this world, not even me. I gave up counting, and waited.

The noise of mixed bombers and fighters seemed to be receding. Was it?

Yes! They were definitely fading away—unless I was growing deaf and dim because of the snake bite. Perhaps a krait bite deafened you as well as calling the heart out on strike for better pay and conditions.

The aircraft noises were fading out altogether. "I do believe we've fooled them," I said, starting to rise.

"Stay down, keep down," Strand shouted.

"What—"

"They will come back, I'm sure of it. Stay still."

Four minutes later: "They won't—" I began.

"Please. Just one more minute."

Sure enough, only a few seconds later there came the low muttering and whistling sound of a gliding aircraft, and a shadow flicked over the ground.

The aircraft must have throttled back miles away, hoping to catch us bending. If we'd moved they would have sent another squadron to strafe us. We would never have survived another attack.

The inspecting aircraft—Gotha—restored power right overhead. The sudden bellow of the engines coming from only a few feet away almost finished me off right there and then, with shock.

And then it was flying into the distance, climbing, fading.

We were still alive. We had survived eight hours of bombing

and machine-gunning. I marveled. And marveled that in all that time we had hardly more than glimpsed the aerial assassins between tatty branches and stabs of light.

Silence, glorious silence, broken only by a hissing and crackling from the still burning tourer, and discontented mutter from John Derby.

Slowly Strand sat up, shielding his eyes from the low sun as he checked the western horizon. I sat up too, but I was looking at my feet; staring stupidly at the ragged bullet hole in the trousers near the right ankle.

It was not a snake at all, but a very near miss. I felt quite faint at the thought of how near I'd come to losing a foot.

Strand was brushing sand from his cropped scalp. The brisk movement of his hand was arrested as he looked at Derby.

Derby had been stirring too, so I had not paid much attention to him until now. Now I saw the splotch of blood. I crawled over, calling his name. He had been hit in the neck.

An hour or so later we were across the border. And still about eighty miles from Djelybad with no means of communicating with the capital.

There had been no doubt that it was the border. Half a company of Khaliwar troops had marked the spot, encamped on either side of the road near a guard post identical to the one that Khooshie was to have been lured across. From the cover of a tangled hillock we had watched them for several minutes, and to our relief we had concluded that they were not on the lookout for fleeing monkeys, as some Indians called us white chaps. It appeared that Khaliwar communications did not extend to this post. The green-turbaned soldiers had looked somnolent in the heat of the evening. So we had little difficulty in circling past them, and rejoining our favorite road a mile inside Jhamjarh.

This despite Derby's heaviness. As I supported him from the left and Strand from the right, I was convinced he was steadily putting on weight. He really had been extraordinarily lucky, though he didn't agree about this when I told him. The bullet had hit him in the back of the neck and, as I informed him, passed through the sterno mastoid, missing the external carotid by a millimetre and "tearing itself out through the trapezius." " Jesus Christ, do you have to be so graphic?" he complained. Even Strand looked a bit squeamish. "There's considerable tissue discerption and laceration at the exit wound," I told him, or I started to, but, "Shut up, shut *up*," Strand said, wincing like mad.

Though most of the damage was muscular, there was enough bleeding to make me apprehensive at first that the artery had been nicked; but, "The gouts of blood seem sluggish enough," as I whispered loudly to Strand. The main problem was how to treat the injury when there was nothing to treat it with. We had only the tatters we were wearing. I couldn't use them for bandages, they were so foul with dirt and sweat. And of course there was no water to clean the wound. Everything had gone with the car. So I used urine— though there was precious little of that, either. "Now I really know what you think of me," Derby said as I trickled onto his neck.

Sterilizing the wound in this fashion—it wasn't my fault if some of it splashed into Derby's earhole—was accompanied by a little homeopathic medicine when, after some foraging, I fell across a broad-leafed plant of no known make. I made a poultice and dressing out of the leaves, moistening them, too, in the only available fluid and then clamping the mess to both sides of John's neck with whippy branches padded with other leaves. "I think I'm turning into a tree," he said. Fortunately we were well over the border before fainting administered a temporary anesthetic. After days of incarceration with little to eat I was in no condition to carry him further, so Strand heaved him onto his back and staggered on down the road; and on and on we tramped, and hours gibbered by. No, it couldn't have been hours, the sun was still above the ragged edge of the world, spraying horizontal light. I was sweat-drenched, sand-bagged by heat, Strand was panting like a donkey engine, and when he shook his head, the moisture sprayed from his face. Was that an airplane? Was it? I couldn't look for it. If you looked up the light stabbed to the back of your head. The sound faded out. I forgot I had even thought I heard it. I was distractingly stinking and filthy. The tatters of my Russian shirt and trousers could absorb no more sweat. My cardboard boots which had been scorned even by the jail guards were barely holding together. Inside they felt as if I was walking in excreta. And Derby was growing delirious. "Binky's too yellow to climb the clock tower," he said suddenly and very clearly, from Strand's back. "Pardon?" "He's not coming with us. Sucks to him."

There were thousands of villages in Jhamjarh and finally we reached one of them, a collection of small white houses and bazaar stalls. It was scattered between this secondary road south and a wide, shallow river. Around it were flat, cultivated fields. As we reached the one and only street, Derby fainted again. There was not a soul in sight but that was hardly surprising, I thought, as souls were invisible. For a despairing moment we thought we'd reached a deserted place, like Daja, the leper place, now presumably seething with poised dacoits, ready to shoot and slit and hack my air and ground people, my men and officers, my friends and my fiancée. The impression of emptiness was reinforced by the view into the nearest house. It wasn't a house but just a wall, with purple light, the color of the sky behind. No, wait, there were a few animals, the inevitable cow, helplessly wandering, with hardly the strength to flick at the flies. I hoped I'd never be treated with reverence. Silent monkeys gathering on a flat roof, peering at us while they nipped for fleas. Then children appeared, with stick-thin arms and brilliant eyes. And then grown-ups ventured into the wandering, dusty street. Now here was a line of street traders. Images of juice-seeping mangoes for sale drove us another few steps. The nearest stall sold brass pots. The villagers were surprised to see us, and stared. After a while a young man who had been sitting on his front steps reading *Vogue*, came forward and soon understood that a donation of water would be much appreciated. By the time we had trickled a little down Derby's gullet, and forced ourselves not to gulp the astonishing, cool, gliding, loving, mystical, anointing, baptizing, life-restoring *pani*, about fifty villagers had gathered round, to gaze in awe at the three mangled sahibs with the second-degree burns and lips like overdone sausages, and at the bloody man with the leafy necklace. The young man who spoke some English said his name was Rangovajan and that he had once been the servant of a memsahib. He offered to put Derby in his own bed, much to the dismay of his young wife; though she looked a little more reconciled to the arrangements when Strand gave her husband five rupees and I promised that if we had to leave the sick man with them, they would be amply rewarded. It certainly looked as if Derby would have to stay. Now that I could examine the wound less hectically I saw that it was much worse than I'd thought. The muscles of his neck and shoulder were badly torn, and he was now feverish and shocked. In the gloom of the house with its flaking walls, his pupils were about the diameter of pin points. He was hot and dry to the touch. His overalls were black with sweat but his skin was quite dry. Rangovajan disappeared. He had offered to fetch an old man, a great healer, who had arrived just the previous day and was now parked under a banyan tree on the outskirts of the village. The old man would heal Derby in a trice. He had raised a young girl from the dead, it was said, some years ago. I told Rangovajan not to bother, but he went anyway. Having received some tolerably clean cloth from Rangovajan's wife, I changed the dressings, and sponged Derby, and trickled more water onto and into him, which was about all that could be done at the moment. Strand, meanwhile, had gone out to investigate the transport situation. He came back to report that nobody in the village had a cart. There were plenty of bullocks but nobody in the village seemed to have a cart. "We'll never get to Djelybad in time, now," he said, but I had been questioning Rangovajan and he had said that there was a railway station about thirty miles away. "With a telegraph office?" I didn't think it likely, but going for the railway line was our only course of action. "And a train will be waiting to whisk us to Djelybad in a couple of hours? Which is about all the time we have left? You're in no shape to walk down to the river and paddle, let alone go thirty miles," Strand said, sitting on Rangovajan's shapeless mattress.

Derby moaned and rolled his head feebly. "Anyway, it'll be dark, soon." "The stars are brilliant these nights, and there'll be a moon. I'll just follow the road." "What road? There happens to be a road that leads straight to this railway station?" I hadn't thought of that. I was delirious with fatigue. "Going through a night infested with *pi* dogs, snakes, and baboons? Crazy." "I can't just stay here and hope something will turn up."

It was Rangovajan who turned up, and his healer, who turned out to be the Sadhu I had encountered in the mango grove such a very long time ago. "We are meeting again, Bandy Sahib," he said in his sing-song. After all, Sadhus were continually wandering the length and breadth of the subcontinent, so there was nothing particularly surprising about finding him here in this remotest of remote villages. "I have come to help you," he said, "for only"—he gestured indifferently, as if picking a number, any number, at random, "five rupees. You want to go home? I will guide you. I will guide you through the darkness, Bandy Sahib."

There was a funeral in the village. Drums were beating, invisible people wailing. Strand had purchased water, rice, and curry from a stall further up the street. I had drunk plenty of water but could not force down more than a grain of rice, or two at the most, but I felt remarkably clear-headed now, as if my brains had been packed in salt to keep them fresh.

Naturally the Sadhu was unaffected by the heat. He was not just dry—he was dusty. "I have walked for days without water," he boasted from the rubbly street. The sun, burning through a glassless window, was setting fire to the iron gray of a far-off banyan tree. Intense black shadows clutched far into a river-irrigated paddy. Vultures, golden, lovely in the spirit-leveled sun, surveyed in circles.

"I will warn them somehow," I said.

"Come. Come," the Sadhu said, gesturing strangely.

I stood in the street. "We need water if we're to go thirty miles."

"I have it," the old man said, indicating the goatskin that so

affectionately embraced his left shoulder. I could have sworn
that a moment ago he was naked and unencumbered but for a
G-string; but there it was, bending and swashing over his
shoulder, with texture and weight.

"You're sure you know the way to the station?"

"Of course, of course. Have I not said."

"I must get there. It's desperately important."

"I will get you where you must go."

Now that the moment had come to set out toward the night
and its frightening fauna, I hesitated. "Why are you helping
me?" I prevaricated. "You're sure as hell not going to all this
trouble for five rupees which I don't even have on me."

He was fiddling with the tip of his belly-button-length beard
and glittering at me with his malevolent eyes. "It is not because
I like you or have any respect for you," he sneered in sing-song.
"But you are special."

"Thanks."

"It is not a compliment, I never make compliments," he
shouted. The goatskin over his shoulder rippled, and the swash
of the water caused him to sway forward. "Come!"

I wouldn't go with him. Strand was right, it was ridiculous.
What time was it now? Sunset. Ten p.m. Even if we walked fast
as a marathon it would take eight or nine hours to travel thirty
miles. And in the darkness. Among scorpions and vipers and
the dreadful wild dogs. And even then I'd still be three dozen
miles from dawn and catastrophe. It was absurdity to the
power of n.

"Come!"

I walked. I followed.

At least I followed until I could no longer stand the sight of
his wrinkled haunches, whereupon I pulled alongside, as he
trod at a remarkably brisk pace considering his bare feet,
toward the wide river.

"Where's your personal assistant, holy man, your *chela*?"

"I have no *chela*."

"Yes, you have, I saw him."

"In that case, I have a *chela*."

I plodded in silence. I had started perspiring again after

drinking so much water. Sunset and it was still suffocating. I felt as if a sweaty sock had been pulled over a miniaturized me.

As we neared the river the noise increased: the shrieks and wails of mourners, touting cries of fakirs, roaring pant of fire-eaters, clack of jugglers, piping of snake-charmers. Smoke filled the air, cinders stung the eyes. There were hundreds, hundreds of people along the river bank, in the sun the water the color of blood, glistening, viscous, animal blood.

"It is a sacred river."

"Is there any river in India that isn't?"

"It is sacred by special dispensation. The Brahmins have decreed it. It is said that ultimately it joins the Ganges."

"Are you a Brahmin?"

"I am nothing."

On the stone bank of the river there was a line of dying humans on bamboo litters.

"Have they just been left there?"

"Dying in this river they will go straight to paradise."

Further on, the burning ghats. Noise, splashings, cracks and protests. The stink of burning flesh, singeing hair and smoldering cloth. The Sadhu went on toward the ghats. Tamarind trees hung in the hot, fetid air. A slow rain of ash from burning corpses. Bodies were being brought from afar to the sacred-river-by-special-dispensation, each brought down the steps to the ghats and laid on slabs of concrete near the river edge. We drifted closer. Some of the groaning mourners had brought their own wood, others purchased small bundles of dried sticks from sellers on the spot. A woman with a painted forehead had arrived with bearers carrying her deceased, rag-wrapped husband on a litter. The Sadhu paused so that I could watch while the cloth was peeled back from the husband's feet. Her attendants lifted the body and dipped the feet in the river. The woman washed them in the sepia water. Further on on the slimy bank, two dogs fought briefly, their snarls like collapsing buildings. Hawks flapped and screeched, mourners howled. The woman hulloo'd to the barge on which prepacked bundles of wood of varying sizes were going at the going rate. Rupees and wood were exchanged, two bundles piled round the body.

For a moment the feet stuck out, glistening wet, then disappeared under twigs and dust. We were in the middle of the ghats, surrounded by bodies, most stained with red dye, some already burning. "Must have been a bloody epidemic." The holy man varied the theme of, "See the burning ghats, Mr. Bandy, see the bodies setting out for heaven on the river, hear the holy din, smell the burning ghats," for the umpteenth time in his hypnotic sing-song. Not a few of the bodies were being inadequately cremated, and we seemed to be staying there long enough to see the smoldering embers being doused with water, leaving blackened untouched bones and human roast to be flipped into the river for the diving fish hawks, and perhaps later the crocs. The Sadhu cupped his hands and brought up soupy river water. "Drink?" he invited, and drank himself, chortling. I could see the soup strands on his chin, liquid trickling. "Why are you doing this to me?" I asked. But—doing what? It was dreamlike, but it wasn't a dream, I was there, conscious, all senses functioning though I wished they bloody weren't. There was a shard of broken glass at the edge of a concrete block. Before I could remind myself that the air and all surfaces under it must be itchy with foulest bacteria, I had picked it up and dragged it across my forearm. Lips parted and blood welled. I was here.

A screech of parrots whirled and settled in the tamarind trees. A bereaved son was busily cracking the skull of his dead dad before setting fire to his pyre, the fire brought from the official flames that were being kept eternal by a blue-robed Brahmin, the fire transferred by torches of crackling elephant grass. In mid-river a white bundle drifted. Perched on it, a vulture. It was tearing at elastic entrails, wobbling slightly as the bundle yawed. "See the leper in the river. Lepers are not burned but are put into the river as they are, as they are." Mourning noises rose in pitch and volume. The woman who had brought her husband to the shores of heaven was wailing, her head uncovered, shaved. Brown smoke was twisting up from the funeral pyre. Suddenly her husband sat bolt upright. Hissing, smoking sticks were scattered by the retraction. The rags had burned from the blackening face, the mouth lopsided.

Was I never to escape from this sort of thing? I'd been seeing dreadful dead since childhood, then in dissecting rooms, then at the Front, or in crashed aircraft, and back again in the hospitals in Moscow and London, in ancient, acrid basements. This was almost as bad as the Western Front where the mud had been half human. Was I never to forget all that? "See," said the holy man, and drew a snake as thin as a pencil from his pot belly and fed it into his mouth and drew it, a moment later, out of a nostril. I saw him do it. I refused to see it. I saw it clearly.

Now the Sadhu was continuing along the river, past a red statue of a baboon, past a temple. I touched a wall. Gritty stonework, hot to the touch in the direct light of the sun. The sun was still above the horizon, though at least an hour seemed to have passed since we had set out. Now we were walking along a line of beggars, Sadhus, yogis, fakirs, swallowers of props. My eye wept, offended by a cinder. If a cinder offend thee, pluck it out. The population of beggars increased, crowding around, silent among idols of gods as elephants, birds, baboons. I staggered against a man whose eyes were dangling from their sockets. He was demonstrating for pay, though my filthy pockets were barren. He replaced his eyes, grinning, the eyes oozing slowly back into place like shellfish into shells. "Stop it," I said to the Sadhu. "I'm not special, I don't deserve this." And now that the silent awe was over with, the beggars barked and whooped and belched as if the sounds were their trade marks.

The entire bank of the river on this side was crowded with dwellings, temples, concrete platforms, steps to the river; yet on the far side, sand. "If you die on the right bank of the river, you are certain to come back as a lowly beast, but if you die on this bank you will return in a higher state." "The bank promotes you?" He wheezed.

I was being forced to gaze at his withered nates again. Also a boil on his shoulder. That was comforting somehow. He was not totally immune from being human. The ash on his body was thicker than ever. His slipstream stank. I drew level with him again as he trod onward along the river, his bare feet grinding over stones. "Are you sure this is the way to the railway?" I demanded. "It looks to me as if you've detoured along the river. What for, to revolt me? I'm revolting enough as it is." " You are weighed down by your own personality. You are a great man. You have been and will be written and talked about. But—" "But—yes, I knew I'd be butted sooner or later." "But what have you gained?" I had no come-back ready just at the moment. "So," he said, and his lips slid back from his rotten teeth in a hideous rictus, and he pointed at one of the turtles in the river. Or perhaps he was summoning it. And the turtle came, dragging out of the water, an enormous gray creature. Over the shouts of birds and the ululation of relatives and a distant hell choir of hyenas, it sucked its way across the slimy mud at the edge of the river, making for me. There was a long narrow bundle in its mouth, white, stained red with dye. It was being brought to me as an offering. And the bundle in the jaws of the great, greasy turtle in the foul brown river was, I knew, a leg. I was cemented to the spot, looking straight into the turtle's ancient eyes, soulless ancient eyes, as it flipped closer, closer, first squelching over the mud, then through the balding yellow grass with a sound like a knife-sharpening, then scratching over the stony ground I was cemented to. "Do you give up?" the Sadhu demanded. "Do you give up?" The turtle, slimy with the stuff of the river, was only seven or eight feet away, huge mouth clamped on the articulated bundle with the red dye streaks, it was still staring fixedly, and I could hear its paddles dislodging stones, and see the stones in miniature avalanches, and could smell its putrid smell, and the faint hiss of its breath behind the rag-wrapped limb. Five feet away. "Take it away," I requested, reeling, reeling for an awful moment, I thought, towards rather than away from the ghastly, inexorable reptile. I landed on my back, not at all unpainfully, and I was back in the stony street outside Rangovajan's half-ruined house, and no time seemed to have passed, because the sunlight through the glassless window was still slashing across the street and illuminating the banyan tree. Unless, of course, this was tomorrow.

Strand was rushing up, pointing up.

"Do you hear it, do you hear?"

"What?"

"Listen, listen!"

The buzz of an aircraft, already halfway toward us from the south, flying at just a few hundred feet, precisely following the road and a hundred yards to the east of it. It was a DH9.

"One of ours. . . ."

We staggered into the middle of the street, waving. In the light of the horizontal sun the light blue fuselage was turning silver. Helmetless heads were easily visible. They had their faces turned our way, the observer shading his eyes.

They hadn't seen us. The biplane droned past. The ground was in shadow, black. Oh, God, the despair, the despair. They would never see us unless we could get into the sunlight. There was only a minute of sunlight left. In India, the dark came with bewildering speed. One moment, daylight. Next, click, night. The sun, after hanging round hallucinatingly for an hour or so, was plopping behind a distant hill. The purple in the sky was now indigo with slashes of orange. We raced along the street toward open ground at the edge of the village where the parched rice paddies began.

We were too late. The biplane had continued down the road toward the border. It was already half a mile away and the crew were still making it almost impossible to see us by placing themselves down sun. Strangely, though I could see the DH9 disappearing, the sound of its engine was growing louder.

With a leap of the heart I saw why. There was another DH9 following behind. And it was up sun.

It banked sharply. Toward us. And flew overhead. And circled, gliding, throttled back, the observer waving. He was waving. He had seen us. He had seen us.

Night Shots

Sigridur was waiting for me when I finally reached the air base in the middle of the night, and it was typical of her that she would put treatment before sentiment, insisting on emergency rations of water, salt, and sugar, and making sure the leg wound was not infected, and treating my sunburn, before deciding to have a good cry. The tears sloshed against my cheeks as she pinioned me helplessly in her arms.

"Oh, Bartholomew...oh, Bartholomew."

"Wot?"

She was babbling, castigating herself for having neglected me almost from the moment of her arrival, she didn't know what had gotten into her, India had had such an effect from the moment she had stepped ashore in Baroda and had seen such poverty, and such indifference to the sufferings of animals and humans, and such terrible treatment of small girls and new wives and old widows, and such superstition and thoughtless cruelty, she had been overwhelmed and she had only felt like herself again when she heard I'd gone missing, and as the days had passed with no word from or about me she had become inconsolable, blaming herself for not looking after me properly, neglecting me....

"Neglecting me? Nonsense. If anything I was neglecting you while I dealt with paltry things like national security—"

"And I kept thinking," she said, turning away to mop her

face, "that I never told you how much you meant to me, and now it might be too late to tell you, to tell you how much I loved you.... Do you remember when we first met?"

How could I forget? Splashing down into the fiord in Iceland in my Gander high-wing amphibian. Being tossed like a salad in the choppy waters, maneuvering into the harbor with cautious bursts of engine, cautious to avoid the Reykjavik smacks, lashed at by the rain, practically petrified by the half-day freezing flight from Labrador; and after blatting helplessly this way and that for minutes, being towed ashore by this oilskinned sou'westered chap in a rowboat who turned out to be this astonishing woman, this Erica the Red.

"M'm, I think I remember."

"Did you never wonder how I happened to be down at the harbor in the pouring rain? How I happened to be there in the rowing boat just when you steered your airplane past the beacons at the harbor mouth?"

"I'm just happy that you were."

"I'd gone down to the harbor because I was almost frantic with...restlessness, and I got into the boat because somehow I had to get rid of some of the energy. I'd just graduated and I had a secure future ahead of me with one of the richest men in Iceland—"

"Agnes."

"Agnar. He'd helped support me through medical school and now he was going to get his reward—me; and he had already built me a new surgery, attached to his house, with a dispensary and waiting room and everything. He had everything planned, right down to the jar of tongue depressors."

"I remember he got the waiting-room benches from a local undertaker."

"And he told me how much everything cost, and everyone said how lucky I was, and it was true, it was wonderful. But that day, suddenly I couldn't stand everything being so wonderful, and I had to get out, and that's why I was down at the harbor, leaning on the oars, and gazing out over the sea and wondering if this was all there was. And then your airplane appeared, and you half dead with cold and fatigue, but it didn't stop you from being rude and impertinent—"

"Me—rude and impertinent? I'm never rude and impertinent."

She laughed, sobbed, and hicupped almost simultaneously. We hugged each other. I held her wet cheek to mine.

"But in spite of you looking like a disreputable horse, complete with whinnying sounds, only hours later I was so much in love with you that I was quite alarmed at myself. It was not possible to fall so instantly in love, it. . . I had no wish to love you, you seemed to be such a fake.

"But I did," she said, wiping her face again, this time with the back of her hand in a gesture so innocently childlike that it almost had me blubbering as well. "But it wasn't until I thought I might have lost you that I realized how much. . . ."

"Darling. . . ."

And then she said briskly, "Anyway, that's enough of that. And now that you have recovered, we can take you to hospital."

Luckily it didn't take long to convince her that there were priorities ever higher than my welfare. As I performed the fastest ever shower, shave, shampoo, and change of clothes, I summarized the situation, and warned her that an attack was coming, perhaps in as little as two hours.

"Where are you going?"

"Emergency meeting."

"I'll come with you."

"You'll need to get the hospital and operating theatre ready, Sigga."

She stared at me for a moment, then, faintly: "There really is going to be a battle?"

"If there was anywhere I could send you, I would, but. . . . Wait—what am I thinking about? I could fly you out!"

She tilted her chin. "Don't be silly, darling, I volunteered to be your M.O. and that is what I shall be."

I'd been about to rush to the door. I turned, and embraced and kissed her tenderly, hands, cheeks, lips, taking plenty of time about it, nearly five precious minutes, and I murmured, and she murmured back, and cried a bit with, the idiot, happiness, not knowing how terrible it was going to be when the casualties started arriving at the hospital.

After which I rushed to the door shouting, "Strand, Strand, where the hell's Strand?"

It was well after midnight before Strand and I had finally reached the aerodrome, flying home in one of the DH9s that had spotted us at the village near the border. Just before total darkness blacked out the earth, the DH9 had managed to bump down in one of the flat fields near the village.

That only left the problem of getting off again in the dark. While this was being organized, I found out how the DH9s happened to be in the vicinity. They had been sent by Hibbert to investigate reports of intense aerial activity over the Khaliwar border; and of distant explosions occurring under what appeared to be multi-engined bombers. It appeared that in their determined efforts to stop us, the Khalis had made it possible for us to get home in time.

Take off was finally accomplished by recruiting the villagers as runway markers: lining them up in the starlight and having them hold aloft flaming sheafs of elephant grass. I flew the airplane out myself, with the German in the observer's seat. I promised the stranded crew that we would be sending help as soon as possible.

This had now been seen to. A Vimy crew had volunteered to fly their five-place bomber, loaded with flares, to the village to pick up Derby and the pilot and observer who had been left there. But as home base would soon be under attack, they were not to return to Djelybad but continue on to the RAF Charanwad, where Derby would have a better chance in the RAF hospital.

During the flight back, one of the dozens of thoughts flashing through the old synapses was—how on earth was I going to rouse everybody on the base in time, as it would be long after midnight when I arrived. I needn't have worried. Everybody was up and about, partly because they were unable to sleep in the sweltering heat, but mostly because a creeping barrage of rumors had been bursting over the aerodrome all day.

When Strand and I got to the operations centre and I led the way inside, I was almost electrocuted by the tension. They already knew some of my news, that Khaliwar was about to attack, and that the enemy were already at the gates; that the aerodrome might come under attack at any moment. There were about a hundred men in the main office as I stood there blinking while my eyes adjusted to the glare. They converged like iron filings to a magnet. Among them were Roland Mays who looked uncommonly anxious, Hibbert, who seemed to have aged several years since I last saw him, and a number of pilots, flight leaders and squadron commanders. And—was that Francis Postillion at the back?

"And just where do you think you've been?" Cot McNeil asked, hands on hips like a ruffled mother; but for once nobody laughed with him.

"Suffice it to say that I was held prisoner in Khaliwar, and that I escaped with the help of this man here, Heinrich Strand of the Khaliwar Air Force."

They darted mistrustful glances at Strand who, like me, had been freshly outfitted in light blue shirt and trousers.

While everybody was thus engaged, I said quickly to Hibbert, "Derby got shot. In the neck. I think he'll be all right."

"What's that?" others said. "Derby shot?"

"Who's Derby?" a female voice asked.

I looked around, couldn't see her.

"Who was that?"

"Who was who?"

"I heard a woman's voice."

"As I'm the only woman present, I guess that must be me," the voice answered; and as the mob parted there stood Petronella Spencer, outfitted in an Australian hat, an African bush shirt, American slacks, Moroccan desert boots, Swiss binoculars, and a German camera.

"Mrs. Spencer."

"Hi."

"What are you doing here?"

"Covering what looks like might be a hell of a story."

"Oh."

"I told Mr. Mays it would be okay with you if I hung around. That we'd gotten acquainted on board ship."

"M'm. Well...as long as you understand that you'll be in the middle of a battle by four this morning," I said.

I should like to have been a little less abrupt and a little more welcoming, but there was no time. I turned to Hibbert. "Hib—organize a conference right away in the map room. All squadron and flight leaders, armament, maintenance chiefs, security—most especially Major Neale. Everybody directly concerned with ops. Right away."

"Yes, sir," Hib said vaguely. Almost immediately he recovered. "Right," he said, and shoved out of the crush of bodies.

"Bax," I shouted over the noise, "you'll take over Two Squadron from Derby. Okay?"

"Sure...Right."

"Roland."

"Yes, Bart?"

"You'll be at the conference, of course, but start getting the base on a war footing. We'll be under attack in maybe two hours. Get everybody to their usual stations. Specific orders will follow the conference. Got it?"

"It's true, then?" Mays asked. Things were moving too rapidly for him.

It was hard to concentrate in this bedlam and in the concentrated heat. The ops building was vibrating with fearful excitement. People rushing, barging, colliding, shouting, field telephones being angrily cranked and smashed down. Cigarettes being agitatedly lit, and forgotten—cigarettes burning on desk edges. Feet thudding on bare boards, people slashing urgently through sheafs of paper and scribbling on smeary blackboards. From a small room along the corridor came the squeal of radio interference and the dit-dash of call signs, endlessly repeated.

I was being lambasted with questions. Jolting rumors had been abroad since late afternoon: stories of heavy military traffic inside Khaliwar. Mysterious, widespread air activity.

Increasingly urgent messages from New Delhi. Rumors of things going wrong, of sabotage.

Somebody in a sweat-soaked white shirt and cricket bags came pushing through. It was Francis Postillion. And good Lord, he was wearing a tie.

"What exactly is happening, Bandy?"

"I'll save it for the conference. You're invited."

He had been despatched by the Viceroy to the Jhamjarh air base to oversee the transfer of our aircraft to the RAF, to ensure that we carried out the orders to the letter. He had been here for several days, along with the RAF signals unit that was supposed to keep him in touch with Government House in New Delhi using a radio link through Charanwad.

I started to force my way toward the map room. I was shivering with excitement, the sort of sensation I used to get just before aerial combat; but it was peculiar to experience it in a heat that had hardly abated since mid-afternoon the previous day. My fresh blue shirt and trousers were already saturated, as were my canvas shoes, and I could feel sweat streaming down my ribs.

Outside, a silver crescent moon had risen, and stars pricked through a slight haze. It was almost bright enough for night flying without the use of runway oil pots.

"You wanted me?"

"Ah, Major Neale."

"I was on my way to the map room."

"A word first, to save time. Do you know that leper village a couple of miles west of here, Daja?"

"Yes?"

I told him as rapidly and tersely as possible about the threat from Sharif-ul-Khalil's criminal force. "I still want you at the meeting, but I thought I should give you advance notice. I'm putting you in complete charge of the defense of the aerodrome."

He took this as calmly as if I were offering him a candy. "Officially I've only forty men under my command. I'll need to conscript everyone not on ops—and I do mean everyone—clerks, cooks, medicine-and-duty men—"

"You have total authority."

"Can you give me an estimate of the size of this enemy force, sir?"

"No. All Strand can tell us is that it's hundreds."

"We don't have all that much in the way of weapons in the armory—"

"There's a bunch of spare Lewis guns in the armament section, taken off the Bristol fighters, and spares."

"Is that so? That'll be a help," Neale said, the light of battle already singeing his eyelashes.

He hurried off to issue preliminary orders. Immediately his place was taken by a sergeant clerk.

"We really are glad to see you again, sir. We thought you were dead."

"Yes, yes. Baker isn't it? Look, get through to the City Palace, Baker. It's urgent I speak to the Maharajah. I do mean urgent."

"I'll do my very best, sir."

"I'll be in the map room. Put the call through there."

The map room was actually the Operations Centre, but that seemed rather too pretentious a name for a room with a few maps on the wall and some wobbly furniture joined together to form a conference table.

Apart from Major Neale, all essential personnel were present when I walked in. The tense audience included Postillion and Strand. Strand was standing apart, repelling everyone with his arrogant stance.

I rather admired that. A weaker man, aware of the hostility toward him as a German, an enemy, and a turncoat, would have attempted to ingratiate himself. Strand stood there proudly defying the lot of them.

"Gentlemen," I said, without wasting a second—except to congratulate myself on making a good start with that 'gentlemen.' All war conferences began with that word (usually followed by the warning that the military situation was hopeless). "Gentlemen, we have very little time to spare for discussion, so every comment must be brief—except mine, of course, because I'm the boss and I can talk as much as I like."

This sally was greeted with not the slightest hint of amusement from the thirty officers present. So I cleared my throat and made a mental note—a very brief note—not to give way to frivolity for the time being. "Yes," I said. "Well." And as succinctly as possible I gave them a summary of the events of the past few days to establish that what I had to say was based on a certain amount of direct experience.

I then introduced Strand. "As I've already mentioned, Strand is a member of the Khaliwar air staff, so he knows what he's talking about, too. I have much to thank him for. He enabled Derby and me to escape, for one thing. Most importantly, he apprised me of certain details of the Khaliwar plan of attack. But I'd like you to hear about it for yourself. So, Strand—pray speak."

Strand replied in his most authoritative voice, "It is understood that I am telling you all I know in return for an immediate passage home and certain expenses?"

"Yes, yes, how many times do I have to promise that, Heinrich?"

"I was making sure that your men understood it also." He paused, perhaps for dramatic purposes, as part of his life's campaign to make the world properly aware of Heinrich Strand. Then: "The Khaliwar Army," he said, "has four well-equipped and highly trained mobile divisions led for the most part by German and Russian officers."

"Russian?" Postillion said sharply.

"There is a strong Soviet involvement in Khaliwarian affairs," I said. "I've experienced some of it myself."

Postillion grew haggard before my very eyes. Extra dots of sweat burst from his brow. The others fell into a breath-snatching, sibilant mutter.

"The second 'Akbar' division is to cross into Jhamjarh at five o'clock this morning. Two mobile divisions are to attack northward toward Delhi, with one division in reserve."

"Jesus," somebody muttered.

Postillion turned to me. "Exactly what do you mean about Russian involvement?" he asked.

"I haven't time to chat about that now, Postillion—"

Strand interrupted. "The Russian who is most senior is called Panyushkin."

"Panyushkin?"

"He is the Soviet Government's chief representative in Khaliwar."

"Panyushkin?" Postillion said again. "Pavel Alexeivitch Panyushkin?"

"That is the man."

Postillion had evidently heard of Panyushkin. He looked as if a battering ram had been driven into his solar plexus.

"Anyway, we've no time to discuss that now," I said. "What most concerns us at the moment is the infiltration that has already taken place in Jhamjarh in advance of the Khaliwar attack."

"Infiltration?" somebody asked nervously, just as Major Neale entered the map room, and made himself as inconspicuous as his ferocious face would allow.

Now Strand was talking again, and I could see from the surrounding expressions that he was being very convincing, as he described the Khaliwar plans to storm the City Palace.

The audience looked even more impressed when he got down to the threat to their own lives. "It is a very strong force that must now have been assembled in the village of Daja," he said. "They are men of several criminal tribes who have been trained for this one task, and are being led by Pathans. Because of the circumstances, the operation being an infiltration tactic at long distance, there is no precise timetable. They have just one order. They must attack this base no later than four this morning and kill every European in it."

In the ensuing shocked silence, somebody drawled, "That's okay by us—we're from North America."

"I meant everybody," Strand said, not realizing that this was supposed to be a joke.

I noticed that Mays was looking particularly unhappy. As for Postillion, he was staring blindly through a window into the silvery moonlight—though in his case he was probably worrying more about the political than the military implications.

"Right. Any questions so far, before I get to the bad news?" I asked.

We were interrupted by the sergeant clerk, who sidled in, blushing. He backed along the wall and whispered self-consciously.

"What? Speak up, man."

"We've lost contact with Djelybad," he said, horribly aware that he was the focus of everybody's attention. "The technical johnnies think the telephone line has been cut."

Somebody swore nervously. I looked at my watch. I didn't have a watch. "Can anyone lend me a watch?"

It was 2:45 a.m. already. I felt as if I'd been injected with 5 cc.s of despair. The Palace might already have been taken.

But there was no way I could abbreviate the talkfest. We hadn't even got all the essential information across yet.

"Baker."

"Sir?"

"Get onto Chiefie Sparrow. I want a two-seater wheeled out and ready to go in five minutes—preferably a Harry Tate."

"Right."

"What was that just now about bad news?" Cot McNeil asked. "You've just told us that Khaliwar is about to invade, it's ready to attack the Government of India, the Maharajah is about to be killed or captured, and probably at this moment a thousand dacoits are creeping up on us in the dark. But now you say you have some bad news?"

Someone laughed; a bit hysterically, I thought. "Yes. Tell them, Strand," I said. But, too impatient to wait: "Strand informs me that simultaneously with the attack from Daja, the Khaliwar Air Force will be bombing us with at least half their air force at five o'clock—about two hours time."

Funnily enough there was not much reaction to that, apart from a pilot's, "I may be bombed long before then." They seemed to think that an aerial bombardment was the least of their worries. But it concerned me most of all. I had faith in Neale, but bombers always got through. And if the Jhamjarh Air Force was lost, the whole of India could go.

Which reminded me: "I have to go in a minute," I began.
"Wait," Postillion said.

"I can't wait," I shouted angrily. "Unless we get moving we'll all be dead in two hours." Steady. That wasn't like me. But then, what was? "Yes, what is it, Mr. Postillion?"

"You've been putting us in the picture, Mr. Bandy. I just wanted to do the same for you. I've been in touch with New Delhi all afternoon—RAF Charanwad has been relaying our messages—"

"Yes, I know, get on with it."

"New Delhi's been receiving reports all day of troop movements inside Khaliwar, and they're not receiving any explanations from Lampur Kalat." He twitched as Strand hissed contemptuously, but kept his eyes on me. "They're particularly alarmed at some RAF reports of troop trains and concentrations of vehicles and personnel along the northern border of Khaliwar."

"Perhaps now they might start conceding that we were right."

He looked embarrassed. "I'm afraid—well, the fact is, they're refusing to believe it."

"They're—*what*?"

"Refusing to believe the reports."

In the ensuing silence, Strand said calmly, "Don't worry, they will believe it very soon, *ja*?"

Ignoring him, Postillion continued, "I sent them another urgent signal suggesting that in the light of these reports, the arrangement to hand over the Jhamjarh aircraft to the RAF tomorrow—no, it's today, isn't it—should be urgently reviewed."

"Well, that's something, anyway."

Postillion hung his head. Very appropriately, I thought, as he now muttered into the incredulous silence, "The orders about your aircraft are to go ahead."

I just looked at him.

Somebody knocked and entered with an urgent query. It was referred to Hibbert. I noticed Petronella Spencer, quietly taking it all in, her expression rapt, her mouth a scarlet slash of lipstick.

Though it was quite outrageous of her to have sneaked into a top-level conference, I was too preoccupied to waste even a minute on her.

"I presume you agree," I said, pinning Postillion to the wall of the map room with a heartless stare, "that the Viceroy's order should be ignored?"

He hesitated, then: "I'm sure that you'll ignore it whatever I say."

"Of course."

"As it happens—I concur."

I really didn't know what to make of Postillion. Sometimes he could be hidebound, then next free as a flea; a concrete pillar of the System one moment, India rubber the next.

I turned to go; then twisted back, feeling quite desperate.

"I can only give very general directives until I get back from the palace," I said. "These are, one, I'm putting Major Neale in complete command of the defense of the aerodrome against the attack from Daja. Two, I want every aircraft on the base fueled, armed, and bombed up, ready for take-off at four-thirty—or before, if possible. Every single machine we've got must be in the air by the time the Khaliwar fighters and bombers arrive. Got that? Mays? Hib?"

"Yes."

"Yes."

"That's basically it. Except to say this: unless we survive as an air force, the Khaliwar offensives north and south will almost certainly succeed.

"But our immediate objective is to survive. That is our only aim—to survive for the next few hours. For the time being we can do nothing about the land attack—the Jhamjarh Army will have to deal with that."

"Goodbye Jhamjarh," somebody murmured.

I lowered my voice. "Just one more thing that I hope you'll pass onto your people. We all have just two choices: to run away or fight. As we're all volunteers I won't stop anyone from running away. But you should remind yourselves and everybody under you that you might not live long if the rest of us fail. And at least we're giving ourselves a good chance, thanks to Strand's advance warning—and because frightful Major Neale is going into action."

The conference ended with a burst of nervous laughter.

View of the Palace

At thirty-five minutes past three in the morning the palpitating heat had finally abated. The air, whorling and eddying past the windscreen of the RE8 seemed almost chilly, now. And the heat haze had gone, leaving a perfect Indian sky, a Stephens' blue-black inky firmament hung with a million trinkets, with the centrepiece of a sterling silver moon.

As we approached the City Palace, I throttled back, and glided up to the gates at a good twelve hundred feet in order to make a hushed approach. If the dacoits had not yet attacked, I had no wish to alert them with the dramatic bellow of a sway-backed biplane.

As I peered over the side, Strand did likewise, gripping the coaming, nervous as Nellie. Like most pilots he hated to be flown by others. Together we examined the contents of the massive seven-mile walls below. Under the brilliant sky-lighting, the fountains, the buildings, the pools, and the grass, even individual trees, were brightly edged in silver, sharply delineated. I was grateful for that, feeling in no shape for a landing that required much concentration.

We paid particular attention to the great carved gates. They were wide open. But that told us little, as they were always wide open. They were closed only when a Maharajah died, and even then only symbolically, to be opened exactly one hour later. It was thought that disaster would befall the State if they were ever shut for any other reason.

Hindus were sticklers for tradition, like the British. On one occasion when the ruler was ailing, the gates were inadvertently shut before he actually expired, so he'd had to be throttled.

We continued to sigh down through the warm air. Seven hundred feet and the main palace building titled into view, with its tall, strange central tower surrounded by worshipful cupolas. No sign of a commotion yet. The palace presented a peaceful appearance with just two of its many windows gleaming, the light cut into narrow strips. The golf course, concourses, piazzas, parade grounds, playing fields, lawns, paths, gardens, pools, temples, all silver-plated by the moon, all deserted. No, wait: there were two sentries at the front entrance to the main palace building. We could make them out easily. They were leaning against the wall, discussing Geulincz' Theory of Occasionalism. Their rifles were propped against a white wall.

I banked sharply and came round again. No wind, so it didn't matter which direction I came in from. Coming out of the turn I crossed the controls fully, and heard Strand gasp as the aircraft sank under him.

The warm air hissed over the surfaces, and the altimeter unwound rapidly. Ahead, the lawn widened. Strand continued to dig his nails into the padded coaming, knuckles phosphorescent.

The undercart squeaked as the wheels thumped down, then bounced and thumped again. The tailskid scraped, the machine came to a stop, engine belly-rumbling. I looked around quickly, about to a taxi closer to the main entrance. I decided against it. The brief roar of the engine would not likely rouse anybody in the building but the dacoits might be close and be motivated to advance their schedule.

As we climbed out, the two sentries hastened up. They had left their rifles behind, I noticed.

They appeared to recognize me, and salaamed. Their grins

faded, though, when they saw us removing a rifle, a haversack full of ammunition drums, and a machine-gun from the airplane.

As we busied ourselves, I tried to tell them that the palace was about to be attacked. I might just as well have played the zither. They looked blank, knowing little English, and I hadn't been long enough in the country to learn Hindi. Well, yes, I had been here long enough, and I had a gift for languages, but I'd been too lazy.

They couldn't even grasp the name of their commander-in-chief. "Pertab, Pertab! Get! Bring! Fetch! *Impshi*! Oh, shit."

The guards were even more upset when I gave up and raced toward the main entrance with the Lewis over my shoulder, Strand pounding after me. They were still shouting as I barged through the front entrance—wide-open, of course—almost falling over the sleeping doorkeepers.

Inside I considered firing a burst into the painted ceiling to get everybody's attention. Instead I made for Khooshie's rooms, upstairs and at the front of the palace. Guards and servants stirred, jumped up, called out. Turning a corner I bumped into a terra cotta goddess. She fell with a crash.

She had her uses. The noise woke Khooshie. He was sitting up on his low couch, rubbing his eyes, and lighting a lamp when we barged in, shouting.

"Khooshie, let's get your father. Now. It's urgent."

"Bartholomew! Where have you been?"

It took another ten minutes to reach the Maharajah's quarters on the second floor at the front of the building. By then the whole palace was in an uproar.

"It's quite all right, I was getting up anyway," the Maharajah mumbled, as if I'd apologized for waking him this early. Then: "Mr. Bandy! You have come back!"

I explained hurriedly, as briefly as possible.

"Mr. Strand is a Khaliwar pilot?" he asked.

"Your Highness, he helped me to escape," I said, and rushed on with further explanations about Strand's part in the affair, and that I had assured him that the Maharajah, would pay him well for his help and for the information he had already provided.

"Yes, yes, of course," the Maharajah said, looking brightly at Strand. "How much would you like, Mr. Strand?"

"Well, I was thinking of my passage home, and two thousand English pounds."

"Ah. Certainly, that is very reasonable, Mr. Strand, very reasonable."

Strand immediately looked discontented, wishing he'd asked for more.

"But do you understand, sir?" I said. "We could be attacked at any moment. It's nearly five to four."

"I make it two minutes to four," Khooshie contributed.

"Do you?" The Maharajah looked at his bedside alarm clock which was ticking like a disapproving aunt. "I make five past-eleven—but perhaps I forgot to wind it last night."

"But in that case it would not be ticking," Khooshie pointed out.

"That is true, dear son, normally speaking. But you see yesterday I wound it when I got up, so that—"

"Your Highness, please—we've got to get you away," I said, just as the Dewan came hurrying into the room, pulling on his ivory coat and Gandhi cap.

"Mr. Bandy," he cried. "What is the meaning of all this? You have greatly upset the palace staff with all your shoutings, and rushings about with mean looks on your face, and—and what is this, all these guns and things? You should not have brought them into the palace, it is not allowed. His Highness will not have it, I tell you."

I was too busy restraining myself from shaking the Maharajah to pay much attention to this. "Please, sir," I said, "you must hide—they could be here at any moment."

"Are you listening to what I am saying?" the Dewan cried. Apparently not. Nobody answered him.

"Sir, what about my money?" Strand asked. "Is there any chance of getting it right away?"

"Money?" Khooshie said, regarding Strand with dislike. "What for?"

He had not been listening to a word we were saying.

"For telling you about the attack," Strand replied.

"But you didn't tell us. It is Mr. Bandy who is telling us."

"*Ja*, but I told him."

"I did not hear you do so."

"I told him on the way here. I gave him the information."

"Well, there you are, then. If you *gave* him the information, then why should you be paid? Or are you some sort of an Indian giver?"

"Khooshie," I began.

"No, I'm sorry, Bartholomew," Khooshie said, stubbornly compressing his lips, "but I see no reason why we should pay this man for information when it is plainly you who is providing it."

"How many times to I have to tell you—"

"It is no good shouting, Mr. Strand. My father has no intention of forking out, have you, Father?"

"Of course not, dear son."

"But you just said you would pay me!" Strand screamed.

"Yes, that's true."

"But Father, he expects us to pay him for information when he has hardly opened his mouth—except to demand money," Khooshie pointed out.

"You Indian fool, is it my information I money for am demanding!" Strand cried, his English going all to pot.

"Well, now you're *certainly* not getting any money," Khooshie said with a sniff, "after all this shouting and irrational behaviour."

I was running from them to the window and back, and then back to window. Apparently feeling that I needed a rest, the Maharajah reached out and almost touched me. "Mr. Bandy," he said, "come and sit down, and you must tell me all about your adventures since you so very mysteriously disappeared from the train. I must say it was most strange. One moment you were lying in your bunk in your lovely red pyjamas, and the very next moment you were vanishing into thin air."

"Sir...Sir: don't you believe us when we tell you this palace is going to be attacked at any moment?"

"Oh, yes, we would never doubt you for a minute, Mr. Bandy. We are trusting you implicitly, aren't we, dear son?"

"Oh, yes," Khooshie said warmly, " there is nobody in the whole world we trust more than you, Bartholomew."

"Well, then, please—please—you must hide."

The Maharajah smiled and lay back contentedly on his single pillow. "You want me to hide in my own palace, Mr. Bandy? No, no, I'm afraid not, no. This is my home that I love. I don't hide in my own home, you know. It is not seemly."

At which point we all became aware of a strange sound, an ominously rhythmic crunching, rapidly growing louder.

Strand ran to a narrow window, I to another. It was not easy to see out the window, but by jamming my head against the right hand side of the window and staring left, I was just able to make out the cause of the noise. It was a squad of men in perfect column of four, trotting toward the building with the most dismaying precision, rifles at the port. Already they were a mere twenty feet away, a relentless approach of dark men in *dhotis*, indistinguishable from civilians provided you did not recognize the green and black turbans and notice the rifles.

Just behind them another group of trotting men were drawing a heavy machine-gun on wheels.

Khooshie crowded up for a look. "Who are those men?" he asked. "Those are Khaliwar turbans. What the devil do they mean by it, making that noise at this time of the night? Damn cheek."

"Serve you right when you are killed," Strand shouted at him. "Serve you right," he repeated, just as an outbreak of gunfire was heard, mixing with shouts, and a scream, abruptly cut off. And then another sputter of gunfire.

"Strand," I said. "I'll pay you two thousand pounds—if you'll help me get them to safety."

"It was not part of the bargain."

Now came the deep, slow chung-ing of a heavy machine gun, firing in bursts.

The Maharajah tilted his head to one side. "I say, Mr. Bandy," he said, "What is that noise?"

"It's the Khaliwar attack, Your Highness."

"No, that cannot be," he said. "They promised not to."

"On the other hand," Strand said with a twisted smile, "they have orders to kill all whites, so it is in my own interest to help, and hide myself as well."

"Strand, you may not have much of a sense of humor, and you may be a trifle rough, arrogant, contemptuous, money-grubbing and insensitive, but you are a man after my own heart," I said, clapping him on the shoulder before hurrying back to the slit of a window.

The view was less encouraging than ever. The front of the palace was seething with dhoti'd figures summited with green turbans who seemed to be in the process of taking up defensive positions in case of a counterattack. And the heavy machine-gun was now mounted on the parapet. Even as I watched, it fired a brief burst. Two lines of tracer streaked out, and into the darkness.

It was far too soon for even an efficient army to be mounting a counterattack, so they were probably just firing the machine-gun for fun, or to keep up their courage.

There was another doorway in the Maharajah's bedchamber. It was shaped like an onion. I darted into the room, which appeared to be his office. A desk and chair stood in front of a carved screen. There was only one way out of the office. It led back into the corridor.

I rejoined the others, suddenly realizing that I was feeling more vigorous. Perhaps because the temperature was dropping, or I'd got my second wind, or at least second breeze. Khooshie and his father were talking in their own language, their eyes now darting about nervously as the din of gunfire increased.

"I say," Khooshie said, "perhaps after all we had better find some sort of hidey-hole, don't you think, Father?"

Now that it was essential for the Maharajah to agree with his beloved son—he failed to do so. "No," he said, wrapping himself more firmly in his bedsheet. "I am not hiding in my own palace."

The martial commotion increased. The quality of the sound suggested that it was coming from inside the building: loud metallic shots—somebody screaming.

Strand and I looked at each other. "They're in."

"Yes."

We held a rushed, tactical conference. Carrying a rifle, Strand sped into the corridor, brushing past the Dewan. Since the shooting had started the Dewan had gone rigid. He seemed bolted to the spot, his great, plum-sized purple eyes bulging with shock. Perhaps he hadn't been told about the storming of the palace. Perhaps he was beginning to realize what he had done.

The flat, echoing gunfire grew louder. "No," the Maharajah was saying to his son.

"We will not be hiding exactly, Father," Khooshie said impatiently, "but merely transporting ourselves to a rather more tranquil spot, that's all."

The gunfire grew louder still. In the confined space of the corridors and with so many unabsorbent surfaces around, of hard plaster and marble and polished marquetry and parquetry, the noise was terrifying, an agony on the nerves.

I darted round the Dewan to check the corridor. Strand was waiting in an alcove further up on the corridor, rifle leveled in the direction from which the dacoits were certain to come. I scurried back into the bedchamber, grabbed Khooshie's arm and rushed him through the office next door and to its exit to the corridor.

Further along the corridor to the right it intersected another passage. I pointed. "Where does that lead?"

"That? To the *zenana*."

I rushed him back to his father. "Sir," I said to the old man, "if you don't try to escape then Khooshie will have to stay here, too, and be killed. He won't go without his father—will you, Khooshie?"

"Uh. . . ."

"So he'll die as well. And you've no other heirs. Is that what you want, is that what you want for Jhamjarh?"

All three of us jumped as shots crashed out, a few feet away. Strand was firing.

"Oh, all right," the Maharajah said. "I am nothing if not a reasonable man, as you know. It is just that I am not going to be bullied into anything. But there you are—you have twisted my arm."

Shouting at the Dewan to follow, I rushed them both into the office and to its exit. Along on the left Strand was firing his rifle from the hip, working the bolt with practised speed, empty cartridges tinkling to the floor, smoke building up in front of the muzzle. Way down the corridor, bodies were sprawled. Even as we watched, he ran out of ammunition, withdrew into the alcove, and slapped another magazine into place.

I signaled to him, then turned to Khooshie, indicating the other corridor. "Soon as I say go, get down there as fast as you can."

"On, no," Khooshie said, appalled. "That is the way to the women's quarters."

"That's where we're going. You and your father first—you must rush him across. Ready?"

The dacoits stared firing down the corridor. In the next room the Dewan let out a shriek, though he could not possibly have been hit.

The Maharajah turned, and was about to go back. "The Dewan," he began.

"I'll look after him. Get ready to go."

The Maharajah, dazed and confused by the noise, kept looking back toward his bedroom as if he felt he would be much safer in there. The comprehension was beginning to drain from his eyes.

"Get ready."

Khooshie swallowed convulsively, looking frightened—and thank God for that.

I swiveled out of the doorway, Lewis gun aimed left, but well away from Strand's alcove, and fired a long burst.

"Now! Go!"

The gun was kicking up. The roses in the corridor ceiling were being pulverized. Clouds of dust descended. A five hundred year-old carving of a god on a pedestal disintegrated. I could hear glass breaking at the far end of the corridor. There was no return fire. My ears rang with the crash of the gun in the hard, narrow space.

Half-blinded by the flashing of the machine-gun, which had been stripped of its tubular jacket to make it easier to handle, I sensed rather than saw Khooshie and his father running with utter lack of dignity across and into the *zenana* corridor. Then I was shouting to Strand that I would cover him—immensely grateful that, like me, he had been an infantryman before he was a pilot.

Strand waited, looking amazingly calm as there came a storm of return fire from way down left. I had swerved back into the bedroom again to change the drum, bumping into the Dewan in the process. He had not moved an inch since the firing started, his eyes bulging and unfocussed. "Get ready to run across into the *zenana*," I told him, but I didn't really care whether he heard or not.

Bullets pounded the inlaid work of the doorway in front of us. Carved woodwork splintered, a strip of wire came loose and hung, shivering. I waited for a brief lull, took a deep breath, feeling ridiculously calm considering I would probably be hit in one second if they were still firing when I took up battle stations again—and took up battle stations, firing carefully past Strand in short bursts, the flash of the gun bright enough to illuminate about thirty feet of corridor.

"Now!"

Strand darted out of the alcove, down the corridor, and into the *zenana* passage. I kept firing. Bullets from the Lewis were punching along one wall, chewing pillars, screeching off tiles, ploughing into plaster, augmenting themselves with splinters from the floor.

I thought of the Dewan. I wanted to leave him behind, but I'd assured the Maharajah that I would look after his first minister. So I bellowed to him to join me in the doorway of the office, ready to dart across, and he obeyed, but unhappily for him, he emerged from the wrong door. He stepped into the corridor from the Maharajah's bedroom instead of the office, turning toward me and saying something in a high, almost petulant tone.

It was bad for him, but good for me. His considerable bulk intervened between me and the dacoits just as they returned fire. At first I thought he had grown frivolous or gone mad, crazed by the noise. He started to dance, quite nimbly, in fact. As he cavorted I glared, considering it a highly inappropriate moment for Terpsichorean activity. I mean, the way he was twirling, quite gracefully along the corridor toward me, now turning with arms outspread and wrists bent as if demonstrating a step to a class of duffers. A waltz? No. As rifles shatteringly clapped behind him, he was punched into a pilaster at the edge of an alcove, and then he sprawled, spraying bright red blood onto cerulean mosaic.

After firing a last long burst, I managed to get myself into the *zenana* corridor without injury, and with the haversack of drums bouncing unpleasantly against my hip, ran down it to where it ended at a doorway set into a carved wooden screen. I was through in seconds, knowing I should have held off the pursuit for another few minutes to enable the others to get further away; but the din in the confined space had teased my nerves into shreds and I couldn't face it. So I went into the women's quarters instead, skittering into a hall filled with ten thousand screaming females.

At least that's what it sounded and even looked like. They had been roused by the shooting long before we burst into their sanctum. They had hollered loud enough when they saw the ruler and his handsome son, but it was nothing to the racket they kicked up when they saw me. And Strand, presumably. The women were fleeing in all directions. Most of them were dressed. Two who weren't were standing in an onion-shaped doorway, stark naked. They covered their faces. One old woman, holding silk in front of her as if threatened by the Gorgon, was shrieking at me in a fingernails-on-glass voice.

As I continued along another corridor the screams faded. Khooshie seemed to be leading us toward the rear of the palace. That was uncommonly sensible of him. Even if the dacoits had thought of guarding all exits, we might be able to fight our way out, and there were a thousand places to hide in the vast palace complex.

And then I found that he was leading his hobbling pater upward, not down to the ground floor. I couldn't believe it. But I could hear them plainly, clattering up a narrow stone circular stairway, with Strand gasping in the rear, gasping and shouting, presumably shouting the same sort of things I'd be shouting if I was close enough, like, "You fool, down not up, we'll be trapped." Oh, Christ, how could I have given Khooshie the job of guide dog?

Obviously I had to follow, to discover the worst: that the circular stairway of stone led to nowhere but the very worst place of all, the roof. I think I would have riddled Khooshie if he'd been in front of me at that moment.

Coughing from cordite, palming the wall with a wet hand, I staggered into the open, to find myself in the centre of a cupola, which was little more than a dome supported by eight columns, the columns barring the lustrous night sky.

Half-doubled up, coughing and rasping from a meal of too much smoke, I gazed blearily into the night through the pillars, and saw that this cupola was one of an elaborate complex of cupolas on the flat roof, with that central tower, or minaret, or whatever that tall structure was, a sort of celebratory center-piece or architectural climax. Everywhere I'd been in India I'd seen that major buildings, palaces, temples, mausoleums, mosques, tombs, forts, and even hotels shared this feature, these graceful cupolas built to excite flat roofs, each with between four and eight columns, rising from substantial mosaic bases, and supporting decorated domes. They looked most magical in this silver moonlight. . . . There was no time for wonderment. As I stepped out of the cupola, half-deafened, Khooshie approached and spoke agitatedly, plucking at my sweat-stinking shirt. I couldn't hear properly. I saw the Maharajah sitting on the plinth of another columned cupola. He kept hauling up a corner of his nightshirt to chew it, then, realizing what he was doing, letting go; and then chewing it again.

Now he was taking out a tin of his favorite toffee, but his hands were shaking so much he couldn't get the lid open.

I looked around for Strand, just as that wrinkled Teuton came trotting out of the starlight. He had been reconnoitering.

"No other way off the roof," he growled, slapping another magazine into his rifle.

I was relieved to see that he, too, was panting. It would have been rather annoying if he had continued to show so much less wear and tear than me.

"You're sure?"

He didn't bother answering, but turned on Khooshie. "Why did you come up here instead of going down?" he shouted. "Now we are trapped."

Khooshie straightened his narrow shoulders and tilted his head so that he could sight down his nose at Strand. "Don't be afraid," he said loftily. "Our army will rescue us."

"In the next few minutes? Because that's all the time we have before they shoot us."

I took Khooshie's arm and led him closer to his father. When I was sure I had their full attention: "They have orders to take you alive if possible," I said, wondering if it was true. "So when they come storming onto the roof, put your hands up and don't move, and you should be okay. Have you got that?"

The Maharajah's fathomless eyes stared at me in the darkness, but they were already looking into the next world. I sincerely hoped that his gaze was premature.

Khooshie was saying excitedly, "You don't understand, Bartholomew. I keep telling you, there is a place for us to hide."

Strand was covering the cupola that provided access to the roof. "There is nowhere," he said. "I have looked all over the roof."

"It is why I was heading upwards, you see," Khooshie said. "I used to come up here when I was a child, and often I would hide from the *chowkidars* for fun, and they were never able to find me." He was jumping up and down with glee and excitement.

My throat was so dry from fumes and exertion I had to say it twice before it emerged. "Where?"

"In there," he said, pointing at the roof's central tower.

"I saw no doorway," Strand said.

"I'll show you. Come on, come on!"

"You two go," I said. "We'll hold them off here as long as we can."

Khooshie was tugging at my shirt again. "But it is not necessary," he cried. "We can all hide—there is tons of room, tons."

I turned to Strand. "I'll check. Back in a minute," I said, and threw him the Lewis gun and the haversack.

Khooshie darted off through the classical landscape, urging his father to hurry, hurry. I caught up with them as they reached the high, circular base from which the central tower reared sixty feet into the glowing dark.

Optically tilting to its capped summit, I became aware of a faintly perceptible lightning of the sky. Dawn? False dawn? I squinted at my watch. Four-fifteen. Four-*fifteen*? After all we'd been through?

After discovering that the battle had lasted for only a quarter hour, I didn't think I could possibly feel any further surprise. But by God I did, when I perceived what had not been obvious from ground level or even from the far end of the roof—that the central structure was no ordinary tower.

It was yet another Indian *lingam*.

The palace's central tower, rising from its high, decorated base, was nothing but a damn great phallus.

Worse, I was now able to make out the nature of the designs in the six foot high circular base on which it was mounted. There were eight designs carved out of the circumferential face of the base, all identical, all forming a ring round the *lingam*: eight *yonis*, each snug within a finely carved stonework representing pubic hair.

Panting blankly, I stared incredulously at the tower, but

confirmed beyond a shadow of doubt that, yes, it was a phallus all right: a sixty-foot, preposterous, prepuce-capped penis soaring from an adoring ring-a-rosies of bronze twats.

I'd glimmed many such celebrations of fertility in India, male members rising basely from practically every available surface, as well as being represented extensively in temple carvings, and on the entire facade of this very palace, and had averted my eyes from quite a few of the female equivalent as well, as they lay plastered to the ground. It had sometimes seemed to me that the whole bloody country was sex-crazed, symbolically at least—nothing but John Thomases as far as the eye could see. But I'd observed none on quite such an extravagant scale as this monument to overpopulation.

As for the encompassing female organs in curlicued bronze which were mounted vertically in the circular base at regular intervals—I had no wish to dwell on them.

Except that I was forced to, when Khooshie whispered, "This way," and hurried to one of the moonlit *yonis*, the one at the two o'clock position; and reaching up, pushed at something unmentionable inside the sculpture, which promptly released the labia, so that a slight push slid them back just far enough to allow a person to slip through, sideways.

Feeling queerer than ever, I went back for Strand. As I dreamed over the roof, sashaying through the fancy architecture, he whirled, aiming the Lewis gun; then trained it back on the wide opening in the cupola where the dacoits would gain access to the roof.

And they would be doing so soon. We could hear them coming, calling to each other on the stone stairway.

"Come on."

When we got to the sculpture—*bas relief?*—Strand quickly took in the nature of the opening though which he was expected to enter.

Whereupon, he demurred. "But that's a . . ." he began; but stopped out of delicacy.

"Hurry, they'll be here in a minute."

"I'm not going in there," he said; and then repeated it: "I'm not going in there."

"It's all right," I coaxed, pointing up at the phallus. "It just leads to that."

It was only then that he realized what the tower was. He started up at it. "Jesus Christ." he said.

"Come on, come in, they'll be here in a moment."

"God-damned filthy Indians."

"Strand, for God's sake—"

There was shouting from the far side of the tower. The dacoits were on the roof.

"I've got some dignity," Strand said.

"Oh, don't be such a prick! Damn it, Strand, it's only a sculpture."

"I don't care. It's disgusting, it's indecent."

"Wouldn't you rather be indecent than dead?" I hissed; and when he failed to answer immediately: "Well, wouldn't you?"

"I'm thinking about it."

The voices and clatter of feet and weapons was getting close. "Well, I'm going in," I said, and abandoning all modesty I slid into the opening.

After a few seconds, Strand followed, emitting unclassifiable noises. After I'd hissed at him again, he closed the entrance behind him with considerable reluctance by pressing the...a stone button.

We found ourselves sandwiched between brick walls, the slightest brush against which dislodged showers of dust. Feeling rather like a sperm I wriggled along the brick passage. It sloped slightly downward for a few feet before opening out into the tower thing. It was dark in there, the only illumination being provided by a slit in the prepuce sixty feet up.

"Is that you, Bartholomew?" Khooshie whispered from a few feet away. It was certainly capacious in the scrotum.

"Amazing though it may seem, yes," I said in a surly tone, for I was not enjoying the experience any more than Strand was.

The four of us stood there in the dark, trying not to breathe noisily; though the attempt made it worse, for every now and then somebody would have to compensate for stifling their natural breathing by issuing occasional gasps for air.

We could hear movements and talk outside with alarming clarity: shouts, clicks, shuffles, whistles.

"Of course—" Khooshie began in his normal voice.

"Shhh!"

"Of course," he said, remembering to whisper, "it is always possible the *chowkidars* were just *pretending* not to find me, and that they knew the way in here all the time."

I glared at him; which didn't do much good as he couldn't see me.

"They were always wonderful to me when I was a small boy," he whispered. "They were like children themselves. I didn't appreciate them until they were sacked."

"Shut up," Strand hissed.

"Don't you tell me to shut up—"

"Shhh."

"Shh, Khooshie, please."

He fell into an offended silence.

Outside, various untranslatable sounds seeped through into the tower; but gradually they faded. Footsteps receded, shouts grew faint.

Feeling my way to the wall, I slid down to a squatting position. As my eyes weren't being used for the moment I closed them and fell to wondering at the idea of a palace dedicated to conjugation in all its convolutions, with a phallus on the roof whose testament to sex was large enough to accommodate two mercenaries and a ruler who didn't want it and a son who couldn't have it. After which, I contemplated my life for a while, wondering about my propensity for concealment, behind curtains, in cupboards, in attics and dugouts. For an awful moment I was tempted to give in to the urge to be sick, to suffer from claustrophobia, or to laugh aloud at my life, not necessarily in that order. And then I thought of the awful death of the Dewan, and it was at that moment I realized fully that the Sadhu had been his sabotage. That he had tried to render me ineffective by using the holy man with his powers to create such a massive and sustained illusion. At least I sup-

posed that the induced panorama was illusion, yet it seemed to
have happened. But what exactly was 'happen'? After all, I had
seen, smelled, felt—not floated, sense-deprived, in a dream.
Aches, cuts and burns had remained, a nail had worked loose
in the tattered remains of my boot, and every so often during
the experience—but what was 'experience'?—it had dug into
my foot. It still hurt. Was I to believe that the Sadhu incorpo-
rated this jabbing into an induced sensation along with the
stink and the scenery? And the wafts of heat up tattered
trouser legs, parched palate, strained muscle, and prickly heat?
Undeniably—apparently—it seemed—perhaps he had. I could
feel my cut forearm in the darkness. The dust had not risen, the
sun hadn't stood still. Sixty minutes had passed and no
minutes. There had been a river all right, but it was no Ganges
depiction, but a withered water course, crossable without
wetting the thighs. There were no crowds—even for Indians it
was too hot to mill. So, happen? Illusion became just another
angle on reality. What else was reality but what we maintained
it was. Perhaps it was that deliberate induction revisited, or the
strain of the hours, or perhaps—appropriately paradoxically—
it was the nature of the symbol in which we were concealed,
but I felt as if I'd suddenly become a spiritual kite, darting and
swooping high, though still attached to a bodily existence, and
perceiving that, extrapolating from the personal experience,
man was no more than the product of what he thought he was,
and that if he happened to think differently, he would become
something different. That physics was there only because we
thought it was all there. To deny the electron was to ensure
that objectively it was not there, and did not exist in physical
fact. One moment there; denial; not there. And that similarly
the universe existed only because we had decreed that it
existed. Descending to the personal, I now discovered myself
to be a pendulum, swinging a trillion years to the understanding of what we really were as humans, presently uncompre-
hended because the human imagination was still a governed
engine. But the most amazing discovery of all was that God
existed after all, not just as the engineer of the body, greatest of
the miracles, but as the anti-architect of the universe whose

presence every now and then some special human being might glimpse for a millisecond through a lightning flash of inspiration. The governed imagination with its leaps and intuitions and spiritual insights, braggartly modest in its assumptions—for example, that other worlds existed—was hardly even at the beginning of an understanding of what it had told itself was the physical world of works, thoughts, print, measurements, but which, I now divined, was God, and was therefore real as the thousand lives that Hindus implored themselves towards. And so, being absurd, the Hindus were right, and all the rest, with micrometers and treatises, joysticks, shopping lists, coffins and cakes, soap box orations and lectures on Heidegger, radio, radioactivity, activity—simply didn't understand.

We remained silent, then started to whisper. Outside they whispered and then there was silence.

We waited. The watch ticked and ticked. We hissed and listened, and argued in whispers, and finally peered out as if giving birth to ourselves, and under the lightening sky saw that the roof was deserted.

General Pertab's troops fought their way into the palace twenty minutes later.

Sigga, Outside Hospital

After saying goodbye to Strand, I belted over to the Harry Tate and took off, and headed low down flat out across the fat city walls. Usually I was respectful toward aero engines. Today I didn't care if this one melted so long as it got me to the aerodrome. I wanted to find out if I still had a fiancée, a few friends, and a job.

It didn't look too promising. Two minutes after the airplane had whizzed over the bungalow'd suburbs of Djelybad, the aerodrome smudged onto the horizon, and much of it was on fire.

The RE8 roared onward at full throttle, bellowing above the yellow plain, vertical smoke stack blowing hot, thin smoke. After yesterday's temperatures, the early morning ground was radiating heat into the still cool air, throwing the aircraft about like a ping-pong ball on a jet of water. The sun was scrawling pink grafitti in the sky. I found myself leaning forward in the cockpit to urge the airplane onward, dreading what might greet me, filled with doubt that even as bonny a fighter as Major Neale would be above to defeat a force greatly superior in numbers. His defense comprised a security force of only forty, plus whoever could be persuaded to switch their allegiance from wrench, tensionometer, or typewriter, to rifle, pistol, or machine-gun. Even before I flew off, some members of the ground staff were sullenly asserting that they were being paid to service aircraft, not to imperil their lives in a foreign cause. Neale, making no other attempt to persuade them—unless that deadly smile of his could be considered a persuasion—had offered them the alternative of being massacred when the base was overrun. Some of the men had looked rather aggrieved at such a limited choice.

As I hurtled headlong toward the smoke, the rocky yellow earth scurrying just below the wings, the picture grew more dismal still. The whole of the western side of the complex was aflame. Great rolling banners of smoke announced a calamity. Most of the buildings on this side of the base were sleeping accommodation. Those that were not on fire were devastated, as if they'd been shelled or mortared. And as I climbed for a more comprehensive view, I saw that the central part of the aerodrome too was affected—canteen, shops, dhobi, housey-housey hall. Smoke swirled between the buildings. Even as I watched, the roof of a building collapsed in a slow shower of red sparks.

My dismay deepened. I had assumed that at least part of the devastation was the work of the Khaliwar Air Force. But they were only now arriving. As I swept in to land on the far side of the complex, I saw them coming out of the north, spread across the sky at a couple of thousand feet. Dozens—no, scores of fighters and bombers, all in neat formations of threes, fives, sevens. So the devastation of the western end was solely the work of the Daja force, and the Khali Air Force had now arrived to finish us off.

There was just one hopeful sign. Apart from a small number of unserviceable aircraft, there were no Jhamjarh aircraft visible on the ground. Which was how we'd planned it: half an hour before the enemy was due, our airworthy machines were to take to the air and make themselves scarce until there was work for them to do. They would now be five miles eastward, waiting for the signal.

As I made a tight turn onto final for a fast landing, I was set on by a pair of bright green Fokkers that reminded me of the screaming parrots. As the wheels of the RE8 thumped onto the scraped plain, one of them opened fire from a hundred feet. I shoved on the rudder to change direction.

The fighter rasped overhead while the Harry Tate staggered, greatly upset at being asked to veer sixty degrees at full landing speed. It lurched toward a hangar. It didn't quite get inside. The wing hit the side of the hangar. The scenery whirled madly. The propeller struck something. Bits of laminated wood flew about.

As I leaped out, the same, or another pair of fighters came charging up, shooting away profligately. Some of their bullets were tracer, wisping through the hangar, others were explosive, crackling and smelling. As I ran out the far, open side of the hangar, the RE8 blew up. A few seconds later the canvas hangar was ablaze.

Behind the long line of hangars, pits and trenches had been clawed out of the stony ground. I jumped into the nearest trench. It was already occupied by a ground-crew man. I fell on top of him.

"Boogering 'ell."

I remembered his ugly, cheerful face but not his name. "Do you know what's happening?" I asked.

"Aye, you boogering stepped on me."

"I mean, how the defense is getting on."

"Well, there's been a boogering lot of noise from t'other end."

I stared up, panting, already soaked with sweat though the sun was hardly up, trying to get a useful impression of what looked like hundreds of aircraft as they wheeled and darted about from 2,000 to zero feet.

Now the bombs were starting to whistle untunefully. They were being aimed at the operation buildings and at the long line of hangars. The ground trembled as bombs burst in rapid succession. The hangar just to our left heaved and billowed. Shrapnel tinkled on the stony ground.

We cowered in the trench. Great Gothas, looking as if they were barely moving, were directly overhead, three of them in V formation. The earth shook again as more bombs exploded, thump, thump, thump. Half the hangars had gone already, burning, rended, collapsed. Now the enemy were turning more of their attention to the buildings, judging by the debris being hurled into the air.

I grabbed my companion's arm. "Your name's Clapper, isn't it?"

"Bell, sir. Tommy Bell."

"Are you sure it's not Clapper? I distinctly remember associating your name with tintinnabulation."

"Eh? No, sir, it's Bell."

"Anyway—" I waited until another shower of bombs had quietened down—some distance off as it happened, but you could never be sure they weren't being aimed straight at you— "is there any transport around here?"

He stared uncomprehendingly.

"Anything—car, truck, steamroller, anything?"

"Soapy Staines 'as got a bike in the next 'angar, if it's still standing. . . ."

Waiting for a lull, I jumped out of the trench and sped off in the direction indicated. As I passed other hastily dug trenches, voices called out. The voices sounded angry, as if it were their safety I was risking rather than my own.

As I darted into the hangar, the ground made like a minor earthquake. Then a heavy, distant explosion.

There it was, a bike leaning against a fitter's bench. A senior ground-staff man scuttled into the hangar after me.

"I'm glad you're alive, sir. We saw you running past."

"Yes. I'm taking this bike. Do you know what the situation is?"

"I was going to ask you, sir. The fighting at the other end seems to be getting closer."

"Yes." I looked at the other's anxious face. "Don't worry. They won't beat us as long as we have an air force," I said, wondering, as I cycled off, where the air force was, and when the hell it was going to intervene.

The air force appeared as I was pedaling along the straight track on the south side of the base; or at least the fighter element arrived—the thirty-two Vimys and DH9s had been ordered to circle high to the east until summoned by morse to join in the fighting. I was apprised of the arrival by the sight of a Fokker coming down out of control. And when I looked over my shoulder I was in time to see another, spinning into the ground.

Now a third. It was trying to pull out of a dive, with a Snipe on its tail. Oh, good, sirrah, good Snipe. The Fokker DVII's nose was coming up as it vanished behind an admin building. The Snipe veered off in a vertical bank. The enemy did not reappear.

Another, a two-seater, was twisting down, smoking. It smashed into the ground. One of its wheels bounced a prodigious height, curving and wobbling.

The sun was now fully out of bed. I could feel the heat increasing every second, and once again its brilliance was making it difficult for me to scan the sky without scalding the retinas. I had to make do with an impression of an arriving Jhamjarh Air Force rather than the actuality, a scene in a steamy mirror, glints of light against the morning blue, millisecond flashes from wings banking into different shapes, vertical trails of smoke, dots before the eyes. And noises, the hot patter of machine-guns, the two- and three-second bursts of fire joining into a continuous, overlapping popping, and the snarl of straining engines, the scream of engines in death dives.

We had about seventy fighters. The enemy had perhaps as many as 150, perhaps even 200, and as three-quarters of their total strength was involved, then the greatest air battle ever must be taking place overhead. And I could hardly see a thing in the morning glare. Just a chaos of disconnected sights and sounds, snarling engines, slashes of smoke, bump of bombs, popping of guns—My God, look at the huge Gotha, one wing on fire, red flames trailing into black smoke—the great biplane rolling slowly, infinitely slowly onto its back, and drifting to the ground, and at the last moment flattening out, but too late, and disappearing behind a building. And then a tremendous *bang*! And thin debris.

Even though he was an enemy, the heart shriveled a little at the sight. Was it because the stricken machine was so large? While that Halberstadt over there, half a mile away on the far side of the field—the one diving straight into the ground—created no other feeling but triumph?

A ball of dull red fire was going up from behind the building. The Gotha must have had a full load of bombs aboard.

At least the battle at this end of the aerodrome was going well. There could be little doubt that the KAF had been taken by surprise. It must surely be a slaughter.

Though I could see little, I knew just what was happening up there. The great Khaliwar fleet thundering out of the north, confident that they had us at their mercy. Their attention would be focused on the higgledy-piggledy ground targets, especially the long line of hangars, which they would assume to be filled with our aircraft. They would not know until it was too late that our fighters were already aloft, sailing above the dawn-stoked furnace of the sun, invisible in the glare until they came warningless along the horizontal sunbeams with spitting Vickers: sixty-nine Camels, Snipes, and Bristol fighters. And the shock and surprise would more than compensate for the Khaliwarian superiority in numbers.

But though I was sensing a victory up there in the new-born morning, it was the battle at the west end that would decide the fate of the state and the Jhamjarh Air Force. If the dacoits from Daja had succeeded in securing a foothold in the camp we were doomed whether we won the air battle or not. And it was more than possible that we had won the battle at this end of the aerodrome and lost it at the other.

I was now cycling into smoke. Gunfire was sputtering behind the smoke. My heart bulged painfully. The noise seemed to be coming from the direction of the hospital.

The hospital stood between the pumping and generating stations. Toward which I pedaled, frantic in the denser smoke. Smoldering yellow grass appeared. I identified it as the triangular patch between the generating station and the laundry.

The hospital solidified through the smoke. I saw Sigga immediately. She was wearing a white coat. She was crouching beside a stretcher. There was a long row of stretchers outside the white hospital building, and several volunteers were pottering—putting umbrellas over the wounded to shield them from the rising sun. The scene suggested the hospital was already filled to capacity. The volunteers, Indians, kept glancing apprehensively eastward at the sky.

Sigga saw me, and her expression of frowning concentration turned to one of joyful relief, to match mine. I jumped off the bicycle, allowing it to collapse in a heap, and hurried forward to embrace her. Her face was strained and there was a fresh streak of blood on her long cotton gown. Otherwise she looked her usual composed, beautiful self. Queries, requests for advice, were coming at her from all sides. Her replies were so calm and incisive that you could hardly help being steadied, and feel your heart rate slowing. For a woman of twenty-six experiencing her first battle she was doing magnificently.

I asked her if she knew what was happening, but all she knew was that she was in a rush. She was determining which of the patients on the stretchers should be first into the operating theatre. She was coming to the conclusion that she could no longer treat all the Khaliwar casualties, as otherwise she would have to neglect our own people.

It was only then when I looked along the row of stretchers that I realized that most of them were Khaliwarian dacoits, some still wearing their green and black turbans.

Only one of them was white: Albert Jones. Burly, hearty, and forty, with a red face and massive chin. Senior mechanic. That is, he usually looked red and hearty. At the moment he was deathly pale and unenthusiastic.

"Hello, Albert."

"Mr. Bandy. We was worried about you."

I looked under the blanket as I talked to him. There was a field dressing over his bare abdomen, so saturated with blood that the red stuff was trickling down his side and round the back, out of sight.

"Can't get rid of me, I'm afraid, Albert. And looks as if we won't be able to get rid of you, either."

As soon as I could I turned back to Sigga. I had to wait while she conferred with her only qualified help, the Hindu doctor who had told me that westerners smelled because they ate so much meat.

"Of course our casualties must come first," I said.

"It's an awful decision...that's official?"

"It's an order. Our men are to be treated and operated on first, the Khalis only after you've seen to our people."

"All right," she said with a regretful tone, but unable to suppress her relief entirely.

"I must go."

"So must I," Sigga said. Her eyes were already straying to a new stretcher case. The man was moaning.

"I don't even know if we've been overrun or not."

She gestured eastward. "They suddenly stopped bombing. What happened?"

"Our air force arrived. I really must go."

"Yes. I love you."

"Me too."

"Oh, sorry." She realized that in embracing me she'd streaked blood onto my shirt. She tried to wipe it off.

I pedaled off, plucking a saturated and now slightly bloody shirt from my ribs, feeling as if pixies had built camp fires in my eye sockets. The sun was only just above the low hills to the east but already its rays burned. I was not wearing a hat. I would have to do something about that very soon, assuming that it would matter whether I had sunstroke or not.

Back into the white smoke of burning buildings, expecting to run into a dacoit at any moment. After all, it was now only a hundred yards or so to the western boundary of the camp—the enemy must surely have penetrated this far. Yet despite the smoke and disorder, there seemed to be no great sense of calamity in the air. Was it possible that the infiltrators had been stopped? Now that I thought about it, the orderlies and volunteers at the hospital had been working urgently but not, so far as I could tell, with fear or anxiety. People can sense it when there is disaster in the air.

I wondered if I dared hope. Even the shooting seemed to have died down.

The smoke thinned, and the long accommodation huts came into view. One of them had almost burned out, sending up just a few puffs of red sparks.

Another upsurge of shooting—the phut and crack of rifles, the tat-tat of a machine-gun; but when the noise died down it seemed quieter than ever. Now I saw bodies, bodies everywhere, heaps of them at the entrance to one of the long huts. Everyone of them seemed to be Khaliwarian. Green and black turbans had unraveled over the ground. I halted the bicycle and stared down at one of the bodies as it lay on its side. Apart from the loss of the turban, it looked unharmed. I was not tempted to roll him over to find out how he'd died. In the war I had seen too many bodies that looked whole at first, until you moved them and they fell apart.

I picked up his rifle. Mauser, was it? Then I put it down again.

The battle seemed to have died out in the sky, as well. I shielded my eyes and scanned the skies, but couldn't see a single aircraft. It was always like that in battle. One moment a skyful of aircraft, the next, emptiness.

Major Neale arrived. He was standing on the running-board of a small lorry. He was having himself driven around to survey the damage. He jumped off and came forward.

He was *strolling*.

"Morning," he said, patting his pockets. He located a cigarette and lit it.

"So, what's been happening while I was away?" I asked, trying to sound as casual as he, but rather spoiling it with a coughing fit.

"We managed to beat them off."

"Oh, good."

"In fact I think we could safely say, Brigadier," Neale said, inhaling with evident pleasure, "that the enemy has been routed."

The plan, briefly discussed before my flight to the palace, had worked far better than we had hoped. Neale had allowed the dacoits to storm evacuated buildings. No doubt the enemy had been informed by their spies that these were accommodation huts, and at four in the morning were expecting the aircraftsmen to be asleep and to cooperate in their own slaughter.

Instead the dacoits had found empty beds but a hell of a lot of dynamite. Which was set off as soon as it was felt that enough of the enemy had been netted. Neale estimated that he had wiped out over a quarter of the attacking force in that one coup.

Other members of the Daja force had been thrown into further confusion when the defenders opened up on them from both sides with everything we had: rifles, machine-guns, grenades, anti-aircraft guns, even Very pistols, all firing into the perturbed, nightgowned figures in the green and black turbans.

"At the moment," Neale drawled, dislodging ash from the cigarette with his pinkie, "the survivors appear to be heading back toward Daja in some disorder."

"Presenting a suitable target for our bombers, Major?"

"Indeed," Neale said, looking at his watch. "They should be passing overhead any minute now."

It was nightfall before the full extent of the aerial victory could be tallied. Seventy-two Khaliwar aircraft were claimed. Ultimately this proved to be an overestimate, but forty-four were confirmed. Khaliwar had lost a fifth of its air force in ten minutes.

Among the victors, Douglas Brashman was credited with four aircraft, all confirmed, and Fetch and Carry on their first combat engagement had one between them.

Our losses amounted to nine aircraft, three of them repairable crash-landings. In the other six, two pilots had died, two were injured, and two had landed safely by parachute, one of them from a flamer.

"By Jove, you were right after all about parachutes," an observer observed wonderingly.

The celebration in the mess that night was modified only slightly by the news that the Jhamjarh Army was falling back on the capital in such disorder and so rapidly that the enemy could hardly keep up with them.

Ironically, after doing their best to destroy us as an air force, the Government of India now urgently called on our help. The moment that atmospheric conditions permitted it, communication was re-established with New Delhi. The first item of news passed to us was that the RAF station at Charanwad had been bombed shortly after dawn, and that there had been casualties and nearly all their remaining equipment had been destroyed.

As for Khaliwar's northern offensive, it was making astonishing progress. One alarmist had estimated that if sustained, the attack could see Sharif-ul-Khalil—yes, they believed at last that Sharif was behind it all—ensconced in New Delhi within a week.

At first the brass regarded this as arrant nonsense. No pair of army divisions, however well-equipped, could cover that amount of ground so speedily. Nevertheless, it was recognized that the situation was serious. There were no significant forces available even to impede the Khaliwarian advance, let alone halt it. It was estimated that it would take the only available combat troops, the 8th/15th Rajput Regiment, over a week to reach Delhi from the North-West Frontier.

Accordingly the Government wished to call on the services of the Royal Jhamjarh Air Force. "The Air Officer Commanding, India, is on his way from Calcutta to take charge of the operation, but in the meantime Government House has ordered the Jhamjarh Air Force to take action against the Khaliwar ground forces in the north. Latest reports have established the enemy in the Gwalior region," Postillion informed me when I was summoned to the RAF wireless unit in the ops building. "They want an indication of how you propose to transfer your flying machines north."

"Do they indeed?"

"They're waiting for a reply," Postillion said encouragingly.

I had managed to get some sleep that afternoon, and was feeling a bit more like my old self. "Do they indeed?" I said again. "Well, you'll have to tell them we're sorry, but the RJAF is fully engaged in defending the State of Jhamjarh."

"You can't say that," Postillion said, looking shocked.

"Why not? It's true."

He recovered quickly, and uttered a brief laugh. "But it's an order, Bandy," he said, plainly expecting that this reminder would cure my mental glaucoma.

"My dear Postillion," I said, thoroughly enjoying my blindness, "we're not subject to their orders. We're in the exclusive service of the independent state of Jhamjarh."

"But you've already recognized Delhi's authority," Postillion pointed out. The mulish expression on my face was beginning to make him look apprehensive. "You were all set to hand over your air force to the RAF only yesterday."

"Only because the Maharajah ordered it. But now he expects me to defend Jhamjarh. He told me so. So that's what I intend to do," I said, "exclusively."

After a further bout of obduracy, Postillion was finally forced to send my response to New Delhi at 22 words per minute.

An hour later came a message from His Excellency himself announcing that the Royal Jhamjarh Air Force had been placed under the command of the AOC, RAF, on whose behalf the Viceroy was demanding immediate cooperation with and subjugation to the Government of India.

I stated again that the Government had no authority to annex the RJAF and that under no circumstances was I prepared to transfer authority or personnel, or to hand over a single item of equipment. I would not provide the Government with such much as a pressure-pumping propeller—so there.

The argument with Francis Postillion grew distinctly acrimonious. He was finding it difficult to believe that the imperial authority could be defied, and at one point actually regarded me with a kind of objective awe, in the same way, perhaps, as a Roman senator might have regarded a common citizen who had contradicted a Claudian Caesar.

"You've made almost a profession out of defiance, haven't you, Bandy," he observed. "But has it ever occurred to you to ask where it's got you? Half the countries of the world seem to have kicked you out. You're practically an exile from your own land. A year ago you were in dire poverty. A year hence you could be in jail."

I started to reply. He held up his hand. "I'm not trying to threaten you, my dear chap—"

"What d'you think you've been doing for the past half hour, darning my socks?"

"—But just to draw your attention to how very little you've actually achieved of a reasonably permanent nature after seven years of your hatred of authority."

"Hatred?" I replied, shocked. "I don't hate anyone."

"You may not have admitted it to yourself, but from all the reports we've received on you, I think you hate everyone you feel was responsible for the War. I think that's the fundamental reason you're refusing to help—because the help is for the kind of man you hate most of all, Field Marshal Blount."

"Has it not occurred to you," I said loftily, "that even if I was willing to help, I couldn't? The Khaliwar forces in the north are well out of range of our aircraft."

"Nothing to stop you operating from RAF Charanwad, is there? And there's an airfield near Delhi."

"And what about Jhamjarh? Am I to abandon the state that I'm being employed to defend?"

"Oh, don't worry about that," Postillion wheedled. "They'll understand."

"They'll understand that I'm betraying them?"

"Of course. They should be used to it by now."

I stared at him. After a moment: "Unless we can stop them, the Khaliwar Army will be in Djelybad in three days, so there's no question of pulling out before Djelybad is safe and the state is secure. However, once that has been achieved, I'm ready to come to the defence of Delhi—assuming of course, that I have the Maharajah's permission."

"Yes, yes," Postillion said eagerly, "there'll be no difficulty there. Go on."

"So I'll do everything I can to help New Delhi."

"My dear chap—you don't know how relieved—"

"On condition."

"Condition? What condition?"

"On condition that the Viceroy makes a personal request—no appeal—a personal appeal to me for help."

"A personal appeal. From His Excellency."

"To me personally."

Postillion's friends in his posh London club would have been amazed to see him now, gape-mouthed as a village idiot.

"Let me see if I've understood this," he said at length. "You'll help us to defend India but only if there is a personal appeal to you from the Viceroy of India."

"Right."

"You're mad."

"M'm."

"It's outrageous," he said, positively gasping. "Do you think for one moment...he hates and despises you, man!"

"I'm sure he'll get over it if he makes the effort."

"Don't do this, Bandy. You'll just bring disaster on all of us."

"You mean it's not already upon us?"

"Bandy, you're the very last person he'd ever ask for help. The very mention of your name enlarges every visible vein and artery in his body. I think he'd die before appealing to you, to you of all people."

"Then," I said with what I was sure was a really nice smile, "he's made his bed...." And I gestured, in lieu of the remainder of the old saying.

I don't know what Postillion told New Delhi, but the reply came remarkably promptly: a demand that Postillion arrange matters so as to remove Brigadier Bandy as head of the Jhamjarh Air Force and replace him with a responsible and loyal officer who could be relied upon to place a higher priority on patriotism than on his own selfish interests.

Postillion came in with this signal into the map room where we were holding yet another emergency conference, this one to hear from a senior officer of the Jhamjarh Army about their attempts to regroup in front of the capital.

After communicating the contents of the latest message from New Delhi to a shocked and silent assembly, Postillion went on to underline the gravity of the situation in New Delhi. In some quarters the atmosphere was close to panic, as reports continued to flood in from commissioners, political agents, aides-de-camp, lieutenant-governors, and Indian and British observers in contiguous, independent states and British-controlled territories, on the progress of the Khaliwarian offensive. They had already cut the Bombay-New Delhi railway supply line in two places, and at the rate they were progressing, they would be in New Delhi in another six days.

The situation was desperate. Accordingly, Postillion said, His Excellency the Viceroy had formally ordered that an amenable officer be appointed head of the Jhamjarh Air Force. "And in discussions with you, Colonel Mays," Postillion said, turning to our most upper-crust colleague, "I have decided that the person should be you. I believe that in the British Army you were second to the Paymaster General?"

"Yes."

I noticed Petronella Spencer scribbling away frantically. "Might it not be advisable to ask a certain foreign journalist to leave?" I suggested; but Postillion seemed determined to eliminate me verbally as well as officially; so I fell silent, got down from the platform from which I had been addressing the assembled air and ground officers, and sat down on a hastily vacated chair at the front of the room. From there I listened to the ensuing discussion with some interest.

Not that there was a great deal of discussion. Postillion had it all wrapped up. "I have been authorized to promote you to Brigadier," he told Mays, "with full Army pay and allowances, and I am to assure you that a senior officer's pension will be forthcoming once the emergency is over."

Mays had hardly rippled a sinew since Postillion had offered him promotion. He did so now. He blinked. "That's very gratifying, sir," he said warmly. "I always wanted to be a general. When you retire, it can get you onto all sorts of boards of directors, with excellent remuneration and no responsibilities worth mentioning. Thanks very much."

Postillion's relief was audible as well as visible. He issued a sigh, and turned as relaxed as if he'd been dead two days.

"But a knighthood would come in even more useful," Mays hinted with a smooth smile, ignoring Hibbert's look of burning-eyed fury and the shocked silence of the rest of them.

Even Postillion looked a bit taken aback. "Well, I...I suppose that might be arranged," he faltered.

"And perhaps a Victoria Cross, or some such award for bravery?"

"Well, hardly a Victoria Cross," Postillion said uneasily, "but I think a DSO could be...."

"But couldn't you make me a full General?" Mays pleaded, "Or even a Field Marshal?"

Even Postillion was beginning to look at Mays with contempt. "I don't think this is quite the right time to discuss that, Mays," he said, trying really hard to sustain a smile. "All I need at the moment is your formal agreement to take over responsibility for the Jhamjarh Air Force, so I can signal New Delhi immediately to that effect."

"My formal agreement to take over from Bandy," Mays said thoughtfully over the tense silence.

"Yes, so we can get on with the planning for the transfer of equipment and personnel to Charanwad."

"Ah." Mays touched the distinguished gray hair at his temples. "Yes, well, of *course* you can have my formal reply," he said warmly. "My reply is that you can go and jump in the lake."

"...what?"

"Even if you have to travel some distance to find a lake." Mays' smooth, gentlemanly face hardened. "And that goes for New Delhi as well."

At which, after two seconds of stunned silence, an outbreak of cheering arose from an audience that, during the last few minutes, had been augmented by a number of other ranks— and Sigga. I caught a glimpse of her halo of curly hair before she disappeared behind the crush of bodies in the doorway.

When the tumult had died down sufficiently to enable him to be heard, Mays continued somberly, "I'm not saying I'm totally in sympathy with Mr. Bandy's opinion of New Delhi. It's true that they have been quite extraordinarily ostrich-like in their views. But they are, after all, our people, and it's now obvious that they desperately need our help.

"But, Mr. Postillion, so does the Maharajah who created this air force. Which deserves greater loyalty, Mr. Postillion—his prescience, or the Viceroy's skill in throwing sand in his own eyes? It's not just a matter of who is paying us. It's a matter of a loyalty that I feel should transcend the kind of patriotism you're calling on us to acknowledge."

"Good on you, Maysy," said an Australian voice at top volume, and there was another outbreak of applause; in the midst of which a pilot leaped onto the platform and shouted and waved his arms until he could be heard. "I don't know anything about that," he shouted, not making it entirely clear what it was he didn't know anything about. "All I know is we'd all have been massacred in our beds if it hadn't been for Bandy getting back in time with that Jerry of his, and I'm with him, and bugger all Field Marshals, it was they who killed my brother, and my best friend in school, and gassed my father, and, and. . . ." But at that point he either lost confidence or the thread of his speech, for he faltered. But his place was taken by another pilot, a Canadian, who said, "I got to admit the Brig is one of the oddest characters I've ever met—" there were cries at this, whether of protest or hilarity I couldn't tell—the former, I trusted—"but everything I've ever heard about him says he's one hell of a leader and he's got guts, and gets things done, and there's no horse shit about him—in spite of his face—"

The rest was drowned in a fresh uproar, interrupted by yet another speaker, who also said some amusing though not particularly complimentary things about me, but also one or two things to my credit; which brought on yet another demonstration in favor of keeping me hitched up instead of being put out to pasture.

Last to contribute to the discussion was Hibbert, and perhaps because he spoke most quietly, though with uncommon passion, his words seemed to have the greatest impact. "What astonishes me is that someone as intelligent as you, Mr. Postillion, would go along with this idea of substituting an unknown quantity, militarily speaking, for a man who has demonstrated his extraordinary abilities over and over again." He glanced at Mays before turning back to a now decidedly pale Postillion. "I'm sorry, Mays, but I must be honest."

"Well, if you must," Mays said, waving his hand.

"It would take too long to list his martial achievements," Hib continued, "except that once again we've seen the sort of person he is, fighting his way back from captivity against fearful odds, to save us from massacre—and let's have no illusions about that. We would all be dead by now, if it weren't for him. I know that Major Neale devised and organized the defense of the aerodrome, but it was Bandy who picked Neale, trusted him, gave him the clear, simple orders of the sort that only great commanders know how to give, and then left him to it."

"Right—I let him do all the work," I put in.

Hibbert ignored the interruption. "Personally," he said, "I see that as the finest kind of leadership, and I know that's just how Neale sees it as well." Several faces turned to check whether Neale agreed with this or not. Neale, in the far corner, must have felt it was not the right moment for controversy, for he nodded faintly. "And you dare," Hibbert said, his usually phlegmatic voice quivering with anger, and glaring at Postillion with volcanic eyes, "to try and bully and blackmail us into replacing a man like that? And at a time like this when his experience, and his original and unconventional qualities are perhaps all that can save us from being overwhelmed? What I say, Mr. Postillion, is, how dare you. How bloody dare you."

At which point I spoke the words that eliminated any doubt that I was the right man to lead them to death or glory.

"I need a drink," I said. "Will somebody fix me a chota peg?"

Bamm Bridge

A t first, even the most urgent messages from senior representatives of the Raj had been dismissed by Government House as ludicrously exaggerated. The Viceroy reminded his advisors that he was a Field Marshal and knew something of military matters. No army could possibly advance as rapidly as the hysterical signals asserted. Militarily, geographically, mechanically, logistically, it was utterly impossible. But as the reports continued to crowd in—or, ominously, failed to come in, suggesting that some official centres were no longer in a position to communicate—the Viceroy began to suspect that all was not as it should be. Even so, it was not until he received rather more direct evidence in the form of a stick of bombs dropped in the gardens of Government House that the reality of the situation was forced upon him. A piddling independent state with a past record of doubtful loyalty to the Raj was actually challenging the might of the Empire. But damn it, it was contrary to the evidence. Had the brasshats not seen for themselves that the Khaliwar Army was an ill-equipped rabble? That its official ruler, Mohammed Farookhi, was a rather disgusting fellow with pederastic rather than territorial ambitions? But with the bombing of his official residence, the Viceroy and his advisors could have no further doubt that they had been systematically fooled over the true state of Khaliwar's military preparedness.

The civilian population proved to be rather more alert to the realities. By the afternoon of the second day of the northern offensive, wealthy Indians and members of the despised British commercial class started moving out of the capital, and many a boxwallah decided to investigate commercial opportunities in other parts of the subcontinent. A third of the shops and market stalls in Old Delhi failed to open on the following morning. Army and Civil Service wives who had prided themselves on their steadfastness in remaining by their husbands' sides, braving the heat of summer, quickly rediscovered the attractions of Simla. Minor looting broke out. Frightening rumors spread that the Government was making contingency plans to evacuate senior civil servants. While the truth was beginning to sound even worse than the rumors: the Rajput Regiment which was supposed to be rushing to the rescue had covered exactly one-eighth the distance traveled by the Khaliwarians in the same period, or five miles to the Khalis' forty, at which rate the 8th/15th would end up not defending New Delhi but having to retake it from the enemy—assuming that even the finest regiment was capable of dealing with two highly mobile divisions trained by German officers and motivated by ruthless commissars.

That was perhaps the worst news of all to reach Delhi—that Soviet Russia was involved. When Postillion first reported on his interview with Strand and I, it was just one more item for the Government to pooh-pooh; until the arrest of an Indian clerk in New Delhi on quite another matter revealed that he was acting as an agent for the GPU, and had in his possession a number of documents confirming Soviet Russia's active interest in Khaliwarian affairs.

The confidence expressed in the captured documents that Khaliwar was certain to capture Delhi and that the only worry was whether Sharif-ul-Khalil had the means to secure it against determined counter-attacks, was the most alarming revelation of all. It led to yet another attempt to expropriate the RJAF. However, on this occasion there was a distinct change of tactics. Having failed to conscript or replace me, they now attempted to persuade me to volunteer on the grounds of self-interest and self-preservation. And as the man on the spot, Postillion was given the job of appealing to my greedy nature. There were no direct bribes, of course; just hints that friends in the right place, presumably meaning the City, would be my safest investment in the future.

"Exactly what friends are you talking about, Francis? Lord Blount?"

"Good God, no—I mean, not exactly, old man," Postillion said with a really nice smile on his fair English face. "But there are other people in the Government besides him, you know."

"He's not ready to make a personal appeal to me, then?"

Postillion shoved the hair back from his intellectual brow with an impatient sweep. "Bandy, you really must take my word for it—he'll never do that, never."

"Then there's no point in talking, Francis. A personal appeal to me is the only way he's ever going to get help from the Royal Jhamjarh Air Force."

"Good God, man, you can't do this! For one thing, you're putting yourself on the same side as the Bolsheviks you're supposed to hate so much!"

"I've told you," I said, looking terribly reasonable, "I'm quite willing to do all I can. Assuming we survive in this neck of the woods, I'm ready, considering the gravity of the situation facing Delhi, to give you maximum possible air support—in return for a simple letter to me from His Excellency. All he has to do," I concluded, spreading my arms to show how reasonable I was being, "is to write me a letter asking me as a favor to aid the old country in its hour of need, and I shall come to his rescue in a trice. He doesn't even have to acknowledge that the Maharajah of Jhamjarh warned him repeatedly about the danger from Khaliwar or confess that he was blinded by suspicion of Jhamjarh and prejudice against me. He doesn't have to make the slightest confession of his own incompetence. All he has to do, Francis, is say pretty please."

He lost his temper. "You damn fool, he'll never do that! He hates you from your horse-face to your clopping feet!"

"Well, it's either me or disaster," I said equably.

"Some choice," I heard somebody murmur; while Postillion

looked around desperately, at Hib, Mays, Cot McNeil, Brashman, and others in the hope that they might support him; but
though some of them considered my attitude to be a trifle
mulish, none of them were prepared to say so or even meet
Postillion's eye.

Postillion turned and walked out; and this time he seemed
to have given up. Two hours later he left the base, taking the
RAF signals unit with him.

For the next twenty-four hours I hardly moved from the map
room except to sleep, eat, look at photographs, bathe, change
my underwear every few minutes, visit the hospital to see how
Sigridur was coping with the rush of business, and puzzle out
what was happening on the road to Djelybad.

All that afternoon and evening, Khali fighters had been
patroling a stretch of the central route from Khaliwar so
diligently and at such strength that we could not get close
enough to find out what was interesting them. Every time our
aircraft approached they were driven off by a truly astonishing
concentration of enemy warplanes—up to sixty Fokkers at a
time, according to Douglas Brashman.

One of our more enterprising Bristol fighter pilots decided
to follow one of the bunches of aircraft that were being
relieved every couple of hours by fresh supplies of fighters.
Keeping well back in his photographic Bristol, he followed the
Fokkers over the border and saw them drifting down to a
landing field just two or three miles inside Khaliwar. He
managed to expose half a dozen photographic plates before
being chased away.

This was the first we'd known of it, that the KAF was using
an advanced landing field—though if we'd had time to think
about it we'd have realized that their aircraft could hardly be
operating from distant Ujipatan valley and still be able to hang
about over Jhamjarh for two hours at a time. That evening at
sunset the hastily processed plates were examined with considerable interest. They revealed that it was not just a landing
field, but an extensive if temporary aerodrome with a runway,
tarpaulined areas of what we took to be fuel and ammunition

dumps, a transport park, and lines of assorted tents in a nearby field. We counted seventy tents.

"So that's how they're managing to operate so freely over Jhamjarh," Hibbert exclaimed.

"And maintain almost constant air cover over the road," I mused.

But what was the air cover covering, that was the question. According to the latest reconnaissance report, even the forward elements of the Khaliwar Army advancing down the central highway were still twenty-five miles from Djelybad. So the fighters were not directly protecting their ground forces.

I crossed to the map of Central Jhamjarh, and had just asked somebody to pinpoint the area that the KAF was so dedicatedly patroling, when a clerk stuck his napper through the doorway and called out that there was an Indian geezer here to see us.

This turned out to be the captain who had been appointed liaison officer between us and the Jhamjarh Army. He was usually to be found in the billiard room trying out various pots to lay a snooker. In fact he had his cue with him right now.

It turned out that he also had the worst news of the war.

To begin with, he informed us, nearly all of the Jhamjarh army bases had been bombed, even the recruiting depot far to the south, and the establishments were still in chaos. And the new hospital in Djelybad was overflowing with casualties. The liaison officer had seen this for himself when he went to see his brother, who had been trapped for hours in a bombed building, and had lost both legs.

"My dear chap," Mays murmured sympathetically.

"What?" the liaison officer asked.

"I was being sympathetic," Mays explained.

"But it is my brother who has lost all his legs, not I."

"M'm. Anyway, carry on."

"Well, as I was saying before I was very politely interrupted, the hospital is so full that all the latest casualties are being put in the gardens; and that is one reason I have been asked to report to you, Brigadier Sahib. Supreme Headquarters, Northern Operations, are in dire need of umbrellas."

"Umbrellas?"

"To keep the sun off all the wounded people who are out in the open, you see."

"Oh. Well, we'll see what we have, Captain, but...surely the Maharajah has lots of tents in the City Palace."

"No, no, it is umbrellas that we are wanting."

"But wouldn't tents be better?"

"Put up a tent over each casualty, you mean? I don't think even His Highness has that many tents."

"I meant, you could put several casualties in each tent."

"Oh," said the liaison officer, thinking about it. His face lit up. "Of course," he exclaimed. "What an absolutely wonderful idea. I will pass that on to Supreme Headquarters, Northern Operations, immediately," he cried, and turned to dash off.

"Wait. Didn't you say you had an important item of news?"

"Oh, yes," he said, potting an imaginary ball with his billiard cue, and went on to describe some other problems that General Pertab was facing, "not counting his narrow escape from death."

"My God, what happened?"

"To General Pertab?"

"Yes."

"The C-in-C?"

"Yes, yes. What happened to him?"

"A shell landed on his advance HQ, you see. Had General Pertab not been elsewhere at the time, engaged in vital discussions with his astrologer, he would almost certainly have been killed."

"Captain."

"Yes, sir?"

"You're not related to a station master named Chatterjee, by any chance?"

"Good heavens, no, Sahib. Only half-castes do that sort of job. Why do you ask?"

"Oh, nothing. What are the other problems General Pertab is facing?"

"Let me see, now. Oh, yes. The driver of our tank is claiming that he is in no position to take part in any counter-attacks, as he is unable to start the engine—even though," the liaison

officer exclaimed indignantly, "the tank was working beautifully just the other day when it was being used to plough
General Liaquat Khan's betel field near his bungalow. Also,
members of the Army's elite Hotstream Guards have been
caught trying to buy second-class railway tickets to Bombay.

"Let me see, now, what else did General Pertab wish me to
say?" the liaison officer mused, diligently chalking his cue
before potting somebody's cigarette lighter. "Oh, yes, the
ammunition dump at Fort Dudley has been blown up by a
person or persons unknown—possibly the commandant, who
was recently passed over for promotion on account of his
camel. That is why we have not been able to explode the Bamm
bridge, you see. There is no more dynamite available."

As he continued to pot everything in sight with his cue, he
seemed oblivious of the shocked silence that had descended
on the map room; except that silence seemed such an inadequate word to describe that profound, motionless, breathless
stillness that followed the captain's throwaway line.

"Also," he went on, "I am to convey an invitation from the
commander of the new division. He is getting married, you see,
and—"

"Wait a minute. Say that again about the Bamm bridge?"

"Yes, that is the principal thing General Pertab wished me to
explain, Brigadier Sahib. There is no problem as regards the
Bamm *railway* bridge further along. That has been thoroughly
destroyed, don't you worry. But so far as he knows, not a great
deal has been done about the road bridge."

"You're telling us that the Bamm road bridge, five miles
north of Djelybad, is still intact?"

"My God," Hibbert said faintly. "*That's* what they're doing
over the road—guarding the bridge until their army gets
there...."

I looked at the map, and nodded, feeling chilly in the heat.

"But don't you worry, Brigadier," the captain added. "As
soon as we get ourselves sorted out, we'll give these Khalis
what for, eh? Give them the jolly good hiding they deserve."

I'd had to sit down. I stared at him.

"However," he went on, busily disassembling his cue with

his neat brown hands, unscrewing each section with delicate movements, "to achieve the inevitable victory, General Pertab requires a small favor. He would be much obliged if you would demolish the bridge as soon as possible, just in case the Khalis are thinking of using it—"

"Wait. I really do have got this straight, have I?" I asked. "The *rail* bridge over the Bamm river gorge further up has been demolished—even though we use it and we've had no reports that the Khalis are using the railway line. But the Bamm *road* bridge, on the road that the Khalis are concentrating their entire effort, has *not* been demolished?"

"That is so, yes."

"...Thank you...Just wanted to get it straight, that's all," I said.

"You're welcome," said the liaison officer.

By dusk we were whelmed with so many problems, crises, and emergencies that they were in danger of combining into a mush of unidentifiable ingredients. The worst news was the report from the crew of one of our battered RE8s that the Khaliwar Army was not twenty-five miles away as we'd thought, but had halted for the night just eight miles north of the Bamm river. Presumably at sunrise their armored cars would make a dash for the bridge. It was almost certain to be in their possession by six in the morning.

Meanwhile their air force continued to protect the bridge right up to dusk before returning to their advance base. So we had no time to mount an attack on the bridge before dark.

As for bombing it after dark, we had done a little night flying but no night bombing practice. It had not occurred to us that it might be necessary.

Nevertheless we agreed that we would have to make the attempt. Volunteers were called for among the DH9 and Vimy crews.

They were scheduled to go out shortly after midnight.

At eleven-thirty the field telephone connecting us with the City Palace rattled, and the ruler himself came on the line to inform me that he was calling an emergency meeting at the palace, and wished me to be present.

I explained that it was impossible. Was he aware that the Bamm bridge was intact? He was. Then he must know that unless we succeeded in destroying it before the enemy got there at six a.m., Djelybad would be in their hands before noon. We were busy at the moment, planning that attack.

He understood. Nevertheless, I must attend the meeting. It was important. "After all, Mr. Bandy," came his squeaky but irrationally calm voice down the line, "Your officers managed quite well without you while you were gallivanting around Khaliwar, did they not? Just give them the usual orders, Mr. Bandy, and let them get on with it. After all, you are always saying that a commander should encourage everybody to do all the work and take all the risks while he gets all the credit."

"Well, I...I tend to exaggerate sometimes. I—"

"By the way, I myself have paid Mr. Strand his two thousand pounds," he said in a wheedling tone, as if that bit of news might make me more amenable. "And he has gone off hot foot to Bombay."

I was glad that Strand had got away—he would have suffered a bit if Panyushkin had collared him when, as now seemed likely, the commissar rode into Djelybad tomorrow; but I had other things on my mind. "But sir," I said, "we have a lot of other decisions to make in the next couple of hours—"

"No, no, I must have you here, Mr. Bandy, and that is all there is to it, please, if you don't mind," the Maharajah said with uncharacteristic firmness; an infuriating firmness considering that this was the one time I needed him to be weak and vacillating.

"But, sir," I said despairingly.

"As soon as you can get here, Mr. Bandy, Please."

I racked my napper for excuses, and trotted them out one after the other, ending with the brainwave: "Ah. I really want to attend your meeting, Your Highness, I really do. I'm awfully disappointed I can't be there—but you see it's too dark for me to land in the palace grounds."

"You did so the other day, Mr. Bandy."

"Yahbut there was a bright moon then, you see. But there's no moon at all tonight, you see," I said, quite truthfully.

"That's all right. We'll see to that, Mr. Bandy."

"You'll supply a moon?"

"Khooshie will arrange to illuminate the polo field for you, he says."

It was hopeless. He had an answer for everything.

I'd never heard the bugger speaking so incisively before. In fact he sounded strange, as if the incisiveness was disconcerting him as well.

"At least let me see the men off at midnight, Your Highness," I begged.

There was a pause. I heard tinny voices. He was consulting somebody. I could guess who. Then the sound went all muffled, as if the Maharajah had covered the telephone mouthpiece with a racing gauntlet.

Two more precious minutes elapsed before he came on the line again. "Very well, Mr. Bandy, but we shall be expecting you very soon after midnight," he said, and actually hung up on me—decisively.

Hibbert, Mays, and others had been listening to all this, so at least I didn't have to waste time filling them in. "Well, at least it gives me an excuse to see for myself how the bombing goes," I said, mopping my face with a towel and, always concerned with economy, squeezing the towel over Hibbert's favorite rubber plant. The sweat pattered noisily onto the broad, shiny leaves.

"Don't do that," Hibbert said irritably. "All that salt's not good for it. What do you mean, see for yourself?"

"I'll accompany the bombers, to see how they get on, and fly on to the palace from there."

Either Hibbert was too annoyed over my treatment of his rubber plant, or too tired to manifest his usual concern for my safety or wellbeing, but he made no attempt to dissuade me. So I called for my personal mount to be wheeled out of the hangar while I changed into fresh blue shirt and trousers—which remained dry for a good four minutes before the sweat started gnawing again at the fibres; and ten minutes later I was taxi-ing through the night with the DH9s and Vimys, and testing the magnetos while I watched the others taking off one after the other in rapid succession between the two rows of flickering oil pots.

Night flying always made me a bit nervous. As I lifted the biplane into the hot, starlit sky, I had to force myself to relax and concentrate on flying the twenty or so miles to the Bamm river without crashing into any of the other machines; though as it turned out, they were visible even by starlight alone.

As was the bridge when we got there—from a thousand feet a dismayingly narrow target. The first bombs were already flashing around it when I got there. But they were bursting as far from the target as five hundred feet. And I knew right away that short of a suicide dive with a full load of bombs, we weren't going to succeed.

Perhaps for some odd security reason the meeting that early morning was held in the stables adjoining the polo field.

Naturally these were no ordinary stables, but a city of wood and horseflesh. It housed hundreds of horses—Khooshie alone used seventy polo ponies during the season, and the building was scaled accordingly, an enormous wooden structure radiating spokes, the interior decorated with carved and polished woods, Jackfield tiles, and the inevitable acreage of marble. Even the feed bins were carved.

The meeting was held in a large wooden chamber with a quarry-tiled floor in green and brown. In the centre of the room a lonely-looking octagonal table had been placed; and to indicate the seriousness of the situation, the Maharajah was seated at it. He was actually sitting on a western chair.

Also present were the new Dewan, over-respectful towards everybody, General Pertab, looking very subdued, and Khooshie, who was pacing, animal-like, over the green and brown tiles, and refusing to look at anybody.

And of course, Francis Postillion. He was standing at a window, gazing into the starlit night. Every now and then he would rise onto his toes, then apply his heels to the tiles again with an unsynchronized click. Click-click.

I looked around, waiting for somebody to speak. Nobody spoke. The Maharajah hung his head.

I could guess what was coming. To postpone their bad news for as long as possible, I thought I'd give them mine. "I guess you'll want a report on our progress re the Bamm bridge, Your Highness," I said.

"Yes, yes, of course," he said listlessly.

"Well, there's no progress, sir. We've just attempted night bombing, and it's failed. We'll have to wait 'til daylight. But the problem is—"

"Yes, well, I'm sure you'll manage all right, Mr. Bandy."

Staring at him, I felt my way into a chair. Manage all right? Yes, we might manage all right. But there might not be much left of the air force by the time thirty to sixty Fokkers had finished with my bombers.

I tried to inject a little realism into the atmosphere.

"You realize, of course, that if we fail, the Khaliwar Army could be here by mid-morning?"

"I'm sure you won't fail, Mr. Bandy," he said. In contrast to his businesslike tones over the telephone he was now sunk in profoundest melancholy. "You are much too resourceful for that."

Christ. We were faced with a desperate engagement, and he was talking as if he were sending me to market for some radishes.

"It's all academic anyway," the old man went on; and announced that the Royal Jhamjarh Air Force was to be handed over to the government, lock, stock, and barrel.

In the silence, General Pertab glanced up guiltily, before resuming the important task of polishing his pince-nez. The gray hair fringing his shiny summit was awry, as if he'd been running his hand through it a few times.

"Of course I'm sure you will be allowed time to destroy the bridge before the transfer," Postillion said from the far window. "I'm sure that New Delhi will understand the necessity for what, when I explain the circumstances."

"The circumstances being that we'd all be dead by noon, otherwise."

"Precisely. We'll need a few hours breathing space before the move to RAF Charanwad. Arrangements have already been made to receive your aircraft and personnel there," he added smoothly. "Your pilots will, of course, continue to fly the machines until such time as RAF personnel become available."

I could hardly believe this; that they were arranging for the certain defeat of Jhamjarh as if it were the most natural thing in the world.

I looked at the Maharajah. "It is a direct order, you see, from the Viceroy himself," he said.

"I see."

"But they are promising to return the aeroplanes the moment they are no longer needed in the emergency," he added. "I have Mr. Postillion's firmest assurance on that, don't you worry."

"Your equipment is more urgently needed than ever," Postillion said, now joining us at the table. "The latest information we have is that by tomorrow the Khaliwar Army will be within ninety miles of the imperial capital. New Delhi simply cannot be allowed to fall, Bandy. Two thousand years of Indian history suggests that whoever holds Delhi controls the subcontinent. And with the Russians involved, however unofficially...well, we can hardly ignore the fact that they live just the other side of Afghanistan."

I stirred. Everybody tensed, as if I'd pulled out a gun. "May I see you in private, Your Highness?" I asked.

"You may not," Postillion said. "Anything you have to say must be said to this committee at large."

"Oh, this is a committee, is it?"

"For the purposes of expediting the transfer of the Jhamjarh Air Force to the imperial authority, yes. That is the only subject we are here to discuss."

"So His Highness no longer has any say in his own state?"

"I'm not saying that at all."

"Yes, you are."

"No, I'm not."

"Yes, you are," Khooshie burst out, halting for a moment to round on us fists clenched, eyes bulging with fury.

But the fury was making him incoherent. After a frightful inner battle it forced him to shut up and resume his frantic pacing.

"We can do nothing," the Maharajah said dully. "He is the Viceroy."

In the distance a horse whinnied; while I looked around at them, and realized that no amount of logical, sensible argument was going to sway them, even though I was a past master at it.

There was only one thing for it.

"Your Highness," I said, taking out my pipe in order to show off my strong, lean, reliable fingers, as I tamped down the burned embers, "I've saved Khooshie's life three times, isn't that right?"

"This is no time to bring that up," Khooshie said, hardly able to force the words from his constricted throat.

Seeing what was coming, Postillion tried to interrupt, but I overrode him. "Well, here is the perfect opportunity for you, sir, to completely discharge your debt," I cried cheerfully.

"I must warn you, Your Highness," Postillion began; but the Maharajah gestured him to a halt.

"What is it you want, Mr. Bandy?" he asked.

"I want you to make me chief of the Air Force—"

"But you already are."

"With sole responsibility for it. I want you to give me the sole right to make all decisions concerning the Air Force. So all the decisions and the consequences will be mine alone. And the government will not be able to blame you, whatever happens."

"What utter rubbish," Postillion cried. "Sir, you cannot evade an invoice just by putting somebody else's name on it."

"I don't see why not," General Pertab said, beginning to look quite interested. "I do it all the time. I put the Army's name on all my bills."

"You established the Air Force, your treasury sustains it, so you answer for it," Postillion snarled at the ruler. "You can't evade the responsibility that easily."

"He's not evading it, he's fulfilling his debt of honor to me," I said.

Lord, I hated saying it, but it was the only way. "His Highness places the obligations of honor above all other considerations, don't you, sir?"

"Uh..."

"Whatever the short-term discomforts of Viceregal disapprobation," I added, while thinking to myself, gad, that was a good point—the Maharajah was in favor of long- rather than short-term objectives—spiritual ones, at least.

Thus the argument raged back and forth, if 'raged' was the right word to describe a pretentious debate between a scheming counter-intelligence tout masquerading as an inverted Philistine civil servant, and a colonial charlatan disguised as a parfit knight with no axe to grind except the one he used to pry open treasure chests, locked doors, chastity belts, etc; until finally Postillion lost his temper completely. "That's not fair," he shouted at me. "You're making it a personal matter when he should be thinking about what's best for the state."

"The personal matter *is* best for the state."

"Shut up! Sir, can't you see he's blackmailing you?"

"I'm far too gentlemanly," I said haughtily, "to allow this discussion to descend to the gutter level of personal recrimination."

"Thank goodness," said the Maharajah, looking quite distressed.

"The implication of your remarks," I continued, "is that you know what's best for this independent state. Well, sucks to you with knobs on, Cuthbert, I don't think you know what would be best for a flea in a paraffin factory. While I, on the contrary, have unqualified respect for His Highness' ability to do the right thing by his—"

"And I say he shouldn't allow his personal obligations to outweigh the broader considerations of—"

"See, he's doing it again," I cheated, turning to a dazed

Maharajah, "he's not only telling you what to do, now he's telling you what to think."

"Oooh, you unprincipled cad, I am nothing of the sort! You're making me look—"

"Look who's calling the pot unprincipled, you kettle!"

"You dirty pot!"

"And you're nothing but a grubby spy."

"And you're a moldy Colonial!"

"Shut up, yuh yellow-eyed maggot!"

"You shut up, you carthorse who thinks he's a thoroughbred!"

"Gentlemen, gentlemen," said the C-in-C in his reedy voice, and agitatedly removed his pince-nez to massage the grooves in his beak. While the new Dewan said, "This is not the sort of behavior we expect of you people."

"Well. . . ."

"Well. . . ."

"You must set an example to us natives, you know."

"They are setting it," General Pertab said, "that's the trouble."

The Maharajah had been covering his sunken face with one hand. "The trouble is, Mr. Bandy," he said, "that we greatly owe loyalty to the office of the Viceroy, even if we're not particularly taken with the chap who's in the office. Whereas my debt to you, my dear Mr. Bandy, is only personal. Which, as Mr. Postillion indicates, should be subordinate to principle."

Postillion smirked. Khooshie keened.

"On the other hand," the Maharajah said thoughtfully, "I am indebted because you saved Khooshie's life. And Khooshie is the future embodiment of the state. Therefore my debt to Mr. Bandy is not personal at all." His beautiful dark eyes shone. "Yes, yes, I see it now," he cried. "In acceding to Mr. Bandy's request, I am supporting a principle, the principle of the state. Why, there is no conflict here at all! And so I can decide what is best for Jhamjarh without any trouble at all.

"So I have made my decision," he said looking around proudly. "Which is, that it is up to Mr. Bandy to decide what to do with the Air Force. That is what I am deciding," he said, and leaned back in his unaccustomed chair with a look of profound satisfaction over so elegant a solution.

After I had confirmed that under no circumstances would one single item of Royal Jhamjarh Air Force equipment be transferred to the imperial authority—"Neither a lender nor a borrower be," quoth I with sententious gravity—Postillion started for the door. Halfway there he turned back and approached, wearing solicitude on his sleeve. "By the way, Bandy," he said softly, "I have some bad news for you."

"That'll make a change."

"For you personally. I was notified just last night. Your friend Derby died of his wounds at Charanwad."

I didn't say anything. Khooshie's head turned sharply, his brief glee at the turn of events fading.

He drew closer, his face softening into pain.

"It wasn't the injury you know about," Postillion continued. "I believe you sent him to the RAF station there, so he could receive prompt medical attention?"

"I...yes."

"Well, I'm afraid you sent him to his death, Bandy," Postillion said, holding a flop of fair hair out of his eyes with one hand. "He got there just in time for the bombing of Charanwad. The rest of your crew are all right, but Derby, it seems, was killed just outside the hospital."

He removed his hand. The hair flopped back into his eyes. "I just wanted to let you know," he said, so sympathetically.

But then his face betrayed him.

At the very last moment the fair features under that intellectual brow hardened into a look of pure vindictiveness.

Group Shot

Before I set off for the palace we'd had a hurried discussion on our options in the event that the bombing attempt on the Bamm bridge was a failure. Many of us suspected that we had not practised enough night-bombing to succeed, and the results had now confirmed those suspicions. The truth was that even our day-bombing left a lot to be desired.

So we had considered all kinds of alternatives, many of them quite desperate. We thought of despatching Major Neale in a fast car with bodyguards and a demolition expert, but there were two drawbacks to this proposal: one, Major Neale was not available, as he was out clobbering dacoits, and, two, nobody knew how to demolish a steel bridge. Besides, it was unlikely that they could have reached the bridge in time. And among other schemes we considered piling enough explosives into a giant Handley Page, landing it on the road, and blasting the bridge by sheer brute power as an alternative to employing a little engineering skill. This alternative, too, was abandoned when no volunteers could be found to land an aircraft packed with high explosives in pitch darkness.

They were still discussing the situation when I reached the operations building shortly after three in the morning, and they had reached the conclusion that we would have to attack the bridge at first light with every bomber we possessed, escorted by every fighter we could muster.

"No," quoth I, leaning against a table in the map room and puffing away at my pipe. I don't know why I was puffing my pipe—the tobacco tasted vile at that time in the morning. "I've been thinking."

"Oh, no."

"With the fleet that the KAF will certainly muster at the bridge at first light, there would be a slaughter. They know just as well as we do how vital that bridge is. We could easily fail, end up with heavy casualties, and have nothing to show for it."

"I don't see what else we can do," Mays said. "We've been gassing about it ever since the first lot of bombers got back. The only alternative we can see is to get out while we still have a chance. Evacuate the base, before their army gets here."

"No," I said, "we're not going to evacuate the aerodrome *or* throw everything we've got at the bridge. This forward base of theirs, just inside their border—that's where most of us are going, gentlemen.

"At four o'clock, in less than an hour's time, I'm sending every machine that's not needed for the bombing to attack the forward base at first light: a few DH9s, all the DH4's, and all the Snipes, Camels, and Bristols, with wing racks loaded.

"The rest of the bombers will deal with the Bamm bridge unescorted."

The heat, which had hardly abated for days now, was probably responsible for the harsh, intemperate reception this little speech received. I continued to puff at my pipe until the noise had subsided sufficiently to make myself heard.

"I know it's a risk," I said.

"A risk? It's madness."

"It's out of the question," a flight commander said hoarsely. "What if we got to the forward base at dawn and they weren't there—they were already on their way to the bridge? Christ, there really would be a slaughter, then."

There was a surge of agreement. "Good God, Bart," Cot said, "they'd knock down every one of our planes."

"It's a totally unjustifiable proposal," Mays said with heavy authority. "Far better to concentrate our strength at the bridge and hope for the best. At least we'd have a chance of destroying the bridge."

"Hib?"

"I must say I agree, sir. If *we* can fly to *their* advance base in the dark, they're just as likely to fly to the bridge in the dark—with the inevitable results."

"We'd not only arrive with nobody to bomb but we'd have gone on a wild-goose chase, leaving our bombers at their mercy," somebody else shouted from the back.

There was a chorus of agreement.

"I know it's a major gamble," I began.

"And we're trying to quit gambling!"

"But we *must* gamble, we *must* take the risk," I said; and when they'd quietened down somewhat: "Look, even though we've given the KAF a hell of a pasting, it's grinding us down as well. Have you looked at the status board? In just a few days we've lost a third of our strength from one cause or another." I took a deep, unsteady breath. "The point is," I said more quietly into the general consternation, "that we can go on the way we're going, fighting well but conventionally, and draining a strength that can't be recharged—while the enemy still has a substantial air force. Or we can compensate by using guile, by being cunning, by being speedy, and above all by doing the unexpected.

"I ask you to imagine what it'll be like otherwise, if we all gather at the river, brethren," I said as forcefully as fatigue would allow. "Unbearable casualties with no certainty that they would be worth while.

"Well, I'm not prepared to make that kind of sacrifice," I went on. "I had enough of that in the war." I looked around at their strained, exhausted faces; and I wished I could have taken them all in my arms and embraced them all together, at the moment. "But," I said, "if we can catch them on this temporary airfield of theirs at the first hint of daylight before they can take off—and I don't think they can take off early, for the simple reason that they *are* a temporary airfield and not set up for night-flying—I think we'll not only get the bridge but deal the KAF a blow they'll never recover from.

"Gentlemen—isn't that worth the risk—when the alternative is heavy casualties anyway?"

After that, some of the vehemence went out of the argument though they trembled at the thought of unprotected bombers at the mercy of dozens of Fokker DVIIs; and a compromise was sought whereby the bombers would not set out for the bridge until the fighters signaled that the attack on the advance base had been successful. But the trouble with that proposal was that the attack on the bridge would be delayed and the Khaliwar Army might be across by the time the bombers arrived.

I couldn't agree to that. And in the end it was decided to take the risk.

"Actually the bombers won't be entirely unescorted," I said with a pretence at insouciance. "I'll be going with them in my trusty Bristol fighter."

"Oh, well, there's not a thing to worry about, then," someone said sarcastically.

After yet more frantic activity in the steamy heat of the night of 29-30 May, every available aircraft we had was loaded up with 112- and 230-pound bombs, and sent off into the dark night north; and less than an hour later every remaining machine took to the air as well: fourteen DH9s and four big twin-engined Vimy bombers, and a single Bristol fighter containing me, with Hibbert as observer; and the top rim of the sun was just peeking over the low hills, casting spearlike shadows over the tawny earth when the aircraft lined up on the bridge at the agreed altitude.

I circled widely, heart painful with apprehension that the gamble might be lost and the Fokkers would come tumbling down on us at any moment; and I watched as one bomb after another missed the target by scores of yards. And worse, the dust kicked up by the explosions was starting to obscure the target.

The bridge, its ferrous geometry totally intact, was growing fuzzy in the horizontal floodlighting. And though the air was breezy enough to pitch my Bristol about like flotsam in a storm, there was no wind to push the dust away.

There! No. Bombs had exploded close to the steelwork over the deep gorged river. I thought they might have hit. But no.

Now it was the turn of the great Vimys. They were just banking into position, lining up on the road. The bridge was almost invisible through the dust.

I looked around. Hibbert was gazing around as well, eyes apprehensive behind his goggles.

No enemy in sight, yet. And the sky was already bright.

Bless them—the Vimys were going round again without laying their eggs. They were waiting for the dust to settle.

Here they were. They'd descended. They were at less than 800 feet, slow as cows. Surely their 230-pound bombs would shake the bridge into the gorge?

No. When the smoke and dust cleared, the structure was still intact, unshaken. I jerked my head around again, imploring the Fokkers not to turn up now, to give us a last chance at the bridge which was their last obstacle to victory over Jhamjarh.

Now the sun was daubing the eastern sky. How I wished I had wireless so I could communicate with the other Vimys, to suggest that they wait just a few minutes until the sun was higher and was illuminating the bridge with a little less optical tomfoolery. Though I couldn't blame the pilots for trying to get the job done as quickly as possible, in case the DVIIs presented bouquets of tracer and explosive bullets. Still no sign of them. But. Were they just late for work or had Brashman and his fleet actually managed to stop them getting off?

I turned back to the second pair of twin-engined bombers, and was just in time to see it lurch and bob in the warm air as it released a foursome of wobbly bombs from its squarish fuselage. I was able to follow the black teardrops part way down until I lost sight of them in the horizontal light. The bombs seemed to be curving short of the bridge. Hell, hell. The target was tall, setting geometry questions with its girders high above the river channel, but it was narrow, narrower even than the road it carried whose width was paltry enough, God knows.

In a moment we would have to rely on the last four DH9s. Their crews had agreed to bomb from dangerously low levels if the bridge was still intact when it came their turn. And it looked as if their daredeviltry would be needed, as the third Vimy, groaning along on its sandwiched engines, had failed—

Wrong. Not all of the Vimy bombs fell short. Two of them burst on the road, creating helpful craters. The third hit the bridge a few feet in from the river bank; and the fourth, oh magnificent aiming!—which Vimy?—letter U—make a note— the fourth bomb also struck the bridge on the far side; and the entire structure slowly buckled into the river, leaving hardly more than a few twisted girders jabbing impotent from concrete.

One moment gray dust was erupting, and concrete chunks, and lengths of something; then confusion; and as the dust cleared, a glorious gap appeared, and what was surely a tangle of metal way down in the shadows of the gorge. The sun had not been obliging enough to shine right down into the depths, but I was sure I could see a jumble of metal in the water, and further along the aquatically impoverished watercourse the flow was unruly, disturbed by debris.

It looked as if a gap of a hundred feet had been created; and my heart felt as if it were expanding to the size of a football, and I yelled and waved as I darted alongside the triumphant Vimy, whose crew of four waved back, grins hacking their faces. The giant biplane wings waggled with elephant slowness. Then we were both banking round for another look at the damage, to make quite sure—*Jesus, I was being attacked*! I kicked the Bristol into a dive and twisted sideways, splitarsing frantically, heart pounding, I'd sensed a sudden rush of aircraft. Fokkers! My old war reflexes had taken over.

But it was just the last of the DH9s, joyfully diving and zooming around me.

I glanced back a bit guiltily at Hibbert. It was no fun being wrenched about by another pilot. But he was still grinning, cheering.

The rest of the formation were also celebrating, dancing wildly in the sky. A DH9 dived alongside, the observer standing up in the cockpit to wave, the pilot snatching off his goggles and swishing them over his head, excalibur style. I waggled the wings, still looking around carefully—the sky still empty of enemy—then throttled back and dived, but gently, remembering Hib. In seconds the air went from warm to hot, and I could taste the dust that still hung in the air. The yellowish ground spread out on all sides. I restored enough power to keep airborne alongside the river. I wanted to make sure that the bridge could not be mended readily.

The sun was starting to illuminate the bottom of the ravine by now, and, yes, there was the bent metal, with water swashing over parts of it, while at the top a few supports of steel were sticking out of the concrete on one side. So nothing was going to get across there for a few days—or weeks, if Pertab fulfilled his promise to establish a defense line that would dominate this twisted site.

An hour later the fleet that had been sent to discourage the Fokkers returned to report a success at least as great as ours. They had arrived at the advance base before sunrise, but there had been enough light to enable them to make out long lines of Fokker DVIIs and a few two-seaters, dozens of them, all lined up with Prussian precision. They were already warming up for a mass take-off, and some were already moving to the rudimentary runway.

It was Brashman's opinion that none had survived the low-level bombing—they had been so conveniently arranged that even a mistimed bomb, missing one target, was almost bound to hit another.

The three squadrons under his command had suffered just two casualties: a young Snipe pilot had been a little too close when the ammunition dump exploded; and a DH4 had gone down with engine trouble on the way back to the aerodrome, but the crew had survived.

Otherwise the surprise attack had been a total success. The runway had been cratered, and after the bombs were used up, Brashman had led his two squadrons of fighters onto the tents using mixed tracer, explosive, and armor-piercing ammunition, which must have done a dreadful damage to whatever Khaliwar personnel were still under canvas.

I was so relieved at Brashman's report that I turned pale and had to sit down for a minute or so. Unless the Khalis had established a satellite airfield that we did not know about, they would now lose days in repairing and reinforcing the border base. Otherwise the Jhamjarh theatre was now out of range of all except their Gotha bombers.

Brashman who rarely speculated, guessed, or offered an opinion, and in fact hardly ever said anything at all, now cleared his throat and said, "We've smashed them."

"What?"

We all gazed at him in wonder, hoping he would continue. But of course he had said it all. As far as the State of Jhamjarh was concerned, the KAF was finished.

It was Roland Mays, unhappy about my refusal to render aid to New Delhi—he could not help siding with the Establishment, however hard he tried not to—who pointed out that the KAF was still unchallenged in the north, still able to biff the British unhindered. But I managed to change the subject before anyone else became too patriotic.

It was easy to change the subject, for we had one more urgent job to do before we could get some desperately needed rest. Just as we had anticipated, the Khaliwar Army had reached the Bamm River shortly after dawn. A reconnaissance Bristol reported them as being logjammed before the broken bridge. So now we had an opportunity to deal their army a heavy blow as well, and I was determined to deal it. Accordingly after yet another frenzy of rearming, and refueling of tanks, stomachs, and spirits, I took one of the Snipes and led a mixed force of fighters and bombers back to the Bamm.

By then it was midmorning on another blistering day, and the jam of military traffic had tripled in length as following units of the Khaliwar Army kept barging into the rear of the queue. In the lead, halted at the very edge of the Bamm ravine, were several armored cars, machine-guns aimed impotently over the gap; then a number of canvas-topped lorries crowded with green-and-black-turbaned troops, mixed in with supply

wagons. Then more armored cars, field guns hitched to ammunition vehicles, more troop transports, more miscellaneous
vehicles, more armored cars—and a single automobile containing a turbaned driver, two white officers and one Indian
officer in sun helmets. More and more vehicles were arriving
every minute, to extend the traffic jam by another mile.

As with the attack on the air base, our plan was to hit the
column first with bombs from the Vimys and the de Havilands,
and afterwards go to work with machine-guns. Until it was
their turn, the Snipes would provide cover, just in case any
surviving Fokkers appeared. None did.

The attack was another slaughter. The vehicles, crushed
nose to tail on a road that was difficult to abandon because of
the rough ground on either side, had no chance whatsoever.
Every bomb that landed within twenty feet of the road or
upon it was certain to cause damage. A hundred and fifty
bombs were to rain down on the trapped column within
minutes. Green turbaned figures scattering into the rough died
by scores as sticks of bombs burst among them. Many others
were killed where they cowered in the armored cars and
trucks, or as they tried to shelter under them. Ammunition
wagons blew with spectacular effect: black storms of dust and
debris, with shoots and tendrils in white and green as shells and
bullets, flares and signal lights and mortar bombs went up.

After dropping my own load from the wing racks, I intended
merely to keep an eye on things generally; but my attention
became fixed almost exclusively on the car with the officers,
and when I saw the black vehicle extricate itself from the
traffic jam and charge off through a patch of elephant grass
and nose into a clump of olive-drab trees, I banked clear of the
other aircraft, then flipped the Snipe upside down and pulled
back the stick, with thumb on engine button. The racket of the
rotary faded, to be replaced by the sound of explosions from
below, and the hissing of hot wind. The wispy horizon swung
and leveled again.

The nippy Snipe hurtled down, revolving half a turn on its
axis. On one side, clouds of smoke and dust rose from the
road, cuddling dim flashes of fire. Fuel was exploding in gouts

of dull red flame, and though I was a good hundred yards off the road, the Snipe was almost flipped onto its back again by the disturbed air. The target jumped into the ring sight. I got a whiff of explosives from the hot air that was bending past the windscreen. I had time for only a two-second burst from the twin Vickers before the trees whipped underneath.

So I went round again, flying level through air that felt as hard and undulating as a funfair ride, and through billowing smoke and alongside flames made almost invisible by the piercing sun. Now I was lining up for another strafe, and firing again at the dark shape among the trees, my occasional tracers spitting into the middle, tracers whose accuracy made me wonder again how the Fokkers had managed to miss me time and time again for hour after hour, when I could send a storm of bullets into the middle of a target after only two passes, a target that I hoped included Panyushkin. I hoped that Panyushkin was one of the occupants of the car. I felt sure that he was one of the senior officers in the car.

Later that day, after a rest, reunion with Sigga, wash and brush up, and fresh clothing, I returned to the City Palace, this time in an automobile. I had an appointment with the Maharajah, but he was busy meditating in the temple beside the ornamental lake. However, I could wait, if I wished, at the nearby Guest House.

While I was sitting on the veranda, keeping the insects away with my pipe fumes, Khooshie drove up in a roadster, braked to a halt in a shower of gravel, jumped out, and ran over. "Bartholomew," he panted.

"Good Lord, Khooshie," I exclaimed, "what are you doing in that?" He was wearing a Jhamjarh Army uniform.

"I have appointed myself colonel," he said, gesturing impatiently. "It is my contribution to the present crisis."

"And you look splendid, Khooshie," I said, admiring all the red and gold bits and pieces.

"I considered making myself a general, but modesty overcame me."

"M'oh yes?"

"But never mind that now," he said, and asked to see the report I had brought for his father.

I handed it over, and while he read, I refilled a tumbler with lemonade. I should have preferred ice-cold beer now that I had managed to take up drinking again, but alcohol was not permitted in the grounds of the City Palace, except the rubbing variety.

After hardly more than a couple of mouthfuls of lemonade the sweat trickled out as if I were a sprinkler system, and my blue shirt with the wings, rings, and ribbons slowly blackened and bonded to my skin. And this in spite of a cooling trend. There was even a hint of cloud on the horizon, giving a month's notice of the monsoon to come.

The smell of camels drifted across the razor-edged light, and for the umpteenth time I made a mental note to buy a pair of smoked glasses. The light was painful even in the shade, stabbing to the back of the head.

It took Khooshie ten minutes to read the report. When he had finished he glanced sideways and said, "Then there may be no need for me to fight with the army?"

"I shouldn't think so."

"Thank goodness for that. I don't mind sticking pigs and shooting the occasional tiger, but to shoot at men, I think that would have made me very sick."

"The trouble is that people like Sharif sometimes make it necessary."

"What about their offensive northwards, Bartholomew? We have heard that it is going very well. Very well for Khaliwar, that is."

"Seems so. Nobody's doing much to stop them."

"Serve them jolly well right, that's all I can say."

"M'm."

"Good riddance to the British, I say."

"Do you?"

"Not really. Us princes wouldn't last long if Congress took over."

He was looking at me with suspiciously shiny eyes. "I really don't know how we can ever repay you," he said at length, gesturing at the report.

"You and your father are always saying that. I'm thinking of trying it on my tailor."

"You have served us without stint, and at great cost to yourself, I think."

"Oh, no, it's cost me very little."

"I think you have tired yourself out in our service. And father thinks so, too, and that some of the cost has been spiritual. That you have lost so much of the conviction of what's what, the certainty that enables you people to achieve so very much, materially."

I glanced at the prince then away, then back again interestedly, because he looked different. His light brown face with its curly eyelashes guarding eyes dark as graphite, had firmed, and the gaze had steadied. I hoped that this was a sign of maturity. He would need it over the next few months, in the aftermath of the conflict with Khaliwar.

"You have been a far more dedicated and self-sacrificing servant of Jhamjarh that we have had any right to expect, Bartholomew."

"You've paid me very well, Khooshie."

"Even so, it seems to both father and myself that you have given us a loyalty far above what we might have expected from mere banknotes. We are most deeply grateful, Bartholomew."

"You're welcome."

"But I have thought of a way to repay you."

"Oh, good," I said, imagining thunderstorms of diamonds, rubies in platinum, sapphires in silver, emeralds set in twists of gold.

"It is some advice."

"Oh, good."

"I know you think I am not very experienced in life, even though I am fully nineteen years old, and have traveled widely from brothel to brothel—"

"Is this going to be about the facts of life, Khooshie?

Because if it is, I learned all about that, months and months
ago."

"Do stop being silly for a minute and listen," the boy said.
"What I am saying is...well, actually it is what father is saying,
but he is too shy to tell you himself. You see, we have been
talking about you, Bartholomew, and father thinks, and I am
concurring, that...."

"What?"

He took my hand, and his soul shone through the hatching
of his eyelashes. "That the war interrupted your faith and
completely ruined your belief in any sort of authority and your
respect for it." He paused, then asked anxiously, "Do you
think we are on the right lines there, Bartholomew?"

I didn't like having my hand held, it made me feel too
emotional. At the same time there was no doubt that it
enhanced the conductivity of communication.

"Possibly," I mumbled.

"But we agree, father and I, that you are the sort of person
who is receptive to Brahman. We sense that in spite of your
many reservations, which in fact many of us would share, you
harmonize with our Hinduism, which is not a religion but a
way of life.

"So we are thinking it is time for you to report to the great
Commanding Officer himself, Bartholomew."

"You mean it's time I died? *Well.* So that's all the thanks I
get."

"No, no. It is just that we think you will continue to go
running downhill like a runaway train unless you can report to
the one whose orders you can accept, at last, faithfully and
without question. We think that is what you need."

"You do?" I asked politely, but: *Great Commanding Officer.*
Good God.

When another twenty minutes went by with no sign of the
Maharajah, I tucked the report under a moist armpit and
strolled around the ornamental lake; except that it was not
quite as ornamental as it had been, for the firefighers had
almost emptied it, to expose a rusty English pram half embed-

ded in stinking ooze, and—I hoped there was no heavy symbolism here—a dead dog, ivory with putrescence.

I walked up to the temple on the far side, removed my shoes, and went inside; but the Maharajah was not in there. Just an elaborately worked bronze statue of the elephant god on a simple dais.

As there was no seating, I sat on the floor and enjoyed the cool marble, and thought about myself for a while in relation to this mysterious world. Like the stillness of the night after a violent day, I felt strangely poised, floating along some obscurity, ready to drift with the mystery to its mystic delta. That damn Sadhu. He had loosened the old underpinnings, creating flashes of straight light and insights about the hanging lamp stars. The moon, and that burning sun out there, really were illusory in that they existed only because we had established that they existed, just as Dalton's atom was real only because we wished to prove that it was real. In trying to sabotage me in my head to make me less of a servant to the Maharajah, the Dewan had perhaps done me a favor, though I was still not grateful for it. With the loss of faith in the concrete came a rolling mist of doubt that I was always right and that it was always other people who were guilty of meanness, greed, or acts of injustice, and perhaps most of all came a doubt that what had dictated so many of my actions and attitudes since the Great War was justified. Postillion had been right when he said I hated. I had seen the comfort of staff officers while their men drowned in human soup, seen them delicately sipping Champers while their junior officers sickened for want of clean food and water, known generals who ordered disgraceful attacks because that was what had been planned and so must be done, met politicians who...no, I had better not get onto that, I'd been a politician myself for a while. No, but for seven years I had raged against the interests that had so lavishly expended half a generation of clever, foolish, poetic, vile, and noble men—and women, my beloved Katherine—and raged against the interests elbowing for commercial position, which was partly understandable, for that was the engine of mankind, but unforgiveably, it seemed, they had all gone on and on in demented obsession until you felt that something far worse even than the war had happened to the world, and that from now on only wicked growth would come to replace the former cultivation. I'd been filled so often since with rage at the sight of begging limbless men being eased aside by profiteers, by congresses dedicated to efficient betrayal, and had known the effect in myself, the heart turned into a pneumatic drill by fright unjustified, and felt depression's drifting cloud and the eroding enmity for the System. But...who were the hated but us? For whom was the war a release but you? Who expressed the exultation when war came but the poets? Who went to the war with bellicose rejoicing? Me.

I wept for the first time since July of '18—anxiety some, but release from fatigue and tension, perhaps, after frantic days. And after I'd recovered I resolved to cease this farcical insubordination. What I had reacted to was not reality any more than the Sadhu's greasy turtle had been real. So when I finally encountered the Maharajah and told him, he actually embraced me, approving purely for my sake, and then I went to find Postillion and told him. If the men consented, we would go to New Delhi's aid with every man and aircraft we could spare, now that the Khalis had almost certainly been halted at the Bamm and their air force was now much inferior in numbers to ours, and there would be no need for the Viceroy to write a word. It was a purely selfish decision on my part, I told Postillion, though I didn't bother telling him why.

Home Again, Again

L ately, spring had been going out of fashion in Canada. One moment winter, a giant ice floe, the next, summer, hot as charcoal. This year, though, spring had been laid on specially for our homecoming, a season decorated with bright forsythia and smelly May blossom.

The folks had been waiting for us. They emerged from the farmhouse the moment the taxi emptied us onto the driveway, and shuddered off, tires spitting gravel.

I was rather taken aback to observe how greatly the parental postures had angled since I last fled the country. And, as it turned out, the parental attitudes. The Reverend Mr. Bandy had always regarded me with critical astonishment as if unable to believe that I was really his son and not an obstetrical error, or a changeling imposed on him by a fallen angel—fallen on account of its bad taste. As for mother, she was actually smiling a shy welcome. I hadn't seen her looking so deferential since the bishop visited us back in 1910, and had to be put up for the night when father caused him to miss his train, and the bishop was just getting to sleep at four a.m. when the cat came in and made a mess in the corner.

They tried to shake hands with Sigga, and looked flustered when she embraced them and said warm things.

"Come in, come in, my dear, you must be frozen," father said, Sigga's instant slave. Age had thinned his blood as if to make it go further. To him, chilliness was any temperature below ninety Fahrenheit. "No, no, leave the bags, my boy," he said to me. "Your mother will bring them in."

Sure enough, though it was a pleasant spring day, a conflagration was burning in the kitchen grate.

Soup bubbled in a cauldron. So did the lacquer on a side table.

"The mayor wanted to greet you with a banner and a brass band," mother panted, "but we didn't know exactly when you would arrive."

"You're looking very distinguished, Bartholomew," father said wonderingly.

"'M'kew.'"

"It's very nice to meet you at last," Sigga said, crossing a silken leg and exposing a dimpled knee. "I've heard so little about you."

There was a puff of flame and smoke as the lacquer on the side-table caught fire, but fortunately the teeny fire soon went out. I felt my underwear growing damp.

"What did the banner say?" I asked.

Mother looked at me enquiringly.

"The banner you mentioned? I suppose it said *Welcome Home*, or something like that," I suggested.

"I suppose so."

"And the brass band. What was it going to play?" I asked, to keep the conversation going.

"*Nearer, my God, to Thee?*" Sigga suggested.

Mother looked at Sigga's glorious face. Father tried not to look at Sigga's knees.

"I guess it would have been quite a reception," I mused. "A banner reading *Welcome Home*. A brass band playing something stirring and romantic, the bandsmen with eyes bulging under the pressure of their uniform collars. Nosegays of ladies in their Sunday best eager to be presented to the Hero of New Delhi and his highly respectful wife, and little girls demure in pink enviously eyeing the raucous whelps of romping, horse-bun-slinging lads. Boot-polished farm workers in awkward collars scowling in that Canadian fashion to show they're as good as toffs any day, and various other citizens including the entire Gallopian Establishment, Cluck Hipsey, Rosalie Hipsey, old lady Hipsey, and the like, all curtsying and bobbing like apples in a barrel, and the Mayor of Gallop with a scroll of welcome, comparing me favorably with Clive of India."

"I can smell liquor on your breath, Bartholomew," mother said.

"M'oh yes. Yet another cause for celebration, eh? For months I fought the terrible temptation to remain a temperancer, Father, and finally triumphed with a celebratory binge in the mess that will be talked about as long as there are tankards and shot glasses."

They both looked at me. Mother lowered her eyes. Father leaned over to poke the fire in the ribs, causing fresh calories to burst from the grate and scorch the vine-leaf-and-trellis wallpaper.

"But despite these and other victories over vacant stoicism, you mustn't feel overly deferential toward me, not even socially," I persuaded. "Underneath I'm still the same modest, self-effacing, and, above all, simple lad who first set off for war pure in heart, mind, and habit."

"You mean," father enquired, "we don't have to address you as Sir Bartholomew?"

"Of course not," I laughed indulgently. "At least, not when it's just among ourselves."

"Actually," Sigga said, undoing all the damage I was trying to do, "he mostly keeps quiet about his knighthood. I think he's afraid they'll take it away from him."

"No," I went on, ignoring this, "just because I'm now Sir Bartholomew Bandy, Knight Grand Commander of the Star of India, as well as recipient of other orders and awards too numerous to mention—the CBE, the DSO, the MC, the DFC, the Croix de Guerre, the Legion of Honor, the the Order of St. Mary of Vaitiekunas, the Albanian Medal for Gallantry, 3rd class, the Tiberius Good Conduct Medal, the Grand Cross of the City Guild of Wasp Keepers, the St. Leger Rosette, the—"

"Wouldn't you like to rest, Bartholomew," mother said, "after your long journey?"

"Yes, I was about to suggest that," father said; and, in one of his loudish undertones to Sigga: "Is he *d-r-u-n-k?*" he asked, actually spelling out the word.

"No, don't worry, Mr. Bandy, he's just having another breakdown. He has one a day nowadays."

"Anyway, the fact that I am now perched on the very pinnacle of success doesn't mean that I'm not still highly approachable, you know," I said.

"Provided you have an appointment," Sigga slipped in.

"In fact I'll let you into a little secret, Pater and Mater. I very nearly did not receive this latest honor from His Majesty at all. At one point he, or rather his advisors, would have preferred not so much to tap me on the napper with the royal sword so much as run me through with it, because I was so tardy in coming to the aid of the Government of India when they were so close to being overrun. In spite of my unbelievable heroism and generosity it was only the intervention of the Maharajah that gained me my knighthood. He refused to accept his own KCSI unless I received one, and when that didn't work, he threatened to grant an embarrassingly comprehensive interview to the American journalist Petronella Spencer, the one who has made me as famous as D.H. Lawrence of Arabia—and a good deal richer, as Lawrence is now just a low aircraftsman in the Royal Air Force, while I am as wealthy as I am renowned. So you see, Mater and Pater, there's no need for you to look upon me with such awe and untrammeled admiration. I haven't *really* changed, you know."

"We were rather hoping you had, dear," mother said.

"Well, what do you think of them?" I asked Sigga that night, in bed.

"Your parents? I like them."

"I think they'll love you as soon as they get over their amazement that their son could have acquired such a beauty," I said, and hugged her—but not too warmly, as I suspected that father was lying awake in his bed rigid with terror that he might hear us engage in marital relations. He had read in the *Method-*

ist Scrutineer that long sea voyages were conducive to lust, even among married couples.

"I got the impression from you that they were practically ogres. They're not at all."

"I seem to have got a new angle on a lot of things."

"An obtuse angle?" she enquired.

That was one reason why I had such respect and affection as well as love for Sigga—her ability to pick up and employ a phrase like that, betokening a quick and original mind. I leaned up on one elbow, kissed her and stroked her cheek for a moment. Her face was just visible in the light that blazed from the back porch and seeped through the window blinds. Somebody in the neighborhood had been stealing mother's undergarments from the clothes line and this had made her nervous, hence the nocturnal illumination.

"What are you stroking me for?" she asked suspiciously.

"No particular reason."

"Because if you're thinking of what I hope you're thinking of but don't wish you to think of, because you know how noisy I am, and your parents might mistake me for a pack of howling wolves—"

"And they might come in and blast us with a shotgun? No, it's not that. I was just thinking I love you more and more each day."

A tear gleamed in the blind-light. "You're always taking me by surprise, saying things like that," she snuffled.

"To answer your question—"

"What question?"

"About the new angle. I've never spoken about this before, Sigga, but somehow India made me think about myself a bit. I was never too keen on that before, suspecting that I wouldn't much like what I found out. And I was right; I didn't much enjoy discovering that I had a fiendishly deep-rooted belief that I didn't amount to a row of beans, and also that I had auditioned revenge for the principal role in my life."

"Revenge?"

"M'm. I've always striven to get my own back. In my time

I've driven quite a few people to drink, distraction, or the Northwest Territories."

I lay back on the pillow again and tucked my hands behind my head. "And I haven't told the truth much, either. I've invariably presented my retaliations as being purely accidental and so forth. But the fact is that I usually engineered the dreadful things that happened to my opponents, while pretending that their comeuppances were the results of chance or ill-luck, or the like."

"Like when you raided your own trenches and took your own battalion commander prisoner? It wasn't an accident?"

"Oh, yes, that was an accident, after Captain Karley put rum in my water bottle and I had the first drink, or the first ten drinks, in my life. But when I dragged the colonel into No-Man's-Land, I always told people that I hadn't recognized him before I hit him with my tin hat to keep him quiet. In actual fact I *had* recognized him."

"And when you ran over your RAF brigadier. That was on purpose too?"

"Oh, no. I didn't know him well enough. But later, after he tried to kill me with a parachute, I'm afraid I quite deliberately drove him into a breakdown in an outdoor privy."

"What an absolute beast you are," Sigga whispered, chortling.

"I know. I'm so ashamed, now."

"Yes, I can tell, by the complacent note in your voice."

"I ran down Mackenzie King with my floatplane on purpose, too."

"Who's he?"

"The Prime Minister."

"Shhh. Give us a kiss. M'm. But you know, darling, you're worse than you think. Because you inspire fury and frustration in people on purpose with that haughty face and that awful voice of yours. You deliberately try to bring out the worst in people. And now you tell me you deliberately get your own back on people—after you goaded them in the first place. That's really terrible."

"That's not fair. I bring out the best in a lot of people."

"Oh, yes, as a military man. But everybody else—I mean, even your parents tonight. Though they started out thoroughly awed by your knighthood and your fame and fortune, they were grinding their teeth by bedtime at some of the things you were saying."

It was now her turn to lean up on her elbows as a sudden thought occurred to her. "Was that why you were insisting on the Viceroy humbling himself in a letter? Because he had injured you?"

"Yes."

"But then what made you drop the demand?"

"I've tried to tell you, Sigga."

"Well, you haven't tried hard enough, because I can't see he's any different from all the others, the generals and prime ministers and such."

"He's not, I'm the one who's different. To get my own back I had to feel I was in the right—to have a certainty about what it was all about."

"But what exactly made you uncertain?"

"I can't explain any more, my love, except to say that the sum total of India, and the Maharajah, and the Sadhu's illusory sabotage, which was part of the Dewan's plot to draw my fangs and make me less of a threat to his masters in Lampur Kalat, jolted me into visions that seemed to be insights into the nature of us and the world. Isn't that utterly pretentious? Good Lord, a mystic Bandy. It's *horrible*."

Sigga stopped laughing suddenly when she realized that she was causing the bed to thump and creak lasciviously.

"But I did understand for a moment an indivisibility of flesh and spirit, and that God exists because you realize he exists. After that, Viceroys become trivial."

"But thinking that way, couldn't you end up accomplishing nothing in this life?"

"Oh, no, I'm not that perfect."

Sigga continued to gaze down at me in the dim porch light, possibly trying to work out what the hell I was talking about, or perhaps mentally shrugging her shoulders over the impracticalities of men.

"Anyway, I'm not thinking of changing too much," I said, lifting my head to kiss Sigga's plump, juicy lips, then turning over and uttering a contented sigh, secure in the knowledge that the anger was over with, and that I had regained that amazing human phenomenon, belief, which could triumph over demolition as surely as a flower emerging from a crack in the concrete.

THE BANDY PAPERS COMPLETED